Love & Death
In The Miskatonic
Valley

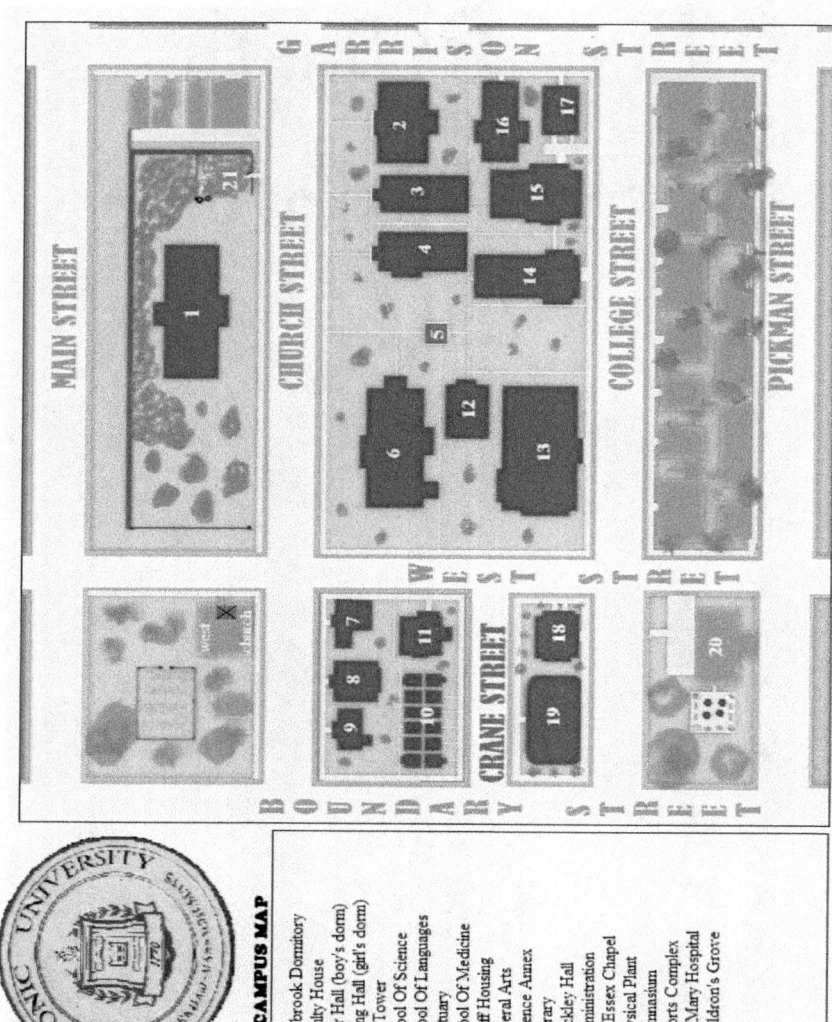

CAMPUS MAP

1. Pembrook Dormitory
2. Faculty House
3. Dyer Hall (boy's dorm)
4. Loring Hall (girl's dorm)
5. Bell Tower
6. School Of Science
7. School Of Languages
8. Mortuary
9. School Of Medicine
10. Staff Housing
11. Liberal Arts
12. Science Annex
13. Library
14. Lockley Hall
15. Administration
16. St. Essex Chapel
17. Physical Plant
18. Gymnasium
19. Sports Complex
20. St. Mary Hospital
21. Waldron's Grove

Love & Death
In The Miskatonic
Valley

R.C. Davis

Cover art, campus map, and title page icon, by: Cosantoir Fere McDaeid
Contributing Cover Artist: Tyli Jura

Dedication

This story is dedicated to Daisy,

my faithful writing companion

of sixteen years.

I will miss you forever

2007-2022
R.I.P.

1

The Sky, A Vaporous Flame

A familiar eagerness bubbled inside me as I prepared for my student job. After a day filled with books and research, I was ready for a little physical activity. Leaving the administration building by the west door, I didn't get more than a couple steps on the cobblestone walkway before coming to an abrupt halt. The sky had been clear all day, and now, caught up in the pinkish afterglow of the sunset, several wispy, mare's tail clouds heralded an approaching storm. Something like Déjà vu wriggled into a corner of my mind like a reticent little mouse and then scampered away. Something about that picturesque horizon troubled me.

I racked my brain for a memory, but like that elusive word that sticks to the tip of your tongue, it failed to come forth. To make matters worse, instead of getting a satisfying revelation, a foreboding washed over me like a cold ocean wave. I shivered and felt fearful that the forthcoming tempest might have more to do with my life than the weather. But the annoyance of not being able to decipher that foggy recall, put me off the whole matter. I truly enjoyed walking the campus in the evening with my German Shepherd, Sarge, and I wanted my thoughts free of the undesirable. I figured I'd worry about it later and got on with my assigned duties.

I soon passed through a group of giggling, teenage girls. In just about every hand, a complimentary, spiral-bound notebook plastered with the red and white university logo. It was a freebie given to new scholars upon their arrival. A student council idea, and most definitely, the badge of a freshman. They were obviously finishing up their first year and still hadn't lost their enthusiasm for university life. Whatever excitement remained was apparent and helped lighten my mood.

1

Exchanging greetings with some, I weaved my way through the sea of cardigans. Then, one of them had to go and utter that one particular remark that has dogged me my entire adult life, "Oooh… sooo Tony Curtis."

I looked back to meet the eyes of the smitten as the others giggled. Slapping a hand over dark red lipstick, her eyebrows rose, and she blushed. Hurrying away, she pushed through the others and disappeared.

I get that all the time—but I couldn't disagree. The resemblance was uncanny. The movie star and I shared the same face shape, blue eyes, dark hair, and wide smile; dimples included. Tony's crime drama, *Six Bridges to Cross*, had just been featured at the Arkham Mystik back in February. It had set off an avalanche of wisecracks and remarks; as expected. Yet every flash flood has to dissipate. They would get tired of it, and then I could fall back into my usual level of obscurity.

I slowed to a stroll and breathed in the perfume of the lilacs and pink flowering crabapple. The birds sang a eulogy to the dying sun as students crisscrossed the green. It was April now, and 1955 was shaping up to be a warm one. With summer break a little over a month away, I suspected the majority of the students couldn't wait to get home.

I had accepted the so-called position of 'Campus Caretaker' way back in my freshman year. It came to me as one of the many available student jobs. Now, as a second-year grad student, I could, very well, drop it and go full blown Teaching Fellow. But I liked it so much that I wanted to keep it—at least until the end of summer break.

My adviser would rather I stood in front of a classroom full of freshman English majors, than be out acting the quasi-watchman. To appease him, and the others, I did teach on occasion. I must admit, it was a point of contention. Having to get up in front of all those eyes was still a little unnerving and on occasion brought about a touch of stage fright.

I understood where Dr. Strang was coming from, but we both knew I needed a little more time to let go of the caretaker position. I am sure if I was more consistent about appearing in the classroom, it would boost my confidence level. I was going to make this upcoming August the month to buckle down and get serious.

A student caretaker's job was to turn on the many outside lamps (and a few inside ones) that filled the 140 plus acres that was Miskatonic University, lovingly referred to as M.U. here in Arkham. Most of the light fixtures required a key in order to dissuade the mischievous. As lamps were added and the campus grew brighter, new keys joined the others, and the watchman's ring, entrusted to me for two hours nightly, grew heavy.

There was also the occasional door unlock in the ivy-covered academic buildings, or the infrequent request for access to a closet in the recently refurbished gymnasium. But that was actually the duty of Lyle Umberling, the full-time night watchmen—and only after I'd handed over his jingling mass of brass.

His shift ran from six at night until six in the morning; eight until eight during the summer months. My job would start about two hours before he came on duty, and it took me just about as long to complete my obligation. I could finish sooner, but I always stopped to chew the fat or grant a favor by unlocking a door at someone's request. I had to pay close attention to the time, and the hourly toll from the Bell Tower came as a helpful reminder. Lyle needed the keys to get inside to punch the clock. If anything drove him ape, it was having to wait for me to show up so he could.

Upon arriving back at the admin building, I would find his portly body leaning against the outside door, cigarette in hand, and a scowl on his face. He would let out a long sigh, remove his grey, eight-pointed cop cap, and scratch his head as if perplexed. Rumor had it, he drank too much. I believed it because I could see the alcohol taking its toll. His bulbous nose had purpled over the years and was now riddled with broken capillaries. His skin had gone a bit yellow, and there seemed to be a bourgeoning forgetfulness. I wondered how much longer he would last.

He'd worked at M.U. for as long as I'd been alive. His position required a great deal of walking. During the course of any evening, I'd see him huffing and wheezing about the campus, sweat staining the armpits of his ash-colored frock coat. I always heard him long before I saw him.

Dean of Students, Lucas Farr, had offered me Lyle's job, once. It had been at a small gathering just after my senior graduation as I stood in a group that included Dr. Strang, my mother, and several other members of the faculty. Lucas's proposal had caught us off guard. He tried to pass it off as a joke, but the beseeching expression on his face said otherwise. Farr knew full well my goal was to complete my education and teach English with hopes to receive tenure. Later, after giving it some thought, there came a realization that I had gotten a glimpse into his desperation.

Dean Farr started exhibiting a certain nervousness when in Lyle's presence. There had been times when I had caught him covertly stocking the watchmen during the evening hours. So, I made veiled inquiries about Lyle to different staff members. My most loyal source of information was Betty Teselsham, the head cook and manager of the school cafeteria. She told me of Lyle's tardiness in unlocking doors, being discovered in rooms where he didn't belong, intoxication while on duty, and worst of all—lewd comments made to female students in passing. I suspected Dean Farr was growing anxious to replace him, however, his conscience was getting in the way.

Besides the soon to be abandoned caretaker position, I also acted as Dormitory Assistant (DA) in Dyer Hall, the boy's dormitory. I took the job because it granted me free rent. All I had to do was coordinate with the housekeepers in maintaining some degree of cleanliness, look out for the undergrads that lived there, and report to Dean Farr. Then there was—Palance Kilham.

Palance lived up on the third floor and was the backup DA in case I had to be away. He gave me a lot of crap about the way I did my job. The boys hated him. A grad student over at the School of Medicine, Palance was a Teaching Fellow like me. He also spent a lot of time working the university's morgue, which always seemed to come off as a rather morbid fascination.

Palance never conversed, Palance complained. The best thing you could do was stand, nod, and then excuse yourself as quickly as possible. His latest complaint—which had nothing to do with me or the dorm— was the pilfering of chloroform over at the School of Medicine. Somebody with regular access had helped themselves to a gallon of the stuff.

4

"Just you wait and see, Sterling, I'm going to get to the bottom of this. That stuff doesn't come cheap," he said the day after the theft was discovered. I just smiled and wished him good luck.

I was kept plenty busy with the two jobs and my schoolwork, but that didn't stave off the loneliness. My girlfriend and I had split just last year. She had been coldhearted and manipulative, and more often than not, I still felt alone even when we were together. My dog proved to be a much better companion than she.

Sarge accompanied me almost everywhere I went. He had been a gift to my father from the university when Silas Martin, the watchdog handler, died. The university closed their kennel soon after. Sarge's two brothers and three sisters had been gifted to other members of faculty and staff. Louis went to live with President Morgan up in the French Hill district and Marie-Louise to Dr. Goldman, the university's physician who resided over in staff housing with his wife. Pauline now belonged to Alice Payne, the head librarian, and Joseph went to Dr. Corning; both of them to live in Faculty House.

Sadly, the rambunctious Joseph had been hit by a car and killed. Now, Pauline was never allowed off leash. Alice, who had been witness to Joseph's death, never allowed anyone else to walk Pauline and kept her as far away from the city's streets as was possible. Dean Farr, who had taken in sister number three, known humorously as: Josephine Two, told me one afternoon that it had been part of the plan all along to phase out watchdogs. Silas's passing had just made it easier.

Sarge continued to live with my mother after my father's death. She revealed her dislike for dogs late in September of that year and taking care of him was more than she could handle. She would often lock him in the cellar or tie him at the back stoop. To keep himself occupied, he barked and dug, simply doing things that dogs do. One day when I came to visit, she let it slip that she was going to have him put down at first opportunity. By that time, I had taken my position as DA of Dyer Hall. So, I rescued him. He proved to be well behaved, especially when shown some love and attention.

I'd seen him around as a younger dog in training, and I sometimes stopped to pet him when I came to chat with Silas. The aging handler told me he named him Sarge after a favorite NCO back in World War

5

II. "A man with a steady gaze—nothing got by him!" Silas boasted while pointing to a faded photo of the sergeant tacked above his desk.

Sarge would endure many a long wait outside the door of any shop or restaurant that did not find canine's acceptable customers. Of course, that didn't include any one of the buildings owned by the university— except the cafeteria. Everybody knew him and if I was present, he was expected to be right by my side.

Sarge was descended from a long line of prominent German Shepherds. His great grandfather, Napoleon, had been the one to take down the infamous Wilbur Whateley who had burgled the university's library back in 1928. The strange and grotesque looking Whateley had attempted to make off with M.U.'s dilapidated copy of the Necronomicon, an ancient book of magic authored by the mad Arab, Abdul Alhazred.

Napoleon confronted Wilbur there and ripped out his throat, leaving the decadent Whateley to bleed out a malodorous, sticky ochre on the hardwood floor. The powers that be, suspected he had not been entirely human. That had been confirmed when the 'Horror' came to the nearby village of Dunwich shortly thereafter—so my father said.

The Necronomicon is now on display in the reference room. One can find it in a locked case, resting on wine-red velvet beneath thick glass within a framework of heavy brass. Somebody thought it a rare treasure and that it should be on display. I had questioned my father about that decision and he just shook his head and muttered something about university politics, adding that I should just stay out of it.

I also knew that the malodorous, leather-bound monstrosity sat upon a pressure switch. If moved, it would set off the burglar alarm high on the north wall, just outside. I gained this little bit of knowledge only because Lyle (being something of a know-it-all) felt compelled to pass it along during my caretaker training back in 1949.

Walking in through the huge, wooden doors of the library, I located a tiny, forked key on the ring and pushed it into a slot in the wall plate left of the entrance. Levering it up, the pole lamps on the steps flashed on along with the ceiling fixture above my head. The inner vestibule doors stood open, as usual, and I moved through to be enveloped by the background noise of a busy library and the smell of old books.

6

Sarge panted as we made our way toward the checkout desk, his toenails clacking on the dark boards of the floor. Bobby Corey watched us through the thick lenses of his black plastic framed glasses and grinned. The freckles on his boyish face contested his prematurely graying red hair. There was one of him in everybody's life—the kid who tried too hard.

"What's up, Daddy-O?" he said. Then looking down at my dog, he added, "Hey, Sarge, what's cooking, you big hunk of German Shepherd, you."

"Bobby Corey, you know how dumb that sounds coming out of your mouth? Save it for the beatniks, huh?" I said and chuckled.

"But Sterling, I don't know any beatniks. Well… except for you."

"Come on, you little nosebleed, I barely fit the mold."

"Close enough in my book."

Raising his eyebrows at me several times, I shook my fist at him in a playful manner and he rolled his chair back just out of reach.

"So… working hard?" I asked.

"Naw, I hate this gig. Checking books out of this place is not my thing. Helps pay the tuition, though, as you know. Hey, I got to take a dump, can you watch the desk for me? I can't find Beasley anywhere. He's supposed to be helping me, but he disappeared up into the stacks. Probably up on the third-floor necking with some chick. So… can you?"

"Sorry, still got lights to light and a dissertation to work on. I have to get back to admin by six and then over to the dorm."

"Ah come on, Sterling, I think I'm going to explode if I don't go soon."

"Well… that would be interesting. I'd give a couple Washingtons to see that."

"Oh, ha-ha. Come on, Ster, five minutes, what's five minutes?"

"Okay, but let me get the rest of the library lights and then I'll come back. But only five minutes, got it?"

"You're a lifesaver, Ster. But make it quick, huh? I'm starting to cramp."

"Hold your horses, I'll be right back."

Sarge, anxious to move, was already on his way into the Reference room. I followed and making my way through the big, open archway, I watched him receive a much-appreciated petting from several girls at a nearby table. An added perk of owning a dog—the girls loved him. That always gave me the opportunity to see if they might love me, too. Not that I intentionally used him for that purpose, I loved my dog. Our loyalty was mutual.

I crossed the room to the far wall and unlocking a small wooden panel right in the middle of the bookshelves, I pulled it open to reveal a breaker box. Flipping on just about every switch in there, I lit all the lights in the public areas of the building, chuckling at the student's varied reactions to the sudden illumination.

Shutting the panel, I turned toward the back of the vast, book filled space and my eyes fell on the exhibit in the corner. I should've just walked away, and more often than not, I would have. But tonight, I felt the compulsion to risk approaching the Necronomicon in order to view the display board behind it.

Walking over with a degree of caution, I eyed the large greenish-brown book. It exuded wicked vibes right through the glass. Their effect was almost instantaneous. A slow growing melancholic malaise started to overcome me as if the book exuded a contagion. My mind wanted to succumb to a dark intoxication, and I had to concentrate hard on staying in the now. Wicked thoughts flitted in and out of my mind, trying to steal my focus. I would have thought it just me, but others had voiced similar feelings while in its presence. Then there were a few who remained unaffected; people like Lyle Umberling, who always threw me an inquisitive look if I mentioned it.

Retreating a couple of steps, I immediately felt more like myself, grateful that my eyesight was almost perfect so I could view the eight by four-foot pictorial presentation on the wall behind it. It was framed in decorative mahogany and gold leaf. Along the top, just below the large brass letters declaring, 'The Champions of Miskatonic University', there hung three large framed portraits in black and white. Below them, a multitude of plaques and narrative plates making statements about the men and their deeds.

On the left was the smiling face of Dr. Francis Morgan, in the middle and set a little higher, hung a larger picture of the sage-like Dr. Henry Armitage, head librarian at the time of the Horror. Then, there was the

8

third man to his right. The reason I had even bothered to risk standing in the presence of that wicked book. Before me hung the likeness of the onetime Professor of Languages, Warren Rice—my father.

He had firsthand knowledge of the Horror and had told me the entire story. Old Wizard Whateley, of Dunwich, had been trying to summon the 'Old Ones'. They were supposed to be some kind of powerful deities who had once ruled the earth and now existed in a different dimension. The Wizard's daughter, Lavinia, had somehow managed the virgin birth of twins, Wilbur—and his unnamed brother. It was said that they were not of this world and were to be the acolytes for the Old Ones on this side of the veil.

The Wizard died, Lavinia disappeared, and Wilbur was left to finish the work of bringing those supernatural beings through that cosmic gate. He needed the Necronomicon to do it. Once through, The Old Ones goal would be to wipe out the human race and reclaim the planet.

Unfortunately for Wilbur, he was killed by the watchdog in just about the same spot where I now stood. His so-called brother, who they discovered later was even less human than Wilbur, was left to fend for himself. Busting out of the Wizard's house where he had been kept, he, or should I say, 'it', sought to satiate its appetite. People and animals disappeared in the night and buildings that stood in its path were demolished.

My father shared with me that the Horror was invisible. It was the wide swath of destruction that it left behind as it lumbered across the land that told them it was as big as the two-story house it had broken out of. Trees were found severed or bent, underbrush was flattened, and the earth plowed up. There had been numerous elephantine sized prints, big and round as whiskey barrels, pushed deep into the soil, evidence the monster they pursued slogged along on more than just two feet. It also left behind a foul-smelling tarry substance on everything it touched. "It was the stench of the thing that told us we were getting close," my father had declared with disgust.

When the three of them cornered it at the altar stone up on Sentinel Hill, they were able to bring it down with a chant concocted by Armitage from his feverish research of the Necronomicon. The tale left me to suspect that the good doctor must have suffered terribly because he had to actually touch that damn book.

Dr. Morgan had brought along his big game rifle, which they determined later would be worthless against their adversary. My father had been in charge of the sprayer that doused the Horror with a white powder so as to bring it into view. He confessed that he regretted that moment, for what he and the others saw would haunt them for the rest of their days.

My earliest memory of my father (that didn't involve the Dunwich Horror, or M.U.) was the day he came into the kitchen, his stocky frame heavy on the floor of the university owned cottage. He had been in a particularly good mood at the time, and taking me from my highchair, he put me in my Radio Flyer and pulled the little red wagon through the house making motor noises as I giggled. Our fun lasted only until my mother made him stop. She complained that the wheels might scratch the floor and then she would have to wax again.

The look on his face in the portrait was one of consternation. People were always going on about what a great presence he used to be. I only remember a man with few happy days and who's nervous paranoia increased with age, but also, a man struggling to be a good father and husband. His hair had been an iron grey at the time of the photo, however, when he passed away, nearly two years ago, it had been as white as the snowdrift in which he died.

He had collapsed while walking across campus during a blizzard and was discovered later by a post-storm frolic of some undergrads. They admitted their shock at finding it was a member of the faculty who lay buried in the drift of snow that stretched across the cobblestones of the walkway. Doctor Goldman said he'd had a heart attack. But why he was out wandering in a snowstorm, nobody had a clue. My mother nearly lost her mind, and nothing has been the same since.

She had been born Elsie Myra Grangerford and came from somewhere in Tennessee, just a few miles south of the Kentucky border along the Mississippi river. She had been traveling with a man-friend heading north to Maine, who was looking to find a job on a fishing boat. The ne're-do-well had abandoned her at a general store down in Salem. She attempted to follow him on foot, but only got as far as Arkham.

10

Admitting she had no money and feared traveling alone, she sought employment with the university. Housekeeping had an opening, and after being hired, she was assigned to Staff Housing, which included my father's cottage.

He told me once that he had never planned to marry. That was until that terrible day over in Dunwich. Elsie had come to clean a week later and found him in a terrible state. Offering sympathy and compassion, she had been rewarded with a home and a husband. They married in February of 1929. My father had been fifty-one at the time, she, just thirty-six. I came along in March of 1931 and would remain their only child.

Remembering Bobby's request, I gave the portrait one last look and turned away, only to stop and study the floor. The place where Wilbur Whateley had taken his last breath. It is said that he simply melted away; not to leave a trace.

I remember at age ten, being with my father here in the reference room. He had been looking for a particular book and after finding it, he gently ushered me to this corner. Looking toward the south windows as if gauging the light, he then cocked his head and searched the floor.

"See it there, Sterling? You can just make it out when the light is right. That's where Wilbur Whateley met his end, good ol' Napoleon saw to that."

"Who's Wilbur? And who's… Napoleon?"

He went on to tell me the story as we walked out with me looking back several times to see nothing but a well-polished floor. I came back, time and time again, hoping to see what he had been referring to. Then, on one particular day, the sun's rays must have been coming in through the front windows at just the right angle—and there it was.

I could just make out a greenish-yellow hue to the wood of the floor. The stain was over nine feet long, and maybe a third of that in width. I tried to imagine what this Wilbur had looked like, and after weeks of that, I demanded my father give me a description of the famous burglar. He was reluctant, but finally gave up what he saw that night after the watchdog killed Whateley, having shredded his clothing in the process. I would suffer in silent regret for a long time after my father's disclosure.

11

Supposedly Wilbur kept his attire well buttoned and only his facial features and his unusual height said that something was amiss. The odd-looking brute had spent a great deal of time on campus at the library, studying Abdul Alhazred's evil book. It was when he demanded they loan him the ancient volume to take back to Dunwich, that things took a turn for the worst.

It was mentioned that Wilbur had made acquaintances of other students here at M.U. while seeking the Necronomicon. Strangely, every one of them who arrived at the Whateley house for a friendly visit, dropped out of sight, and no amount of inquiry by the state police produced any evidence of their whereabouts. It was my understanding it had been the same for many young folks that had called Dunwich their home. People who got too close to the so called 'decayed branch' of the Whateley clan, ultimately, disappeared.

I kept the fear of the Wilbur monster I had conjured up, all to myself, not wishing to inspire guilt in my father. I was a glutton for punishment, though, and went as far as to press him for a verbal portrait of Wilbur's brother, the supernatural thing they had vanquished atop Sentinel Hill. That's where he drew the line, adamantly refusing to give me the slightest bit of information. I always felt it was because he couldn't bear to bring forth that memory from wherever he had buried it. And if he couldn't endure it—how could I?

With my eyes still on the library floor, I stood as if in a trance. A shiver racked my body and pulled me out of it. Hurrying away, I called Sarge over from his giggling audience of undergrads and headed back to the checkout desk.

Bobby was still there, but now dancing in place. I suspected Beasley hadn't returned to relieve him as I had hoped he would. Seeing me coming, Bobby dashed away, and heading for the door on the opposite wall marked, 'Library Staff Only' he hollered back, "Thought you forgot!" This was followed by a painfilled, "Oh, brother!" as he disappeared through the door.

Directing Sarge under an adjacent table, he lay down, head on paws. Dropping the huge ring of keys onto one of the many piles of papers scattered over the top of the desk, I put my derriere in the chair and waited. It didn't take long for me to start fidgeting, my eyes constantly

12

straying to the mammoth grandfather's clock. Only twice did I have to check out any books as Bobby's five minutes turned to ten. Stamping date plates and recording names on note cards wasn't that difficult. I had the choice of taking this very job back in my sophomore year instead of continuing with my caretaker position. Yet being cooped up inside wasn't my idea of something I could have done for three years straight. The freedom of walking and breathing fresh air had its allure.

The entrance door was jerked open and a girl burst in. I didn't know her, but she looked irritated. Scanning the room, her eyes fell on me and she stomped my way. She had the face of Shirley Temple straight out of The Blue Bird, but the body of a short Elizabeth Taylor. That childlike face could have easily led me to believe she just might be some kid who had gotten lost and was seeking directions. But the textbooks tucked up under her arm and that well-developed physique, said no. Her denim pedal pushers were tight. Her white blouse, with its sleeves rolled up, remained untucked following the latest trend. Then there were the bobby socks over black and white saddle shoes.

I grinned as she approached, thinking, here comes another little sheep following the fads. No sooner had I thought that, then I remembered I was now sporting a pompadour style haircut. It had been an experiment. I didn't like it, and the thing required more grease than I cared to use.

Subduing the hypocrite within, I decided to keep my sarcasm to myself. She caught the smirk on my face before I could wipe it off, and said, "What in the hell are you grinning at? Is there something funny?"

She tried to show me that she meant business, but her high-pitched voice was working against her. However, the scowl, along with the daggers in her eyes, told me that I had better try. So, I forced my lips into a more neutral position, and she scrutinized me with a squint. Even though she was trying to act tough, she seemed a little flustered, like something about me had put her off balance. Her eyes fell to the large ring of keys on the desk and then looking back at me, she said, "You look familiar. Like… famous person familiar. Where do I know that face from? Oh well… are you the security man? The watchman for the university?"

I lost control and chuckled, my mouth blossoming into a full-blown smile. She huffed and set her books down hard on the desk. That got my attention—and everybody else in the room, the sound echoing off the high, vaulted ceiling.

"Please answer my question."

"Sorry, so… yes, and no?"

"Yes, and no? You must be. I've seen you around. You and that dog… and that crazy ring of keys."

"Well, I…" was all I got out when she blurted, "Oh! I know now… you… you remind me of Tony Curtis."

It was my turn to scowl and squint.

"And…?"

"Oh! Right! Sorry, got distracted… so, anyway, yes, or no? Are you the man, and can you help me?"

"No. I mean, I'm not him… the watchman. I'm just a grad student. I work as a campus caretaker, and… how can I help you if you haven't told me what the problem is? But first, who are you? I know a lot of people here at M.U., and you're not one of them."

"Claudia, Claudia Osborn," she said, sticking out her little hand in an abrupt but nervous fashion. The fire in her eyes dwindled as I took it and gave it a shake. Her skin was soft and warm. It had been a while since I'd held a woman's hand. I didn't let go right away and she jerked it back, giving me a hard look, saying, "And you? What's your name— Mister… Not Really A Watchman?" It was strange to hear sarcasm in a voice like that. But she wasn't going to be messed with and was willing to go the discourteous route to prove it.

"No need to get rude, Miss Osborn. I'm trying to do my best. Sterling Rice here—no middle name. Student of the English language, part time lamplighter, and lover of dogs."

She glanced down at Sarge, who was now giving her his full attention as his overly long Shepherd's tail thumped the floor. A good sign. He didn't feel she was a threat, and maybe he sensed I was already starting to like her.

"That name sounds familiar. Hmmm… Rice? Where have I heard it before?" Taking a hand off her books, she put a finger to her lips. I waited as she pondered her own question, her face tilted to the ceiling. She brought it back to me in quick fashion, her eyes opening wide to show their amber-like brownness. She grinned and pointed the very same finger at me.

"Professor Warren Rice... that's it!"

"Very good, he was my father."

"Crazy. Something of a celebrity, then?"

"No, not even."

"Sure you are! Whether you like it or not. Everybody here knows the story. You can walk right into the other room and read it on that board above that horrid book. That Necro... Necro something or other."

"Necronomicon—and yes, it is a horrid book."

Bobby suddenly appeared, tucking his red plaid shirt into his beige slacks. Pulling a comb from his back pocket, he moved it through his Brylcreemed hair. Then adjusting his glasses, he grinned at Claudia and said, "Hey Sterling, who's the dolly?"

"I beg your pardon," she said, turning her squint to him.

"Oh, don't get frosty, babe, I'm just a little cranked by your looks."

Coming to my feet, I glared at him. I felt an overwhelming desire to knock him on his annoying butt. Turning my attention to the clock, I concluded he had been gone almost half an hour.

"Five minutes, huh? More like five hours."

"Ah, geez, Ster, it was almost a screamer... must have been the goulash I ate in the cafeteria."

Claudia gave him a look of disgust and backed up a step like she feared she might get something on her. Looking past her out the window, I saw it was fast growing dark. I still had the whole western part of the campus to do and Lyle would be waiting. I wanted to grab a couple burgers and a malt over at Dean's Corner Drive-In before I gave my dissertation any attention. I already felt beat, and my motivation for homework was fast diminishing. Grabbing the watchman's keys, I called Sarge to his feet.

Happy to be moving again, he did a kind of doggy dance, and taking my wrist lightly in his jaws, he pulled me toward the doors. I was sure he wanted out so he could baptize a few hydrants. Letting go of me, he ran for the exit, looking back to see if I followed.

"Thanks, Ster, I owe you," Bobby said.

"Yeah, you sure do... and I WILL collect. And stop calling me, Ster."

Halfway to the doors, I heard him say something to Claudia who spouted, "Take a hike, jack!" then added, "Hey! Wait! Ummm... I'm not done talking to you." I felt her presence behind me and then the clonk of her shoes on the limestone steps.

"Would you please hold up for just one minute?"

I slowed for her, watching Sarge water the decorative cast iron borders around the flower beds. Catching up, she plodded along beside me. Not only was she short, but she seemed a little clumsy. For some strange reason that appealed to me. She was the total opposite of Sandra Heinz, the last woman I dated. A person who seemed to float along with a kind of obscene grace. Sometimes, I would imagine a large book balanced on her blonde head as she moved, leaving her to wonder what I was grinning about all the time.

Looking down at my companion, I asked, "So... what do you want, Claudia?"

"You know... maybe it would be better if I talked to the actual watchman, or the Arkham cops."

"The cops? It's that serious? I'll tell you right now, ol' Lyle's not going to do you any good. Don't let that uniform fool you. If this means involving the police, then he could do no better than to telephone the cop shop for you. But now that you got my attention, how's about you tell me what's going on and make all your hassling worthwhile."

"Hassling? Am I hassling you? Pardon me, your highness. Maybe I should just walk away right now since you're being such a jerk."

She was right. I hadn't eaten since breakfast and fatigue was taking over, making me grumpy. "Okay, sorry... I just need to get my work done and I'm getting a little annoyed at all the interruptions. So, ask me, and I promise I'll stop being a so-called jerk."

We stopped next to a lamp post just outside the northwest corner of the library. She seemed to be studying my face as I rifled through the ring looking for the right key. Finding it, I stuck it into the switch plate high above my head and twisted. The large carriage lamp at the top flashed on, putting a gleam to Claudia's golden-brown hair. We made eye contact and for some reason her face softened and she said, "Okay, let's start over." Sticking out her hand again, she pretended as if we had just met.

16

"Hello, my name is Claudia Osborn. I need to talk to someone about my roommate."

I took the hand again and this time she didn't jerk it away. "Glad to meet you, I'm Sterling Rice—sounds like a job for the Housing Office—not security, or the police." Releasing her hand, I moved across West Street toward the Liberal Arts building.

She followed, saying, "Okay, so… it's just, I haven't seen her all day. She hasn't been in class and it's not like her to not be there to tell me all of her business. Her name is Elspeth… Elspeth Houghton, from over Aylesbury way. She's Dr. Houghton's niece. Maybe you've seen her around? She looks a lot like me, except taller, or… should I say, bigger? We could almost be twins. The other girls are always making fun of us because of that. So weird! I always thought it was strange that Housing had put us together in the same room. Oh! And she's also missing the little toe on her right foot. Her uncle, he's a doctor, had to cut it off because a horse stepped on her bare foot and smashed it flat. Anyway, I got a feeling she's missing."

I stopped and stared at her. That was the last thing I wanted to hear. The memory of those mare's tail clouds caught up in the afterglow came back, and my chest tightened. I felt like I'd just finished off a mixing bowl full of hot chili. My stomach knotted, and I actually belched. "Oh man! Sorry," I said as she glanced my way and grinned.

I had pushed her to reveal her concerns, and now, wished I hadn't. It unleashed the ghosts that I had worked so hard to lock away in that big box in my head. I tried to conceal my unease, but changing the subject would put us back at square one.

She now stood looking at me like she was expecting me to belch again. I decided it best to soldier on until she finished voicing her concern, and without any more interruption. That way I could make some suggestion and try to get her off the subject. But even if I succeeded in soothing her concerns, it wasn't going to soothe mine. Not now.

"Okay, so… when the weather is warm, she likes to go hang out on the back terrace just before bed. If you remember, it was pretty warm last night but was going to rain. She always wore this flimsy, sleeveless nightgown—completely see through. Something I never would have

17

worn outside. But she's kind of flat chested, so… she didn't care. You know what I mean? That was another weird thing, she should have had the bigger… well, you know."

I wasn't sure why she added that last part, and as hard as I tried to keep my eyes on the side of her face, they strayed. Traveling down, they took in the cleavage at her open collar, everything enhanced because she was hugging her textbooks tight to her chest.

She had her eyes on Sarge as she talked, but then looked up to catch me doing what I believed she wanted me to do. Our eyes met, and she grinned. I didn't want her to think that I would be duped that easily, so I tried to make her believe I had some other reason for focusing on that area.

"You've been carrying those books for a long time. Want me to haul them around for a while?"

"Ummm… sure. If you don't mind. I mean, it's not your problem. But if you'd like?"

I still couldn't tell if I had fooled her or if she had seen right through me and was just being polite. The thing is, the look she gave me when our eyes met was not one of disapproval. The grin had been somewhat mischievous, leaving me to believe she had been testing me, and I had failed. I also got the impression she was proud of her bust, and just might be one of those girls who had a more liberal view on things sexual.

Claudia handed me the books, and I nearly dropped them. I wanted to suggest she get a cart if she was going to lug weighty text books around, but I decided against it.

She sighed and wrung her hands. "Wowzah! Got to get the blood flowing again. Thanks—you're a rather noble guy. That's a good quality, don't lose that."

Grinning, but feeling like a fool, I adjusted my load as she continued with her story. "So, I was on my bed reading some crap about Alfred Wallace and how he influenced Darwin, when Elspeth told me she was going out to the terrace. No big deal, except, I figured she was going to get wet. Then I fell asleep. You know, that face in the book thing where you slobber all over your homework? Well, anyway, I woke up this morning and even though she had turned down her bed before going out, it was never slept in. Now, it's been almost twelve hours and no

18

Elspeth. So, I'm a little worried. I was hoping you could give me some idea what I might do. I mean, because I thought you were the actual watchman, and all."

"Did you go to anybody else? Like, your DA… or maybe, somebody over at admin?"

"Yeah, both in fact. But they blew me off. Some grouchy woman over at the President's office told me they knew all about it, and besides that, it was none of my business. But they thanked me for my concern. So, I figured the next step would be security, or the cops."

"Hmmm… that must have been ol' lady Samuels. It does sounds like a job for the police—not me, or the watchman. There's not much you or I can do, except to wait and see. I don't know what they'd do in this kind of a situation."

That was a lie, I did know. I had lived that experience. It was all coming back now as memories escaped that cerebral lockbox in my head. The clouds at sunset coming as the usual omen, the Déjà vu, and then the foreboding. All because of Elspeth. Time to drop the subject. I suspected Claudia wouldn't want to, though, because it was a pretty serious matter. But all we could do was worry, and I had nearly a lifetime of that, already.

Trying hard not to show my unease, I said, "I suspect the cops are already on it by now. I know one of them pretty well, I could always ask him?"

"That would be great, would you do that for me?"

"Well, since it looks like you and I are going to be friends, why not?"

Claudia didn't say anything and just smiled. That statement, designed as a solution to bring the subject to a close, had also created a conundrum for me. I didn't know if her reaction was more about me accepting her as a friend, or because I was doing her a favor. She put a finger to her lips and focused on the ground as we walked. She was sure giving it a lot of thought; whether the former or the latter.

The liberal arts building loomed up on our right, and beyond that, staff housing. It was a double row of twelve cottages, a story and a half in height. Six faced Crane Street and the six behind faced the opposite direction, their front yards, the back lawn of the school of medicine. Every one of them had a cobblestone walk and a pole lamp out front.

19

Coming up on the first one outside of Doctor Goldman's place, Marie-Louise barked at us from the front window. Sarge stopped and barked back. The good doctor soon appeared behind her and after giving us a wave, pulled her back and shut the curtain. Sarge ran to the Goldman's porch and peed on a corner of the steps, making Claudia giggle.

I strolled away, turning on each lamp as I went. Coming to the last cottage in the row before turning north to do the other six, I stopped just outside my mother's cottage, or should I say, my father's. He had been given the bungalow just days after the Dunwich incident. I suspect he had accepted it to get away from the prying eyes of the other residents at Faculty House. A place of his own would allow him to suffer in silence from whatever trauma the Horror had wrought.

My mother had been allowed to remain after he passed, a benefit bestowed upon the good widow of Professor Warren Rice. She could reside there for as long as she wished. It was my childhood home. So, I hoped it would be a lifetime.

I looked back at Claudia and it appeared as if she had lost interest in the topic of our conversation. Being free of her books, she now played tag with Sarge. The tightness in my shoulders dissolved away and I was glad to stuff all those related images back in that box and mentally lock the lid of that gloomy coffer.

Waiting for Claudia and Sarge to catch up, I couldn't help but notice birds arriving in twos and threes to land in the shrubbery between my mother's cottage and the one next door. It seemed like they were forming for a convention. I presumed they were coming in to roost for the night, but this left me wondering what kind of a bird roosted on the ground, and why there?

My mother had all her drapes pulled, her silhouette moving across them periodically. The parlor went dark and within minutes, the bedroom light lit up the window shade, telling me she might be heading to bed early.

"What are you looking at?" Claudia asked as she came up. Craning her neck, she leaned forward to look in the same direction.

"Um… nothing really. Did you see those birds?"

"Yeah, so? Just birds," she said, and looking at me, her eyes showed a mischievous twinkle.

20

I suspected she now awaited my response so she could send some sarcasm my way. Not wanting to get into another exchange, I just shrugged. That's when Sarge came up from behind and goosed her. She jumped, yelping. Spinning around, she swatted him away. He danced just beyond her reach and then came over to sit beside me with his tongue lolling. I fought to keep from laughing and quickly said, "Sorry about that, he's got terrible manners."

Sarge looked up at me and whimpered, wagging his tail. Then returning his gaze to Claudia, he rocked back and forth, throwing her a little, "Woof." This eliminated any doubt whether he liked her or not.

"It's okay, I forgive him. But... don't YOU get any ideas, mister!" she said. Her expression, once again, conveyed the opposite of her words and then she grinned, revealing an overbite filled with pearly white teeth. She was confusing me more by the minute.

I couldn't tell if she was truly interested in me or if this is how she treated every guy. Claudia wasn't the kind of girl I would normally have been attracted to—her short stature, her little girl voice, her choice of clothing, and that childlike face. But she had somehow gotten a foot in my door. I felt my adoration growing.

"Shall we get on with your duties?" she said, interrupting my introspection. Walking away, she motioned for me to follow as if she knew the route. A slight breeze blew, and I caught a whiff of her perfume. It was 'Accomplice' by Coty. Strangely, a perfume that had come to my mother at the hands of a suitor just last year. My mother had bragged about it, and her wonderful new man-friend. But she only wore the perfume once and never again, later telling me that she didn't like the fragrance. It soon joined the other unused bottles lining her bathroom shelf.

It dawned on me that Claudia could have said goodbye and walked away at any point since our meeting, however, she chose to hang around. She must have realized, at this point, that I had noticed and just might be asking myself why. I could just simply address the issue, but I feared that might be too forward. She might take my concern as rejection, and I didn't want that. I mean, at first, I wanted her to be on her way, and bringing that unsettling news about her missing roommate, didn't help matters. Now, I didn't want her to go. We had connected, and it just seemed so natural for us to be spending time together.

I followed Claudia around to the cottage behind my mother's, and after lighting the lamps in front of the other six tiny abodes, we headed for the School of Medicine. She swung her arms as she walked, and looking back, she smiled and slowed down so I could catch up. Perhaps what I had perceived earlier at the library had been anger, or bravado expressed in the face of anticipated adversity. She had been rebuked by her dorm assistant, and then ol' lady Samuels. So, maybe, she had expected the same from me. I sensed I was seeing the real Claudia now, a person of jovial affability.

We worked our way along the north side of the campus with Claudia and Sarge resuming their play. I finished up with the School of Science, and just as I stepped down onto the cobblestone apron at the base of the steps, I heard a whip-poor-will start to call. Others soon joined, and the rhythm in which they piped was peculiar. It rose and fell—like breathing. I thought back to when my father had died. My mother complained weeks before of whip-poor-wills keeping her up at night. My father remained silent on the matter, but projected a high degree of anxiety, his eyes filling with fear when she brought up the subject. I wondered if he knew something we didn't. Something from his Dunwich experience.

"Whip-poor-wills," I exclaimed.

"What?"

"Those birds… whip-poor-wills."

"Oh… yeah, we had tons of them where I was born," she said with disinterest. "Hey, would you walk with me to Pembrook? I know it's out of your way, but…"

"Certainly, I can do that."

"Yes… but do you want too?"

I gave her my, 'Why wouldn't I want too?' look, and said, "Of course, it would be my pleasure." The request brought me a degree of excitement as she smiled in a triumphant kind of way.

"So, your D.A. is actually a house mother—Warden Mordechai?"

"Yep, ol' Warden Mordechai. Why? Did you think I lived at Loring?"

"Yeah, I guess. I thought it might be Sandra Heinz. But I suppose, knowing them as I do, they'd both blow you off if you came to them with any kind of a concern."

"Well, I knew Mordechai would, but I don't know Heinz. So, you think she would have, as well? Do you know her?"

"Ummm, yeah, she used to be my girlfriend."

"But... not anymore?"

"That's right, we are done. Just me and Sarge now."

"So—no girlfriend?"

"Yep, that's what I said."

She skipped several steps ahead and then twirled. Sarge and I stood watching, and I could tell even he was baffled by what had just happened.

She skipped back and took the books from my arms. "What was that all about? The twirling thing?"

"Oh, nothing. Something I do when I'm happy."

"So, what are you happy about? I mean, a little bit ago you seemed pretty upset about your roommate."

"Yeah, I still am, but... something else has happened, since."

"What was that?" I asked, hoping for a confession.

"Oh, wouldn't you like to know," she said, playfully taunting me. Then peering into the sky, she tried diversion. "Wow! Look at all those stars. Have you ever seen so many?"

"Yeah, lots of stars," I said flatly and decided not to pressure her to reveal her secret.

Crossing Church Street, we walked through the vast front lawn that was Pembrook's. Claudia's dorm was twice the size of Loring and sat right in the center of the block north of the quad. It was surrounded by spacious green on three sides and a lot of old trees. The back of the building butted up against a wooded area. That, and Waldron's Grove, which borders the property on the east, is all that is left of Waldron Park. It had once covered the entire block before the dorm was built. Beyond it. lay the warehouse district and the Miskatonic River.

The building wasn't even ten years old, but was already starting to show its share of the Boston ivy that clung stubbornly to the walls of

23

most of the buildings on campus. Pembrook had been built to handle the overflow from Loring Hall, the first girl's dormitory.

Some very smart person anticipated an influx of female students after World War II and had it built to accommodate them. It had been constructed of brick and mortar in the Federal style, matching most of the buildings on campus; unlike the popular post-war designs that were popping up everywhere else around Arkham.

It had high windows on the first floor, shorter ones on the second and third, and dormers festooned both slopes of the slate covered roof to light the attic rooms beneath. Under its high canopied veranda, supported by massive columns, there hung a huge chandelier that swung slowly in the breeze. Dean Farr shared with me, some time ago, that M.U. had underestimated the cost of the dorm. They had to use money slated for the tennis court and swimming pool that was supposed to replace the timbered space behind.

They still had a housemother (yes, a housemother!) who managed the building, as well as the girls. The matron's rooms were accessed through a door from the vestibule, and another that opened into the commons area. It had its own bathroom. I didn't have anything to do with the lights over there—or anything else. It was all up to Matilda J. Mordechai, and that suited me just fine. I kept my distance, mostly because of my disdain for authoritarians.

Walking Claudia to the front steps, a curtain in the window to the left of the front door opened about an inch. Light spilled out and a single eyeball scrutinized us. Mordechai. It wasn't quite eight o'clock, and the curfew for the girls was eleven bells. So, I had no reason to expect a confrontation with the 'Warden'.

"Well, thanks, Sterling. If you make any discoveries, let me know, will you? Especially if you get a chance to talk with your cop friend. I can track you down and you can let me know what you've learned. Okay, remember… Claudia Osborne. My room number is two-o-eight, on the second floor. Give me a bell, will you? You know the number. Of course, you will get Madame Pushy, but… press on, huh?" Claudia turned and glared at the opened curtain. With one hand on her hip, she tapped her right foot as if annoyed. The drape fell shut and the light went out.

24

Turning back, she walked to me and stopped within inches, looking up into my face, her perfume filling my nose. Sarge moved to sit beside me, ears up, his tongue lolling and tail wagging. It seemed he had taken an interest in what she had to say.

"If you call, just tell the old bat to give me a yell, and I'll come down and take the call in the commons. Sound peachy?"

"It does. So… I'll see you around? Ummm, maybe we can get together and just talk, and… not about Elspeth."

"Well, I'm not going to forget about Elspeth, but you're going to speak with your cop friend, right? I mean, because you told me that, it gave me a little hope. I expect you to stick to your word. Like I said, you're a noble guy. So, I'm positive you will. You know, I plan on being at the library tomorrow morning. Can you stop by? It'll save you a phone call."

"Yeah, I have some work to do over there. So… see you then."

Bringing her chin down to the edge of her books, she looked at me out of the tops of her eyes. I swear I saw them sparkle. "Sounds keen, jellybean," she said, and flipping her hair, she turned away to do a kind of hopping dash up the short set of granite steps.

I strolled away, smiling to myself with Sarge sticking close. I hadn't gotten ten feet before I heard, "See yah later, alligator." Looking back, I saw Claudia had stopped at the top to watch me leave.

"After a while, crocodile," I said, and after giving her a grin, I continued.

That was not a typical retort for me. I couldn't explain why I did it, at least not without a great deal of thought. I needed time to think about the whole event and put all the pieces together. Here I met this girl, I am with her for less than two hours, and I didn't want to leave her. I looked back one more time. She now stood just inside the door with her face pressed to the glass. I waved, and her hand came up to wag fingers at me. Turning my attention back to the main campus, I forced myself to push on.

I passed the occasional couple out for a stroll, small groups of giggling girls, and clusters of obnoxious boys. Most of them knew me and said hello; petting Sarge as they passed. The rowdier bunches would come along later, but that would be Lyle's concern. As I made my way across the grass, I could just make out his shape as he stood waiting under the light at the west entrance to admin. He checked his watch and adjusted his cap. I gave him a grin when I arrived and handed off the keys.

"Right on time tonight, thanks kid." Without another word, he unlocked the door and slipped inside, leaving me and Sarge to go about our business. Hoofing it back the way we had come, we turned east between Faculty House and Saint Essex Chapel enroute to Garrison Street. Crossing over, we went north and did a fast walk up the block to Dean's Corner Drive-In.

It wasn't that lively on a Wednesday night, so I decided to stay and eat inside. Sarge planted himself in his favorite spot, right in the middle of the walk—directly in front of the double, sliding doors. Dean left them open in the warm months for the carhops to skate in and out. Sarge lay in his usual position, belly down, head on paws, his eyes envious as they followed me inside.

Dean's sat in the middle of the block, it's huge parking lot stretching to the same street I'd come in on. An alley, bordered by an ancient hedge, separated its back door from other businesses and residences. Large windows wrapped around the front and ran halfway back on each side. Red vinyl booths formed a horseshoe shape in each of the two front corners and could seat eight people. The ones in between, along the front wall, could seat four, with the smaller tables, for the love birds, sitting out on the floor in the open space between the booths and the counter, in two rows of four. That left the single stools at the counter where I would sit if I wanted to yak it up with Dean. But my favorite was the big booth in the far front corner. I could sit facing the parking lot as well as look out on River Street to my right; keeping track of all the action.

As a teenager, sitting there with my clique of classmates, it gave us the opportunity to see who pulled into the lot. Then, in my undergrad years, when aimlessly driving up and down the main thoroughfares was becoming a thing, I could entertain myself with the flow of car jocks returning to Dean's on River Street after they had taken several circuits. The popular route was to take Main as far east as possible up into the French Hill District before turning back, to honk at, and harass, the lovers parked along the Miskatonic River.

One of the carhops I didn't know, came up on her skates to take my order. A new girl who Dean must have just hired since the last time I was there. She was young, maybe all of sixteen. There were blond pigtails, braces, and just a hint of makeup. I wondered how long it would take for her to quit. I think every girl I knew in high school wanted that job; it was glamorous and if you were good at skating, you got to show off. It didn't take any one of them very long to realize it was actually hard work, especially on the real busy nights here at the drive-in. The turnover rate was high and only the tough ones stayed. Dean was a good boss—but the customers would tear you to shreds.

The girl popped her gum with an expression of annoyance as she fought to keep upright on her skates, her little pencil poised above her pad. After taking my order, she zoomed away, and slapping the guest check on the counter in front of Dean, she grabbed up a tray of food and sped out the doors saying, "What's shaking, big dog?" Sarge looked up at her, wagged his tail once and licked his chops.

Watching her go, I caught a familiar face rolling up to the open doors and heard, "Hey, Sarge." He never budged an inch as she skated one complete circle around him before gliding inside to spin once and fall back to lean against the counter. Her eyes went wide as they fell on me and "Oh my," escaped her lips.

Regina Duncan, one of those tough girls I was talking about.

Strands of chocolate brown hair had freed themselves from the loose bun at the back of her head. Her red bellboy cap sat in front of that, offset to the left. Her light green eyes bored into me, accompanied by her impish grin.

"Two burgers, fries, and a malted milk, now up!" Dean hollered.

Looking my way, he threw me a little salute before turning back to the grill. Regina didn't miss a trick, and taking advantage of the situation, grabbed up my order and rolled over to my table.

"Hey, Sterling, what's cooking?" she said, her toe brake squealing on the checkerboard of black and white tiles. Setting my tray down, she stood with hands on hips, ogling me.

"Hey, Reg," I said, and grabbing one of my burgers, I took a big bite to give me an excuse not to converse. Returning her gaze, I tried to smile with my eyes as I chewed away. I was avoiding small talk and anything that might give her an excuse to start in. It didn't take much with her. She was known to be 'easy', and bolstering that belief, she hit on me every chance she got. I just let it roll off. I'd known her all of my life. We were little kids together and we had always been, 'somewhat friends'. My mother did her best to see we didn't hang out together. I suspect she thought Regina was trash and would rub off on me.

Regina held the status of founder for the 'Arkham Harlots', a local girl gang. There were only five of them, but that was too many for a town this size. I still remember the fight she had with a boyfriend over a year ago. She bested him, and he had sped away in his coupe with a bloody nose. Dean had let it slip to me that he had hired Regina because she could hold her own against belligerent customers, especially drunk ones after midnight. If she liked you, you were safe. If you were smart, you stayed on her good side. I always treated her like a lady but resisted her advances in a passive manner.

"Don't feel like chewing the fat, huh? Oh, wait! I see you already are."

She laughed at her own pun in her usual raspy voice, adding, "You know, Sterling, you get me cranked… EV-ER-REE time I see you."

Turning to a forty-five-degree angle, she stuck out her chest. Popping her gum, she gazed seductively, raising her overly plucked eyebrows several times. The predictable flirtatious grin came next, with the exaggerated wink showing blue eye shadow. Nodding once hard enough to stress the bobby pins holding her cap in place, she clicked her tongue at me.

Swallowing my bite of burger, I risked saying, "Sorry, Reg, no time for talk, got work to do back at the dorm. Got to get done and get the hell out of here. Just finished my rounds and I needed to rest my feet."

"You want to talk about feet? Skate a few hundred miles in my shoes, kookie."

"You win, hands down, Reg. You don't need to convince me."

Projecting her lower lip, she blew the strands of loose hair from her face. "Yeah, but I know you also put in a few miles, too, and I respect that. No rest for the lamplighters, or… was that the wicked? Oh, hell, maybe it was wicked lamplighters. Anyway… okay… so, you don't want to razz my berries? Have it your way, Jose. You don't know what you're missing. Later, gator."

"See you, Reg."

She skated away with a heavy sigh. The pink poodle skirt she wore was standard uniform. She had taken hers up well above knee length, and now I saw it had somehow gotten hitched up in the back, probably from leaning on the counter. The tops of her nylons and garters were now on display to the world. If she bent over, it would expose a whole lot more. Dean required the carhops wear a petticoat—but not Reg. She'd been with him the longest and she could get away with a lot more than the others. I figured Dean was afraid if he said anything, she would quit. Regina was loyal and would show up when the others wouldn't. Dean could call her anytime and she'd come. On the opposite side of the coin, Dean's Corner Drive-In was her life. I suspected she would be there until the end, hers or Dean's.

Heading out the door, she looked back over her shoulder and grinning, she gave me a wink. Then she did bend over a little too far in patting Sarge on the way by; giving me a glimpse of red lace. I quickly looked away and brought my attention back to my burger. I felt pity for Regina because of the obvious rough life she lived.

Finishing what I wanted of my food, I left the rest for Sarge. Starting in on the malt, I mulled over my day. Claudia's face kept coming back with its many expressions and that Shirley Temple smile. Then came her words running through my head, expressing her concern about Elspeth being kidnapped. My stomach did a little flip-flop and Claudia's face melted away to become—Aubrey Celestine Rice.

Aubrey's round, sunny face with its milky skin and freckles came back to haunt me. A ghost wafting from that box in my head that was labeled: 'Things I don't want to think about'. With wide blue eyes over a perpetual full lipped smile, her auburn hair was always braided in one style or another and wrapped around her head with a different configuration every couple of days. Her flowery summer dress flowed out as she twirled on the lawn outside our cottage, the little silver necklace with the blue stone that I had bought her, swinging out from her neck. She always smelled of lavender and innocence. That's how I will always remember my dear cousin.

She was from Aylesbury, and that image was almost twelve years old now. Where she might be at the moment, was the mystery. The common belief was: a lonely, unmarked grave deep within some dark woods. The thought made me shudder. I imagined her lying dead next to a hole in the ground, waiting to be tossed in like some worthless piece of trash. It sickened me, and tears welled up in my eyes.

I realized that if I didn't stop this train of thought, I would do that one thing that I didn't do in public. The very reason I had wished for Claudia to change the subject. Wiping at my eyes, I sucked on my straw and tried to think of other things. I failed miserably.

At the age of ten, I was sent to live at the prestigious Wentworth House for Boys, a boarding school in the countryside just north of Boston. Every year, on the first of June, I would return to Arkham to spend the summer with my parents. Aubrey would travel over to be with us during the hot months.

My folks thought it good for me to have a companion during that time. Aubrey was the most willing, and we became very close. She was allowed to take the second bed opposite mine upstairs in my room, and we would talk and joke late into the night, or until one of us fell asleep.

Aubrey was how my parents coped with me. It was how they kept me busy and out of their hair. My mother had her social engagements, and my father was caught up in his devotion to the university. He hadn't handled fatherhood very well and spent his time either nestled in his cluttered office or with his cronies over at the Arkham Clubhouse Lounge. Rather than stay home with me and my mother, he would be out for drinks, discussing the philosophy of one thing or another—or politics. I don't think he wanted me born as much as my mother wanted to have a child. The thing is, once you make an appearance, it's too late. I have to give them credit, though, they did their best.

It was the end of my second year at Wentworth when the headmaster summoned me to his office and told me to pack; I was going home a month early. His manner had been brusk and he seemed nervous. All he told me was that my parents wanted me home and that was that. I wasn't going to protest because that's where I wanted to be.

I returned to Arkham earlier than I anticipated in April of forty-three, happy to be away from the rigors of boarding school and the cruelty of its inmates. I knew I would have to make up some of my schoolwork, but I could handle that when I returned in August.

Starting my break early brought a great deal of excitement. I could hardly contain my twelve-year-old self as I watched the pinkish mare's tail clouds rising up in the sun's afterglow, my young face reflected in the window of an Arkham bound train.

I fully expected Aubrey, with her old brown suitcase, to grace our front porch sooner than usual. I couldn't wait for her to throw her arms around me and say, "Oh! My dear Sterling!" Something she never failed to say at any initial meeting. Three words that never failed to raise my spirits.

We would soon be planning our adventures for the summer and maybe come up with new places to go within hiking distance of Arkham. Devil's Altar Island out in the Miskatonic River, or the vast woods beyond Hangman's Hill were a couple of them.

Of course, that jubilant frame of mind that I had the entire distance between Wentworth and Arkham, disintegrated as soon as I entered our little cottage. The sky was going to fall, and I could say goodbye to innocence.

I should have suspected something serious had happened when I saw the two brand new state police cars parked at the curb in front of our cottage. My mother greeted me as I walked into the front parlor. Tears flowed freely down her face as she hurried over from the two troopers standing in the corner with her expensive china coffee cups in hand. I remember the sound her shoes made on the wooden floor as she moved to embrace me. Wrapping my arms around that familiar waist, I looked past her to see my father sitting straight-backed on the sofa. The courageous Warren Rice, stone faced and not a single word for his twelve-year-old son.

I remember my mother ushering me over to him and sitting me at his side, she told him he would have to be the one to explain. I looked up into my father's face as he turned to me and said, "Sterling, my boy, your lovely cousin, Aubrey, has disappeared. We fear… she has been kidnapped."

31

11

Leering Through Dead Branches

Kidnapped is a terrible word. I felt there was nothing worse than being forced against your will to leave all you knew, stolen, maliciously removed from the comfort and safety of your loved ones. As soon as my twelve-year-old mind understood what had happened to Aubrey, I started to fret. I begged my parents and the police to find her. They had come to the university to question my folks and me, looking for information and clues, things that we may know that could help them piece it all together. My uncle Walter had called to break the shocking news and to seek permission to send the lawmen. They questioned me for over an hour. Afterwards, I pleaded again for them to bring Aubrey back safe. "We'll see what we can do," repeated over and over again, brought me no solace.

Two years passed before I realized what that statement really meant. It was not so much, "We are going to find that girl or die trying!" it was more like, "We are going to see if we have the ability to find missing people, and maybe, we'll get lucky." The heartbreak bordered on the unbearable.

By memory, it was the worst summer of my life. The war in Europe lagged with no end in sight and it affected everything. My folks were always nervous and unapproachable during that time. Their discussions always turned to the Fascists, or Japan, always bringing the question, "What if?" But all I wanted to talk about, was Aubrey.

"Will you please go out and play!" became the most commonly spoken phrase in our house that summer. The days just dragged until my return to Wentworth and the tedium of what I knew as boarding school. My comfort would come from my books. Fiction could whisk me away from the present and all the woes that went with it.

A red custom roadster intruded into my thoughts as it raced by on River Street, sparking annoyance. I always felt it odd that once I started reflecting on the one thing I didn't want to think about, and then got disrupted, how it always brought my ire. The driver honked his horn at the others who sat parked along that side of the lot. The 'Owooga' vibrated the windows, as a variety of different horns responded. I snarled a, "Thanks, buddy," as I watched the roadster speed to the corner to start his next, seemingly pointless, circuit. This brought my attention to the Miskatonic River that flowed by at the bottom of the short grassy slope on the other side of the street. Its waters gleamed as it rippled and flowed. That brought another terrible thought, and I wondered if Aubrey's abductor had sunk her body in the river all those years ago. I caught myself whispering a resigned, "No child deserves that." A hopeless kind of lethargy overcame me as I imagined the terror Aubrey must have felt in the clutches of her abductor.

The river's motion was hypnotic, and it easily carried me back into reverie. I recalled lying in my bed one night, listening to the words of my parents conversing in the dining room downstairs. My mother had lamented how Aubrey's window screen was discovered lying on the lawn, the old wooden ladder still leaning against the wall, and Aubrey's bedroom in shambles. 'Why didn't anyone hear?' and, 'Why did they let her play in the woods behind the house? Anyone could have been watching.' My father's response came low and almost inaudible. He seemed to dismiss it all, saying things like, 'Calm yourself, Elsie, it's out of our hands.' I hated him for that, believing at the time that I was the only one who really cared about Aubrey.

Obsession would grab a hold on me when I got older and I soon started my own investigation. My free time was spent perusing archived copies of the Arkham Advertiser, and other newspapers, for anything related to Aubrey's disappearance. I even sought out retired cops who had worked the case, mostly state policemen who were still riding horses at the time. I wrote them letters, called them on the telephone, and occasionally, met them face to face for a quasi-interview. Because some M.U. students, a few citizens of Dunwich as well as Aylesbury,

33

had dropped out of sight at the time of the Horror, it made me wonder if there might be some connection.

I realize now I wasn't very thorough. There existed a great sense of urgency which obstructed any attempt to be methodical. My work was sporadic and undisciplined. Then there was always a gnawing fear that while in pursuit of information, I would uncover some ghastly detail that I really didn't want to know. That fear may have intruded in a subconscious manner that caused me to create roadblocks. It was like I was trying to convince myself that I was doing good, when in all reality, I was just slogging through the mire. I never learned much of anything earthshaking and gave up my quest the year I entered university. It was all too much to bear, and after creating that imaginary trunk in my head, I dumped it all inside, closed the lid, and tried to get on with a life less gloomy.

Dean dropped a spatula on the grill, and I resurfaced. My eyes focused and I saw that Regina had moved to the row of hotrods along the River Street side of the lot. She now stood in my line of sight, bent over, leaning in the window of a black coupe with fake flames licking its sides. She was busy yakking up the driver, the pale skin of her thighs exposed to the world. She looked in my direction and waved. I presumed she thought I was admiring her legs. Grinning, she confirmed it by licking a fingertip and pressing it against her bare flesh. She then pulled it away like it was hot to the touch and I imagined the noise of a drop of water hitting a hot griddle. Even at that distance, I could see her throw me an exaggerated wink.

The driver of the car glared back over his shoulder; a face full of contempt. I looked away to Sarge, who lay gazing at me, head up, ears erect. It was like he sensed something was wrong and grew anxious to come to me. Getting to his feet, he woofed and wagged his tail while dancing in place.

Time to go.

Leaving a few Washingtons on the table, I grabbed what remained of my burger and made for the door.

"See you, Dean, got to get back to campus."

"See you, kiddo. Come back when you can stay longer."

I grinned and gave him the same salute he was always throwing at me. Coming out onto the walk, I tossed a piece of the hamburger to Sarge. Leaping to catch it, he expressed a dog's glee as he wolfed it down and begged for more. I obliged him with the remaining.

Balling up the wrapper, I tossed it into the garbage can as I moved out past the corner of the building. Breaking into a fast walk, I stuck my hands in my pockets and hunched my shoulders, hoping Regina wouldn't notice my departure. No such luck.

"See you, Tony... I mean... Mr. Curtis... ummm... I mean, Sterling," and lowering her voice, "You dreamboat, you."

A rough sounding, "Who's that cube?" rolled out of the roadster's window.

"He ain't no cube. That guy's cool. I've been fishing for a make out session—but he ain't biting."

Not wanting to hear anymore, I playfully jumped at Sarge and roughed up his coat saying, "Hey, boy." That put him in a frisky mood, and he pranced around me with playful growls, sometimes lightly grabbing the cuff of my sleeve with his teeth, sometimes jumping up to lick my face.

The air had grown cooler and I now wished I had brought my jacket. "Come on, boy," I said and took off running. Mischievously yanking at his tail when he took the lead, we crossed over Garrison Street. Jogging up the walk past the shops that separated me from Waldron's Grove and the Pembrook lawn, I thought how some of those places had been there since way before the turn of the century. There was the drug store, a beauty salon (new since 1946), a printing shop, and Adam's Clothier. On the other side, McNeal's shoes, Davis & McGuire's Bookshop, Sharp's Hardware, and then there was Gott's mom & pop grocery store, sitting kitty-corner from the quad. You name it, Arkham had it, but mostly up in fast-growing French Hill.

A chuckle slipped from my lips as I thought about how people (especially classmates at Wentworth) always referred to Arkham as a 'Dark Town'. Well, what town wasn't at night? But I knew that's not what they meant. They alluded to its dark past—the panic of the typhoid outbreak in 1905, Herbert West-the mad scientist, the horror from

35

Dunwich that everybody knew so well, and other such strange events wrought by past denizens of the town of Arkham and Miskatonic University.

I supposed it was because I had lived here all of my life that I didn't see it. Kind of like when you never notice how the inside of your house smells until you come home after being away for a long time. Our cottage—roses and cleaning fluid, Professor Hale's—old books and pipe smoke, Widow Waite's—cooked cabbage and cat piss.

I've visited other towns in the USA and Europe, weighing the difference, but to me, it seemed as normal as any other town or city. The way I figured it, Arkham had nothing on Transylvania.

I crossed Church Street at the corner and made for the lighted veranda of Dyer Hall. It had always been the men's dorm. The university had changed its name prior to my freshman year. I couldn't even remember what it was called before then. It was my job to lock the front door at midnight when everyone was supposed to be in their rooms. I knew if I forgot, Lyle would do it for me—and without complaint. Late arrivals had to ring the doorbell for admittance. One of the many annoyances a D.A. had to put up with.

My room was just inside the vestibule to the left, much like Pembrook, except, I didn't have my own bathroom or kitchenette. Its location allowed me to monitor the front door. If the boys arrived after lockup and I had to get the bell, I would just throw open the door for the latecomer, make some off the wall joke about their inability to tell time, and then walk away. I felt it better just to aid the undergrads when they needed it, not be their parents on campus. M.U. didn't need another Warden Mordechai.

Switching on my desk lamp, I delved into writing summaries. Sarge, as always, jumped onto my bed to lick his balls and sleep. He'd raise his head to look at the door every time someone came in, and with his ears at full attention; he seemed to be waiting for a knock, which rarely came.

Midnight arrived as a welcome break with the Bell Tower's peel confirming the hour. I walked out into the entry hall to peek into the first commons room. As usual, Casper Jenkins, a freshman, was seated in a chair, his stocking feet stretched out onto an ottoman. He looked up from Tolkien's *The Lord of the Rings* and grinned.

"Hey, bean, how's the book?" I said.

"Oh, hey, uh… Mr. Rice, ummm… not as good as The Hobbit… but I'm sure it'll grow on me."

"Casper, I told you to call me Sterling. Mr. Rice was my father."

"Oh, sorry, still can't get used to all this freedom. I'm hoping my sophomore year will be better."

"I'm sure it will be. So, is Alex still keeping you out of the room?"

"Yeah, well… it's okay. He's got a girl, you know? Hell, if I had a girl, I wouldn't want my roommate creeping around."

"You want me to say something?"

"NO! He'd hate me forever. Because, well… he'd know I was complaining. It's better this way. Sofa's pretty comfy and no one seems to mind that I'm in here all the time. Or… do you?"

"Naw, it's okay, make yourself at home."

"You know, it's not like I can't ever go up to my room. He's gone most of the day."

Casper struggled with everything. The product of a sheltered life. He was probably smart enough for Harvard or Yale—just not thick-skinned enough. Miskatonic was perfect for him. A small-town university with a weird background, but a lot more laid-back. This place could be considered right at the line for Ivy League. Casper was probably from one of the small towns around Arkham. M.U. was convenient for those overbearing parents who wanted to keep their kids close.

"Say, Mr. Ri… uh, Sterling, did you see that weird guy hanging around outside?"

"Weird guy?"

"Yeah, standing around over at the Bell Tower, smoking. Looked like he was watching the girl's dorm, uhhh... you know, Loring Hall? He looked kind of nervous. I could see him out of the window in my room. Then he went over toward Pembrook, and I didn't see him anymore. Looked kind of creepy, if you know what I mean."

"Well, if you see him again, let me know… or tell Lyle."

"Okay, but… that guys kind of creepy, too."

"Casper… everyone's creepy to you."

"Yeah, well…"

"Got to go. Talk to you later," I said, feeling the need to break away.

Alex Ryan's girlfriend spent more time in his, and Casper's room than her own, a violation of dormitory rules. The same rule I broke a dozen times myself back in 1949 when I was going steady with Francine Morgan, a girl who happened to be the university President's daughter. But there was no good place to go for any kind of an intimate liaison. The back of a Mercury wagon, Christ Church cemetery among the tombstones, the Grove, or, spooky Hangman's Hill for a little added excitement. Students got creative when it came to finding places to make out. That stretch of river bank east of Dean's was townie territory. No M.U. student wanted to be discovered making out there unless they were looking for trouble.

As D.A. of Dyer, I trusted my residents to be covert in their actions in order to give me plausible deniability. Alex and his girl did a real good job avoiding me when inside the dorm. But I couldn't see raising a fuss about things that were simple human nature. However, I expected complete transparency on more serious issues like—anything that might include loss of life. The majority of the residents knew the difference and we functioned like a well-oiled machine here at the dorm.

Strolling toward the kitchen I came into the second cavernous commons area which served as the television room. I turned off the unattended Admiral Regency and closed the cabinet doors to the giant console TV/Stereo. I arranged the couches and chairs back to their original (and recommended) positions. Slipping through the pocket doors into the large kitchen, I noticed it needed a good cleaning.

Checking the list tacked to the frame of the door, I looked to see who had kitchen duty. Felix Spater, and wouldn't you know it—Casper Jenkins. Grabbing an apple from a cheaply made basket someone left on the countertop, I went to rattle the backdoor to make sure it was secure. Then moving back to my room, I thought to remind Casper of his kitchen duties, but he now snored away, his book open, face down on his chest. He talked in his sleep between snores, and I'm sure I heard, "Mommy…" once or twice.

I woke Sarge for his final visit to the hydrant before bed. Moving out onto the front veranda, I stood and watched him sniff his way out to the very center of the lawn to water a newly planted tree. The air was cool, and the first vestiges of fog were just rolling in. Gnawing at my apple, I thought about what Casper had said. Stepping out onto the walk that led up to the front door, I moved to where I could see past the girl's dorm. The base of the tower was free of bodies, leaving me to suspect the creeper had given up for the night.

Sarge, on his way back, changed directions and ran out of sight between the dormitory and Faculty House as it sat, huge and ominous, just outside my room's east looking windows.

Stepping back up on the veranda, I moved to the end to lean out over the railing and peer around the corner of Dyer. In the ambient light, I could just see Sarge taking a dump along the chapel wall.

There came giggling and I moved to take cover behind a rather rotund column supporting the porch roof. Peeking around it toward the street, I watched four girls cross over from Gott's Grocery. Too proper for jay walking, they came straight over to the opposite corner via the crosswalk and slowly strolled along the sidewalk on the opposite side. Stopping just short of the gate to Waldron's Grove, they began to debate some issue.

The 'Grove' was a wooded swath of ground that separated Pembrook's lawn from the backs of the shops that I had passed earlier in the evening in my return from Dean's. It was a well-manicured park-like area, close to two hundred feet wide that extended north along a high brick wall. It terminated at that forest like area behind Pembrook.

There were assorted flowering shrubs in beds scattered among the trees, benches placed for meditative purposes, with everything sandwiching a winding path of pea gravel bordered by red brick cobblestones that ran from one end to the other. The Grove was mostly used for making out because it got quite dark back in there. The street lights on Garrison sent some rays of light between the roof tops into those trees, but that only added to the surrealness of the place.

The brick wall served as a barrier between university and private property. There had been a discussion among the board members about tearing it down, but the shop owners had rose up together in protest. So, the wall remained.

It ran north from Church Street and stopping about three hundred feet shy of Main, it took a left and continued on to West Street, where it met a tall, wrought iron fence that ran back toward the quad. The two, together, encompassed Pembrook and the woods behind it. Several round topped gates, made of heavy planks, had been built into the brick barrier and shortly after the Wilbur incident, large steel padlocks had been put in place, securing the gates for good. At one time it had been a requirement for the campus caretakers to check them during the Friday evening lamp lighting session. But that was back when I first started, a requirement that was soon ignored by all the caretakers. It took about half an hour to complete the task, something I always hurried through in order to deter the ever-growing fear of being caught back there after dark; something I considered odd because as a boy it never troubled me. There seemed to be an unspoken agreement among the caretakers to just let Lyle handle the gates. The university furnished him with a hefty, four cell, Burgess brand flashlight. Student workers had to find their own.

With my eyes still on that group of girls on the other side of the street, I watched them move at a snail's pace, their loud discussion turning into an argument. I heard one say, "No, Lucy, let's just go back to the room. It's late and we're probably already locked out." Another one humphed and said, "Well, you wanted to go to the late showing of that stupid army movie. Good ol' Van… whatshisname. What a germ."

"Oh, shut up Gertie, you don't like anything," the one in the lead said as they crossed over and headed for Loring.

They didn't even get to the curb on this side, when something swirled the mist at The Grove's gate. Focusing my eyes, I could have sworn I saw a tall, dark shadow, in the shape of a man, step out as if to follow. He appeared to change his mind and fell back in among the tree trunks. I waited, hoping to catch another glimpse.

The girls saw and greeted me loudly as they stepped up onto the porch at Loring Hall. One of them giggled and whispered loud enough for me to hear, "Oh… it's the Tony Curtis guy." The leader hissed an, "Oh, shut-up," as she rattled the doorknob and then rang the bell.

"See, I told you so," came from the girl at the back. "Locked out— as usual." Someone was quick to answer the door, but I couldn't see whom. I suspected it was Sandra. The girls were inside in an instant, and the quad grew quiet again.

Bringing my eyes back to The Grove, I was rewarded with a match erupting back among the trees. The glow of a cigarette increased and then faltered, followed by a cough. Idiot! If you're trying to hide, you don't light up!

Lyle told me once that criminals were the dumbest people in the world. I remember telling him I was glad for that, otherwise, civilized society was in trouble. I feared the 'Shadowman' would see me, so I thought it better to cozy right up to that roof support.

Something warm and moist assaulted my right hand. Spinning around with a gasp, I found it was only Sarge tasting me with his overly large tongue.

In an agitated whisper, I said, "Sarge, you're cruising for a bruising. Geez, dog, you scared the crap out of me."

He just wagged and looked into my face, his eyes searching. I was glad he couldn't understand English. I had the privilege of cussing him out and he didn't understand a single word of it. He was a good dog, though, and I feared the day I'd lose him to old age. The very reason I decided not to send him across the street to sniff out the stranger. He might have been courageous, but he wasn't blade or bullet proof. The odds were, I could enjoy his company for a good ten years or more—if I took care of him. Pushing it all out of my mind, I said, "Let's get inside, buddy, I've got work to do."

He tilted his muzzle up and made a strange, whining gurgle, like he did understand something more than just, sit, stay, or heel. Locking up behind me, I glanced through the window in the door one last time, but the glow of the cigarette was gone.

I decided to call Lyle and tell him about what had happened. I went to the telephone on the small, round table next to the dark wainscoting of the stairwell and dialed the watchman's closet. It rang a few times, but no answer. Hanging up, I decided to wait awhile and then call again. Moving back to the front doors, I noticed the fog was thickening. The lights over at Pembrook were only a glow through the ground bound cloud. I thought of Claudia. What was she doing right now? Working on some boring biology crap? Chatting with the other girls? Having a pillow fight? Perhaps, already sacked out for the night? My imagination went into overdrive.

I pictured her snoozing, cozy under her blanket, lying on her side, knees pulled up, with a slight smile on her face. The image soon evolved into something more erotic as it changed to a bird's eye view of her lying on her back without a blanket. She wore a white, baby doll PJ top and her left knee was up, allowing a view to a white, 'V' shaped patch of panty. Her hair was perfect, sporting a small, light blue bow opposite the part. The fingers of her left hand caressed her belly just above her pubic bone as the other ran up and down her bare thigh. She smiled seductively and closing her eyes, she kissed up at me.

My fantasy was brought to an abrupt halt as shoes thumped on the short section of stairs that led down to the first landing. Sarge gave a low "woof" as I swung around from the door to catch Alex Ryan, his comb frozen halfway to his bright blond hair. His eyes showed more white than brown as he stared back in fear. In that same moment, a sock free foot in a pink pump came into view as it stepped down onto the next tread.

I gave Sarge the command to stay as Alex stuttered out, "Oh, uh… hey Sterling." Then turning, he dashed back up, the pink pump going with him. I figured he must have picked the girl up and carried her along as he ran. But then they stupidly stopped in the upper hallway to address their situation—as if I couldn't hear.

"What's going on, Alex?" the girl said.

"Ummm… baby, I hate to say it, but Sterling is standing right down there at the front door."

"Who? Sterling? Who's that?"

"Oh, you know, the D.A.? Hey, you know…"

"The ducks-ass? I thought that was a haircut?"

"No, geez! D.A.? Dorm Assistant, get it? Goofball."

"Hey, don't call me that. That's not nice. So… you mean that, ummm… Tony Curtis guy?"

"Tony Curtis guy?"

"Yeah, you know…? The Tony Curtis guy… goofball. The grad student that lives downstairs."

"Geez, Sissy, you drive me nuts… and don't call me goofball."

"Okay, so what are we going to do?"

"Let's just go back to the room. You can spend the night and leave early."

"What? And give you a chance to make it to home base?"

"No, we'll just sleep. I'm tired anyway. Casper will be coming up soon, so… no time for hanky-panky. We can be under the covers by that time, and besides, I'm a little worried about the weird guy hanging around the quad."

"Yeah, he was kind of creepy, especially with that hat. I wonder who he was?"

"I don't care, as long as he doesn't come back. Probably just some peeping tom that wants to get a peek at you naked."

She giggled, and he hushed her as their footfalls echoed down the hall. I heard a door open and close, then a mock growl that gave rise to a playful squeal. It left me glad she decided to stay. I thought of what Casper had said and then what I had just experienced. If the Shadowman was still lurking about, Sissy might not fare so well out of doors, especially if she was a Pembrook girl. That could turn into a perilous walk through the fog.

It had been a long time since there had been any kind of trouble on campus. But if Elspeth had actually been abducted and hadn't just run away, it was better that Sissy remain until dawn and suffer Mordechai's wrath. A good bawling out was better than dead in a ditch, any day.

Going back into my room, I locked the door. Sarge jumped on his bed in the corner and was out cold in no time, running, and whimpering in his sleep. I returned to my work and remained there until the grandfather clock in the first commons room chimed two in the morning.

Moving from my desk to the end of my bed, I pushed off my penny loafers, and dropped my slacks. I lay them over the back of my ancient club chair and then pulling off my shirt without unbuttoning it, I threw it and my socks into the laundry basket by the door. Sitting down in just my skivvies, I tried to clear my head of its research related clutter.

Claudia's face popped in there from that moment when she said, 'Wouldn't you like to know?' Well, Claudia, yes, I would! I already presumed what it might be that had made her happy enough to cause her to twirl. I felt a slight twinge of excitement knowing I would see her later this morning and maybe get some kind of confirmation that it was being with me that had brought her that joy. It had been the best part of my Wednesday, something that didn't end just because the day did. Now, I had something to look forward to other than PhD work, visiting with faculty, and lighting lamps.

I reminded myself that I needed to stop being so picky about who I dated just so I could please my mother. Elsie expected a visit this morning. I could never get over how she only wanted to see me two days out of the week—and only for a few minutes on holidays, just so she could give me a care package that consisted of a homecooked meal. She had made it very clear after my father's death that I shouldn't show up unannounced. Tuesday and Thursday only. If I couldn't show, then I should call because she needed to make other plans.

It was also ironic that she had been a humble housekeeper upon arriving in Arkham back in the 20's, and by simply marrying my father, she had been propelled into the house of the M.U. elite. With no higher-education and only her southern etiquette to shield her from the intellectuals, she had struggled to be accepted. Yet over time, she became part of that world—the wife of Warren Rice, champion of Miskatonic University.

My mother now cavorted with the Arkham gentry, many of whom I detested. She did fundraisers, luncheons, a book club, a music club, and a cooking group. She took singing lessons, violin lessons, and was also learning French. She had many suitors, mostly men looking for a free ride. Every once in a while, she would receive an invitation to attend an M.U. dinner, showing up only to represent my father. Most of the time, she acted like she was better than everybody else, too superior—even for me.

Sitting in the dark, dreading my visit, I heard a noise at my window. Sarge was snoring so loudly I could barely hear what sounded like scraping at the sash. I had left the roller shades down all day, so I couldn't see who, or what, was out there. Potted plants would not have been very happy in my room.

The windows were about six feet apart, multi paned, and reached nearly to the ceiling. There were four of them, two at the front and two at the side facing Faculty House. The noise came from the one farthest away from the street at that side. It sounded like a mouse gnawing at the wood. In the daytime, it would have been so immersed in the other sounds that it could have easily been missed. But at almost three in the morning, its only competition was the steam pipes in the winter.

My heart climbed up into my throat, but I went to the window, anyway. I stood just off to the side. A silhouette vacillated across the thin material of the shade. I pinched an edge to pull it back just far enough to get a peek. That's when Sarge jumped up and blasted me with one loud bark.

I felt like I had been shocked with a large dose of electricity and the hair stood up on the back of my neck. The adrenalin rushed in, and I inadvertently jerked the spring-loaded shade, causing it to roll up with a snap. I must have looked a fright as I stood there staring at—nothing. The fog churned as if someone had left in a hurry. Tiny chunks of glazing compound littered the sill, and in the grass; something gleamed. It was a pocket knife with one blade open.

Part of me wanted to go out and retrieve it, but another part of me said that the smart thing to do was to stay put. My gut protested, though. Coward! Go out and grab it! Resisting my inner caveman, I pulled the shade closed and moved back to my chair. Forcing myself to sit, I waited to see if the creeper would come back. Sarge, taking advantage of my empty bed, curled up in my blankets. I felt shaken, but I soon dozed off, and for the first time since I was a kid, the Wilbur monster came back to haunt my dreams with a vengeance.

III

The Presence That Marches

I woke with a start and leapt from my chair. Sarge, sitting at the door, watched me over his shoulder. Seeing that he got my attention, he scratched at the panel a few times and gave me his, "Hey, I gotta piss," whimper. Events from earlier in the morning came roiling back to me and reassuring Sarge with a, "Yeah, just a second boy," I let my curiosity lead me to the window. Lifting the shade, I saw the chunks of glazing compound were gone and so was the knife. A line of tracks showed in the dew-covered lawn coming from the direction of the chapel. The grass in the area below the window had been smashed down and three lines of footprints were either coming or going from that spot.

My old, brass alarm clock sitting on the nightstand told me it was 6:40 in the morning. I still had time to do a little investigating. I slipped into my slacks from the day before and pulled on a dark colored cowl necked sweater from the closet. Sticking bare feet into loafers, I snatched my door keys from the desk and headed out. Sarge stayed one step ahead of me and the second I opened the door, he bolted for his favorite tree. I launched myself over the railing at the end of the veranda where I'd stood the night before and walked slowly toward my window, studying the ground.

There were two different sets of tracks. The footprints coming from the chapel were larger, and within each one, the grass blades lay nearly flat. This told me they were the most recent. Close examination revealed they were made by walking shoes with a wide flat sole and heel. The other set, coming from and returning to Church Street, were made by a square toed boot. The grass inside the prints had sprung back nearly vertical. My curiosity drew me toward The Grove, and whistling for Sarge, I followed the tracks left behind by the boots.

A slight breeze blew, and tiny grey clouds scudded by overhead, turning pink with the rising sun. Stopping briefly at The Grove's gate, I studied the interior before going in. From what I could see, everything appeared as normal. The pea sized gravel of the path was soon crunching under foot as Sarge moved in and out of the trees ahead of me, squirrels mocking him from the branches overhead.

I came across several burnt matchsticks scattered over the path. Moving my eyes in an ever-widening circle, I discovered the butts from hand rolled cigarettes littering the mossy loam at the back of a large hickory. A well-worn trail curved back from that spot to run along the wall. With the rain we had on Tuesday, it had been fairly well muddied up by that same pair of boots, and now, a peculiar nail pattern showed at the heels.

I walked along the wall, listening to the sound of the shops on the other side as they prepared to open for the day. Sidewalks were being swept, awnings were being cranked down, and stock boys were cussing and conversing in low tones as they brought in deliveries. Coming to the first of the two round top gates in that section of the wall, I found the dated padlock still in place. The wood showed its age in the form of rot and the fungi that grew on its surface. There was no damage. Continuing, I found the next one in the same condition. So far, so good.

The rough trail I'd been walking soon came to a short, rusty fence of cast iron. The turn of the century decorative barrier, mimicking ivy, ran perpendicular from the brick wall toward the dormitory to terminate at the east edge of the Pembrook lawn. The trail continued just on the other side of the thigh high obstacle, telling me, whoever was using it, had just stepped over instead of going around. That would allow them to avoid detection if anyone were watching from a dormitory window.

Sarge, who had been behind me, ran over to where the curving, pebbled path ended at the freshly cut lawn. Two large Grecian flower urns had been placed there, one on each side of the walkway. Stopping between them, Sarge raised a leg to one of the large metal planters. Upon completion of his task, he dashed around the fence and disappeared into the undergrowth on the opposite side.

I too chose to step over the fence to avoid the prying eyes of Warden Mordechai. It was risky business because I chanced snagging a certain part of my anatomy that would definitely send me into the mud to writhe in excruciating pain. Once over, I breathed a sigh of relief. Pulling my hand from the fence, my eye caught the shiny surface where the point of a metal ivy leaf had been broken off. Blue denim threads still clung to the jagged edge along with a hint of dried blood. I suspected the prowler had snapped it off in their haste, paying the price for moving too quickly through the dark without a flashlight.

Arriving at the inside corner of the wall, I found yet another well-worn spot where someone had stood for a long time. This one was larger than the first, almost as if the watcher had been given to pacing. There were more matches and cigarette butts, along with gum wrappers and what looked like wood shavings as if someone had indulged in a little whittling while they waited.

This particular spot offered a clear view through the trees, straight to the terrace at the back of the dorm. Somebody was not only watching Loring Hall, but Pembrook as well. I walked back and forth in alternating lines, studying the ground, looking for anything new. I soon came across another set of prints with a wider, half-moon shaped heel. It was a shape I had become quite familiar with at the Wentworth stables. Riding boots. Their indentation was deeper than the others, telling me the wearer carried a few extra pounds. They appeared to have come from the west, and stopping where I now stood, they had done an about-face and went back.

Moving on, I kept my eyes peeled for anything that would give me a clue as to who these people might be. My old tree house soon came into sight, the short boards I'd nailed to the side of the tree to be used as a ladder, now hung askew, one or two of them missing completely. We had also built a fort further to the west, a makeshift castle of crates and planks that, over the years, had been consumed by nature. Animals like deer, raccoon, rabbits, opossums, and squirrels had found a home in what had become one massive thicket. I wondered when M.U. would get around to leveling the place for their swimming pool/tennis court project. I made a mental note to ask Dean Farr.

Coming to the first round top gate in the north wall, I found it in the same condition as the two before it. But, from where I stood, I could see the next one, at the center, swung freely. I trotted over to find the hasp and padlock hanging from the staple at the jamb. The long metal screws that once secured it to the gate, now lay bent and broken on the ground. The nail pattern I'd seen in the heel print of the squared toed boots was stamped into the wood at four different places on the outside. Someone had kicked the gate until it gave.

The ground there was trampled into a quagmire as if a multitude of feet had congregated in the opening. They all seemed to have moved toward the west, smashing the grass, and leaving a good many divots in the soil. Only the riding, and square toed boots went the opposite direction to the eastern, inside corner.

Sarge startled me when he broke from the underbrush. Coming to stand beside me, we gazed out the opening and down the well mowed slope to Main Street. I could see the backs of the warehouses and the Miskatonic River as it flowed toward the Atlantic. Stepping just outside to ponder the situation, it didn't escape me that the little trail I'd been following now dissected the lawn as a stripe of well-worn grass. I moved down to the street and saw that it continued on the other side, stretching to River Street and then through the buildings just beyond.

I was gradually putting the puzzle together, and it all started to make sense. Whomever utilized this path was doing it on a regular basis. They would have easy access to a car parked at the curb where I now stood, or a boat farther down at the dock. I suspected the latter. A gap between two warehouses offered a straight shot to the river. I thought of Elspeth. Had she been bound, gagged, and forced to stumble her way down to the Miskatonic where she was loaded into the bilge of a small motorboat?

Cars passed, and the people inside watched me watching them. The early morning commuters going to work over in the French Hill district reminded me that I needed to get back to the dorm. After doing a fast walk back inside the brick wall, I pushed the gate shut and looked around for something to brace it with. I pulled a fat branch from a pile of brush, exposing a limestone paver covered in moss; the remnants of a narrow walkway that had once divided Waldron's Park. It had run from the gate, straight to Church Street. Outliving its usefulness, the walkway was now blocked by fallen branches, brush, and itself, dissected by a large dormitory. Using it would only lead to a serious case of aggravation, but I knew it would bug me all day if I didn't try. After bracing the gate shut with the branch, I took a deep breath and pushed into the tangle.

Sarge, seeing that our outing wasn't quite over, gleefully followed me in. Not quite as adept as my dog, I struggled to force my way forward. The damp clay had all but consumed the large stepping stones and made for some slick walking. It had captured a number of animal tracks, and not surprisingly—a few hobnailed heel prints.

The path proved as difficult as I had predicted. Deciding I had all I could take, I turned back with a claustrophobic urgency. A frightened dove rocketed from a nearby briar patch, and I tracked a single, tiny feather as it floated to the earth.

I watched the miniscule plume tumble across the ground and get hung up on a tuft of grass just off the side of the trail. When I got to where it had been snagged, I bent to pick it up, only to stop mid act. A small, bare, footprint showed in the clay. Closer examination disclosed that the foot that made it, only had four toes. Elspeth! The absence of drag marks told me she had not been towed or made to stumble, but had, instead, been carried. Perhaps she had been set down for a second, or someone had dropped her. She would have surely screamed or cried out, unless she was unconscious. I needed to tell somebody what I had found.

Moving back to the brick wall, I took a left and followed the trail of tracks to the tall, wrought iron fence at West Street. Passing the last gate in the wall, I didn't bother to check it. I'd already gotten what I came for. With no choice but to take a left, I continued to follow the trail created by all those feet. When I got to where the wooded area stopped and the swath of lawn that served as a backyard to the dormitory, I saw that all the prints had turned left toward the terrace's giant stone stairway.

I continued on toward Church Street, breaking into a slow jog. Sarge danced ahead of me, thinking it all good fun as he frolicked, spun, and barked. Crossing over the dew damp cobblestones of the street, I found the quad was just starting to stir as staff and faculty moved toward academic buildings in preparation for their day. I maintained my speed, stopping to rest only when I arrived at Dyer.

Stepping up onto the veranda, I paced slowly from one end to the other and back, trying to still my racing heart, analyzing all the while, what I had discovered. Stopping at the Loring side of the porch, I bent over at the waist to try to catch my breath. Doris Day's 'Secret Love' poured into my ears and looking up, I saw the window to the shower room on the second floor of the girl's dorm, was wide open. So typical.

From where I stood, I couldn't see inside, but the boys upstairs with rooms adjacent, could. The two dorms were separated by a street's width of lawn, a cobblestone walkway running along at the center. The buildings were still close enough to offer arousing details of any unclothed occupant and, without the aid of binoculars.

Sandra had mentioned that she had taken to adding the little 'No-No' of leaving the window open to her speech for first-year girls. She would also be sure to give occasional reminders to the rest. Because her charges chose to ignore her, she had complained incessantly when we were together. She couldn't understand why any proper girl would allow it. Sandra just couldn't seem to grasp that not all girls were proper—and neither did they care. She had asked me many times to censure and discipline those I caught indulging in voyeuristic behavior. I never told her how even I had been duped into joining a group of peepers my first year.

I was standing in Kevin Blyth's room with a raucous bunch of boys and we were carrying on about something. Kevin, and Billy Peel, (two football players) sandwiched me between them, and picking me up under my arms, they turned me around and ushered me forth to the open sash. I thought for sure they were going to toss me out. But instead, I was faced with 'Sing, Sing, Sing' by Benny Goodman as it flowed out of the window from Loring's shower room radio.

I was stunned to find Lori Saunders there in all her glory. She danced to the beat while toweling herself dry. Looking my way, she grinned as I felt the blush creep up my neck. I wanted to get away, but the two lettermen held me there for a few minutes longer amidst a hail of laughter. Then Sean McCabe demanded his turn and I was allowed to flee.

I wasn't a so-called virgin by any means as I suspected many of them were. I just never felt compelled to intentionally involve myself in such activity. Yet I suspect that was as close as many of those boys were ever going to get to experiencing a girl while at college. I wasn't going to be the one to deprive them of that. Thinking back on it now, I know Lori was an exhibitionist of the most extreme kind. It would have been useless for me to try to convince Sandra otherwise.

Sarge soon joined me on the veranda and scratched at the door, a sign he wanted fed. Going inside, I gave him a scoop from the bag stored inside the closet and refilled his ceramic water bowl from the untouched glass of water on my desk. Taking off my clothes, I dropped them in a pile and donned my threadbare robe. Grabbing my keys, a towel, and toilet kit, I made my way to the second-floor bathroom, leaving Sarge to crunch away at his dish. Half an hour later, I returned to find him passed out on the bed.

Dropping the robe and slipping on my underwear, I decided this time I was not going to dress to please my mother and donned clothes from the 'already worn' pile. Being somewhat of a fan of Jack Kerouac, I opted for his style of dress. Looking more like a common laborer than an Ivy Leaguer, I felt it a much more comfortable wardrobe choice. There would be enough of sports jackets and ties whenever I got around to teaching. My present outfit gave many people the impression that I was one of the 'Beats'. Which, even though many of my beliefs were comparable—I wasn't. Sure, I wrote poetry and other things, but I felt pretty lame compared to Jack and his troupe.

As I stood in front of the mirror and tried to manage my hair, my stomach rumbled, reminding me that breakfast should happen soon. Leaving Sarge to snooze, I exited and strolled through the quiet commons areas to find one of the kitchen doors propped open. A nearly full box of Sugar Jets sat on the counter, with no one around. Helping myself to a bowl and the last of my milk, I made a mental note to go over to the grocers if my mother's weekly care package didn't include the white of the cow.

She was expecting me about eight. If I arrived late, I would suffer a scolding. I dare not knock early, though, because I would get the same. I would have to hang out on the porch and wait until her mantle clock, visible through the front window, struck the hour.

With thirty minutes to kill before I had to be there, I dumped my unwashed bowl in the sink and left by the back door, almost running into Lyle as he trudged on by. I suspected he was putting in some overtime, but for what reason, was beyond me. He should have been gone by six. Samuels and President Morgan wouldn't be in until nine. His appearance behind Dyer Hall at that time of the morning made me suspicious.

Lyle wasn't allowed into the President's reception before hours. So, a drop slot had been added high in the wall of his converted, coat closet office. All he had to do was drop the keys in the slot on his side and they would slide down the chute to the box on the other, where Samuels could collect them. Control was her thing. The ring would remain stashed in her drawer until a caretaker, or Lyle, showed up to retrieve them prior to her leaving for the day.

"Hey, Lyle, heading home?"

"Well, if it isn't Sterling Rice. How are you, kiddo?"

"On the stick, as always," I said. "So… I wanted to tell you something."

"Walk with me, will you? Heading back to my humble closet to drop these keys."

"So, there was this guy standing around over at the Church Street entrance to The Grove last night. It was like he was watching Loring Hall. Then, a little after two this morning, I heard a noise at my window. When I went to check it, whoever it was, ran away. I figured he was scraping at the putty on the sash with a knife, trying to take out a pane of glass without breaking it."

Lyle didn't reply right away, which told me that he had to think about it. Opening the outside door to the building, he followed me in. As we walked to his closet, I turned to add something, but he beat me to it by saying, "Anything else you noticed?"

"No, that was pretty much it, except I think he came back to clean up his mess... for some weird reason."

Lyle unlocked the closet door and pulled the chain to the bare bulb hanging at the ceiling. I moved to the front of his tiny desk as he laid his big silver flashlight on a shelf at the back. After dropping his wide black belt in his chair, he threw his sweat-stained uniform frock onto one of the old coat hooks next to the shelf. It slipped off and fell to the floor. Grumbling, he picked it up and put extra effort into making sure it stayed the second time.

With his back to me, he said, "Okay, well... I'll make a report and pass it along to the cops. Then I'll get a work order over to the Physical Plant to get your sash fixed. They might be able to get to it before the end of the day. Who knows? Those lazy bones are slower than molasses in January."

Just when I thought he had accomplished getting the frock hung up, I watched it slither to the floor a second time. Lyle caught it and said, "Damn it all to hell." Using a different hook, he angrily worked at getting the frock to stay put.

Waiting for him to turn back to me, I ran my eyes over the top of his desk. A Staghorn handled Barlow knife lay there on a pile of daily reports. Picking it up, I saw that someone had tried to scrape away some initials engraved in a small, silver plate riveted to its side. There had been three initials. The first two were indecipherable, but the last one had definitely been an 'R.' Turning it over, I found, 'C. K. Whateley' scratched into the staghorn side plate. A chill ran through me as the knife slipped from my fingers and clattered onto the desktop.

Lyle spun around and reaching across he snatched it up, throwing me a scowl as he stuck it in his pocket. "Wondered where I'd left that damn thing. Not good to be without a pocketknife, you know. A man never knows when he's going to need one."

The tone of his voice was indifferent, but the look on his face was malevolent and told me, 'Keep your paws off my shit.' I suspected the knife to be the one I saw gleaming from the grass. I knew about Barlow knives because Aubrey had one. Something she had saved money for, so she could buy one at the general store over in Aylesbury.

She told me she was going to buy me one for my thirteenth birthday and have my name engraved on it—like hers. She never got the chance. The one Lyle had was the exact same kind, except for the 'C.K. Whateley.' I needed to get the hell out of there or say something to change the subject.

"Oh… something else I wanted to ask you before I go. Did you hear about that missing girl over at Pembrook? Elspeth something or another…"

"Who told you about that?"

"Oh, some girl was yakking on about it over at the library."

"Did you know her? The girl at the library, I mean. Maybe I could talk to her."

"No, some first-year student, didn't recognize her."

"Well… keep that under wraps, huh? Can't let that stuff get around. Bad for the university. If you go blabbing it, people might think your word is official."

Ignoring the BS he was spewing, I said, "Anyway, I went over this morning and found that center gate in the northside of the brick wall, behind Pembrook, hanging open. On top of that, there was a bare foot print in the mud."

"You just might want to stay out of there. If that girl was kidnapped, you don't want to be mixed up in that. Hell, the next thing you know, you're a suspect too. So, take it from me, kiddo, let the cops handle it, huh?"

The cops consisted of three men. Chief Solum, Jerry McClean, and Ralph Hutchins. There was Eleanor, the daytime clerk and dispatcher, but she didn't really count as a cop. I didn't have a whole lot of confidence in anyone of the three solving anything, well, maybe except for Jerry. They had a fifty-four Ford to get around in, and the chief sometimes rode an old black mare when he made his rounds in the day. Probably to save fuel so the night cop could have a full tank.

"You hearing me, Sterling? Stay out of it. President Morgan is already up to his ass in alligators, and old lady Samuels has just been a bear. It's only been over a day, and they're not even sure the Houghton girl didn't just run away."

Yeah, because college age girls always run away in flimsy night gowns and bare feet! My bad feeling got worse and I started to itch to be gone. Lyle had turned from a friendly mentor to a potential threat.

I forced a grin and said, "Okay, sounds like good advice,"

"Good," was all he said, trying to hide his relief.

"Got to go, see you later," I said, deciding to leave off the gator part.

"See you tonight, don't be late, huh kiddo? I have a clock to punch, you know."

Leaving by the same door I came in, I strolled back the way we had come, and then west, to pass through the open base of the bell tower. Cigarette remnants and burnt matchsticks littered the ceramic tile of the floor inside. Kicking at them with the toe of my shoe, I moved on. Passing between the science buildings, I eventually crossed West Street, and gaining the sidewalk outside of the Liberal Arts building, I slowed my pace as I approached staff housing.

I was nervous, but that was typical. I would never outgrow that. She was my mother and I would always be her child. I just wished she would accept the fact that I had grown up. Upon arriving, I ran up the steps and peeked in the window. She had opened the heavy curtains in anticipation of my arrival. I could see the mantle clock showed 7:59. With my eyes on it and a finger hovering at the door bell, I waited. When the big hand clicked over, I hit the button at the first chime of the ancient Ingraham.

The bolt was pulled and the oaken door with its heavily etched glass window, opened a crack. That was all she would do for me. Pushing it open, I entered to see my mother in her kimono-like robe, walking away into the dining room.

"Please close it, Sterling, and set the bolt if you would."

"Yes, mother, will do," I said snidely.

She glanced over her shoulder with a look of distain. Her long, dark hair had been brushed straight back over her forehead and was still wet from her bath. With piercing blue eyes, her face and nose were nearly the same as mine, but seemingly etched in stone. Her lips were pinched, so she wasn't happy that I added, "...will do."

"Sterling, you're an English major. Talk like one."

"If it would please you—mother dear."

"It should please, you. People judge you by the way you speak."

56

"Yes, you're right, they do."

"Yes, I am correct, I have no doubt," she said in what could be considered a haughty, New England accent.

Turning away to hang my leather bomber jacket on the rack by the door, an age-old despair flooded in. Along with that, came a feeling of hopeless lethargy. I thought of how her voice had gradually changed over the years from the Tennessean drawl to a more sophisticated, eastern Massachusetts way of speaking. It was only when she was seriously angry and screamed at people that she would revert back. Elsie had been abused as a child, by her father, by her brother, and sometimes, by her mother. She had always made bad choices when it came to companions. That included her lovers. My father had been her first big break. He would always be her god.

I walked into the dining room as she stood pouring tea, and after setting the flowered China pot back on the matching trivet, she turned to find me awaiting further instructions.

"Kiss your mother, Sterling. Give me a proper greeting."

Embracing her lightly, I pecked her pursed lips as her eyes studied mine. She then placed her long slender fingers on my arms, briefly squeezing my left to assure me that she still loved me; even if I might be a disappointment. I felt her frail body through her robe, wondering if she might be ill. I glanced at her face again and noticed her complexion had paled significantly since Tuesday.

She knew I was scrutinizing her and she turned quickly out of my embrace. Gesturing toward my father's chair, she said, "Sit there."

I didn't dare plant my derriere on that seat until she did hers, and only after I held her chair. Practicing etiquette was key in helping keep our encounters civilized.

Once seated, she picked up a spoon and dumped some sugar into my tea. "Just how you like it, Sterling," she said, not looking at me.

"Thank you," I said, even though I knew she wanted me to remain silent.

I put my eyes on my cup, but eventually let them stray across the tabletop to the hand now stirring the contents of hers. She had already adorned herself with her favorite jewelry choices of the day, and all but her thumb displayed a fine ring. Sterling Silver was her thing. No gold, no white gold, every gem housed in silver. It was her passion, and the very reason for my name. As my father had put it once, while he and I were out for a day of fishing, "She wanted your middle name to be Silver. I wouldn't allow it. So, she told me straight from the birth bed—in that case, Warren, Sterling shall receive no middle name."

It was one of the few times my father had ever joked with me, saying maybe she could have, instead, named me after some exotic gem. But Ruby, Opal or Aquamarine, wouldn't quite do it, either. He felt that being saddled with Sterling was enough for any boy to have to deal with.

I sat in my father's chair, waiting for my mother to break the silence. She would have to be the one to start any topic. If I broke the rule, she would change the subject right away, even if it might have been what she wanted to talk about in the first place. Also, I dare not go off on some tangent in an attempt to change it back. That, more often than not, would lead to a request for my early departure.

"Sterling, your dress is unacceptable. Your father would have been furious. You need to dress like a man of importance. You represent Warren while you are here at Miskatonic. You need to keep in mind that you are Professor Rice's son. A man who helped save mankind. Do you remember?"

"Yes, mother, I most certainly do."

"Then... please, stop your Beatnik impression. You are not downtrodden. You come from a family of means. I truly believe you will be a great man, someday."

"Thank you, mother, I appreciate hearing that from you."

"Sterling, you don't think that you're the brother to that awful Jack Kerouac, do you?"

"No mother, I don't."

"Well, thank heavens because, you are better than that."

"Thank you, mother."

And that's how it went for a full hour. I was a captive until nine bells and then I could leave on my own or be badgered out the front door. Lingering in my mother's house was disrespectful.

It was about eight forty when the conversation switched from her fund raising, her woman's group, her singing lessons, her violin lessons, and the last M.U. dinner that required her presence, to: my terrible dog, dumping Sandra, lamp lighting versus teaching, the vow I had made to my father (that I would become a professor), and my progress toward that goal. She finalized it all with her concerns over my insolence, my lack of a proper diet, the Whip-Poor-Wills gathering outside her window at night, and her fear that someone had been lurking in the dark around the cottage.

That's the one that got my attention. I thought it better not to say anything. I feared I would scare her. Besides, she was safe enough, mostly because she kept the house locked up tighter than a drum. Another reason I didn't say anything about the Shadowman, was because I feared it might open the door for her to bring up Aubrey. That would just make me feel worse than I already did. So, I just let her lament, nodding my head, and smiling politely.

"Sterling, I believe whoever has been prowling around the cottage may be trying to see me disrobing. But as you know, I am sure to keep the curtains tightly closed. Last evening, I am positive someone was on the porch. I didn't dare look out, though. I will now keep the front porch and back stoop lights on all night. If you would be so kind to mention it to Mr. Umberling, I would be most grateful. He should be made aware. Also, when you make your rounds for the lamps, you could keep your eye open for people who don't belong, and… oh, yes, maybe you could frighten off those ghastly birds?"

She was done conversing by eight fifty-five and Aubrey didn't come up once. I was anxious to get away and just as much as she was for me to be gone. She confirmed it when she said, "Take your groceries and go, Sterling. I have to prepare for my singing lesson. Mr. Levi is a hard man to please, but he is an excellent instructor, even if he is a German."

"Yes, mother," I said, doubting that our Mr. Levi actually ever set foot in Europe.

Moving to the refrigerator, I opened the door to see that she had bought two of everything. I would be allowed to take half. Pulling out one of the cartons of milk and several small, plastic containers of vegetables, it was obvious that my mother had added Tupperware parties to her list of social engagements. I am certain if I were to say anything, she would remind me that Mr. Tupper was a Massachusetts man, deserving of all the support we could give him.

There were grocery sacks on the counter with 'Sterling' penned across the sides. One had apples, oranges, pears, and a turnip inside, along with napkins, butter, and a carton of eggs. The second held a box of bran flakes and soda crackers. I put the milk and Tupperware in that one and finished it off with a loaf of bread.

"Watch the eggs, they break easily," her voice, matter of fact, floated in from the dining room.

I wanted to blurt out, "You're kidding me? Eggs?" But I contained my irritation as I wrestled to get a solid grip on the bags. Heading for the door, I saw she was already there, holding it open for me.

"Okay, kiss your mother, Sterling, say goodbye in a proper way."

I leaned over my groceries and pecked her lips. She squeezed my arm for the final time. I was only allowed two squeezes per visit. For a total of four squeezes per week, and possibly two more on Sunday—if—she summoned me for dinner at noon. If.

I stepped out onto the porch as the mantle clocked chimed nine. The door closed behind me, and that, was that. No wish for me to have a lovely day, no 'See you later, alligator.' Just an unspoken, 'Get out, I've given you all the time you deserve.' I gladly accepted it, though, mostly because I don't think I could have taken anymore.

On the average, it took about an hour for me to get back to feeling normal after every visit. Yet it wouldn't be the normal I had been before Claudia brought me the news of Elspeth. I needed a beer, but it was too early. Standing at the corner of Crane and West Street, I waited for traffic, feeling pleased that the Gott's had double bagged.

At Dyer Hall, I unloaded the groceries onto the long counter in the kitchen. Bobby Corey came in just as I was folding up the bags to put them in the overstuffed drawer designated for bag storage.

"Hey, daddy-o, how they hanging? Oh! Groceries! About time, I was starving."

"You're always starving, Bobby. Better get a doctor to check you for a tapeworm."

"What? A tapeworm? You think I might have a tapeworm?" he said, his face growing serious as he ran the palms of his hands up and down the outside of his thighs in nervous fashion.

"Uh… yeah… people who want to eat all the time, in all probability, have a huge tapeworm living inside them. You're eating for two."

"Do you think I should make an appointment?"

His eyes were almost bulging in fear, his hands now rubbing each other nervously at his belt buckle.

"Bobby…"

"Yeah?"

"I'm just pulling your leg, bean, calm down."

"Oh! Hah! Okay. You had me cranked, daddy-o."

"Just calm down. Help yourself to some food—just don't drink my milk.'

"Oh…okay, yeah. Hey Ster, did you hear about that girl that got kidnapped?"

"It's just rumor right now."

"I don't know about that. I went joy riding up Main Street last night with some friends. Beasley has a car and we were bored, so we went looking for chicks. We were out pretty late, and it was getting really foggy, but the last loop we made took us down Main Street behind Pembrook, and we passed a whole crapload of cop cars parked at the curb. I think they were the Arkham cops and county mounties. They were running around everywhere back there with flashlights. We'd had a few beers and didn't want to end up in the hoosegow, so, Beasley parked over on Boundary Street and we walked back to campus."

I suspected the cops that he thought were county, were actually state police because Arkham only had one car, and Essex County regularly had only one deputy on duty at any one time. I figured Bobby had exaggerated to make a point.

"Did you see anybody you knew?"

"Well, I think I saw that old bat of a housemother, what's her name? Mordecky… Mardickle… Mordor…"

"Mordechai?"

"Oh! Yeah! That's it. She was standing there at the curb talking to a cop. I'm telling you, Ster, even if it was foggy, you just can't miss ol' Mordunky. I hate that old cow."

"Yeah, I know what you mean. Well, I got to go, Bobby, see you around."

"Later, gator," he said, and then opened a cupboard to see what I had put in there. He zeroed in on a box of vanilla wafers and pulled it out. I didn't have the heart to tell him that they weren't mine.

So, the presence of cops behind Pembrook, last night, explained the multiple footprints running from that back gate, west, and then around to the dorm terrace.

I expected to come across Claudia sometime in my day, but now I made it my goal to seek her out, even if she wasn't at the library. There was no way she could not know something. I imagined her and a few other girls with their heads hanging out of a back window at the dorm, doing a play by play during the event.

Opening the door to my room, Sarge lunged out, and jumping up on me, he started licking my face. Then after dancing around me for minute or so, he stopped to sit at my feet and made a face that said he was disappointed in me for having left him alone.

"Sorry, Sarge. You know I had to go see my mother, and you know how she feels about you. Remember when you lived there? She tried to have you killed. So, my friend, even though she won't let you lay on her porch, it's not your fault. You're super in my book."

He had been staring up into my face the whole time, his tail levering back and forth, his ears pricked as his head cocked left and then right like he was trying to catch every word. I scratched under his chin and when I finished, he let out a low woof and moved to sit at the front door of the dorm. Reaching inside my room, I grabbed my research valise, and after locking my door, we headed for the library.

My advisor, the ancient Professor Strang, approached us from the Bell Tower, exhibiting his typical ungainly walk as he made his way to Faculty House. Even with what must have been a ton of academic papers stacked in his arms, he still stopped to talk. Sarge gave him the usual poke in the derriere with his snout, and Dr. Strang sang out, "And… how do you do?" Then laughing, he refused my offer to help carry his burden. He wasn't one to tote a bag or case. I suspected grabbing up all those papers was a last-minute thought and he probably told himself, "Oh, what the hell…" and took the risk of losing everything to a gust of wind. If he lost your paper, he would, in all probability, just give you an A.

We chatted about my dissertation for a while, and he requested I stop by his office with anything I had accomplished since the last time. Then, waving me off, he continued on his way.

Sarge and I went to the 'Front Campus' taking in yet another lovely day. It was slightly cloudy, but the sun shone intermittently between the large, cotton ball like cumulous that floated overhead, their planate bottoms tinted grey. Thoughts of my mother still loitered in my head, leaving me to wish I could break through that wall of propriety.

Coming around to the front door of the library on College Street, an ambulance raced past toward St. Mary's hospital, its siren blaring. I watched it whip into the emergency entrance and after the driver shut down and things got quiet again, I heard, "Hey, kookie, did you hear me?"

I turned to find Claudia seated at the top of the steps. I smiled and started to speak, but today she wore a poodle skirt—with no petticoat. Because she had seated herself above me, there was no hiding what she wore underneath. She sat, knees wide apart, her underwear visible to the world. I was a little surprised that she hadn't put two and two together.

I pulled my eyes away and studied the bricks in the wall of the nearby gymnasium.

"What? You don't want to talk to me today?"

"Well, ummm… does… 'I see London, I see France…' mean anything to you?"

I turned back and tried to keep my focus on her face and not the 'V' shaped patch of flowered fabric between her legs. She gave me her squint-eyed look and then tilted her face up as if in thought. She remained that way for a few seconds before bursting out in laughter and clapping her knees together.

"Oh, come on, Sterling, you're a grown man. Does that bother you? Do you object to my choice of lingerie, or, are you just a prude? I never took you for one."

"I'm not a prude. It's just… how many people have walked by here and indulged in a veiled view to your private parts?"

"Veiled view? Definitely something an English major would say. But to answer your question—no one. I saw you through the library window and I came out to meet you. Sitting down, well… that was a last-minute thought. I've only been here for less than two minutes and to be honest, I didn't think about the consequences. So… don't have a cow."

"Okay, fine. So, I've arrived," I said, and even though she had closed her knees, it didn't help much. Lowering my eyes, I kicked at a dandelion growing through a crack in the cobblestones.

"So… you're here. But first, before we start a serious conversation, I need your opinion on something."

"Sure, I'm good for advice," I said, bringing my eyes back to hers.

She whipped her knees wide apart and said, "Sooo… what do YOU think of my new underwear?" I must have looked shocked, because she broke out into some serious laughter, exposing that glorious overbite.

I decided directing my focus someplace else wasn't going to help anymore. The mental picture of Claudia's new underwear wasn't going away. I didn't know what to think. She either had a crude sense of humor or trusted me enough to share something even more personal than cleavage. I tried not to be judgmental. I suspected she was coming on to me and this was just her style. I supposed she wanted a more efficient way to show it, even if inappropriate. If that were the case, it worked. Claudia had successfully broken the ice.

Sarge took her action as an invitation. Bounding up the stairs, he attempted to investigate. She giggled and was able to push his head out from between her knees before his nose found its mark. "Silly dog, that's one bed of flowers you don't get to dig. Dig?"

Picking up her large textbook titled: Principals of Systematic Zoology and another book whose title I didn't catch, she stood and brushed off the back of her skirt. "Okay, so enough joking around. I have to confess, I don't do that for… or should I say, to, anyone who I don't feel an above average attachment for. I mean, I don't joke around like that with my parents, Aunt Doreen, or, god-forbid, my Uncle Alijah. I mean, in truth, I hardly know you, but I sure feel like I do. Like... I want to, anyway. You get my drift?"

So, it was the latter. If there had been a question about where our association was going, it had now vanished. I wondered if she was of a Bohemian attitude, or one of those sexual radicals. I knew my mother wouldn't like her, but that was just added motivation.

"Right?" she said again, pressing me for an answer.

"Yeah, I get your drift."

"Good. So, can we talk now? You wanted to talk, right?"

"Sure, just... not about Elspeth."

"Well, we have to talk about that first. Why don't you want to talk about that? Does it scare you? You don't seem to be the kind that scares easy. So, okay, I'll try to keep it short, then we can talk about anything you want. Alright?"

"Sounds like a deal. Where should we go?"

"Let's go up into the stacks on the third floor. Hardly anybody hangs out up there. As long as we keep our voices down, we should be okay. Right? Sound good?"

"Sure, lead the way."

"Peachy! I have something to tell you about this thing that happened last night at Pembrook. It was some pretty exciting crap! You won't even believe it!"

IV

Yet Untainted

Claudia turned to walk inside, and I just stood, watching her go. Seeing that I wasn't coming, she turned, ran down the steps and grabbed my free hand to tow me up to the door. Another student was exiting as we approached and not waiting, Claudia pushed passed him with a giggle. The student actually held the door for me to keep me from getting crushed as she pulled me through. A grin stretched his lips and I wanted to tell him it wasn't what he thought, but then realized that—I couldn't say for sure.

We ran through the front hall, making our way straight back to the large, Gothic framed opening, marked, 'STACKS'. Alice Payne, the head librarian, threw us a scowl as Claudia giggled, her saddle shoes clonking on the wooden floor.

Pauline, Sarge's sister, poked her muzzle out from behind the desk and he met her, nose to nose. Giving her a quiet woof, he then splayed his front legs in a kind of bow, like he wanted to play. Pauline just pulled back, the librarian helping her with a slight tug on the tether that secured her to the chair leg. Alice then put a finger to her lips and issued a, "Hush!" Claudia ignored her, and giving me a glee filled glance over her shoulder, she laughed. Then letting go of my hand, she charged up the stairs with Sarge in hot pursuit.

Claudia was lusty and something of a mischief-maker. She struck me as not only intelligent, but also rather adventuresome. She, apparently, didn't take crap from anyone. I liked her even more for that. It left me to wonder if she had been a tomboy in her childhood. Singing out, "Slow poke!" upon reaching the second floor, she slung herself around the newel post with her free hand and launched herself up onto the next set of steps to disappear from view.

I trudged up the first set of stairs, wishing I had her energy. Glancing up through the balustrade just a few treads short of the top, I caught her in a twirl up on the third-floor landing. Her skirt spun out, exposing everything from her feet to her belly button. I couldn't help but notice how tanned and muscular her legs were. I wondered if she joined the other girls who stayed for the summer and spent their days sunbathing naked upon the widows walk atop Pembrook's roof.

It was something I, and a couple of my pals, had discovered in our sophomore year. We had been fooling around in the woods behind the dorm and had gotten an eye full. There was also the gossip among the present-day Dyer Hall residents confirming the act was still in practice.

Making my way up the last flight of stairs, I watched her drop her books, and forcing her skirt down, back up to the wall, squeaking out, "Sorry."

Two boys and a girl I didn't know, came into view as they made their way down. The second boy in passing, grinned and said, "Hey, Claudia."

"Hey, Carl."

"Still trying to keep that poodle under control?" he said as he turned down the stairs. Grinning at me, he raised his eyebrows several times in succession.

"Ha-ha," Claudia replied, and we all laughed.

Sarge came back into view to stop beside Claudia as she bent to pick up her books, an obvious flush to her face.

"What was it you were saying about consequence?" I asked.

"What?"

"Oh, forget it."

Claudia sneered and stuck out her tongue before moving out of sight behind the floor to ceiling bookshelves, taking my dog with her. I made my way to a small table at the back wall with a view to the science annex. Not a minute after I planted my derriere in the seat, I heard, "Marco?"

I waited, saying nothing. I was not really interested in playing pool tag on dry land. But when she said it a second time from a different location, I thought it better not to drag it out.

"Polo," I said flatly, giving her the response she was looking for.

She then let out a yelp and shouted in mock seriousness, "I told you to stop that!"

Sarge danced backwards into view, his mouth open, his tongue lolling. He appeared to be grinning. Claudia's head emerged from behind the bookshelf as if she were levitating prone, and then turning her face to me, she laughed. Ending her illusion, she skipped out from behind the shelf and came to me, Sarge following. She threw herself into the chair on the other side of the table and slammed her books down on top. That gave me a view to the title of her second book, a well-thumbed copy of, *Sexual Behavior in the Human Female* by Alfred Kinsey.

She saw me looking and said, "Do you know Kinsey? He's my fave. I read about him in Time magazine and then I found his book. It makes me feel like we are all a bunch of ignorant prudes. I think I'm going to do a study on the effect of puritanism on the American population. We've got to loosen up, Sterling, or... I think we are doomed as a nation. We are going to end up right back where we were in the sixteen hundreds if we're not careful. Just an opinion," she said and gave me an exaggerated smile.

"Anyway, so... how old are you, Claudia?"

"Twenty? Why?"

"You sure have a lot of energy."

"Oh, I just like having fun. You're not a party pooper, are you?"

"Never thought I was. How come you're only a freshman at your age?"

"Oh, I'm not a freshman. I'm a sophomore. I'm almost done with my second year."

"Then how come I've only first seen you now? Where have you been hiding?"

"Ummm... I was pretty much a dorm-rat my first year. Which is why I now want to have some fun. It took me a while to realize I was being a drag."

"I'm sure I would have seen you around, though?"

"Oh, I saw you around—a lot. But always from a distance. You know the other kids say you look a lot like Tony Curtis, the actor?"

"Yeah, I know, I get that all the time. But geez, I don't even like the guy."

"Honestly… I don't either. But you're not him. So, that doesn't matter, I can live with it."

"Well, you look a hell of a lot like Shirley Temple, you know? Straight out of *The Blue Bird*. So, what gives?"

"Yes, I know that, too. Of course I know that! I've been getting it all of my life. But I bet you don't know what it's like to have other kids follow you down the hallway in school, singing, 'On The Good Ship, Lollipop' or, 'Animal Crackers in my Soup' while you're changing in the girl's locker room? No, I suppose you wouldn't. But I kind of feel like you and I are in the same boat. Do you agree?"

"Sure, never been in the girl's locker room, though, but if I may ask, what's the attraction? To me, I mean?"

"I needed someone to help me with Elspeth. I saw you, and thought you were the watchman. Nobody wants to talk about it, as you may know. It's supposed to be hush-hush."

She grinned and blushed, adding "But then, I don't know what it is, there's something about you. Something I can't put my finger on. But who knows these things? Isn't it always kind of a mystery? What attracts one person to another? I don't know, but I'm sure Kinsey does. I simply have to read more to learn more."

"So… you seem pretty smart?"

"Yeah, sure, straight A's, so what? Want me to explain Recapitulation Theory to you? I can do it. If you still don't know the Theory of Evolution, or maybe a few concepts of Ethology, I can help."

"No, that's alright."

"Of course! What was I thinking? You're shooting for a PhD in English, I'll bet? So, why would you care? About science, I mean."

She leaned across the table, wiggling her derriere in the chair as she smiled into my face and stared into my eyes. Her breath smelled like Dentyne gum and I caught another whiff of the perfume. I studied that sweet face from less than a foot away, noticing that crow's feet were starting to form at the corners of those amber-brown eyes. A happy person's thing. Not only smart—but funny. A jovial optimist.

"So, where are you from?" I asked as she pulled back and slid down in her chair. Nibbling at a hangnail on her thumb gave her time to form the right words for her answer. When she did speak, it was with a certain degree of hesitation that she said, "I came here from Cambridge."

"Cambridge? So, a Radcliff transfer?"

"No silly, the town."

"Why, the hell, Miskatonic?"

"My mother couldn't afford Radcliff, and neither could my stepfather. M.U. was perfect. It offered everything I wanted in a school, and my folks could afford it."

"So, you were born there, then? A true Cambridge-ite?"

"Oh no, daddy-o. I said I came here from there. I was actually born in Dunwich."

My guts turned to ice. I stared without blinking. Dunwich. The name was almost a swear word in my house. My father's words echoed in my head; his voice as clear as the first day he divulged his nightmarish story of Dunwich and the Horror.

"A terrible place... Dunwich, terrible, terrible place." I still remember his horrified shouts in the night as he fought some demon in his dreams. His episodes were always followed by my mother's soothing voice as she calmed him upon waking. Those events only served to bolster the Wilbur monster in my nightly terrors and I often longed for her to come up and sooth me too. But my cries for her to come to me, went unheeded. I was left to lay shivering in the dark, wishing for the sound of her tread on the stairs.

I remained quiet as my eyes searched Claudia's. "I know what you want to say," she said. "Yes, I know the story. Doctor Henry Armitage, dead now. Francis Morgan, old and grey, living out his last days in Boston. And of course, the great Professor Warren Rice—your father. Yeah, I know, but what you should know is, my father was Joseph Osborn. He owned the general store there and he was a drunk who beat my mother nightly. I was born upstairs to Elizabeth Mabel Brown-Osborn. Delivered by the hands of Dr. Houghton from Aylesbury, assisted by old Mamie Bishop. We were just as poor as the families of the kids I hung out with. The few that still lived in the village, anyway."

70

Claudia sat up straight and planting an elbow on the table, she put her chin in her hand and continued, her eyes studying me as she talked.

"By the time I was four, I was playing with those kids down in spooky, ol' Cold Springs Glen, splashing around in Bishops Brook, and climbing Sentinel Hill. There's an altar up there, you know? And some pretty weird stones sticking up out of the ground. Anyway, by September of my fifth year, we were gone. My mother tried to runaway one other time before that morning. We had taken a train ride down to Brimfield. I remember my folks argued all the way there. They decided to turn around and come home, but before we got back, she took me and snuck off the train in Gowan, waiting until the car started to move before getting off. She couldn't stick to her decision to leave him, though. One night away and she talked herself into going back to him and Dunwich. I remember the black eye he gave her for that little blunder. It was soon after, we left that man and Dunwich behind, forever. She said she wasn't going to let me grow up in that place. I will never forget the night we left. My folks had a really bad argument, all because she wanted my father to sell the store and move down to Aylesbury. He tried to kill her by pushing her down the stairs. They made me go to my bed early and I lay there thinking I wouldn't see my mother ever again. I would be alone with that bastard to do with me as he wished. I remember feeling surprised, but happy, when my mother woke me up at about two the next morning with a suitcase in her hand."

Claudia paused, adjusted herself in her chair again as I stared, listening, hardly blinking. It was a lot to take in. She gave me a fleeting grin and continued.

"So, my mother snuck me out to the woods where she had tied a horse earlier in the evening. I remember a long and painful ride to Aylesbury with me bouncing in front of her on that saddle, all the while trying to hold on to that suitcase. We were so afraid my father would find us and kill us. I thought that ride would never end, but it finally did at the Aylesbury Inn out on the Pike. She met a man there. He loaded us into his big black car, and we drove through the dark, all the way to Cambridge. You see, she had been having an affair with that guy, who, I can happily say, is now my stepfather. Retired Colonel Anton B. Kofta

71

of the Massachusetts State Police. He and a few others were assigned to the Wilbur Whateley case after the weirdo tried to steal that book downstairs. What's it called again?"

"The Necronomicon?"

"Yeah, anyway, they didn't find out much, but he did find my mother. Having stopped in at the store once for a root beer, she just kind of fell for him. Notes started being passed, and well… the rest is history. I don't even know if my real father is still alive. But honestly, I don't care. Anton is a good man, and a big tickle. I think you can best describe him as jolly. I liked him right from the beginning. He's not with the cops anymore, he got hurt and had to retire. He confessed to mom and me that he felt it was time to get out of the business. He owns a coffee shop now, catering to the Beats over in Cambridge. I think his sense of humor rubbed off on me. He cares for me like I am his own. I can only imagine where I would be if we had stayed in Dunwich. What a dump! I'll tell you, Sterling, I couldn't have better parents."

Feeling a little unnerved because of all the overwhelming information, I just sat there, speechless.

"You okay? Looking a little pale, there. Probably should close your mouth before you catch a fly."

"Well, you kind of floored me. I mean, because of my history and… how weird is it that it kind of connects with yours."

"So, Sterling Rice. Let's see, you were born here, right?"

"Yes, over at St. Mary's hospital, and I have lived here all of my life. Well, except for when I was over at Wentworth."

"Wentworth! The boy's private school? That's so boss! I went to Alice Barton. Which, I believe is like five miles east? Oh boy, did I hate wearing pleated skirts and white blouses every day. You've probably noticed that I'm not very mindful of it when I'm in a skirt."

"Uh… yeah. But I get you… about private school, I mean. I don't think I'll ever want to wear another white shirt and tie again for as long as I live. And those blue blazers with the big, red 'W' embroidered on the pocket, oh, man! I secretly burned mine the first year here at Miskatonic. I did it up on Hangman's Hill with a couple of friends lending a hand. We danced around the fire like a mad tribe of freshman, sharing a bottle of whisky. My mother searched high and low for that jacket. She even asked me where it might be. I just shrugged at her. She didn't take it well."

"So, anyway, I know your dad died. Someone told me a bunch of students found him in a snowbank? So, what happened to your mom?"

"She's still alive. Still living over in staff housing."

"Oh! That's the ginchiest. Can you introduce me?"

"Whoa, stop right there. She's kind of a private person. I don't think that's a good idea. You would hate her the minute you met her, because, well… she'd hate you, and then tell you right to your face. Sometimes I think she even hates me, but…"

"Oh, come on now, honestly?"

"I am sure it's all for show. That is, what she does show"

"Kind of frosty, huh? Does it make you feel bad? I mean, that it seems like she doesn't really love you?"

"I didn't say that."

"Ummm… yes, you did."

Her words sparked some anger. I tried to fight it, but I was on guard now. Reaching across the table, she laid her hand on mine. Her face softened and she looked genuinely concerned. Her eyes were comforting. She was ready to hear whatever I had to say, but I wasn't ready to say it. I had never talked with anyone about my mother, or how I felt; not even to Sandra.

But Sandra seemed to understand Elsie. They became friends, but only because she was the kind of girl my mother wanted me to marry. She had accepted Sandra into her heart and her home in just a matter of hours. I recall she raged for days when she learned I had broken it off with 'our' girlfriend.

It would be easy to spill the beans to Claudia, to tell her all about it. It would be effortless, all because of the way she was looking at me. But frustration rested just below the ire, and just below that—the tears. I feared I would break my rule and weep in public, something I haven't done since I was twelve, and that, had been for Aubrey. It dawned on me that Claudia was doing just what I wished my mother would have done all those years ago.

"Okay, I get it. It's okay," she said, "Maybe another time."

73

"Sure, maybe," I said, feeling subdued, but also relieved.

"So, anyway, about last night. You won't believe this. I went to Warden Mordechai because I was worried about Elspeth. What a nosebleed! That woman really rattles my cage. I'll tell you, Sterling, if she were to choke on her shrimp cocktail, I wouldn't even raise a hand to slap her on the back. She demanded to know why I was concerned. Can you believe it? Anyway, she told me that M.U. was aware, and it was in the hands of the Arkham cops along with the state police. I had already called Anton, though. He gave me some good advice and let me know he was on top of it. So, maybe you don't have to talk to your cop friend, after all. Anyway, last night I was in my room with Beatrice Balch from across the hall. We call her Triss. We were in our PJ's, messing with some new lipstick when we heard the warden's battle cry. It came from the terrace at the back. Since my room is at the front, we got up and ran over to Triss's and stuck our heads out the window. The terrace is right below, and you wouldn't believe it! Mordechai was chasing some guy around with the poker from our fireplace. She was in her robe and curlers. It was crazy! The creep was dressed all in black and was trying to hold on to his hat while he was making his escape. She got to the stone stairs first. You know the ones that curve around to the lawn? So, he tried the door to the dorm, but she caught him there and gave him a good whack. I think she only got his shoulder, though. But you should have heard him holler! He ended up jumping over the railing. It's almost ten feet down, you know! We were going to go down there after he ran away, but... well, my PJ's are just the top part of a baby-doll, along with my underwear. You met them earlier, remember?"

Claudia chuckled and raised her eyebrows several times before continuing. "I didn't have a bra on, and my headlights tend to bounce when not slung properly. Besides that, it's kind of see-thru... Oh! Sorry... I guess I could have left that part out." She grinned mischievously and added in a low tone, "So, did I give you a woody?"

Here she was going for the shock-value again. Claudia had totally mesmerized me with her story and then changed directions and popped that question on me. I'd never heard a girl say 'woody' before. Well, aside for Regina's version—but she was the exception. Francine Morgan liked to talk dirty during sex, but never in public. She, like

74

Sandra, felt that they had a reputation to uphold and cared what people thought. Which, I honestly felt wasn't such a good thing. So, maybe it was because I thought of Claudia as a 'nice girl' or worse yet, I was in the process of putting her up on a pedestal, that when she said 'woody', or talked about her underwear, she knocked me right off that ladder of infatuation.

Keeping my voice steady, I said, "A woody? No, you didn't. So, don't worry about it. But you know, Claudia, when you say those things, it makes you sound easy. If you know what I mean?" I gave her a grin, realizing too late that those were my mother's words. Claudia's face became somber, but her response was tempered with just enough caution to let me know she wasn't going to accept being chastised.

"Easy? No. And a kitten? I am not. You should know that, right now. I've only had one boyfriend in my whole young life, and we didn't make it to home base until our second year. He split afterwards. Besides, I'm careful what I say around people I don't know. You're not a child anymore, Sterling. You can handle the humor, right? Like I said, it's because I feel a connection to you. I want to be myself without the judgement. I was hoping you could be the one person who I could do that with. So…?"

"Sure, I can do that," I said, feeling a little foolish.

"I like you, Sterling. You make me feel at ease. I want to get to know you more, and I hope you want the same."

She still had her hand on top of mine. I wasn't sure what to say. So, I turned it palm up and gently took her hand in mine as an act of surrender. Her face went from serious back to relaxed, and for a second, her eyes sparkled. I felt I was going to get an education with Claudia and anticipated that it was going to be the best one ever.

"So, what happened after? At Pembrook…"

"Well, Mordechai had us all come down to the commons. It was horrible. She made us line up in rows, like we were in the army or something. She blabbed away about what had happened and what we were going to do about it. I'm standing there in my flowered underwear and Jenny Davis is pinching at my butt cheeks, making me laugh. I told her to stop. Then she had to go and mimic an old lady's voice, saying,

'Relax, my dear, I'm just picking flowers!' Everybody laughed so hard. I'm sure Mordechai wanted to strangle every one of us. She divided us into groups and assigned us sections of the house to inspect. She ordered us to check all doors and windows to make sure they were locked. Later, I heard her on the phone with the police, yakking them up about the peeper. We are now to stay off the terrace after dark and make sure the French doors are locked all the time with the drapes pulled at night. She wants us to have escorts when we are outside in the evening, and we are to stay out of the woods in the back."

"Well, I'll be your escort, if you want. At least you'll be safe."

"Neato! My own personal bodyguard. Not only are you qualified to light my lamps, but you can now guard my body."

We laughed together and I felt any anger that remained, dissolve away. I wanted to tell her about my experience with the Shadowman, but she continued on with her story.

"Anyway, the cops showed up and were running around out back of the dorm. We went up to Casandra Filberts room on the third floor and watched them out of her dormer window. You know? Those windows on the roof?"

"Yeah, I know what a dormer is."

"So, they were out there for hours with their flashlights, poking around in the fog. Two cops, I think were state police, came up on the terrace and were looking around, pointing at stuff. I think they were searching for evidence. I overheard one of them mention the Houghton girl and something about a kidnapping. So, I think it's official now. Anton said they have to make sure she didn't just run away. I really believe M.U. wants to keep this under wraps. Anton warned me not to gossip and to be cautious. Hey... what time is it?"

After checking her little wristwatch, she looked out the window at the science annex and said, "I see Doctor Ellery is already in the room. I've got to get to class, Sterling. Shall we go?"

"I've got some research to do, so... I'm here for the day."

"Oh, okay, well, maybe I'll see you later?"

"Certainly, give me a bell at Dyer. Leave a message. The boys will post something on my door if I'm gone."

"Peachy! Okay, got to make the scene with Dr. Ellery. Got a two-hour lab, but labs are always fun. I get to play with dead frogs and stuff."

We stood up and she grabbed her books. "I'll walk you down," I said.

"No, it's okay. Got to run if I'm going to make it." Coming around the table, she stood on her tip toes and pulling my head down with her free hand, she kissed my cheek.

I looked hard into her face afterwards and she smiled and said, "Later, gator."

Dashing away, she went to the landing and before going down, she looked back and wagged a hand. I waved. Sarge gazed up at me and whined his concern. "Don't worry boy, you'll see her again. Come on, let's get you outside so you can do your duty."

Going down the stairs, I thought about all the things Claudia said. The man in black on the terrace was probably the Shadowman. I forgot to ask what time that happened. It must have been shortly after I had seen him at The Grove. I was still going to talk to Officer McClean, hopefully he would give up some information about what was going on around campus.

Sarge did his thing and we came back inside. Going to the reference room, I found my favorite table in front of one of the massive windows and sat down. It was a good, sunny spot, hidden from my father's constant stare—and far away from that damn book.

V

Nemesis

When I noticed the sun no longer warmed the tabletop, I decided I had enough of pens, paper, and thumbing through yellowed pages of old books. Gathering up what was mine, I strapped my valise shut and headed over to admin. The campus cafeteria was located in the basement at the south end of the building. I would find mostly faculty, staff and first year students eating there. The food, sometimes questionable, meant I had to rely on good ol' Betty, to pick out the best of what they served. She held the position of kitchen manager and sometimes—my second mom. She knew my father, but had rejected my mother. She would only speak to Elsie out of respect for me and, "Good ol' Professor Rice!"

Going down the wide concrete ramp on the east side of the building, I slipped in the back door of the kitchen. Sarge wasn't allowed in, so he sat just outside to sulk with the promise of a treat upon my return. It was supper time, and the place was hopping. I spied Betty moving among the cooks, dishwashers, and student workers. Her chubby round face was red and wet with sweat. Her hands were always fluttering, sometimes stopping to tuck lose strands of greying dark hair back in under her hairnet. Steam rolled up, food smells filled the room, and the clatter was close to deafening. Seeing me standing at the back, she grabbed a small brown bag, the bottom spotted with grease, and held it aloft with one hand as she motioned me over with the other.

Moving in close, she yelled, "No time to chat today, hon, we had to throw out all the goulash and redo it. So, I made you a BLT and stuck in some fruit and oatmeal cookies. Oh! And there's a pint of milk to go with 'em. Sorry about the goulash, don't know how many times I've told Benny to keep that damn cigar out of my kitchen. There was enough ash in that damn pot to… Oh, well, talk with you later, dearie, got to get back to it." Grabbing my shoulder, she bent me down and gave me a big slobbery kiss on my cheek. Then hurrying away, she hollered, "Benny Mitchell, you get that damn cigar out of your mouth, right now."

Moving out of the kitchen into the dining room, I was met with a barrage of, "Hey, Sterling!" from the students, coupled with the more dignified waves from certain members of the faculty. They sat separately, their dining table, a long, wooden monstrosity that had been placed domineeringly at the front of the room. I heard it's been sitting there since the 1800's.

Moving out through the mammoth archway that led to the stairs, I came into a small antechamber where coats were hung. Then running up the wide wooden steps to the first floor's main corridor, I stopped and turned to sit at the top, facing the way I had come. Pulling the BLT from the sack, I let the waxed paper float down to where my feet rested on the steps. I attacked the sandwich with the manners of my dog, thinking all along how lucky I was to have Betty looking out for me. It was about the time I got to the crust that I heard from behind, a familiar, but agitating voice.

"Sterling, you are such an animal. You could sit at a table, you know—like civilized people."

It was Sandra Heinz.

Looking back, I took in her tall, slender body sporting a light blue shirtwaist dress with long sleeves and blazingly white cuffs. A crème-colored belt cinched her waist, giving her a false hourglass shape. I knew from having seen her in her birthday suit that she did everything possible to perpetuate a womanlier figure. Inside that Perma-Lift bra, there was more toilet paper than actual woman. If she hadn't complained so much about what other women had that she didn't, I wouldn't have given it a second thought. But her perpetual grumbling had driven me to sarcasm, and I now used it as a weapon against her unwarranted attacks.

She hugged a clipboard to her chest, probably a subconscious action to shield her from return fire. I looked up into her thin, oval face as her pale blue eyes studied me over her long straight nose. Her thin lips were somewhat pursed on a regular basis, and when she smiled, which happened rarely, it came as a half simper, showing longer than average canines. I always wondered if some dentist had ground all her other teeth flat across the tops at her request. They were so abnormally even that they actually emphasized her fangs.

"Well... if it isn't Sandra Heinz. Care to sit with me... on the stairs?"

"And risk dirtying up my skirt with the filth and possibly catching a case of cooties? No, thank you. Help yourself, though. Oh, wait, you already did. Hanging out with big boobed sophomores again, I hear. That's so, nineteen fifty. I thought you were passed that." Walking down the stairs, she stopped and turned to face me at the half way point.

"Well, Sandra, I confess, I've digressed. I've caught a case of those dreaded cooties and they are eating away my brain, causing me to chase after younger women who can actually walk around in the sunlight."

She whipped her straighter-than-average, blonde hair back, and grimaced at me. You've heard that old saying about being able to dish it out, but not take it? Well... that was Sandra. Taking another bite of my sandwich, I chewed with diligence.

"God, Sterling, why did I ever go steady with you? And for a year at that!"

I stopped chewing and opening my mouth, I showed her the contents. Then clawing at her with my free hand, I hissed like a rabid cat.

"Oh, gross! You're a twenty-four-year-old man, Sterling. Show it, will you? I so liked your mother. It's too bad you're such a germ."

"What are you talking about, Sandra? You are my mother."

"Oh, drop dead," she said, and continued down the stairs.

"What, and look like you?"

Without turning around, she raised her middle finger at me. Unfortunately for her, Professor Bigley was passing the open door at the bottom on his way to the garbage can. I saw him turn to greet her, but seeing her proudly displaying the bird, he quickly looked away, shaking his head.

"Professor Bigley... uh, how are you?" she said nervously. He just walked away without a word. Passing through the dining area, she looked back over her shoulder, a scowl on her face and daggers in her eyes. Then stomping away toward the serving line, I could tell she was trying to control her forthcoming tantrum.

Laughing loud enough for her to hear, I picked up my trash, dumped my sandwich crust in the paper bag, grabbed my valise, and walked away down the corridor. Passing Lyles closet, I peeked through the first window of the president's reception to see Miss Samuels at her desk. I prepared myself mentally for the attack I knew was coming and continued to the door marked #1. Knocking where 'Nathaniel P. Morgan-President' had been stenciled on the glass, I waited for Samuels to wave me in. When she did, I entered to find her in the usual grouchy mood. I learned not to say hello. I would just sign the book, take the keys, and get the hell out. She pulled the ring from the drawer and tossed it on the top of the desk. Then pulling out the ledger, she laid it beside the keys and opened it for me to sign. All the caretaker's names had already been written down in the margin, one for each day of the week. I just needed to put my mark next to 'S. Rice'

I saw I had the weekend off and I nearly shouted with joy. I didn't dare do that, though. Such a thing would lead to a reprimand, and if you ever saw a mature man get a bawling out, well… it's embarrassing.

Taking the keys in my left hand, I risked a smile and a little salute. Turning away, I heard, "You might be Professor Rice's kid, but that don't cut no ice with me."

Fumbling for the knob, I hoped to get out before I heard the rest. No such luck.

"I knew your father; he was a good man. Maybe you can follow in his footprints."

I wanted to tell her that the phrase was, 'Follow in his footsteps' but that would get President Morgan an earful, and I didn't want to be the cause of that. Finally getting the door open, I looked back over my shoulder saying, "Yes, ma'am." She stuck out her jaw, and squinting with her left eye, she opened the right one as wide as she could. I gave her my submissive smile and hurried out of the door, allowing the hydraulic closer to shut it for me.

Not wanting another confrontation with Sandra, I went in the other direction to where the hallway opened into a vast lounge with a high cathedral ceiling. The space was full of comfortable chairs, couches, and small, wooden tables topped with assorted lamps. There were tall plants everywhere and assorted Persian rugs had been lain with care.

It was a place where academics and staff mingled. Some had brought their lunch upstairs and ate it there. Coffee was being drunk, and the Arkham Advertiser was being read. I could have spent hours there, just chatting with everyone I knew, but I had to get going. The entrance from the college green was on the left, but turning right, I went out the east door on the Physical Plant side. Moving along the wall, I whistled up Sarge when I got close to the ramp.

Running to the top, he stopped to study me, looking a little confused because I had come out a different door. Racing my way, he jumped on me and then went to running circles around my legs. Tossing him the remnants of my sandwich, he caught it on the run as we hurried to Dyer Hall. I had about fifteen minutes to dump my valise, use the john and get to my lamps. The note that was tacked to my door could possibly change all that.

Sterling,

Some snobby sounding woman gave you a bell. Said she was Dr. Osborn. Told me to tell you she was sorry she had to cut your appointment short this morning. You are to meet with her on the steps of the Science Annex, Bell Tower side, 6:30 sharp. Wants to get your project started today if possible.

Casper

P.S.-What project? Is it something cool?

I thought, yeah Casper, it's cool, but I expect it to heat up real soon. Looking at my watch I saw it was already four forty-six. Sarge wanted to be fed, so filling his bowl, I left him there and went into the commons. The TV room was going full blast. The Colgate Comedy Hour was on, but the discussion centered more on who had dated how many girls before they came to M.U.

I think every first-year student, who had just returned from the cafeteria, was in there. Slipping up to the second-floor john, I took care of my business and upon passing the room just opposite the girl's shower over in Loring, I saw three boys in chairs, one of them peering toward the girl's dorm through the open window, elbows on the sill, chin in hands—agonizingly waiting. The other two were dozing because they already had their watch. The twins, Allen, and Paul Drexler, were housed in that room, but they were nowhere to be seen.

Sticking my head in the door, I said, "BOO!" Everybody startled into a standing position. This was followed by a lot of hmmming and hahing.

"Oh, hey, Mr. Rice."

I recognized the one who spoke as Jimmy Edsel, the kid who had been keeping watch at the window.

"What's the tale, nightingale?"

"Oh, uh… nothing. We're just talking, ummm… about homework."

"Crazy, keep up the good work. Oh, I just wanted to warn you…"

They grew extra nervous at that and I am sure if I shouted, somebody would have peed their pants.

"It's Sterling. Mr. Rice was my father."

Walking away, I heard a loud sigh of relief and I chuckled. Going down to my room, I grabbed the keys, the rest of my supper, and Sarge. Then heading for the Science Annex, I turned on all the lamps between it and Dyer. I was super curious about what Claudia wanted. My mind was abuzz with reasons and it reminded me of what it was like to be one of those undergrads up there in the Drexler's room. It'd been a long time since I had felt this giddy—and all because of Claudia.

VI

Dwelling In Bliss

The sky showed clear and the air grew chilly. A thin ground mist rose from the grass of the college green. Groups of students moved from building to building, laughing, talking, and arguing. I thought about how spring seemed to offer something to everybody. With that, came the realization of what it had gifted me.

She stood on the steps of the annex, hugging herself like she was cold. Her tan jacket was too big for her, as was the red and black plaid shirt hanging untucked over cuffed dungarees. There were pink anklets with white lace inside penny loafers. The little, blue barrette had transformed into a red one to match her shirt.

Claudia grinned as I strolled up. Cocking her hip, her hands went to her waist, and with mock dismay, she said, "About time you showed up." I smiled and pretending to be embarrassed at my lack of punctuality, I sighed, shrugged, and threw up my hands. Sarge ran to her and she bent down to rough him up a bit. Then clapping his head in her hands, she kissed him between his ears. She was fast gaining points.

Seating himself beside her, Sarge gave me a look that said he claimed her as ours. I just hoped he wouldn't go as far as to lift his leg on her. I watched them for a minute in silence and thought how funny it was that she was only about a foot and a half taller, standing, than he was sitting. She sputtered, wiped her lips and said, "Yuk! Dog hair!"

"Don't blame him, he can't help it. He's had it all his life. We'll just have to get used to it."

A few seconds past before she grasped the humor. When she got it, she giggled, saying, "Oh, you!" I moved up to her but stopped one step shy. She surprised me by wrapping her arms around me. Then laying the side of her head against my chest, she sighed.

After a few seconds, she let go, and stepping back, she grinned, her eyes twinkling. I have to admit, I had never seen anyone's peepers do that before. She started to speak, but I beat her to it by asking, "So, why the meeting? Do you have some news?"

"Uh… no, I just have a free evening. I knew you would be setting out on your rounds and… I was hoping I could walk with you. You don't mind, do you?"

"Not at all, it would be a change. Sarge doesn't talk much."

"Cool! So, shall we?"

"Just a sec," I said, and opening the front door of the annex, I reached in and switched on all of the necessary lights. Then the three of us walked down the steps together with Claudia yakking away about different things that happened throughout her day. Sometimes she'd put her hand on the small of my back, and leaning forward, she would look up into my face while trying to make a point. When it seemed she got tired of talking, she went to playing with Sarge who obviously appreciated the attention.

When I stopped to walk up the steps of any one veranda or lingered at the many pole lamps scattered over the green, the two of them danced around each other in a kind of horseplay. Sometimes they would chase each other in circles and Claudia would perform a mock attack against Sarge, who would run away only to circle back and goose her. Between bouts, they spent a lot of time just standing and panting, waiting for me to finish.

"You're getting your exercise tonight," I said.

"Well, I've never had a dog. I'm kind of jealous. How old is he?"

"Four. He was kind of a gift from my folks."

"Where'd they get him?"

"M.U. had a kennel for watchdogs at one time. Way back in the twenties. They didn't have a watchman, just dogs. One of the first was Napoleon, the dog that brought an end to ol' Wilbur Whateley. That dog sired every puppy since and happens to be Sarge's great grandfather. His mother's name had been Josephine—of course!

"Neat! So, M.U. had a kennel?"

"Yeah. After the library break-in they started a watchman program, coupling the dogs with men. But that went away back when Silas Martin died. He was the kennel manager and handler. M.U. didn't see any more use for watchdogs, I guess. Now the watchman works alone. They gave all the dogs away to faculty and staff. The kennel used to be on the admin side of the Physical Plant. They tore it all down and planted grass. If you look closely, you can still see where it used to be."

"Well, I love Sarge. I've actually made two new friends," she said, and dashed away, Sarge giving chase. She stopped and twirled like before, and he ran past, looking back, confused. He looked like he couldn't figure out what this crazy girl was up to.

We had reached the corner of Boundary and Crane, just outside my mother's place. The porch light was on and violin music emanated from inside. I could see her in the parlor, sawing away in front of her music stand. The other staff houses were ablaze with light, and a dinner party was in full swing at the Goldman's cottage.

"Do you hear that?" Claudia said.

"What? The party?"

"No, the music. Someone's playing a violin, or something. I think it's from this place." Pointing at my mother's cottage, she walked toward it across the lawn. "It's a woman in there, I can see her. I wonder who it is."

"It's, ummm… my mother."

"Your mother! Hey, let's go visit."

"NO! Not a good idea."

I hurried up to her and wrapped my arms around her waist from behind, saying, "Please Claudia, don't." She stopped and rotated slowly inside them, her breasts rubbing my chest. She put her own arms around me, and we stood there, just looking into each other's faces, with me trying to express how serious I was about intruding in on my mother. Claudia just looked up at me, enamored.

It was well into twilight. A nearly full moon peaked over the rooftops up on French Hill. I recognized the tune my mother played as *Beethoven's Moonlight Sonata*. It was one of her favorites and one of the first she had learned to play. She had taken up the violin my last year at Wentworth, and after making that final train trip home, we all celebrated my completion with a glass of champagne and my mother playing that tune for me.

Elsie pulled it off without a hitch. Now, she played it every evening at this time and if I was passing, the romantic tune would float out to greet me. I suspected that late spring day back in nineteen forty-nine had been one of her good ones. She was striving to keep that memory alive.

Claudia's face softened, and she pulled my head down to bring her lips to mine. It surprised me, but I didn't resist. It was a long, soft kiss, unlike any I'd ever had before. Not hard and desperate like Sandra, or overly passionate like Francine, but velvety soft. A kiss given—not taken. When Claudia pulled back and released my head, she whispered, "Finally, I was so afraid that was never going to happen."

"Why? Have I been giving you a bad vibe or something?"

Before she could answer, I realized the sonata had stopped. Looking up, I saw my mother watching us through a window, her face illuminated by a table lamp. It was just enough to reveal the scowl on her face.

"Ah crap! I think we have an audience."

Claudia rotated within my embrace to face the cottage, and resting one of her hands on mine, she waved in a slow genial manner with the other. My mother responded by pulling the curtain.

"What was that all about?"

"I told you, remember? Not the best place for romance. Never was."

It was my turn to tow her along as I walked toward the School of Medicine. I was anticipating a truckload of badgering, complaining, and threats, all initiated with a note to call home, which I could expect to find tacked to my door upon my return.

I realized Claudia wasn't talking. Glancing back, I could see she was deep in thought. Her gaze seemed to be on the lawn as she walked, but her grip on my hand was tight and affirming.

It wasn't until after I turned on the lights at the School of Medicine and we stood together within the Ionic columns supporting the pediment at the front that she said, "I think you're right, your mom's not going to like me. I could see it in her face, even at that distance. And… maybe, I felt it too."

"Don't worry about it. I like you, and that's all that matters. Or maybe I should say, 'we' like you."

Reaching down I rubbed the top of Sarge's head as he sat beside me, staring up. Turning to Claudia, he wagged his tail and reaching out a paw, he rested it on her thigh like he knew what we were talking about. She took it and gave it a shake and then dropped it before moving over to face me. I waited for another kiss or a hug, but all she did was rub my upper arms and search my eyes.

She didn't smile. Her lips remained tight, and in the glow of the lamps, I saw them tremble. She was suppressing an urge to cry. For a brief few seconds they filled with a strange kind of light, followed by welling tears.

Turning away, she hopped down the steps. "Let's get on with it, huh? I've got some studying to do." Keeping her back to me, she wiped at her face. I stayed right where I was, waiting.

There was a down side to every great relationship. I realized that since meeting Claudia, I had come to a fork in the road, and like that Frost poem, I had taken the path less traveled. She was taking me some place; to something I needed. Something I had lost, a long time ago. I was experiencing a feeling that I had not felt since Aubrey. I also suspected I might be resisting, afraid of losing what I had gained by moving too fast.

I thought about my past relationships, realizing they had all been rather superficial. Sandra had only happened because I felt a need to please my mother in order to be happy. Someone had told me I should try to meet Elsie half way. So—I tried.

Sex with Sandra only seemed to satisfy some inner craving. It never brought us closer and the ice queen never melted. I only managed to descend further into some dark place, not even comprehending that I had, least until it came time to crawl out. That happened only after I said, "Fuck it all." Aubrey brought love when she came, and for three months out of the year there was this kind of bliss. It wasn't puppy love. It wasn't a crush. That's what I had for Emma Wheeler, and only because I was required to learn ballroom dancing while at Wentworth.

The girls from the Beacon Hill School down in Boston would be bused up for the day, and I was soon introduced to the waltz and a serious case of infatuation. Emma taught me a great many things, and not all of them dance related. But the loss I felt when dance instruction came to an end a year later, didn't even compare to the pain I felt at the loss of Aubrey.

I hadn't even known Claudia a week, and I felt I could easily drop my guard. A hard shell had cracked and a warm, liquid-like feeling flowed into my gut, bringing the glow that accompanies comprehension. I believe Aubrey was love personified, and Claudia—was bringing it back.

The ground mist was on the rise, a common phenomenon here at M.U. It floated at about my waist, and the people strolling through it, appeared disembodied, their top halves seemingly drifting above it. I walked down to Claudia and she turned to fall against my chest. Her arms went around my waist and she looked up into my face, her cheeks still wet with tears. My heart melted. I mean, it literally felt just like that.

"What is it? What's on your mind. Why the tears?"

She tightened her embrace, moving her cheek to my chest. Without looking up, she said, "Oh, nothing, really. It's just… to be honest, I was so lonely. Then I met you and I thought, wow, this could be it. Goodbye Little Miss Loneliness. But I think I expected your mom to be more like you. I was wrong, huh?"

I tightened my embrace and lay my cheek on the top of her head. The scent of Woodbury shampoo mixed with perfume, rolled up into my nose. Claudia's body heat fed the warmth in my belly and it enveloped us. Tipping her head back, I looked into her eyes as she whispered, "Kiss me again, Sterling."

Our lips met for the second time. Still the same soft kiss, except this time her tongue came to meet mine. I was on fire and perspiration rose to my pores. When we came up for air, I said, "Oh boy, I need to cool off."

"Yeah, I know what you mean."

Stepping back, she fanned her face, adding, "Wow! I didn't expect that."

"You and me, both."

Sarge had sat through the whole thing, just watching, not making a sound. Looking at him, I had to laugh because only his head showed above the rising layer of mist. A surreal, floating dog head. He woofed at me, like he wanted us to get moving and could we please stop messing around.

"I suppose I had better get on with it, I still have a few more lights."

Taking my hand, she walked beside me as I finished up with the remaining pole lamps. We occasionally broke out in laughter at Sarge's head and tail as they sailed across the mist. By the time we got back around to the chapel, it was time to meet Lyle.

Moving up the walk past the physical plant, which had no outside lights, I finalized it all with the single pole lamp at the corner of Garrison and College Street on the Front Campus. Coming in sight of admin's west entrance, I let go of Claudia's hand and tried to appear all business. Lyle was on the steps as usual, his back to us. He was checking his wristwatch and shaking his head.

"Hey, Lyle."

It startled him. Spinning around to face us, he said, "Shit, kiddo… you scared the bejeezus out of me. Running a little behind tonight, I see?"

"Uh… yeah. Had a damsel in distress. Lyle, meet Claudia."

"Hi, pleased to meet you," she said, trying to be polite.

"Hello, little missy… say, you look familiar."

"Yeah, I get that all the time."

"No, I mean like, movie star famous."

"Yeah, like I said."

"Okay, well… got to get inside, going to have to work a few minutes overtime in the morning. Okay, kiddo, how about them keys?" Handing them off to him, he said, "Nice to meet you, missy."

"Same here," Claudia said, now looking nervous for some reason.

We turned away, walking between the buildings toward Dyer Hall. Glancing back, I saw Lyle hadn't moved, even though he'd been in a hurry. "Shirley Temple, right," he hollered. Claudia looked back, waved, and gave him an exaggerated grin.

Something about our little exchange troubled me. For a few seconds, his reaction was typical for a first time meet and greet. Then his face changed. He started looking Claudia up and down like livestock set for auction. I wanted to dismiss the whole thing to movie star obsession, but the bad feeling hung in there. Something in his eyes. Dark, cold, and calculating, like when I had mentioned the missing Elspeth.

As a little boy, I went to see the Hyena at the zoo. It walked right up to the bars, studying me like prey. Those black eyeballs held no emotion. It was sorting out the best way to get to me, waiting for me to make some fatal error. That's what I saw, for a brief moment, in Lyles' eyes. I realized as we walked, I really didn't know him all that well. He was unmarried and lived alone over on Pickman Street, across from the so-called Witch House. I'd walked by many times, but never visited. As a loner, the job suited him. He slept days and prowled nights.

A shiver ran up my spine and Claudia said, "Hey, you okay? I felt that."

"What? Oh, sorry, got a chill. Good thing you have a jacket."

"So, this is where you live?" she said, and looking up, I realized we were just outside of Dyer by my east windows. "Correct! Right behind that glass. Sarge's and my humble abode. Living life with undergrads."

"I'd have you invite me in, but I have to get back to Pembrook. Test tomorrow on Molecular Bonding. Not the kind of bonding I want to do right now, but…" Giggling, she threw an arm around my waist and pressed the side of her face against me. "You will walk me back, won't you?"

"Certainly will… missy."

She laughed and said, "Yeah, what was that all about? Creepy, huh?"

There it was again. First Casper, now Claudia. I thought of the nights I'd caught Dean Farr following Lyle around campus. Then there was the watchman's behavior as of late, the look of nervous suspicion in his eyes, moments he had snapped at me when I asked probing questions, and then—there was that pocketknife. A wariness was growing in me, and I cursed myself for having taken Lyle at face value. I would always be guarded around him now. I wanted to give him the benefit of the doubt, but that was just me trying to be decent, something I felt I could no longer afford him.

It started to trouble me that he walked the night, so to speak, and had access to every building on campus. My thoughts turned to Elspeth, a girl I had never met. The picture that formed in my mind was of a faceless girl that transformed into Aubrey, standing on the Pembrook terrace as dark figures paced the shadows. Wanting to get that image out of my head, I turned to Claudia and said, "We should go over to Dean's some night for burgers, how about it?"

The frightening image that was starting to form in my mind, disintegrated as I took in her face. The trusting smile, the cute little nose, and the lively eyes. All of that framed by her golden-brown hair.

"Sounds peachy, I'd like that. Are they any good? The burgers, I mean. Been at M.U. for two years and haven't gone there yet. Some of the girls say it's a Greaser's hangout, but that's just gossip. Besides, I don't mind Greasers, or Beats for that matter. Anton is always saying, 'It takes all kinds to make a world'. I have to agree."

"Dean's place is cool. A lot of students go there, not just Greasers. I go there... a lot. Have, almost all of my life"

"Well then, we should go there. You and me...oh, and Sarge."

Hearing his name, his head popped up above the mist. Walking back to Claudia, he sniffed her hand.

"Maybe this weekend?" she said, "Saturday night would be good."

"Sounds like a date."

"Sounds boss, is what it sounds like."

With that, she let go, stepped away, and twirled. This time it was more like a pirouette.

"Did you used to be a dancer?"

"Oh, hah! Ballet. Years ago. I think that was the last thing I learned, before deciding it wasn't for me. Besides, my instructor said I was too short to be a dancer. He predicted I could never go 'on pointe' without getting hurt. So, I said, fuck it... oops! That doesn't bother you, does it? That I swore? Sorry."

"No, it's okay, I do it sometimes, too. Not enough to make people think I'm some kind of a ditz, though. I am an English major, you know. There are better words, but sometimes saying fuck is... well, just fun."

"Yeah, I know. So, anyway, I took up swimming years ago. I'm a good swimmer. I've swam competitively. I even have medals. I'd show you, but the Warden wouldn't let you up into my room. So, I'd have to bring them out. I have them tacked to my corkboard and I look at them occasionally when I feel like I'm failing. They remind me to keep moving forward. You know what I mean?"

"Does that work?"

"Yes, surprisingly. So, what did you do? I mean, like competitively? Anything?"

"Well, if boxing, rowing, horseback riding, and fencing, count as anything… then yeah."

"Fencing?"

"Yeah, you know, like sword fighting? Top of my class. I liked boxing a lot, but you know what that gets you. Cauliflower ear would sure hurt these good looks. But maybe I should dig out some of my old metals and hang them where I can see them. Maybe that would work for me."

"Why? Do you sometimes feel like a failure?"

"Well, Claudia… who doesn't?"

"Right, I suspect everybody does at some point."

Holding hands, we ambled along in silence. I caught her glancing over at me once in a while like she was studying me. I wanted to whip my face around, and shout, 'BOO!' But I didn't want to ruin the moment for her. So, I kept my face forward as I tracked the top third of Sarge's tail cutting like a shark's fin through the mist. By the time we reached the veranda at Pembrook, the mist had risen even more. It was now, just above Claudia's head and sarge had completely disappeared.

"Think it would be okay to kiss you good night right here in front of the dorm?" I asked.

Without a word, she came to me and wrapping her arms around my waist, she tilted her head back. I bent to find her lips and a ray of light flashed across us as a curtain cracked open. Because I had leaned down, it took me just below the surface of the mist, shielding us from prying eyes as we kissed. Then pulling my lips from hers a mere fraction, I said, "I think we have an audience."

"Fuck her," Claudia whispered and then giggled into my mouth. Her lips found mine again and moving her hands to my derriere, she squeezed. I so wanted to do the same to hers, but I would have had to bend her over backwards, and I didn't think her spine could take it. She suddenly pulled away and said, "Oh brother, I've got to stop now or this could get out of hand." Dashing up the steps into the light, she grabbed the door knob and looked back grinning.

"See you tomorrow, okay?" she said, and without waiting for an answer, she slipped inside. I watched through the glass as the door from Mordechai's room opened, filling the vestibule with light. But Claudia had dashed away through the inner door and had mounted the open staircase that curved up to the second floor. By the time I heard, "Miss Osborn!" emitted with authority, the fleeing girl's loafers had disappeared from view. So, Mordechai turned her attention to me.

I spun away, hoping to get out of there before the door opened. The hinges squeaked and the rasp of the wood on the metal sill told me she was on her way. I was a good twenty-five feet out when I heard, "Mr. Rice."

She didn't scare me like she did most people. I knew she had no authority over me or anybody else outside that building. A mischievousness overcame me, and I dropped to a knee. Sarge came to me and I whispered the command to 'sit'.

"Sterling Rice?"

Thinking back on Claudia at the library, I couldn't resist and, "Marco?" slipped from my lips.

I heard a huff. Then what sounded like her stomping a foot as she growled out, "Okay, you." The door squeaked shut, followed by the sound of the bolt being thrown. Poking my head up, I could see the foyer was dark now, the large figure of Mordechai, pacing back and forth just inside.

I got up and walked away, hoping she wouldn't cause trouble for Claudia. Knowing the Warden like I did, I expected she would. It would come as an act of revenge. She would first try President Morgan, but wouldn't get past Samuels. Then, she'd ring the Dean and nag on him for a while, getting no results. Next, she'd call Claudia's home in Cambridge. I assumed Claudia's folks would be tolerant toward Mordecai, but she would still not get what she wanted. She would wear herself down with complaining. I knew as a fact she had alienated

94

almost everyone she knew on campus, and perhaps, a few parents. She would then come after me as a last resort.

I would use my privilege to thwart her, but only in the name of justice. Ol' lady Samuels had said that I didn't cut any ice with her, but that was all bluster, just as it was with Mordechai. I decided long ago, I needed to be humble about my surname, taking my lumps if deserving, and taking a stand, if not. With Mordechai, I would bring all my resources to bear in defense of Claudia.

There existed no rule about kissing in public; on campus, or off. I wasn't actual faculty or staff. So, impropriety didn't apply. Sexual behavior in public with the intent of entertaining, versus just getting caught in a romantic moment, were two different things. The Warden would try to make them one and the same, just so she could punish whomever she wanted.

I thought back to Lori Saunders and that morning at the window. Then there was minding your own business, versus minding someone else's. The phrase, 'Do what you want to do, just so long as you don't hurt anyone' popped into my head. I knew if anyone came down too hard on Claudia, I would champion her cause. I supposed, though, nothing would come of it. Mordechai would just have to stew in her own juices. Tomorrow would tell.

VII

Under Sinister Grey Clouded Skies

L eaving the Pembrook green, Sarge and I crossed back over Church Street to the quad. The surface of the fog had a well-defined flatness to it now, like looking down on a layer of cloud from great heights. Every lamp on campus showed a halo of condensation, but visibility above that stratum of vapor remained good. People moved across the quad as bodiless heads. Even though I have lived here all of my life, the phenomena never failed to amaze me.

Laughter and loud voices caught my ear. Arriving at the Science Hall, I stopped to peer over one of the chin high sidewalls that sandwiched the wide front steps. I could just make out a group of lamp lit students between the library and Lockley Hall on the Front Campus. They were playing a version of 'hide and seek', popping up and down within the ground bound cloud as they changed locations. They acted like freshman from a warmer climate experiencing their first snowfall.

Sarge rose up on his back legs and putting his front paws on the wall, tried to look over. Unable to, he dropped back down out of sight and went to licking some part of his body. I remained, leaning against the cold masonry, my chin resting on my crossed arms at the top, just watching the students in their fun, and reminiscing.

There was movement in my peripheral and looking left I watched a man move out of The Grove. He showed a partial limp as he crossed over Church Street to the quad, his long, crude, walking stick clacking on the cobblestones at every step. He towered above the mist and his dark jacket was buttoned to his chin. Passing close to a pole lamp, I could see he wore a black Fedora pulled low over his eyes and sported a beard without a mustache. The Shadowman? Or should I say—C. K.

Whateley? Even though he moved with a confidence that conveyed that he belonged there, it didn't fool those of us who knew better.

Adrenaline coursed in and crouching below the surface of the fog, I turned sideways to the wall and waited. Wanting to give him time to pass, I slowly counted to ten and then resumed my original position. Pushing my eyes just above the capstone, I watched him lumber toward the Bell Tower. Passing students seemed to pay him no heed, either out of disinterest or fear. The man soon disappeared inside the four large decorative piers that formed the base of the tower. A match flickered, lighting up the area inside to make the tiled floor shimmer. A cigarette was lit, and the match went out, leaving only a tiny red glow to tattle on the prowler.

The noise on the college green seemed to be magnified by the weather. Sounds bounced off the buildings, making it difficult to determine their origin. I could hear the students in their game, a few vacillating conversations here and there, and entry doors, opening and closing. One came with a loud creak and I knew that was the north door on Lockley Hall. Somebody came out and moved toward the Bell Tower, a flashlight wagging back and forth. Lyle Umberling!

Okay, time for a showdown. Lyle must have seen the Shadowman from a window and came out to confront him. I prepared to assist, fully expecting there to be shouting and a tussle as the Shadowman attempted to escape. Lyle went directly to the tower base and shined his light inside. It illuminated the taller man's face, but there was no attempt to flee. He and Lyle were having a conversation. Then, stepping into view, Lyle tucked the flashlight into an armpit, the glow now lighting up both their midsections.

I watched Lyle reach into his pocket, pull something out, and hand it to the taller man. The Shadowman took it, shoved it into his own pocket and loudly said, "You can shut the fucking light off, now."

Lyle said something, but his words were indiscernible. The two men exited together on my side of the tower. So, I ducked down behind the wall. Whispering a command to Sarge to sit and stay, I wrapped my hand briefly around his muzzle as his cue to be quiet. It left me grateful that he had been taught a regimental obedience before coming into my care. He always did as he was told.

I held him next to me with an arm around his shoulders. Several times he licked my ear, one front foot pawing lightly at the dirt of the flowerbed where we crouched. I could hear the sound of boots coming closer, so I duck-walked backwards until I felt the shrubbery at my derriere. Sarge had wiggled along with me and lay on his stomach as if ready to pounce. My nose picked up a slight odor of human sweat, tobacco smoke, and what I was pretty damn sure was chloroform. The two men soon passed me, moving toward Church Street on my left. They stopped on the sidewalk about twenty feet away, just on the edge of the light cast from the two pole lamps projecting up from the steps.

"Thanks for grabbing my knife, I thought that kid would snatch it up for sure." The Shadowman's dialect was very much like I remember Aubrey's to be. A backwoods kind of vernacular.

"I'm sure he was thinking about it. Told me he'd seen it lying out there. Probably too scared to go out and grab it. Worked out for the best, though. You got to be more careful. What the hell were you thinking, Whateley?"

That confirmed it, the Shadowman was C.K. Whateley.

I also noticed that Lyle's voice had a hardened quality to it; not like usual. His tone more like one of Regina's older ex-boyfriends that had hung out at Dean's in the past. At no time in my life had I ever heard Lyle talk that way. M.U.'s watchman was living a charade

Whateley said, "Well, I know he saw me over in them trees while out with that dog. I reckoned I'd give him a little scare if I came scratching at his window."

"Stupid move on your part. What if he'd let that dog out to have its way with you? I figure you'd be talking soprano. I used to work with those dogs, they ain't nothing to trifle with."

"You can just shut up with that kind of talk, watchman. I ain't afeared of that mutt."

I felt compelled to jump up and give them a little scare of my own and let Sarge have his way with the both of them. It would be too easy to just command, 'Beissen!' A German word that would turn him from the docile pet everybody knew—into a raging mass of fur and teeth. I'd

98

been witness to Silas's training sessions. There was no doubt, Sarge could become quite formidable.

I peeked up to see them standing with their backs to me and I heard Lyle say, "What about the girl? And what about my hundred bucks?"

"Don't you worry about that girl. You know damn well we grabbed the wrong one. So, you ain't getting paid for that. But that don't matter. We'll get the right one, soon enough. Then I'm sure my pa will get you your money."

"Well, wasn't my fault you grabbed the wrong one, you idiot."

"Hey now! You didn't help matters, no how."

"It's going to cost you more next time. You, and that brother of yours, promised to pay. So, that's the way it stays. There's been enough trouble on the campus. People are getting suspicious. So, I still want that hundred bucks, plus another for the right girl, along with the fifty you promised for that other thing. These students aren't like peanuts from the barrel over at Gott's. Folks are going to notice when they come up missing."

"Stick to your part of the deal, fat man. Let us take care of the rest. You'll get your money soon enough. My pa has a plan and he don't like it when somebody messes with it. You just keep track of that other girl. Her pa paid good money to have her back. As for that other situation, you just keep that key handy... hearing me?"

"I hear you," Lyle answered gruffly.

They stood glaring at each other and then Whateley clicked his tongue and turned away, heading back toward The Grove. Lyle stayed, watching him go. I dropped back down as he mumbled something and then his shoes clonked their way west down the walk toward the School of Languages. The sound of his footfalls changed as he crossed West Street and I took that as my cue. Peeking up again, I didn't see him or Whateley. Patting Sarge's back one time as his cue to relax, he came to his feet, and we did a fast walk toward Dyer. The fog was rising, so I didn't have to worry about them seeing me, and if they did, they wouldn't know who it was.

What I had surmised earlier about Lyle's reaction to Claudia couldn't have been more on the money. I wasn't paranoid after all. If Elspeth had been the wrong girl, then who was the right one? I got a stabbing pain in my gut and I felt as cold as ice. Could it have been Claudia they were after? And the fifty-dollar thing, what was that? I needed help, but I feared the Arkham cops might be involved as well and not in a good way. I needed to be one hundred percent positive before I notified anyone. Also, until I was sure it was Claudia they were after, I didn't dare say anything to her. That may prove difficult. I had to overwhelm her with my concern about the wellbeing of every girl at M.U. in order to get her to start worrying about it. Then I could gradually let her know that she was my biggest concern in the matter. Her stepfather, Anton, might very well be our last resort to get a handle on this thing.

The game of fog-tag seemed to have lost its allure and I could just make out the students now standing in a group, talking and laughing, contrasted by a pole lamp on College Street. The rest of the campus appeared 'head free' and as I passed Loring's veranda, I was greeted by a few boys and girls who had gathered there. Going inside Dyer, I apologized to Sarge for his late meal as I served up the kibble. Sitting down in my rolling desk chair, I swiveled back and forth, pondering what I had just learned.

The front door opened and closed randomly as the boys returned, trying to get in before lock up. There came giggles at two different times and a swish of petticoats as non-Dyer residents were ushered secretly up the stairs. I anticipated there was going to be a couple of roommates sacked out on couches in the commons before the night was over.

I wanted to work on my paper, but my mind kept going back to Lyle and Whateley. Part of my dilemma was, I still had to touch base with him every evening until Saturday. It would be difficult to act like I knew nothing. But I had no choice. I would keep our contact brief, no friendly chat, just a, "Hey Lyle," and walk away. I figured I might have to follow him around a couple nights myself, hoping I didn't bump into Dean Farr in the process.

Spying on the night watchman didn't appeal to me. Not that I felt afraid, it was just, I hadn't been motivated enough until now. I didn't seek high adventure. I preferred the laid back. Not that I couldn't be pushed in that direction—like a few times in my past. The last one being when I and a few other students accessed a door in the library basement that opened into the catacombs under M.U. I left it unlocked, and after getting the keys to Lyle, returned to my partners in crime who awaited me there. The tunnels connected just about every building at Miskatonic University, and we explored them until almost sunrise the next morning.

We had used two flashlights that we found in the librarian's desk drawer and failed to return them. Somebody from our crew had set one down by the tunnel entrance at the library and forgot it. A housekeeper had come across it and made a report. An investigation was undertaken, but we were never found out. Of course, the locks were changed on every cellar door, in every building, and a separate ring of keys was created for just those locks. Rumor has it that the new set was sequestered inside a locked metal box in a secure drawer in Miss Samuel's desk.

Now, at twenty-four years of age, I no longer felt compelled. With better self-control, I believed I was the master of my own destiny. A teaching job, a wife and kids, bright sunny days, and warm cozy nights. That's what appealed to me now. That brought me back to Claudia, her tears, that incredible kiss, and her naïve optimism. Could I live with her for the rest of my life? Is that what she wanted? Could I protect her from the evildoers?

That foreboding feeling from Wednesday came back. Nobody would be safe with Whateley around. Exposing Lyle would cause a serious ripple in the placid waters that was Miskatonic University. Cliff Breckingham was the relief watchman, but he was also a janitor in Lockley Hall. He was a likable fellow and seemed somewhat sagacious in manner. Cliff too, had been here as long as I and was the only person of color employed by the university. He rarely worked in Lyle's place because Lyle rarely took time off. If he was taken into custody for whatever reason and convicted, the caretaker schedule would change as M.U. struggled to fill the position. Student caretakers would be given opportunities to fill the late shift lock up as well as the morning unlock. But there would be no one to watch the campus in the night. Cliff might just have to jump into the mix and let Lockley stay dirty for a few days until they could get a new janitor. But he was the kind of guy who would take on both jobs, full time, out of his dedication to family. He had mouths to feed and neither position paid diddly. The burden of knowing what I now knew about the whole state of affairs lay heavily upon me.

Midnight rolled around, and I was still pondering my situation. I felt Sarge's eyes on me and I snapped out of my rumination. Looking up, I saw him sitting patiently on the little oval rug in front of the door. Having my attention now, he stood up and danced back and forth, nudging the door knob with his nose. Then a particular odor filled my room followed by a discernable fart. Time to lock up.

Moving out onto the veranda, I watched him disappear into the now full-blown fog. The college green was quiet and not even the sound of traffic could be heard. The weather had not only shut down M.U., but the whole town of Arkham, as well. Listening hard for Sarge's paws as they slapped wet grass, I could have sworn I heard a boat motor start up. Not one of the smaller freight haulers, but more like a sportsman's boat. Something like my father's Peterborough Speedster that sat in McCabe's Boat House & Storage down on the river.

I remember the first time my father took me boating. I had just turned ten. My mother in her wide brimmed, black straw hat and white dress, sat mid vessel, trying to read. My father had me seated in the back, teaching me how to fish. In an unusual display of tenderness, he gently placed the rod in my hand and proceeded to explain how to use it. He sat with his left arm around my shoulders, his right hand holding mine as he flicked the rod tip, showing me how to cast. His words had been soft and assuring as he explained the workings of the simple mechanism.

I recall leaning back against his chest and putting the side of my face to the rough tweed of his jacket. For maybe all of twenty seconds, with eyes closed, I soaked him in, his instruction evolving into some kind of a lullaby. I didn't care all that much about fishing, but I did about the closest thing to an embrace the celebrated Professor Rice had ever given me.

A serious case of boredom soon followed that moment and I wanted to jump into the pilot's seat and take control of that Speedster. My head filled with visions of us racing up and down the river as my parents laughed and clung to each other in excitement. I imagined a huge smile on my face as I looked back, revealing to them that I could pilot that craft like an expert boatman. But my father had given me strict orders to keep my hands off the V45-26 HP outboard that hung at the transom. I told him I would do as he wished, but that didn't mean I did.

Several times I'd snuck down to the boat house with Aubrey to treat her to a high speed run up and down the Miskatonic. I became as familiar with that boat as I was with my bicycle. I pleaded with Mr. McCabe not to rat on me, but he required a bribe. I am still amazed that my folks never discovered the missing bottles from our wine cellar. I only took the ones that came as gifts at different events throughout the year. The mediocre ones that got tucked into the single rack far back in the corner, categorized as forgettable. That included a bottle of scotch that had come as a gift from a student. His family had been especially appreciative over the fact that he had actually graduated, and all because of my father's tutelage. There was no way they could have known Professor Rice wasn't a scotch drinker. The bottle joined the ranks of the neglected. That was until McCabe got his hands on it. After that, the old drunkard treated me like I was royalty.

The fog swirled and the motor buzzed. It seemed to be moving westward toward Aylesbury, or—Dunwich. The sound melted away, leaving me to wonder who would be out on the Miskatonic in a fog like this. Definitely somebody who knew the river with its snags, sandbars, and fallen trees, many sticking out from shore like accusing fingers. To be out in this soup, even moving at quarter throttle with a forward mounted spotlight would prove treacherous.

Sarge soon returned and we went back inside. Locking up, I moved through the first floor, checking the kitchen and back door. Snores radiated from couches in the front commons and the television room, all of it backed up by the blaring test pattern on the TV. Turning it off, I counted five students sacked out in both rooms. That meant either someone had lost their room keys and failed to report it, or there were at least five girls upstairs. I decided against hall patrol for the night.

Before returning to my desk, I shut the huge inner doors to the vestibule, isolating my room from the rest of the building. If it got lively upstairs, I didn't want to know. If they needed me, they knew where to find me. If things got bad, Palance Kilham would be at my door in no time to let me know that I was the most irresponsible dormitory assistant he knew, and that he could do a much better job if Dean Farr would just give him a chance.

I doubled locked my room door, secured the windows, and stripping down to my skivvies, I went to work on my dissertation. I didn't even make it to one o'clock and waking face down in one of my composition books, I dragged myself to bed. Sarge followed to lie beside me, reminding me that his monthly bath was due.

My snores would soon follow his, but not until after I went back through every moment I had with Claudia over the day. Then I created a few of my own, fueled by her talk of baby doll PJ's and flowered underwear. That train of thought took the two of us to a place in my head that we actually hadn't quite gotten to yet.

***

I woke up in a cold sweat, my shout still echoing in the room. Realizing it had only been a nightmare, I relaxed and rubbed the sleep from my eyes. The clock said it was eleven minutes after two. Sarge, now in his own bed, lay watching me. I tried to put the dream back together and make some sense of it. I had been sitting on the end of a bed, but the room wasn't mine. It smelled of mold and rot, the floor to ceiling curtains were heavily stained and covered in fungus. The wainscot had fallen away in places to reveal large holes in the plaster. The red eyes of large rats glowered. Claudia appeared before me, her arms out as if seeking an embrace. Then the window burst in with the curtains flying up. Long pale green arms, draped in the tattered sleeves of a tweedy suit jacket, shot through the opening. The huge claw-like hands of the Wilbur monster snatched her up and jerked her out into the thick grey mist roiling outside. She didn't scream, and I didn't try to save her. I just sat helpless, fearing for myself. The picture of me in my mind's eye was that of a coward and a fool.

Pulling my blanket up against the chill of the room, I rolled over onto my stomach, making eye contact with my dog. Taking it as his cue, he jumped back on the bed to lay beside me, his muzzle on my back. His big hairy body, warmed me and I drifted off, thinking about my father and his horrifying stories.

I awoke as usual to the clamoring of the alarm clock. Sarge lay curled up in front of the door, his tail over his face with only his eyes moving as he took in my every move. I stilled the obnoxious clock and took a minute to rewind it. Lyle would be unlocking the library and switching off the lights over there in about an hour, his last task before calling it a night. I wanted to avoid him as much as possible. So, I would take my time, delaying my departure from the dorm until I figured he had left the campus.

The problem with that, Sarge had to pee. Getting to my feet, I put on my robe and we went out onto the veranda. The fog was fast being burned away by the rising sun that now peeked between the stately houses up on French Hill. I could already tell the day was going to be a warm one.

Putting myself back in a corner of the veranda, I kept an eye peeled for Lyle as Sarge squirted on demand. Sandra soon appeared in her light blue robe, broom in hand, her course blonde hair too perfect for the time of day. She went to sweeping Loring's porch as I pushed myself further back out of sight. But Sarge ran by, causing her to look up, and just in time to catch me sneaking back inside. I threw her a wave and she said, "Sterling?" Not a greeting—but a question. I just didn't get it. She seemed to hate me, yet sometimes her face, or voice, said differently.

Fact number one: Her cold-hearted manner did not appeal to young men. Fact number two: Our short-lived relationship happened to be the only one she'd had in a long time. Fact number three: She had a cruel streak but didn't seem to be aware of it. So, like a bully who believes their association with their victim is a friendship, her perspective was rather skewed. I suspect it was because that's all she knew and was unwilling to change—or didn't know how. I felt pity for her. But no way would I ever go back. It would remain a hard lesson. Too bad we had to live next door to each other. Maybe it was time for me to find some kind of housing off campus, or just away from Sandra Heinz.

I opened the inside doors to the smell of cigarette smoke, burnt toast, and boy's locker room. Kicking the doorstops into place, I hoped the housekeeper would throw open a few windows today and turn on the ceiling fans. Something that couldn't be done without a ladder, or the long stick for hooking the pull chains—the one that had been found splintered after a night of horseplay last year. There had been evidence that the residents had been jousting up in the second-floor corridor.

Coming through my open door, I saw the corner of a folded piece of paper, protruding from under the edge of the oval rug. Someone had taken a message for me and instead of tacking it to the door, they had slipped it under the bottom, and inadvertently, under the rug.

Pulling it out, I moved back into the light coming in through the decorative glass of the front doors, and read:

Sterling,

Some crabby woman called, she claimed to be your mother. You're supposed to call her as soon as possible. Wow, Daddy-O, she sounds like bad news. Glad she's not my mom.

Alex

Now, I knew why I hadn't come home to a note last night. I felt torn between giving her a bell at the cottage or going over there to give her a piece of my mind. I knew what it was about, and it was nothing dire. It could wait until next Tuesday. Not the kind of thing I wanted to discuss over the telephone. The entry hall to the dorm would be the worst place to get into an argument with your mother about your girlfriend.

Putting it at the bottom of my mental list of priorities, I went through my usual morning routine of showering, shaving, eating breakfast, and sharing some time with curious undergrads. I finally got around to dressing, and then grabbing my valise, Sarge, and I, were ready to start our day.

Stepping off the veranda, we greeted Professors as they moved by Dyer on their way from Faculty House to the academic buildings. It surprised me to see Claudia crossing Church Street with a group of girls. She spotted me and jumped up and down in a frantic manner, waving, her poodle skirt bouncing to disclose that she had traded flowered panties for plain white ones. Then pointing to her wristwatch, she yelled, "Finals next month! Got to run!" Blowing me a kiss, she continued on her way as her classmates crowded around her with obvious questions, some glancing back toward me with mischievous grins.

Her manner left me with the impression that we wouldn't be getting together today. I felt sad, but I understood that with the summer break coming up, students were anxious to get done and get the hell out. I wondered if Claudia would remain in Arkham for the break. Pembrook allowed it, Loring didn't. The girls who wished to stay over the summer, would transfer over there and then get reassigned new rooms at Loring, come August. That is, if they didn't want to put up with Mordecai, otherwise, they could stay.

Dyer boys could stay, but rarely would. Only a few seniors, I, Palance, and other grad students, would remain. It would get quiet, and soon, an army of housekeepers and maintenance people would fill the halls and rooms for nearly ten hours a day. My job description would evolve into being just dorm security and I'd suffer many a lonely night without my charges. But maybe not this year—not if Claudia stayed.

Going to the library, I took my usual seat and dove into my work. Sarge walked around introducing himself to students, seeking his daily dose of attention. I had to get up on occasion to reference resources or gather books to bring back to my table. I lost track of time and when the big grandfather clock chimed one, there came the sound of heavy boots and the creak of leather. I detected the clank of loosely strapped handcuffs as they moved along the opposite side of the head high bookshelf closest to me. Along with them, the odor of tobacco, sweat, and some kind of foul-smelling aftershave. Things suddenly went quiet and I felt a presence close behind. Looking over my shoulder, I met the eyes of Officer Ralph Hutchins.

His chubby, heart shaped face always reminded me of Lou Costello of the comedy duo. It's just… he wasn't funny. I was now a head higher at twenty-four and no longer intimidated. I had a difficult time taking Hutchins seriously. He had a bad habit of picking his nose. I, and a few of my fourteen-year-old friends, had been sitting in Dean's having chocolate shakes one day back in nineteen forty-five. We had been sitting on the stools at the narrow counter, spinning, sucking on straws, and talking about girls. A much younger Hutchins came in for lunch and sat in a booth at the front by the windows.

Setting our milk shakes down, the whole bunch of us matched him pick for pick. Every time his index finger traveled up to his nose, four teenage fingers followed suit, coupled with giggles and the occasional "Oh yum." He finally turned to us and growling low so no one else would hear, said, "Knock that shit off or you've had it, got me?" That day set the premise for our relationship. He would never forget—but neither would I.

Now, he was the oldest on the force. A veteran of twelve years, next to Chief Solum. He worked from noon until ten. Jerry McClean, the other younger officer, worked from ten until six when Chief Solum showed up. Jerry had replaced Officer Cooper who had been killed in the line of duty. He had been a tall, friendly guy who gave Aubrey, and I, chewing gum from Gott's whenever he passed us on the street. Cooper had been stabbed to death at Tilly's Tavern over on the north edge of town back in nineteen fifty-one. Word has it, the perpetrator, an unknown drifter, was then beaten to death and tossed into the Miskatonic by the regulars. No charges were ever filed.

To see Hutchins on campus, told me he must have been on special assignment. Probably playing detective. I held back a chuckle at the thought. I'd much rather talk to Jerry. He didn't have a history with Arkham. So, we got along just fine. Hutchins was married to Elvira Whateley, of the Dunwich Whateley's. The less she knew of the Rice's business, the better.

"They told me at the front desk you'd be here."

"Well… officer, I am still a student. It's all about school work here at M.U."

"Still kind of a smart aleck, huh? Was hoping you wouldn't mind me interrupting, but now… I don't care. Where were you on the night of April fifth? Around, oh let's say, ten forty-five in the evening?"

"In my room, up to my neck in dissertation. Ever write a dissertation, Officer Hutchins?"

"You be nice, or you're going to get a free ride over to the station. What's it going to be? Yeah… I knew your father… and yeah, I know what he did. But... you're not him, so…"

"You're right, sorry. It's all of this school work, has me kind of irritated."

I supposed Hutchins was the cop I'd best not piss off. I'm sure the chief would set him straight if he got out of hand, but he could, and would, make my life miserable. So, I reigned in my contempt.

"Can anyone corroborate your presence there? Word has it, you were asking around about the missing student."

"Yes, a few dozen pesky undergrads can verify I was in my room, and are you referring to Elspeth?"

"Yeah, that's the one. How'd you know her name?"

"Well, gossip is gossip, kids will talk. I did mention that to the watchman... Lyle Umberling?"

"Yeah, we talked to him too, that's how we know. Say, can we go somewhere else? Kinda crowded in here."

"Finals, next month, everybody's taking their work seriously."

"Come on, let's go outside."

"Certainly, officer. I can step out front to take in a little sun. I need a break, anyway."

There were a lot of eyes on us. The cops were talking to Sterling Rice. So, somebody's in trouble. Sarge was just in sight, lying under a table, sniffing, and licking some girl's saddle shoes. He saw me watching him, got up and came over to sit down beside my table, his eyes locked on Hutchins.

"Hey, I remember that dog."

"Yeah, well... he looks a lot like his mom. He was one of Josephine's. My father gave him to me."

"Yep, been around long enough to know that. So, can we get to it? Got hundreds of others to question. Got to get this done before the summer break. Wouldn't want any suspects slipping away, you know?"

I ignored his statement and getting up, Sarge followed me out with Hutchins close behind. Moving over to the shady side of the loggia, I sat down while Sarge took care of dog business. Hutchins moved to stand in front of me several treads down on the steps.

Pulling a 'Big Time!' candy bar from his frock coat pocket, he tore open the wrapper and took a bite. They were his favorite. I never saw him without one.

"So... am I suspect?"

Swallowing, he said, "Sadly… nope. But because you're kind of staff here at M.U., and because of what Umberling told us, we figured you might have some information for us to pass along to the State boys. They're really on our ass, so we have to do something. We already questioned everybody over at that Pembrook place where she lived."

"You talked with Mordechai?"

"Yep, but she already talked to Jerry and some of the state boys the other night. They had a peeper; you may have heard?

"Or… a kidnapper?"

"What makes you say that?"

"Just makes sense that Elspeth comes up missing and there's also this guy who gets caught poking around behind the dorm."

"Well, you don't know that. Probably just a peeping tom."

Okay, so, my first clue that there might be collusion between Whateley, Umberling, and the Arkham cops. He was ignoring the obvious, or at least, trying to make me think he was.

"So, did Umberling tell you about the guy hanging around the quad and Waldron's Grove?

"Nope, said you saw someone, though, but that's it. Could've been anybody. Kids are always hanging around in The Grove after dark. So, have you ever met this Elspeth?"

"Nope, only heard about her. Lots of kids talking."

"Yep… they do that. Gossip is gossip," he said, mimicking my words and acting like kidnappings happened every day in Arkham. His indifference became obvious. Finishing his chocolate bar, he dropped the wrapper on the ground. Then taking out a little notebook, he started writing. When I caught a glimpse of the page, I could see it was just a list of names with check marks next to them and some doodling of rudimentary horses and horse heads.

"Well… I guess since you don't know nothing about this, I'm going to go talk to someone who does."

He stuck the notebook back in his pocket and turned away. Stopping, he looked back over his shoulder and said, "If you hear anything, call the station, will you?"

"Most certainly, officer," I said, trying to overcome the urge to tell him to pick up his litter.

"You know… like I said, I knew your pa. You don't look nothing like him. What I'm seeing… that's probably your ma, right?" You kind of look like that …Tony Curtis fella, you know? Talked with a student over at Pembrook this morning… the Houghton girl's roommate. She looked a whole lot like Shirley Temple. You know of her?" That little girl actress that had all those movies? Sang a song about lollipop ships or… some crap like that."

He studied me hard for a moment. I decided not to answer and just smiled. He moved down the steps but stopped at the bottom. Without looking back, he said, "Don't like actors much… never did."

Pulling off his cop cap, he wiped at the top of his balding head and walked away toward the gymnasium like his feet hurt, his knee-high riding boots clonking on the concrete. They were made for riding horses, not walking. Their flat bottoms and round heel offered no support. That made me wonder about the doodles and if the chief ever let him ride ol' Tessa. Poor horse.

Going back inside, I found I could no longer concentrate. I thought again of Claudia and toyed with the idea of stealing a few minutes of her time. I could hang out on the Science Hall steps and wait for her to appear and then insist on some attention. I knew I was becoming dependent, but I had resigned myself to it. It was something I wanted— badly.

Packing up my valise, I headed for the door. I got as far as the checkout desk. Dr. Strang's stooped figure appeared before me with his unruly white hair, bushy mustache, and hounds tooth sport jacket. I thought of how much he looked like a short Albert Einstein and smiled to myself. Turning from the librarian, he adjusted the stack of papers in his arms and said, "Oh! Never mind, Alice, there he is."

"Dr. Strang, how are you," I said, trying to appear polite and scholarly.

"Just fine, young man, just fine, but I need to speak with you."

This guy was nearly ninety. He had been here at M.U. since the Victorian era. The Gilded Age if I am not mistaken. He had seen everything, and seemingly, had taken it all in stride. One couldn't have a better advisor, that's for sure. Dr. Strang was the bright spot in my quest for a higher degree. I can assure you, if it hadn't been for him, I would have quit out of frustration long ago. He had been a confidant to my father. The guy who stood at the back of the room, heard everything, but said nothing. Yet, he acted as a fulcrum in the lives of people he thought were worth his trouble. Grateful to be one of them, I knew he would keep me moving forward. Dr. Strang was so well respected by the faculty and administration here, that he could, with just a few words, turn the tide of any negative discussion about Sterling Rice.

"Walk with me?" he said, "I'm going to my office."

"Certainly, professor," I replied with enthusiasm. To be completely honest, I wish I had loitered at my studies a little longer to avoid him. Claudia would have to wait.

I followed him out, and on the way across the green, we chatted about trivial things. The weather, meetings with faculty, staff and students. Then there was the pool and tennis court over at Pembrook, which everybody wanted to talk about, but nobody wanted to act on.

Professor Strang didn't think it was a faculty matter. Yet President Morgan was indecisive on the subject and constantly sought advice from the elder members of M.U. He wanted to be prepared before presenting anything to the board. "Not my business," Professor Strang said, as we entered the front door of the School of Languages.

Dark wainscot covered just about every wall, and heavy cornice framed the ceilings. A massive chandelier hung in the entry hall with ponderous light sconces lining the corridors that branched off of it. It had become like my second home. I had spent many hours in the vast faculty lounge at the back whenever I was there to teach.

Dr. Strang unlocked his office door and we went into a large, corner room with high windows on the south and west walls. The other two had floor to ceiling bookshelves with a rolling ladder and the entry door sat right in the center of the east set. Relics, like brass telescopes, a huge ship's compass, and rolls of maps lay around on massive tables. There were huge chairs, settees with button tufted backs, and a couple of fainting couches for reading. Antiquated lamps were everywhere, and I wondered if Dr. Strang even used half of them.

The room was full of taxidermy and smelled of it. Animals and birds stared at me from every direction. Dr. Strang's favorite, a vicious looking Wolverine, stood resting a paw on a weasel, frozen in fear for eternity. I could tell you the story, word for word, of how it came to be in his possession, but I was sick of it.

"Sterling, please sit down. Coffee or tea?" he said and let his stack of papers slam down onto his massive desk followed by a heavy sigh. Then moving to a smaller table in the corner, he looked back, before pouring himself a cup.

"No, thanks, doctor."

"Very well," he said, and moving to his worn leather chair, he sat down. After taking a sip from his cup, he twisted one end of his mustache, his eyes studying me.

"How is the dissertation going? You were working on it at the library, I presume?"

"Yes, diligently."

"I believe you. We are getting down to the end. Will you be finished on time or will you need an extension?"

"No need for that. I believe I'll have it done on time."

"Very good. So… that is not why I asked you here today, though. I got something to say and I want to give it to you straight."

I felt the apprehension creep in. He looked at me unblinking, his eyes larger than normal behind those thick glasses.

"Please do, I am sure I can take it."

"Sterling… M.U. has an offer. They want to give you a job. It's my understanding that you do want to teach and… you do want to do it here at Miskatonic?"

The anxiety melted away to be replaced with relief. That was something I could deal with. I knew if I didn't like it, I could seek a position elsewhere.

"Sterling?"

"Yes, sorry… thank you."

"So, if I worked toward getting you accepted, you would… as you put it, work diligently on what remains to be done? I will help, as you know, and do everything in my power to get you through it. Don't let me down and I am most certain, barring the unforeseen, you will hold a position here in the year nineteen and fifty-seven. As you may have heard, Professor Chamberlin is retiring at the end of May. They will appoint a temporary Fellow until you can take the reins in August of that year. In all probability, Professor Proctor from over at Bowdish, the private college just north of Salem, will be their choice to sit in. That is until you've completed your education. But he will only take it for that time period. He is a missionary and wishes to travel to South America at the closing of summer break that year. At the end of his obligation. It is in his favor that you be appointed. So, he too will be in your corner, so to speak. At this time, I see no obstacle. But Sterling, understand that you will be somewhat grandfathered in. You will be fast tracked, if I may use the term, largely because of your father, and uh… as much as I hate to say it, your privilege. There are many people here still very grateful to Dr. Rice. I am one of them. Understand though, this may create hard feelings among a few, but they are the minority. What do you say?"

"Thank you? It's all very overwhelming, but you have my promise."

"We all know you are quite capable. Some say, "Sterling Rice is not his father!" Yet I see a great deal of Warren in you. He was a good man, and so are you."

The praise was doing the trick. I felt my self-esteem climbing like the mercury in one of those outdoor thermometers. I felt a warmness filling my chest for the old guy, so I let him know it.

"Allow me to say this, Dr. Strang, I appreciate all that you have done for me. I honestly can say I don't believe I could have had a better adviser."

He smiled briefly like he'd heard it all before and continued in a business-like manner. "Very well, Sterling. Now, let's talk about your progress."

I spent nearly three hours in his office. I had to finally accept a cup of tea, having missed lunch, and afterwards, we both ended up stretched out on adjacent settees, finalizing the discussion. He sent me away, saying, "Time for a little nap before supper over in the cafeteria. Good talk, Sterling. See you again soon, I hope?" That was my cue to get out. It was four thirty by the time I opened the door to leave, with Dr. Strang removing his jacket and matching vest to make himself more comfortable.

114

Sarge had paced, slept, and paced some more. Dr. Strang, moving through his agenda, didn't seem to notice the dog. By the time we had finished, Sarge appeared to be one degree away from a full-blown tango.

Stopping on the steps outside, I had to ponder all that had been said. I had anticipated this moment, but until stated, it was still only a hope. Now in my head, the machine was roaring into action. I had to commit, or a lot of people would be let down. The board was not partisan to my cause. Yet they could be convinced to swing my way. My failure, if it came, would materialize after I took the position. My first year would be a tough one. I had taught an acceptable number of classes last year in the fall, and early winter before Christmas break, and expected to again, come August. The students seemed to like me and my method. I wondered if I would become another Dr. Strang.

After draining his bladder, Sarge gave me that look that asked, "Food?" My stomach had been grumbling for the last half an hour. I felt like I could eat a cow. Slinging my valise over my shoulder, Sarge took it as his cue, and dashed off for the dorm. Looking back and seeing I wasn't following, he came to me, circled, and ran a little farther the second time. Having moved out past the front of the Science Annex, he returned in my direction only to change his mind and rush out of sight around the corner, his tail wagging frantically.

Clearing the building, I saw Claudia sitting cross legged on the lawn. Sarge sat beside her, getting a serious petting. I walked to her, noticing the large stack of books in the grass at her hip. Today her little bow barrette was green, matching one of the colors in her checkered shirt. Her red anklets with white lace trim were folded over at the top. Her blue jean capris were newer than the last pair—and just as tight.

Simply put, she was cute. There was no other word to describe her. A visceral feeling blossomed in me. Some primitive instinct that made me feel a need to protect her or die trying. I realized I would give my life if it would save hers.

"What's the tale, nightingale? Been here for hours waiting for you," she said.

"Liar."

"Okay, well… at least one. I just wanted you to know I put effort into it."

"Hungry?"

"Uh… no, just came from the cafeteria. That food is the worst."

Standing up, she brushed off her derriere. Then bending forward, she adjusted a sock, and bringing her eyes up to mine, she gave me her 'sad look'.

"Sterling… my free time has run out. I was hoping to meet you two hours ago. I've got to really hit the books tonight if I want to go out on the town tomorrow."

"You've been waiting two hours? But…"

"I'm sorry, I wish I could… but I can't." Turning, she picked up her books, but then stood with her back to me as if she was having second thoughts. Putting her books back down, she came to me and looked up into my eyes. I saw the anger, wondering if it was at herself or me. She controlled it well.

In the shadow of the building, her pupils dilated, and my face was reflected in those dark pools. "Sterling… do you see your face in my eyes?"

"Ummm… yeah?"

"Good, because you're going to be in there all night, and I can just bet, studying biology is going to be the hardest thing, ever. I really wish we had met up earlier."

Reaching out, she took my hand for a few seconds and squeezed it. Letting go, she turned and snatching up her books, she almost fell on her face. Sarge followed, dancing circles around her as she walked away. Looking back to see I hadn't moved, he came back and barked at me before making a false dash toward Claudia. Then sitting down, he stared at me like I was some kind of an idiot.

Claudia kept going, and after crossing the street, she looked back once and waved. "See you tomorrow!" she hollered and then tripped over some unseen object in the grass. Catching herself, I saw her shake her head and grin. Watching until she reached Pembrook, I turned away after her tiny image slipped in through the front door. Sarge remained sitting, giving me that look. "What? She's mad about something, and besides, she has to study. So… don't look at me like that, dog."

116

Getting up, he ran for the Bell Tower. I caught up when he stopped to pee on every single foundation pier. Some grounds keeper had cleaned up the cigarette butts and gum wrappers. Which meant, if Whateley came back, I would know. Realizing I had only fifteen minutes to get to Morgan's office before they left for the evening, I broke into a jog.

Samuels was in her usual foul mood. President Morgan greeted me from his office but went right back to his telephone conversation. More talk about the swimming pool at Pembrook. Signing the ledger and grabbing the keys, I didn't speak to Samuels, who 'humphed' at me as I went out the door.

Returning to my room, I fed Sarge and made for the kitchen. A group of undergrads sat watching the four o' clock Looney Tunes, a thick roast beef sandwich in every hand. Somebody had bought roast beef from the deli over on Garrison. My loaf of bread was out on the kitchen counter and had dwindled to just four slices; two of them crusts. Using someone else's mayonnaise in a jar that sat beside the decimated loaf of bread, I made myself a sandwich.

I stopped for a moment behind one of the sofas on my return trip, but then regretted it as the boys piled on the questions. They appeared honored that I had chosen to halt my activity long enough to share a sandwich. Five minutes passed, and it was all I could stand. I left them to argue over who had the best come-on line. I didn't want to tell them that come-on lines were for jerks, but it would be best for them to learn the hard way. Rejection was an excellent teacher.

Gathering Sarge, we headed out. What I was going to do after my rounds was beyond me. I had a free night. I'd spent so much time on my dissertation, I didn't want to do any more of that for at least the next twenty-four hours. I could head over to the Arkham Clubhouse Lounge, the tavern where M.U. faculty drank. A beer and some intellectual conversation with the professors sounded like a good idea.

Starting my rounds at Faculty House, I worked my way south to College Street. Taking it slow, I stopped to stare down Lich Street to see who might be going through the front door at the tavern. If I kept up my pace, it would be dark before I got back around. Afterwards, I could

117

drop the keys with Lyle and then dash off using a meeting at the lounge as an excuse to avoid conversation.

When I got back around to the Church Street side of the Science Hall, twilight filled the air. I still had fifteen minutes to finish up and get back to administration. I walked across the street and stood on Pembrook's green, looking toward the dorm. If I remembered correctly, Claudia said Room 204. I had been inside the place many times during the summer months when the majority of the girls were gone, and when Mordechai was on her summer break. She took the whole month of June, leaving Tabitha Good, a grad student from down Salem way, to run the show until she got back. Knowing the order of the rooms, I counted. I should have figured it would be the most, well-lit window in the wall; the curtains open wide.

Ten minutes passed with no movement. I supposed she sat at her desk, or more than likely, lay on her bed. As a serious scholar, once she started, she wouldn't stop until she passed out. I waited a few minutes, thinking about the look she had given me earlier where my image had floated in the pupils of her eyes. I assumed she had been angry at herself. Her plan to hook up with me had failed. I have to admit, I was impressed at how well she controlled it. That day at the library when I said she sounded easy, she had gotten livid. But she had leveled with me, instead of shouting, like my mother—or Sandra. I felt fortunate.

Cars passed behind me on Church Street as I stood speculating about Claudia's activity. In my head, I pictured myself as some kind of a voyeur. Not the image I wished to project. Bringing my eyes over to The Grove on my right, I wondered if this watcher was also being watched. Time to go. Whistling Sarge over, I crossed back over the street, and while making my way toward Lyle, a feeling of fear formed like a lead weight in my gut.

VIII

Beats The Wings Of Unmerciful Gloom

Lyle greeted me as usual and gave me that smile that I now knew cloaked his contempt. I had always been the enemy. One of those, 'Collegiates' he complained about all the time. It troubled me that all of these years I had never noticed that his smile never reached his eyes. I figured as long as he thought he had me fooled, I would be safe. Wishing him a good night, Sarge and I hurried away.

The Arkham Clubhouse was one of those places off campus that Sarge could go into without a beef. I sat with professors and other grad students in the leather club chairs that circled a large, low, mahogany table; one of many. Sarge lay underneath on the rug, using the opportunity to sniff footwear or snooze. The conversation was good, and I have to admit I had more than one beer. M.U. intellects preferred imports. I never had to pay for any one of the five bottles of stout that had been pushed my way.

Midnight found us at the front door of Dyer, my key in the lock. After securing it for the night, I went to my room, undressed, and fell onto my bed. The beer had taken the edge off of my concern, dulling the events of the day, and to put it morbidly, I slept like the dead. When I woke up the next morning, the sun had worked its way around from French Hill and now hung above the chapel. Its rays slanted in through the gap at the top of the window shade and bounced off the mirror—right into my face. Turning away, I looked at the clock to see it was nine thirty-five in the morning. Groaning, I got out of my bed and putting on my robe, I went out to sit on the veranda steps with Sarge doing the usual. Then, back inside to fill food and water bowls before collapsing back onto my bed—still in my robe. It was Saturday.

119

I lay studying the ceiling, wishing for the hours to zoom by to the moment I would meet Claudia. It dawned on me that we had not agreed to a time. I would just have to give her a bell. The memory of her face, with me reflected in her eyes, blossomed in my mind. At the time, I hadn't thought how peculiar it was that she said, "Good, because you're going to be in there all night…" It had what I can only describe as a poetic quality. A deep-thinking sense of things. A wonderful way of conveying that she would be thinking of me all the time we were apart.

Like a juggernaut, another intense feeling pushed in. There was no question now, I'd fallen in love. That had never happened before, but there was no doubt that's what it was. It left me not sure how to act. I felt excited at the prospect, and hope glistened like a single dewdrop on a blade of grass in the morning sun. But had I not been hopeful before?

Maybe any hope I had for anything being good had dissolved away with the loss of Aubrey. The prospect that despondency may have reigned for almost twelve years without any real awareness of it, saddened me. Had love been missing, too? I felt a kind of love for my mother, sure. I am positive I loved my father, and Sarge, he was a definite. However, it had been Aubrey who had brought the real sunshine. Then some wicked person had come and ripped her from my life for their own selfish motive. Claudia had brought it back, and now, they were trying to do it again.

I felt the anger start to bubble and cruel thoughts of what I might do to any perpetrator who committed an act of violence toward Claudia, cycled through my head. Lyle had joined the ranks of the transgressors and was somebody who functioned within my sphere. Too close for comfort. It seemed my day was cast in shadow, even though the sun outside shone with a brilliance. I needed to get up, get dressed, and get the hell out of my room. Sarge climbed up on the bed as I dressed, and not even a minute passed before his snores filled my ears. Letting him sleep, I left Dyer Hall. I needed a good, long walk so I could clear my head. I vowed that when I returned, I would think about nothing but Claudia and being in love. That would last for the rest of the day.

The usual Saturday automobile traffic moved over the streets, and the sidewalks were alive with shoppers, many of them farmers coming into Arkham for their weekly groceries. People moved in bunches across the quad, most of them townies who passed through from the Hangman's Brook neighborhood in the southwest quadrant of the town. Their destination; either the shops on Garrison Street or French Hill.

I moved north with those people, and crossing over to Dean's, I went inside. He had been open for about four hours, but the carhops wouldn't start until noon. If you showed up before that, you had to eat inside. His two cooks, Juan, and Miguel, two cleverly funny young men, would be there to assist Dean. They would be the ones to serve the food until the skaters showed up. I asked for a cherry phosphate, and took it out with Dean's consent

Sucking on the straw, I strolled down to the river bridge. My goal was to walk over to Hangman's Hill via the riverbank and then move back south to the campus. That should be enough to allow me to sort out a few things. Making my way down to the water, I saw several small fishing boats anchored midstream just off the island. Local fishermen out on a Saturday with their poles, tackle, and ramshackle boats. It was a constant occurrence three seasons out of the year. So, nothing unusual.

Yet those skiffs sparked a thought, and I made my way upstream to McCabe's Boathouse. Moving past a dock down on the shore to my right, I crossed the gravel driveway that also served as a boat ramp. Dashing up a short set of steps to a small porch at the side of the boathouse, I struggled with the door because it had warped and was stuck in its jamb. I gave it a swift kick at the bottom and it swung open. Entering the garage-like repair shop/office at the east end, I passed through and went out the door on the far wall. Stepping out to stand on a narrow catwalk that started at a short set of stairs on my right, it worked its way around the back wall. I moved along it, checking out all the boats slung in dry dock. Their prows bumped up against old tires tacked to the side of the walkway. It created a slow cadence backed by the lapping of water and the squeaking of taught hemp riggings.

The boathouse was rarely attended. Its open front stretched for maybe a hundred yards down the river bank and its roof hung in cantilever out over the water. A single crank and reel were placed in each stall to raise or lower its adjacent boat. Then you could motor or paddle out of the building backwards into the main channel. The only source of illumination came through the open front and a few badly placed skylights. There were bare electrical bulbs mounted on creosoted rafters above, but public access to the switch was prohibited. McCabe, when not completely obliterated by drink, would turn them on at night and off in the morning.

I walked to the end as sleek, little swallows flitted in and out. A family of sparrows occupied the rafters tweeting their curiosity as a startled pigeon flapped from ventilator to ventilator up under the ridge. Gas and oil smells filled the air, mixed with the odor of the river and dead fish. Paddles, oars, and life vests hung on the wall along with the occasional outboard motor chained and padlocked to a long, thick metal rail fixed to the exposed studs. I soon arrived at stall #25 and pulled the cover off the Speedster. McCabe had been taking good care of my father's boat. I suspected my mother was still paying his meager monthly fee.

The manila rope of the slings showed a good amount of wear, but when I lowered the craft a foot or so, and then raised it back, it still moved with ease. So, setting Dean's glass on a narrow ledge, I lowered the Speedster down to where it just floated on the brown water of the Miskatonic. Leaving the slings in place, I climbed in. Sitting down on the hardwood pilot's bench, my hands were drawn to the wheel. I rotated it left, then right, all the while looking back to make sure the outboard swiveled with each turn. I expected things to be a little rusty, or even decayed, but McCabe had taken his job seriously. Everything was waxed and oiled. It appeared as it had the day my father proudly displayed it to me for the first time.

I longed to take Claudia out onto the river—just like I had Aubrey. We could spend a leisurely day on the water, maybe swim in Keziah's Cove, or picnic out on Devil's Altar Island. Ideas filled my head, sparked by a budding enthusiasm. There was so much to enjoy when you had someone to enjoy it with. I found myself smiling at the thought as I climbed out of the boat.

After crawling back up onto the catwalk, I wound the boat to the top, secured the crank, and replaced the cover. Leaving the building the way I'd come in; I slammed the outside door to make sure it re-stuck in its jamb.

I daydreamed as I ambled up toward River Street. A passenger train, the Coast Bound Flyer on its return trip to Gowan and points beyond, made its way west on the other side of the Miskatonic. The sun shone through its windows and I could see the passengers inside the dining car at their breakfast. Damn, Dean's soda glass!

I didn't want to deal with the sticky door, so I made my way toward the short set of stairs just inside the corner where the catwalk began. That way was muddier, but it would take me straight inside.

McCabe had used a bulldozer to scrape a road about fifteen feet wide from the street, straight down to the water where he cut the bank. Then after graveling it, the old drunkard sunk a row of wooden mooring posts with eyebolts into the mud along the water's edge. They had been placed just to the right of the ramp's mouth and stood an equal distance apart. It was cheaper to rent a post, padlock, and chain, then it was to store a boat in the house.

My eye caught the first craft on the ramp side of the boats tethered there. It was very similar to my fathers; just newer. As I stood checking it out, my eye picked up something else. Deep grooves had been made in the mud by the keel rib of another watercraft that had put-in. Somebody had been running their boat aground and not using a mooring post. The furrow's depth and length told me the boat had come in fast. So, definitely motorized. But it was the trait of a lazy boatman. They seriously risked damaging the propeller, all for the sake of keeping their feet dry. There were other impressions in the mire. Somebody had been dropping a round, flat bottomed anchor just forward of where the prow would have been, and whoever that somebody was—they wore a pair of square toed boots with a hobnailed heel.

I scanned upriver for any approaching or departing vessels, and seeing none, I went inside, grabbed that soda glass, and came back out. My curiosity was getting the better of me and I stopped one more time to study the hodgepodge of marks in the muck. I thought about that slightly worn path coming down the slope outside Pembrook's back wall and decided to take the route our devious boater might take. I moved up between the two large warehouses on the other side of River

Street, and then crossing Main, I followed the slightly worn trail up the slope and stopped just outside the gate.

The heavy oaken panel still had not been secured, and once again, it swung free. I could see the terrace through the trees. Several girls either sat or stood there, their conversations not quite as audible as their laughter. I wondered if Claudia might be among them. I thought to risk a short visit, but changed my mind when Mordechai appeared, bringing the terrace to silence.

Leaving the gate as it was, I turned right and walked along the outside of the wall to the end. Instead of turning left to follow the wrought iron fence, I crossed over West Street. Going one more block to Boundary, I stopped at the base of Hangman's Hill. I'd hoped to spend a little time hiking through the trees and reminiscing in its park like atmosphere, but I had spent too much time at the boat house. If I left Sarge alone much longer, there was no doubt he would leave me a large, steaming gift right in the middle of the floor. My reward for abandoning him.

I'd leave the hill for another day. Turning south, I picked up my pace and after crossing Church Street, I walked along the west wall of the School of Medicine. I thought to take a quick left before I reached staff housing in order to avoid being seen from my mother's cottage, but the thought came too late and I heard a loud, "Sterling Rice." Looking up, I saw my mother stepping up onto the sidewalk at the other end of the block.

Her black, well lacquered, wide brimmed, straw hat, gleamed in the sun. It was tipped low over her eyes and she had to tilt her head back to look my way. Her handbag matched the hat, contrasted by her short-sleeved, blue on white polka dotted shirtwaist dress. Elbow length white gloves adorned her hands, hiding the fast-accumulating age spots on her arms. Her book club met for breakfast on Saturdays at Sonia's Bistro and that was the direction from which she appeared to be coming. She walked everywhere she went, even though she could have driven my father's car. But she didn't like cars, or driving, any more than I did. It surprised me that she had called out to me, being that no proper meeting had been scheduled.

Too late to sneak away. I walked toward her and before I arrived, she said, "Good day, Sterling. What brings you over this way? It's Saturday, aren't you usually still in your bed and wasting good daylight?"

I stopped to face her, and she looked me up and down. Her eyes returned to my muddy shoes, and she grimaced before saying, "Kiss your mother, Sterling."

I committed to the usual and stepped back. She looked frail and washed out standing there in the sunlight. When she raised her sunglasses to study my face, I saw her eyes were red and puffy. Her hands were shaking, and seeing that I noticed, she clutched her pocketbook with both of them and looked away.

I waited for the lecture that I knew was coming. After a few seconds of awkward silence, she turned her face back to me and said, "So, where have you been, and why are you carrying a water glass?"

"Just out for a walk to clear my head. Believe it or not, I can walk and drink at the same time."

A fleeting frown crossed her face and she squinted. "Have you been checking my house at night? Those dreadful birds are keeping me from my much-needed rest. It's almost as if they follow my every breath. However, I believe that is just my imagination." She didn't wait for my answer and monotoned a, "So... who was the girl, Sterling?"

"Girl?"

"Yes, you know who I mean. Don't be evasive with me, young man."

"Oh, you mean the night before last?"

"Yes, you stood right over there...kissing. Who is she? Some middle-class floozy trying to take advantage of your good name?"

"Don't remember kissing any floozy... ever. But I was with Claudia, a rather class act, who happens to find me interesting and well worth her time."

My ire was rising, and I knew I had better flee before this meeting turned into a shouting match. However, I couldn't help but add, "And if I remember correctly, you and she share the same kind of a journey from a place of questionable repute. I am going to ask you to please not belittle those who are of similar, or of greater worth to me, mother. It's unbecoming to malign those whom you know nothing about. Sorry, I

125

have to go. I have to tend to my dog, whom I believe will be much happier to see me."

I walked away. She gasped and stuttered out, "Sterling Rice, you come back here, right now!" I kept walking, forcing one foot in front of the other. "Don't you walk away from me, young man!"

I picked up my pace. She said no more, and I didn't look back. Moving out of her sight by veering left in front of the Liberal Arts Building, I cut between the Science Hall and it's annex for a straight shot back to the dorm.

I had actually lectured my mother! Something I had never done before. But her bashing Claudia like that had pushed me over the edge. A showdown loomed. Elsie would either have to accept Claudia or see even less of me than she already was. She would have to change her ways and come down off that damn high horse of hers. I'm surprised that she hadn't rubbed off on me anymore than she had. It wasn't clear what inside of me made me more compassionate, or empathetic than she was. I believed it might be my father. So, maybe I was more like him than I realized.

I found Sarge still sleeping, but the air in the room was thick with flatulence. He looked back over his shoulder as the low hiss of another, ruffled the hair of his tail. The look in his eyes said, "Well? What did you expect?" After setting Dean's glass on my desk, I moved around the room opening windows before taking Sarge out. Running to his favorite spot over by the Chapel, I sat on the railing at the side of the veranda watching him relieve himself. Then the side door of the building opened and Chaplin Parris stepped out. A shout ripped the air and Sarge playfully bounded away.

Parris saw me and yelled, "Somebody might step in that, you know." I just waved.

He threw up his hands in surrender and went back inside just as I started for the cafeteria. Leaving Sarge in his usual place, I slipped into the kitchen. Planting my derriere on the corner of a large, unused prep table, I watched Betty busy preparing chocolate cake for supper's dessert. Cutting the rather tasty treat into pieces, she carefully placed them on small plates. Handing one to me with a fork, she said, "You hear about that girl got kidnapped from Pembrook? Don't think that's ever happened right here on the campus before."

"Yeah, I heard about that, mostly through the grapevine."

"Ain't safe to be a college kid, no more. But I guess M.U. ain't been the safest place in the world. Used to be a lot of stuff went on around here. Why I remember back when I was a little girl, my mama used to tell me how everybody got sick from the typhoid. Allen Halsey was the Dean here then, and he just went nuts… killed a whole bunch of people, including some students. That was before they caught him and stuck him in the asylum. No one talks about that. You ask anyone of those old men sitting out at that faculty table… I just betcha, they get up and walk away without a word."

"Yeah, my father told me all about that."

"Good ol' Professor Rice… really miss that man. So, then there was that time all them young girls was being kidnapped over in Aylesbury and around the valley. Old Martha Whittle, lived over on Powdermill Street, she told me once that she'd just bet it was because of those Dunwich men. I think them, Whateley's… they were looking for wives because there was no one left in that village worthy of a match. That is… worth marrying and having children with. Martha, she despised Elvira Whateley… that Hutchins of the police… his wife. She's dead now, you know… old Martha, I mean."

I stopped chewing. The bite of cake had stuck in my throat. Taking a drink of milk to keep from choking, a terrible feeling washed over me as Aubrey's face filled my mind's eye. As much as it troubled me and as much as I wanted to just jump down and walk out—I stayed. Betty knew something I didn't, and my curiosity overrode my anxiety.

"There were others?" I said with a hint of disbelief.

"You're thinking about Aubrey now, aren't you? I'm sorry Sterling, guess I shouldn't have brought it up. I don't think your folks wanted you to be troubled with all that bad business. That sweet little girl… so sad."

"Yes, but… there were others?"

"Well… yeah. Girls came up missing all over the valley. Five or six if I remember correctly. No, your sweet little cousin wasn't the only one, Sterling. She might have been the first, but she weren't the last. But you were a little boy and not to be concerned about such things. Well, except for your missing cousin. I reckon it went on for about two years or so and then stopped. They never found a one of them. The state police or the Hoover boys, I mean. They always suspected Dunwich, but you know, them folks wouldn't talk even if you stuck them with a hot poker. Most of them girls disappeared from places way out of the way. You know, back up in the hills? The word getting around at the time was they'd just run off. Got tired of being treated bad by their kinfolk or something like that. I suspect the law found out about the others in a roundabout way. I'm thinking since Aubrey was the first, her folks were the only ones to call the law. So, in the middle of looking for her, they found out about all the others. If you know what I mean?"

"I never heard a thing, like…"

"Like I said, you were just a boy, not much on reading newspapers, were you? Your folks wouldn't talk about it, would they? No… good ol' Professor Rice wouldn't want to make it any worse for his little boy than it already was. And I know damn well that your ma wouldn't. Now it seems, its starting all over again, only now, right here in Arkham. Keep your eyes open, Sterling. You're a man now, you can meet it head on. I hear you got a new sweetheart? That snotty little Miss Priss, Sandra Heinz, was in here complaining out loud to everybody, trying to make you look bad. That's how I know. Well… if it's true, you keep that girl close, you hear me, Sterling? Somethings brewing, I can just feel it. Keep your darling close, okay, hon?"

"I will, Betty… think I'd better go, Sarge is waiting."

I finished my cake even though it had become dry and tasteless. Getting down from the table, Betty patted me softly on my back and handed me a small brown lunch sack.

"Here, made this up for you."

"Thanks," I said, and after handing it off, she took me by the arm, spun me around, and hugged me. Then returning to her duties, she said nothing else and I could see by her face that she felt terrible. I patted her shoulder to let her know it was okay, and she gave me a sad smile. "Sorry," she said and went back to her cake.

I left the way I'd come in. The bag held another BLT, an apple, and another slice of cake wrapped in waxed paper. Pulling out a piece of bacon, I tossed it to Sarge. He caught it mid-leap and then stayed close as I walked to the dorm. My day had darkened even more as the ghost of Aubrey Rice followed me down that walkway. Nearly twelve years— why couldn't I let it go? And now I learn there were others? No one ever spoke a word of it. But like Betty said, I was concerned only about Aubrey at the time.

I really wanted to talk to my mother, but that wasn't going to happen. Even if she finally gave in, I'd be lucky to get her to tell me all she knew. Aubrey was a Rice, not a Grangerford. So, wasn't really her kin. She had made that part perfectly clear. The only reprieve from this dark mood would come from Claudia. I wanted to see her so badly that it hurt. She would be the sun breaking through the clouds on a dismal day. Shining brighter than the actual one that now tried to bake the pomade right out of my hair.

I felt the aggravation of having to wait. I, would call her. I could set a definite time for our date and that would help. Perhaps we could talk a bit. I went inside Dyer and as I dug for my room key, the telephone rang. I heard footsteps running from the TV room and Casper slid into view, his stocking feet gliding on the waxed surface of the hardwood floor.

"Oh! Sterling."

"I got it, Casper. You can go back to doing nothing."

"It's probably that girl again. She called for you about half an hour ago."

"Thanks Casper. I'll take it from here"

"Okay, daddy-o. Oh, ummm… I ate all your oranges. I tried that turnip thing, but that tasted like sh…"

"CASPER!"

"Sorry…"

He dashed away as the phone rang for the fourth time. Snatching it up, I said, "Hello?"

"Oh! Sterling, my dear."

Adrenaline flowed in like a flash flood. My brain froze and a strange gurgle rolled up out of my throat. Mustering all of my ability, I was able to find my voice and stuttered out, "Aubrey?"

IX

Village Laid Under

The line went quiet and then, "Sterling? It's Claudia."

It took a minute for what she said to register. Regaining my composure, but feeling a little embarrassed, I said, "Oh! Claudia! Ummm... how are you?"

"Just peachy. The question is, how are you? You sound kind of weird. Is everything okay?

"Yeah, it's okay. Happy to hear your voice, that's for sure."

"Same here... so... can we meet at six over at the Bell Tower? Can't hardly wait. I need a break. Don't think I'm going to do one bit of Biology until Monday. I'm so sick of Larson's theories that I could just barf."

I heard other voices in the background, and then a distant, "Hey everyone, Claudia's on the phone with the Tony Curtis guy." There came the sound of running feet and giggling.

I ignored it and said, "Oh, sure. That would be great. To be honest, I can hardly wait, myself."

"Neato! See you at six. Got to get a shower and wash this bod. Unless, of course, you want to come over and take care of that?" More giggling. "Okay, going now...see you later, alligator. Oh, Sterling?"

"Yes, Claudia?"

"Not that you look like an alligator, or anything." There came the sound of laughter from many feminine mouths and Claudia giggled.

"I got it," I said and chuckled, thinking that she was probably standing in a circle of nosey dormmates right at the moment. All of them leaning in, trying to catch a word or two of what I was saying.

"Okay, bye-bye, kookie."

130

There came more laughter and the click of the handset being returned to the cradle. I hung up, abuzz with adrenaline. I didn't know how to act. I had conjured up Aubrey's voice and that made me feel even more unsettled. I had Aubrey on the brain. The urge to do something about it had become overpowering. But what could I do? I knew a little about Freud and even a little Jung. Psychology wasn't my thing, but it might have to be. I needed to finish my unfinished business. I vowed to restart my investigation and get to the bottom of this. The library now had a vast wealth of historical resources for me to use, plus the two, fairly new, microfilm machines that would allow me to view old copies of the Arkham Advertiser and other newspapers. My dissertation was going well enough that I could take some time off for a different kind of research.

The Bell Tower chimed four and the grandfather clock in the commons concurred. I had two hours to kill. The last one would be for hygiene. So, I could go and start my little research project immediately. Except, I didn't want to be in a foul mood when I hooked up with Claudia. If I filled my head with dreadful things from the past, there would be no getting them out of there for at least a day. I didn't want to come to Claudia troubled. She could help take my mind off such things and the fewer negative thoughts floating around inside my noggin, the better. I felt compelled to keep her happy, that way, she could make me happier. The investigation would have to wait another day.

Going to my room, I grabbed my unfinished copy of James Thurber's *My World And Welcome To It* along with Sarge's chewed up rubber ball. My destination—the college green with intent to laze about in the grass and saturate my brain with humor. But first, a swift and rigorous session of ball play with Sarge, whom I would leave behind this evening. I wanted him full of food and past exhaustion by the time I took off.

The hour went as planned. I pushed back my anguish, using Thurber like a shield. I still had a sense of the angst hanging around just at the corner of my mind's eye, the shadowy shape of Aubrey's ghost lingering in rejection. I felt bad for wanting to push her away, but she needed to understand, it was for my own good. When I started to doze off, I realized I had achieved my goal—time to head for the dorm.

131

I fed Sarge and while he ate, I showered, shaved, after-shaved, and dressed. A black turtle neck, dungarees, and my black loafers should be enough. It was too warm for my bomber jacket, and I suspect I'd be carrying it most of the time, anyway. It would be just my luck to forget I had brought it and walk away from Dean's with it still draped over the back of a booth.

Letting Sarge out for a quick squirt, I stood watching the traffic moving up and down Garrison. The teenagers were starting their joy riding early. Among them, the hot-rodder's teasing the 'Want-To-Be's' who craved for something more than just their daddy's car.

Sarge came back, ran to the door, and scratched on it. After letting him inside, I sat at my desk going over some notes as I waited for the chime of six. I felt my excitement growing. My first date in a long time, and one that I actually wanted to have. There was no apprehension that I might fail to act proper, no fear of judgement, just a wholesome eagerness to be with Claudia. I wondered if she would dress up. It would be odd to see her in a shirtwaist dress that dropped to her knees, or something even more formal. If she did, I may have to stop back, pick up my sport jacket and switch to oxfords with socks.

When the clock did chime, I nearly jumped out of my seat. Sarge was contently snoozing on my bed. So, as quiet as possible, I grabbed Dean's glass and left the room, softly pulling the door shut behind me.

Coming around Loring Hall, I saw Claudia had already arrived. My concern over her dressing-up, melted away. Leaning back against one of the decorative piers of the Bell Tower, with hands in pockets, she grinned, her head cocked to the right. She wore a light, V necked gold colored sweater over a white blouse (untucked of course, sleeves rolled up). Dark blue, denim peddle-pushers exposed her muscular calves and contrasted her white bobby socks and brown loafers. She had replaced the tiny, colorful bow with a turtle shell barrette.

"Wow! All in black tonight? Cool! If I got you a beret you could be a Beatnik."

"Is that what you've been looking for all your life, a Beatnik?"

"Actually… no. I think what I've been looking for all of my life is a kind of happiness that comes from being with a guy who looks a lot like Tony Curtis but acts like Sterling Rice."

I stopped and grinned. Claudia crossed her eyes, stuck out her tongue, and pushing off of the wall, she passed me and walked toward Garrison. She left me perplexed, but it didn't last long because she looked back over her shoulder, smiled big enough to show that signature overbite, and said, "Coming, Mr. Rice?"

"Mr. Rice? Mr. Rice was my…"

"It's what all the other kids call you. So weird. Thought I'd tease you a bit, though."

Dashing after her, she reached a hand back, took mine, and pulled me up even with her. "Is this okay? I mean, for other people to see us holding hands? The gossip has already started, anyway. So, I figured it doesn't matter, right?"

"It's copasetic. They all suspect we are a thing. Especially if my mother, or somebody else I know, has been blabbing."

"Peachy keen! So, we'll just let them if that's what makes them happy. Then everybody's happy. How about you? Are you happy?" Her amber brown eyes searched mine as she squeezed my hand.

"Oh, the happiest… now." Her eyes did that sparkling thing and her face grew soft with gratification.

"So, what's with the drinking glass? You don't want to get cooties, so… you brought your own?"

"Ah, no. Took it from Dean's this morning. Went for an early morning walk and stopped in for a phosphate."

"Oh, okay, peachy. I was concerned you may have a little germ thing going on. You know, kind of a phobia?"

"Nope."

"Good," she said, and we walked in silence with her swinging our hands back and forth. Coming up on Garrison Street, I looked left and then right to avoid getting run down. I thought I saw Lyle duck back behind the shrubbery at the corner of the physical plant. He was trying to hide. Sadly, for him, the illumination from the pole lamp at his back showed his shape through the leaves. With my eyes on him, we crossed over.

Claudia was able to find the only pothole on the entire block and promptly tripped in it. I caught her, throwing one arm around her back and under an armpit—my hand, accidently, coming up to cup her left breast. I immediately blushed and releasing her I stepped back, stuttering, "Sorry, sorry! I didn't mean to do that."

She giggled and crossing her arms under them, she pushed them up, making them even more evident. Casting her eyes down at them and then back at me, she said, "Well, these things are good for something. I mean, besides wasting money on brassieres, anyway. They can cushion me if I fall on my face, or... somebody can just grab them if I've tripped and am falling."

"Hey, I didn't grab them... I just... it was an accident."

"Well, regardless, I'm grateful... ummm... that you saved me. I could have skinned my nose and how would that have looked?" She winked and grinned.

Letting her breasts fall back into their usual position, she took my hand again, and we continued walking with me wishing the flush from my face.

"So, where's Sarge tonight? It's kind of weird not having him around."

"He decided to stay home. Dates are not his thing. All the lovebird talk gets on his nerves. I suspect he gets confused about why there has to be dating at all. For him, it's just, wham-bam, thank you, mam. He's a real he-dog. Romance for him is a drag. That's where we differ—a lot. But... we get along."

"I would have never thought," she said, laughed, and added, "You—a romantic."

I chuckled at her humor and looking back, I saw Lyle's silhouette had gone, but the bad feeling that came with it remained.

"What are you looking at?"

"Oh, nothing. Thought I saw someone I knew. Oh well..."

Turning my attention back to her, we exchanged small talk about the things displayed in the shop windows as we passed. We were nearly to the corner when she skipped away and stopped at Main Street to twirl at the curb. Then she stood scanning the parking lot over at Dean's, her feet set about shoulder width apart. My eyes couldn't help but take in her form as she stood there. Her pedal pushers were tight, showing the curves of her calves and thighs. A breeze blew up the tail of her blouse and showed a well-rounded derriere. As much as I tried not to ogle, it was a losing battle. Something about a woman in tight denim. She looked back over her shoulder and grinned like she was happy that I was eyeing her physique.

"The place is packed, hope we can get a seat inside," she said.

"No need to worry about that. Dean and I are old friends, we could even sit behind the serving counter if we wanted… but he might put us to work. I suspect most everyone there came to sit in their cars, though. Not cool to sit inside. That's for squares."

"So, we going to be square tonight?"

"Yeah, let's keep them guessing, huh?"

"I get you," she said, her eyes wide with excitement. "Wow, this place is fat city on a Saturday. Almost two years at M.U. and this is my first time here."

The lot was full of cars. I watched Regina working methodically through the rows, pen, and pad in hand. Two other girls on roller skates raced around Chevy's, Buicks, and Studebakers, the distress on their faces apparent. University students, more often than not, gathered at the tables out front on the walkway under the windows, and after exchanging greetings with the ones we knew, Claudia skipped away to the open door.

Stopping to survey the room, she stood with hands on hips. Two more carhops were working inside, running orders from the counter to the tables, their poodle skirt uniforms, stiff and bright with newness. I placed Dean's glass on the counter and then came up behind Claudia who had moved to stand at the bar stools so she could watch the cooks work their magic. Putting my hands gently on her shoulders, I watched Dean turn and peer over the top of Juan's head. Giving me his usual salute, he then pointed at my favorite booth and raised his eyebrows as if to ask, "Is that okay?" Turning, I saw Miguel working it over with a damp rag. Taking Claudia's hand, I towed her to the corner.

I looked back to catch Dean's eye and he gave me an exaggerated wink, followed by a thumbs up. I gave him a quick grin and hurried Claudia to the booth. I was trying to be inconspicuous but she had caught Dean's gesture and said, "What's that all about?"

135

"Nothing much."

"Come on, Sterling…tell me."

"I just got Dean's approval."

"For?"

"For you. He wants me to know I have good taste." She rolled her eyes and huffed. "Yeah, okay… but he's an old guy. I wonder what Kinsey would say about that."

"Let's forget about Kinsey for a couple hours, okay?"

"Well… okay, but just two. Then back at it. I'm not letting go of Kinsey. I might need him later. I truly think you will be a lot happier for him… it!"

"What do you mean by that?"

"Oh, you'll see soon enough. So, no talk of Kinsey—time starts now," she said, and giggling, she slid into the booth to sit with her back to River Street, facing toward the open door. I started to sit across from her, but she said, "No… you sit here," and slapped the Naugahyde covered seat beside her.

"Oh, sorry… habit."

Moving over beside her, I left a slight gap between us. She closed it up, pressing her hip tight against mine. "You know that's not fair play, I…" was all I got out when Dean yelled, "Becky!" It startled me and whipping my face around, I saw him nod his head sideways toward us and raise his eyebrows to her in his 'Get to it!' look.

A short, blonde teen with a ponytail rolled our way. Upon reaching a clear space between the tables, she spun like a professional skater. A mother covered her son's eyes as the poodle skirt flattened out like a disc at her waist. But the pink petticoat did its job, shielding the kid from an early education. A little red-haired girl two booths away, clapped her hands, and crowed her glee. Claudia expressed amazement with a, "Wow."

Becky completed her routine and rolled to our table, stopping with precision.

"You're good," Claudia said."

"Yeah… thanks. I'm just as good on ice," Becky said with an obvious Bostonian accent. "I'm at the rink every chance I get. Not much else to do in this town. I want to go back to Boston, but mom says no. She got a job in Arkham, so we're here to stay. Oh well…"

Becky sighed, stared out the window with a faraway look and added, "Can't win for losing. These skates are going to be my ticket out of here. I'm pretty sure I'm Olympics material. So… whata-yah have?"

We placed our order, while Becky chomped away on her Juicy Fruit, her green eyes following the tip of her pencil as she wrote. Repeating the order to us, she pushed off with a toe stop and skated backwards to the counter. Slapping the order down on the Formica top, she turned and zipped toward a couple who had just sat down in a booth by the door. Looking at Dean, I saw a fleeting expression of what I believed to be pride.

Claudia fished a quarter out of her pocket and dropped it in the small, chrome plated Seeburg 'Wall-O-Matic' that hung just below the window. Dean had them installed just last year, saying something about wanting to keep up with the times.

"You don't mind, do you?" Claudia asked.

"Ah, no, have at it," I said as she rolled the catalogue, the small panels flapping. Then gasping with pleasure, she punched two buttons. I heard the barely audible whir of the main unit in the back room as it came to life, and Nat King Cole began to croon, *Unforgettable* through the speaker in the wall unit.

Leaving the rest of her choices untaken, she turned to me and said, "I love this," her eyes gleeful.

She turned away to face the table, and closing them, she dropped her chin and her head swayed slowly back and forth in time with the music. She then wrapped her hands around my upper arm and pressing her cheek to them, she closed her eyes again. I heard a woman's voice saying, "Someone's in love…" followed by, "Isn't that sweet, Richard?"

Claudia heard it to, and releasing my arm, she blushed. Turning to the jukebox, she went to slowly rotating the selector knob like she was going to make her last two selections. About a minute passed before she glanced back at me and grinned. I just smiled, said nothing, and patted her thigh. Becky rolled up to put our order on the table, and then rolled away, muttering, "I hate that song." Ignoring her, we went to devouring our burgers and fries.

Regina skated in and out constantly. Her eyes found mine every time, but her face remained indifferent. On her fifth time in, she shouted, "Dean! Five minutes, huh?"

"Five minutes only, that lots packed, Reg, I need you out there."

"Ok, you old coot, geez, I've been at it since four."

"Five minutes!"

"OKAY!"

Passing Becky, I heard her say, "You... germ." Becky spun completely around one time and stuck out her tongue. Regina ignored her and glided to us, halting her motion by using both toe stops at the same time. Grabbing the edge of our table, she stood there like a ballerina on point. I prepared for the worst, hoping she wouldn't badger Claudia.

"Hey, Sterling! What's the tale, nightingale?"

"Hey, Reg."

"Who's the dolly?" she said looking Claudia over. Claudia just grinned and chewed her burger, a tiny smear of mustard at the corner of her mouth.

"Oh! Hey! It's Shirley Temple! Another celebrity in the house. Tony Curtis is out with Shirley Temple! Hey... is she even old enough for you? Seems I'm more your age... and type."

"Reg... meet Claudia. Second year student at M.U. So, yeah—old enough."

"Crazy," Regina said and stuck out her hand. Claudia took it and continued smiling.

"Can she talk, Sterling? Or is she really just a puppet, kinda like that Howdy Doody fella. Oh! You're Heidi Doody, right?" she said and laughed at her own joke.

"I can talk very well, thank you. So... hey Reg, what's cooking?" Claudia said.

"Crazy! So, you're Sterling's new babe? You must be on cloud nine? I know he sure gets me cranked."

"Number 13's up, Reg! Back to the lot."

"Got to cut out, it's antsville out there tonight. Later, gators."

138

She moved to leave, stopped, turned back, leaned down in front of me, and whispered into Claudia's face, "Don't fake him out, or you're going to have to deal with me, girly. If you love him, then… love him with all your heart."

Regina righted herself and kissed at me before speeding away. Picking up the loaded tray on the counter, she raced out the door with her usual grace. She stared at us through the window as she passed, that familiar look of envy in her eyes.

"Sorry about that. Regina's just a little overprotective."

"No, it's okay. I get it. I've been watching her. She's amazing at her job."

"You didn't say much?"

"With a girl like that, you don't say much. You smile, be polite, and say only what needs saying. Let them think you're some kind of a ditzy cube. The less threatening, the better. Mouthing off to a tough chick only gets you creamed. I also know she wouldn't touch me out of respect for you."

"Yeah, she's also got to protect that rep. Now that we got through all that, back to the food."

Picking up the remaining part of her burger, she chewed thoughtfully. I ate a handful of fries and watched her face. After swallowing, she turned to me and smiled, a question in her eyes."

"What is it?"

"Oh, nothing," she said and went back to her burger.

Hours passed as we talked and chewed, sucked on straws, and took turns picking songs on the jukebox. I barely noticed it had gotten dark until Dean hit the line of switches on the back wall and all the exterior lights popped on. Every parking spot had a white plastic globe mounted on a post, each one marked with a large red number. The customer could hit a button to make the light blink and attract the attention of the car hop. The vast expanse of asphalt was now spotted with little lights, some blinking.

Claudia and I talked about everything. Our lives as 'only children' life in Cambridge for her, and Arkham for me. I avoided speaking of Dunwich and she didn't bring it up. Then it was: swimming, fencing, boxing, horseback riding, and learning to drive. The one thing we both knew how to do, but rarely ever did. Regina skated in and out, glancing our way, grinning and winking every time she caught my eye. Becky called it quits for the evening and packing her skates away in a lavender case, she walked out, her pink jacket announcing 'HARLOTS' across the back in big white letters. So, one of Regina's recruits. An act of desperation, I assumed. A need to be accepted in a new town. Yeah—not much to do in Arkham.

The room gradually cleared out with only a few teenaged couples scattered about in the booths. The parking lot remained busy, but now with fewer families and more of the younger crowd. There was the squealing of tires, rumbling engines, loud laughter, and radio music turned up full blast. Cars raced in and out. Then there was the frequent drag race, drawing everyone to gather on the sidewalk along River Street. Claudia had plunked quarter after quarter in the little jukebox, yakking away about school and life inside Pembrook.

"Sterling?" she said, rubbing my knee and smiling at me.

"Uh... yeah?" I said, realizing I had drifted away as I watched the Arkham police cruiser move past.

"Ummm... who's Aubrey?"

Our eyes met and she smiled submissively. Pulling back a bit, she reached out a hand and pushed a loose strand of hair from my face.

"You don't have to say, if you don't want. But I was wondering because you called me Aubrey on the phone."

Time to spill the beans. I felt I could do that with Claudia.

"Sorry about that. I was thinking about her when you called. For some reason, I heard her voice instead of yours."

"No, it's okay. Don't be sorry. It happens. So... who was she? An old girl friend?"

"No, she was my cousin."

"Was?"

"She was abducted from her bedroom over in Aylesbury some eleven years ago. We were very close. I think she was the only person I ever truly loved."

"Aubrey Rice?"

"Yes—why?"

140

"She was your cousin?"

"Well… the last name should tell you something."

"Yes, I know, but I never put two and two together. Were you exiled to Wentworth at the time?"

"That's right, we spent just about every summer together, even before Wentworth became a part of my life. It was a difficult time. I don't recall ever crying for anyone but myself until that day. I don't think I got that upset even when my father died. With him, it seemed more like a dream. I mean, I shed a few tears at his funeral, but I think it was more because everybody else was. My memories of my father are few. We didn't spend a great deal of time together. I was at Wentworth two hundred and seventy-five days out of the year. And my mother, well… she was always so stoic with this kind of rigid etiquette. I'm sure she felt I'd interfere with her social life if I had remained home. I suspect the school for boys was her idea, and she had convinced my father that it would be best. But Aubrey, she was my life."

"So, I was at Barton when your cousin was kidnapped. I should tell you; Anton was involved in an investigation at that time. But I think it was because she wasn't the only one that disappeared that year. That's what I recall overhearing him telling my mother, anyway."

"So, you know about that, too? How come I never knew about the others?"

"I don't know. How would I know? I only became aware because of Anton and didn't hear about it until the decision was made for me to come to M.U. I mean, being so close to Dunwich, and all."

"Sorry, I guess that question was rhetorical."

"Well, I'll clue you, if you have any questions, I'm sure Anton would be the one to ask."

"I'm wondering if I was so self-absorbed that I just wasn't paying attention."

"I don't know, Sterling. But… I think you were suffering from a broken heart, and still are. That kind of thing leaves a person low. Don't be too hard on yourself. Hey, like my mom's always saying, "Claudia, you're only human, quit thinking you're Superwoman." So, Sterling, stop thinking you're Superman. I understand the pain. Pure tragedy. I also think it would be better for you to learn to let it go. I'll try to help if I can."

I turned my face to hers and looked longingly into her eyes. She blinked and smiled. I cupped her cheek, feeling the soft curls of her hair as they fell over my fingers. Then pushing my hand behind her head, I drew her to me, kissing her full, supple lips. Somebody let go with a wolf whistle, followed by applause. Not bothering to look their way, I pulled my lips from hers and we touched foreheads.

"My turn!" I heard some guy say, and looking his way, I watched some teenaged boy, three booths away, bend his date back toward the window and plant a big slobbery kiss on her. She fought him, saying, "Kenny, geez! You nosebleed. It's our first date. I don't kiss on the first date!"

Sitting back down, Kenny picked up his milkshake and went to slurping it as he cast his eyes to the ceiling. At that same moment, a man suddenly appeared in the open door. He had come from the back of the building, not from the lot. His denim, hip length jacket was buttoned to the throat and his dusty black slouch hat was pulled low over his mean, yellowish eyes. He wore a beard with no mustache. Mud spotted his pant legs and I noticed a knee had been patched.

C.K. Whateley? What would he be doing here at Dean's?

I felt Claudia tense up and a barely audible, "Lister," slipped from her lips.

The man first looked at Dean and his cooks. Then he started a slow scan of the room, his eyes moving from the kids closest to the door, over the other two couples sitting at the front wall and finally, his eyes fell on us. He studied us pretty hard. His face changed with recognition, showing what I felt could only be considered, wicked glee. "Found yah," he said flatly, and stepped inside.

He walked in about a third of the way and announced, "Well, Claudia Osborn. About time I run across you. Your pa would like a visit and he sent me to bring you home. Been a long time since we were young'uns, huh? Still missing that little kitty of yours? So… anyways, you come with me real peaceful like. Your pa is real sick, and he'd like to see you before he kicks the bucket. He sent me to ferry you home. I'll give you a right pleasant boat ride back to Dunwich. Hell, you might even be back to this shithole called a town by the morning, but don't count on it."

Claudia started shaking her head slowly in disagreement and said, "I'm not going anywhere with you, Lister Whateley, especially not back to your town; speaking of shitholes. You can just go back and tell Joe Osborn, I'm sorry, but I'm busy—for the rest of my life."

Lister's grin became even more wicked. Baring his rotten teeth, he said, "Oh, yes you are." That's when a large hunting knife slipped out of his sleeve into his right hand. Bringing it up, he pointed it at me. "Don't you get in my way, boy." Then pointing it at Dean and the cooks, he added, "Same for you."

But Dean had been in war—in fact, the beach at Normandy. He had seen men die in all sorts of ways. There wasn't much he was afraid of. I could tell he was waiting for just the right moment to make his move. His place rarely got robbed, and I've got some good stories to tell as to why.

I felt the adrenaline rush in as solutions for our escape so overwhelmed my brain that it barely acknowledged Regina rocketing past the long row of windows. From that point, everything went into slow motion. The girls screamed, the boys shouted, and everybody, but us, got up and stampeded out the door behind Lister. He didn't acknowledge them because his eyes were locked on us. I remember seeing Juan and Miguel picking up butcher knives and Dean bringing his Louisville Slugger up from beneath the counter.

The surrealness of what was happening made it hard to accept it as an actual reality. But there he was, a man with a foot long, skinning knife, standing within twenty feet of us, demanding that Claudia come with him.

I stood up and stepped out of the booth. Claudia followed and moved to my side. She could have stood behind me, or run down the back corridor to the restrooms and locked herself in. But she chose to stand with me. I glanced at her face and saw she appeared to be more angry than frightened. The words she had spoken at the library, 'I'm no kitten,' echoed in my head. My instinct was to protect her, but it looked like she just might jump into the coming fray right along with me. We both knew

143

that knife could cut me just as deep as her, and I am sure neither of us was any more frightened than the other.

Dropping my hands to the back of a chair, I waited for the right moment to pick it up and hold it lion-tamer style. Lister started our way in a slow, cautious manner. His snake like eyes shifting back and forth from us to the counter. The air thickened with something that felt just plain evil and he said, "You, sonny boy, you go right ahead and try to hit me with that chair, and I'll send you to meet your pa. That's right, I know who you are. I've run across a few of you Rice's, before. So, just git out of the way and nobody bleeds on this shiny checkerboard of a floor."

I watched as Regina rolled slow motion through the door behind him, not making a sound. Bending forward at the waist, she held a metal tray with both hands high above her head. The strange thing was, her and Lister shared the same expression, one that said they really wanted to hurt somebody. She came within a few feet of him and then went air born. Before Lister realized she was back there, she brought that metal tray down so hard on his head that it bent over his face. Blood spurted from his nose and Claudia let out a loud, "Yeah!" just as an "Oh shit," slipped my lips.

Lister's knife clattered to the floor and he followed it down. The metal tray remained attached to his head, his dust encrusted slouch hat acting as the only buffer. Regina then skated around him once before stopping and kicking him hard in the gut with her heavy skate. The escaping air came with an, "Oomph!" followed by a groan.

Dean launched himself over the counter and picking up the knife, said, "You stay put, mister, the cops are on the way."

I turned to see Miguel was just hanging up the white wall phone as Dean rolled the unconscious Lister onto his stomach. Then planting a foot on the attackers back, he held him down as he tapped the tip of the baseball bat on the floor next to the downed man's ear. Regina stood there, one hand on a cocked hip, the other pushing strands of hair back into her bun as she tried to catch her breath. She looked at me like she wanted me to know that she was my champion and that I should be grateful.

144

"Seen him through the window when he came in… it was that knife that set me off. Knives always do that," she said, and chuckled.

Claudia put an arm around my waist and pushed me sideways toward the serving counter and away from the unconscious Lister. I dropped an arm over her shoulders, and she let out a long sigh, collapsing against me.

"So, you know this guy, Claudia?" I asked.

"Yeah, Lister Whateley."

"You know him from Dunwich?"

"Yeah… as kids. I always played with the Curtis's, the Frye's', the Sawyers', and the Bishops'. He was on the other side. Loony Lister, his brother Canaan and all the other Whateley clan. I remember he liked to hurt animals. Killed my cat. It's been a long time, but I still see that mean kid in his face."

A siren drowned out her voice as the Arkham police car squealed around the corner. Whipping into the parking lot, it pulled up just outside the door. Officer Hutchins got out and hitching up his belt, he swaggered to us like the man of the hour.

"What's going on here, Dean?"

"Well, Ralph, this bad hombre was looking to use this pig sticker on Sterling and his girl."

Handing Hutchins the knife, the officer looked it over and then stuck it in his belt. Pulling his hand cuffs from their strap, he latched them around Lister's wrists.

"What the hell is that on his head?" Hutchins asked as he bent to check it out.

"One of my good stainless serving trays, but if it wasn't for Regina here, we might be needing an ambulance for some of my best customers."

Hutchins looked at Regina, who stood defiantly, popping her gum. They eyed each other with contempt. No doubt they had run-ins in the past and I am sure Hutchins would like to see her in jail.

"So, you hit him over the head with a tray?"

"That's right, big daddy. Sadly, it was my favorite. Now I'm going to have to find a new one," Regina said, not trying to hide her sarcasm.

145

Hutchins looked at her like he wanted to wrap his hands around her throat and squeeze. Turning to look at us, his eyes lingered on Claudia. I felt her tremble, but she glared back with insolence. Then turning her chest to my side, she brought her other arm around my stomach and squeezed with both arms, her face unchanging.

"You going to haul him in, Ralph?" Dean asked.

"Sure, but on what charges? Ain't no crime in having a hunting knife."

"Well, the bastard threatened Sterling with it."

"You want to press charges, Mr. Rice?"

"I suppose, if I need to," I said, my attention now on Lister because he had moved.

"Okay, then… well… let's get that tray off his head, first of all."

Hutchins grunted as he got down on one knee and grabbing the edges of the tray, he yanked it off Lister's head, taking the hat with it. Lister screamed in pain and sat up looking around at everyone. His eyes fell on Regina, and he growled, "You the hussy that waylaid me?"

"Yeah, you're not so tough, are you? Knocked down by a girl! Hah! Hillbilly… Mr. Bad News ain't so bad after all." She laughed and her eyes flashed. Adjusting her Bellboy hat, she said, "Got work to do, officer, you done with me?"

"For now, but don't go nowhere. Might have you come down to the station for some kind of a statement."

"Don't go nowhere? Hell, that was the plan right from the start. Just ask my folks," she said and skated out the door.

Laying the bat on the counter, Dean said, "If I need to come down to the station and file charges, I will. Must be some kind of a law says you can't bring a weapon into a place of business."

"Well, Dean… we'll see."

"Take these bracelets off me, mister lawman. I ain't done no wrong here. You can't hold me for nothing."

Hutchins didn't reply, instead he reached down, grabbed Lister under the armpits and picked him up. He let his prisoner find his feet before walking him out to the car. Lister whipped his bloody face around to look at Claudia and said, "This ain't over, Osborn."

146

Hutchins looked back at us, his eyes questioning. Claudia released me and started to stomp toward him. I wrapped my arms around her from behind and pulled her back. Hutchins never bothered to ask me what was going on and why Lister would pull a knife on me. I got the impression, for some reason, he already knew. Opening the back door of the squad car, he pushed Lister inside. Shutting it, he came back to us. Picking up the bent tray and Lister's slouch hat, he said, "Better take this for evidence, and Mr. Rice, you and this little girlie… Osborn, is it?"

"That's right," Claudia said with a bit of cheekiness.

"You must be Joe Osborn's daughter? If I remember correctly, he had a young-un once… yeah… I know your father. Ol' Joe, the grocer. Has that mercantile over in Dunwich."

Claudia, now sounding angry, said, "Is knowing that supposed to impress me somehow?"

"Don't get smart with me, missy. I'll stick you in the backseat with Whateley. He…"

"Thank you, officer, for coming so quickly," Dean said as he stepped over in front of Hutchins. Putting his arm over the officer's shoulders, the cop didn't resist, and Dean walked him to the squad car. Opening the door for him, Dean shook his hand, and said, "Stop in anytime, Ralph, suppers always on the house." Hutchins got in the driver's seat and turned the car around to drive away with Lister glaring wickedly out of the back window.

"Sterling, we've got to go. It's after midnight and I am sure old Mordechai has already locked me out."

Dean walked back inside and going behind the counter, put the slugger on the lower shelf where he kept it.

"Got to run, Dean."

"Sorry about all the trouble, Sterling. Nothing like that's happened in a long time."

"Not your fault, I appreciate all you did. How much do I owe you for the food?"

"On the house, Sterling. Glad to meet you, Claudia," he said and nodded at her.

"Same here," she said, smiling. "And, thanks."

A big grin broke his lips and he tapped the side of that one finger to his temple. "See you, kiddo." Turning back to the grill, he went to scraping it with a spatula while Juan and Miguel flooded him with questions.

Claudia grabbed my hand and led me out. We passed Regina who had rolled up to the garbage can just outside the door. Pushing trash from a tray into its opening, she said, "Tony and Shirley... hey, don't I get a kiss or something? I mean, I saved your lives, right?"

"Thanks, Reg, I owe you."

"You sure do, and I'm going to collect—someday. See you, Shirley. Take care of your man. Because, if you don't—I will."

Claudia turned and grinned at her, giving her a little wave as we walked away. I saw that look of disappointment cross Regina's face again, and pushing off from the garbage can, she skated inside. Claudia and I didn't speak as we walked to the corner. It wasn't until we were out of sight of the drive-in that she broke the silence.

"I'm scared, Sterling."

"Understandably so. That makes two of us. You said that guy killed your cat?"

"Yeah, but that was almost sixteen years ago. I had this little tabby. Ol' Mr. Brauner over at the blacksmiths shop gave it to me. I named it Stripes. But you know kids when it comes to pet names, right? I had him up in our treehouse, which for some reason, we had built right next to the Devils Hop Yard. Your dad ever mention it? Anyway, it was me, Rachel Farr, and Danny Carrier. We could see Lister and Ezra Whateley out there in the middle of that place, digging something up. They seen us too. The next thing you know, Lister pops his head in the trapdoor and starts threatening to beat us all bloody. Stripes wandered over to him, not knowing any better. Before I could grab him, Lister snatched him up by his scruff and took him down to the ground. We started yelling at him, but before I could get down there, he pulled out this fish cleaning knife and stuck it straight through Stripes like it was nothing. Then he pulled the knife out and tossed my cat as far as he could."

Claudia choked back a sob and it caught me off guard. I put my arm around her shoulders and waited to see if there would be more. But she

148

composed herself quickly and said, "So, I started cussing him out, but the son of a bitch ran away laughing and yelled back that if I didn't shut my mouth, his pa would sic Yogsothoth on me and I might just up and disappear. I didn't know who that was, but I didn't care. It was a terrible day. We found Stripes, who of course, was dead. We buried him right there next to the Hop Yard. I told my father, but he didn't care. He just said maybe I could get another cat. Dunwich wasn't even safe for pets."

"I want to know how Lister would know that you were at Dean's, and how did your real father find out that you were at university?"

"I don't know, Sterling. That's kind of why I'm afraid. My mom wouldn't have said a thing. And also, why two years after I came to M.U.?"

"Hey, did that guy that Mordechai was chasing around the terrace that night, look anything like Lister? Do you remember?"

"We'll he was dressed the same, but it was hard to tell. He didn't have a hat on, and his hair was darker and shorter than Lister's. Besides that, Lister wouldn't have run away—fireplace poker or not."

"I wanted to tell you; I saw some guy hanging around the quad. I've got good reason to believe it was a Whateley."

"Do you think that's who our peeper was?"

"Well, the first time I saw him he was standing in Waldron's Grove, he must have seen me too. Somebody tried to break into my room through the window afterwards. Sarge scared them away, and whoever it was, dropped his pocket knife in the process. Lyle just happened to grab it up before I could."

"The watchman?"

"Yeah, I got a look at it out the window when it was laying in the grass. He took it before I could get to it. I found it sitting on the desk in the watchman's closet. It had 'C.K. Whateley' scratched into its handle."

"So, Lister's younger brother... Canaan's a walking disaster. Not as dangerous as Lister, who I think is some kind of a psycho. But Canaan's bad enough to make your life miserable."

"Another thing, I saw Canaan with Lyle acting like they were pals or something."

"Sterling, now you're really starting to scare me."

"Well, that makes two of us. Then Hutchins over at Dean's. He sure seemed interested in you. You want to know who he's married to? Elvira Whateley."

"I remember her, she's Josiah Whateley's daughter. Lister and Canaan's sister."

"So, I wonder why your father couldn't just drop in for a visit like normal fathers do?"

"I don't know, he probably figured I wouldn't want to see him, and he'd be right. If he did show up, I'd have to call the cops and let Anton know. They couldn't pay me enough to even talk to that man. So, he probably figured this would be the best way to get to me. Maybe he is sick like Lister said and can't travel, or maybe, he's dying..."

I didn't let her finish and said, "Maybe he is, but I think something else is going on here. I can just feel it."

"I'm beginning to think so, too," she said, and appeared to drift away into reflection. With her eyes seemingly focused on the sidewalk in front of us, she kept a hold on my hand, but said no more about it. So, neither did I.

When we reached Waldron's Grove, we stopped and stood for a moment, studying the dark interior. Seeing no movement, I figured we were safe for the time being. Taking a tighter grip on Claudia's hand, we hurried away out onto the Pembrook green. The Bell Tower had already chimed midnight. I figured we were in for trouble with the Warden, but she didn't bother me as much as the Whateley's did.

Stopping about twenty feet out from the front door, Claudia pulled me to her and wrapping her arms around my waist, she said, "How about a kiss?" Her hands strayed to my derriere and her tongue found mine. She moaned into my mouth, awakening something primal way down deep inside me. Something that had been asleep all of my years since Emma Wheeler.

I did bend her back this time, but so I could pick her up. She clamped her legs around my hips, her arms now over my shoulders. Our passion increased and her lips pressed tighter against mine. After a moment of that, she moved them to my ear and said, "Kiss my neck, Sterling." I did as she asked, grazing up and down her sweet-smelling skin, not only kissing, but biting as her tongue found my ear. I found it hard to remain standing, and several times Claudia seemed to lose her grip and had to readjust.

Lightning flashed, and for a brief moment I thought it was a product of our fervor, but then the thunder rolled confirming that it was Mother Nature telling us it might be time to get indoors.

Pulling her face back, Claudia said, "We're going to get wet. I'd better get inside."

Setting her down, she sandwiched my head in her hands and pulling it to her, she softly kissed my forehead. Mordechai's light came on, so Claudia let me go and dashed up the stairs. "See you tomorrow? Maybe we can picnic or something. Sound like fun?"

"Certainly, give me a bell, will you? I've nothing to do all day."

"Okay, later... I mean... goodnight," she said and then blurted, "It was the most exciting evening I've had in like, forever. No doubt, you know how to show a girl a good time! Be sure to lock up tight, though. Those Whateley's might be on the prowl."

"You too."

"Okay," she said, and turning to the door, she hit the bell. Light flooded out of Mordechai's room into the vestibule, and the old bat, dressed in her robe, unlocked, and swung open the outside door. Claudia pushed her way past and headed for the stairs as the Warden's voice filled the air with, "Claudia Osborn, you get back here."

I didn't wait for my turn. Dashing away, I headed for the quad. The lightning flashed and the thunder rolled as I hurried across the green. With one eye on Dyer Hall and the other on The Grove, I grew fearful that every strobe would reveal a Whateley, standing in the trees, looking for a chance to pounce.

X

Forked Lightning Will Rend

The rain came down hard, but I was too exhausted to care. After seeing to Sarge, and locking up, I undressed and fell into bed. The lightning and thunder died down after about an hour, but the rain stayed. It beat against the windows, rushed through the gutters, and hammered in the downspouts. I snoozed in a kind of half sleep. The sound of the water as it cascaded down those brass tubes transformed into an intermittent pounding. Chunks of plaster and lath suddenly exploded into the room and a jet of water shot through a hole in the wall. The gusher filled my space and the bed, with me, and a whining Sarge onboard, rose to bob on the surface.

I jerked awake and sat up, feeling the relief that comes with realizing it had all been a dream. I lay back down, hoping for a quick return to slumber. But the pounding came again, only this time it was someone beating on the glass of one of my windows. Launching myself out of bed, Sarge came awake, barking loud enough to tip a seismograph. I presumed it was some student who had been locked out and I hadn't heard the bell. Not caring who saw me in my underwear, I pulled up the shade.

Sarge jumped up to put his paws on the sill and barked at the lone figure standing just outside on the lawn. Claudia hugged herself, her hair matted flat, rain running off her nose and chin.

"Sterling…" she pled.

She painted a forlorn picture standing out there; one I suspect I will never forget. Turning on my desk lamp, a terrible feeling roiled in my gut. Grabbing my robe, I put it on as I worked my way through the doors. Claudia met me on the threshold and threw herself into my arms. I just held her as she sobbed into my chest, the water running off of her in torrents. A large puddle formed around our feet and a small stream ran down the veranda to the steps. Sarge had followed me out and now sat beside us, licking the water that trickled down my bare, right leg.

Fearing we would wake the entire dorm, I picked Claudia up, one hand behind her back, the other behind her knees. Without a word, she put an arm around my neck, and her face to my cheek, as I carried her to my room. Casper now stood just outside the first commons door, dressed in blue flannel pajamas covered in cartoon bunnies. He had a serious cowlick in his hair, and rubbing his eyes, he yawned and said, "What's up, Mr. Rice? Who's the dolly?"

I responded in a ghostly tone of voice, "Casper, this is only a dream. You are sleepwalking. Go back to the sofa, none of this is really happening."

"Oh, okay. Goodnight, Mr. Rice," he said, his voice sluggish with sleep as he trudged out of sight.

Bringing Claudia into my room, I pushed the door shut with my foot. Sitting her in a small folding chair next to the door, I wiped her face dry with the hem of my robe. Then remembering that it had been wash day, I grabbed a towel from a freshly laundered stack in my 'clean laundry' basket. I attempted to dry her hair. Sarge watched bewildered from the bed, his tail wagging briefly every time Claudia sniffed or snorted.

With snot rattling in her nose, she snatched the towel from my hand and said, "I'm grateful, Sterling, but... unless you want to be the one to brush it out, you should let me do it."

Without argument, I kneeled and removed her shoes and socks. Placing them with mine on the mat, I stood and said, "Probably should get that jacket off, huh?" She dropped the towel in her lap and thrust her arms up in the air. "Help me, mommy," she said, followed by a halfhearted giggle. Grabbing the cuffs, I pulled as she wriggled.

"Mommy?" I said.

"Yeah, this is what my mother would do for me. Didn't yours?"

"Ummm... not that I recall."

"Oh, sorry."

Not saying anything, I dropped the jacket on the floor. She stood up and threw her arms around me again. I just held her as more tears spilled out. Ten minutes passed before she calmed down, leaving us to stand silent in our embrace. Then she started to hiccup, a short giggle escaping between each one. I just rubbed her back as she employed the, 'holding your breath' technique of trying to still them. When she accomplished her task, she tilted her head back and gave me a little smile.

"All done," she said and slipping out from between me and the chair, she picked up the towel and resumed drying herself as she moved across the room.

"I'm sorry for all this trouble, Sterling. But I had no choice. That old bitch pushed me out of the front door at Pembrook and wouldn't let me back in."

"You mean, Mordechai?"

"Yeah, what other old bitch do you know?" she said, now glaring.

"Claudia... we have to do something about that."

"No... we don't. She's just doing her job."

"Perhaps, but I'm going to talk with someone, anyway. Maybe the Dean."

"Sterling—don't. If they don't get rid of her, she will only make my life miserable. It's bad enough I have to deal with these Whateley's."

"We... we have to deal with these Whateley's."

"Oh, yeah, of course. So, anyway, it's better to let her think she has won. Besides, I'm safe now. That's not such a bad thing, right? Sure, I'm upset, and maybe a little scared, but I had you to come to."

"Well, I suppose, but..."

"I know you feel like you want to do something about her. That's just that noble thing in you. Forget about it."

"She put you in danger, Claudia. Knowingly."

"Yes, she got angry. I got angry. People do stupid things when they're upset. I told you, Sterling, I am not a kitten. I can be ferocious, too. I can defend myself if I need to. I also know you want to protect me, and I appreciate that. So... I will allow it, but let's not lose our heads over this, huh? Besides, this is partially my fault."

Sighing heavily, she dropped the towel on my overstuffed chair and returned to me. Taking my hands, she looked up into my eyes, seeking conformation that I would just let her handle the Warden.

154

"Okay, just this one time. That doesn't mean that someday when she least expects it… Pow!"

"Oh Sterling, you're so dramatic. I think you're just going to have to get used to experiencing all my failures, all my moments of despair, and well… all that is Claudia Osborn."

I didn't hear that little girl voice, anymore. Instead, there resounded this mature, confident woman-sage. Someone with a life time of wisdom. Then a realization—Claudia at twenty, might be more mature than I at twenty-four.

"Okay, I'll work on it. But… only because you're asking me too. No other reason."

"Good," she said, and letting go of my hands, she walked over to the window and pulled down the shade.

Glancing back over her shoulder, she said, "Still raining out there. But you know what they say about April showers."

"Yeah, something about bringing me a flower?"

"Oh, Sterling, sometimes you're just too sweet. Cheesy… but sweet."

"So, tell me what happened. I need to know. If I'm just going to walk away from this, I need to hear the story."

She turned to face me and sticking her hands in her pockets, she said, "Well, same ol' crap. Mordecai had never followed me up the stairs, ever, before this time. I went to my room to get ready for bed, and that germ came flying in the door, demanding to know why I was late. I told her to get out. She refused, still wanting to know. So, I told her we were detained over at Dean's because of some incident, and the police wanted to question us because we were witnesses. She didn't care. She said that was because I am getting mixed up with you, and if I hadn't stopped outside to kiss, I would have made it in time. Which of course, we know is a lie. I told her that being late wasn't breaking any rules. I could stay out all night, if I wanted too, just as long as I didn't disrupt the dorm. But she didn't like that. I bent over to pick up my jacket and she grabbed me by the arm. Believe me when I say that woman is strong. She pulled me down the hallway and then the stairs. Dragging me to the front door, she shoved me outside, saying, "Well, if you want to be out there so badly, there you go."

"She actually grabbed you? That's against the rules, I know that as a D.A. We are not supposed to grab the students. Especially undergrads, no matter how annoying they are."

"Yeah… so, then she slammed the door, locked it and turned out the lights. I beat on the glass for a while before Beatrice came down in her night gown. Mordecai caught her and forced her back up the stairs. A few of the other girls who came to see what was going on, tried to let me in, but the ol' bat got in their way. By that time, it was raining, well… actually storming. When I realized I wasn't getting back in, I kept thinking about Lister at the diner, and that Canaan, might be hiding in the bushes waiting to grab me. I sat down on the porch back in a corner and just started crying. It was mostly out of frustration, though. I think all the strain from finals and that thing last night at Dean's pushed me over the edge. Anyway, I knew I could come to you. It was such a relief. I was so afraid if I stayed where I was, somebody would sneak up on me and I'd end up just like Elspeth. So, I ran all the way over here."

"Well, I'm really glad you did," I said as I shooed Sarge from the mattress. He rolled off reluctantly and went to his own bed. Claudia started to pace back and forth in the dim light of the room. Figuring we could use a little more light on the subject, I switched on the lamp that sat atop my nightstand and tilted the shade to direct its illumination to the wall behind.

"You should sit down. Sit in my big chair if you want, it's pretty comfortable."

"I'll get it all wet, I'm still kind of drippy."

"Well, I could lay down some towels? Yesterday was a laundry day. Myrtle did towels and bedding. Today, she'll do my dirty clothes. A few more towels won't hurt anything. I'll slip her a few extra Washingtons for cigarettes. She won't mind."

Claudia stopped pacing and just stood watching me. She looked so small standing there. I suspected she wasn't going to grow much taller. Small to me, always meant fragile. I could never hold anybody's infant out of fear I would break it, like little birds that needed to be handled with the utmost care. But Claudia, wasn't that. All that swimming must

156

have toned her up. When she grabbed me, I could feel the strength in her hands. I suspected if we arm wrestled, she just might lead me to embarrassment. Even with the boxing, rowing, and fencing from my Wentworth days, she would give me a run for my money.

"Hey, I have an extra robe in the closet. It was a gift from my mother. I didn't like it, so that's where it stayed. It may be too long for you, but at least you'd have something to wear, while your clothes dried."

"Okay, sounds peachy," she said and pulled off her sweater, dropping it at her feet.

Getting the blue and green plaid robe out of the closet, I pulled off the price tag and shook it out.

"Here, I have to go pee. I'll lay it right here on the bed. You can drop those wet clothes in the corner, okay?"

"Thanks a bunch, Sterling, you're my hero," she said and giggled as she started to remove her shirt before I even left the room.

Pulling the door shut behind me, I stopped to listen to the dorm just in case anyone was stirring. Not hearing any movement anywhere, I quietly bounded up the stairs. The second-floor hallway was vacant, but the Drexler twin's door was wide open, and snores emanated from inside. There were several boys, including the twins, asleep on the floor, in the beds, and in every chair. I could now hear a typewriter clicking away up on the third floor—an obsessive Palance, burning the late-night oil. None of the other three grad students up there worked that hard. I rarely saw or heard from them. They seemed to live a life apart.

After draining my bladder, I went down to the kitchen. Helping myself to a glass of milk, I checked the bolt on the backdoor to make sure it was still thrown and then returned to my room. I knocked softly and Claudia called me in. She stood in the same spot, but now swam inside my robe with more than a foot of it piled up on the floor around her feet. She had to roll up the sleeves several times in order to bare her hands. She grinned, giggled, and said, "Yeah, might have to tailor this thing if I'm going to keep wearing it."

"Nothing a pair of scissors couldn't handle."

The barrette was gone, and her hair now hung in her face. I saw all her wet clothes were piled in the far corner next to Sarge's bed. His head came up when I walked in, and then taking a sniff of her sweater, he pulled it to him and rested his muzzle on its bulk. I thought to say something, but Claudia was on top of it.

"That's alright, it's an old sweater."

Getting my drying rack from under my bed, I handed it to her. She set it up and hung all but the sweater. I suspect she didn't want to disappoint Sarge on her very first sleepover. So, she was willing to grant him one article of clothing. Afterwards, she turned her gaze to me, and we stood there in awkward silence as I tried to come up with something else to say. I realized she might be waiting for me to make the next move, but I didn't think it was mine to make, so I said, "You can have the bed, I'll take the chair… since it's still dry."

"Are you sure?"

"Certainly."

"How about… I take the bed and… you take it with me?" With that, she pulled the belt to the robe and shrugged off the oversized garment.

Now, I'd been with many other girls before Claudia, however, when she stood before me naked, it felt like my first time. I just gawked. She laughed at my expression and putting her hands on her waist, she cocked a hip. Tilting her head, the hair blocking her face fell away to reveal a seductive smile.

Claudia's breasts, even though well formed, were not as large as she had made them out to be, leaving me to believe her perspective had been formed without regard to her small build. I stood there in a state of semi-shock, taking in the firm, round mounds of flesh, their perfectly centered, dime sized, areola, barely contrasting her tanned skin. Pea sized nipples stood rigid with excitement, alleviating any doubt I may have had that, she wasn't prepared for what I knew was coming.

Her stomach was smooth and flat, with an 'inny' for a belly button. The fine down of her pubic hair radiated gold from the lamp's illumination. There was no question that her swimming had paid off.

She turned to pick up the robe and I couldn't help but take in her round and somewhat muscular derriere. I went from a state of shock to obvious arousal. Noticing I had, she laid the bathrobe over the chair and walked to me. Using both hands, she pushed my robe away at the shoulders and let it cascade to the dark boards of the floor. Then taking my hand, she towed me to the bed, and falling back, she pulled me with her as she maneuvered her head onto my pillow.

I soon found myself on my hands and knees bestride her as she lay on her back. Running her fingers up and down my arms, she grinned and whispered, "Nice muscles." Her sleepy eyes and contented smile left me to wonder what her next move might be. I didn't have to wait long, for soon her hands glided up my biceps and came together at the back of my neck. Bringing her legs up, she wrapped my waist and locked her feet just above my tail bone. Pulling herself up, she brought her lips to mine. We kissed in that soft, opened mouth kind of way, leaving me to wish I had the use of my hands. I feared crushing her if I lowered my six-foot, one-hundred-and-seventy-pound frame down to the mattress.

She squeezed me with her legs, and I felt their strength. Her arms stayed strong in their task to support her weight as she hung beneath me. There would be no escaping until she allowed it. Our kiss became even more passionate and moving my lips to her neck, she moaned. One leg came loose from around my middle and slipping her toes in under the waist band of my skivvies, she pushed them down to my knees. Re-wrapping her leg, she whispered in my ear, "Roll onto your back Sterling, I want to have my way with you."

We both chuckled. Yes, she had taken control of the moment, but I felt more than willing to allow it. She rode me over and releasing her hold, she soon sat atop me, straddling my hips. Bending forward, her hands caressed my chest as she levered up her feet to rest their insteps on my thighs. Locking the fabric of my underwear in the toes of both feet, she pushed them off completely, simultaneously sliding her body up mine. Her abdomen moved over my erection, her supple breasts traveling up my torso. Her lips came back to mine, her hands cupping the back of my head as they did.

With her derriere within reach, I took advantage of the moment. Expecting it to be soft and pliant like most, I found, instead, that it was firm, the muscles seemingly vibrating. I took the risk of manipulating it with some force and that seemed to push her to a higher level of ecstasy, as moans and squeaks slipped out from around our lips. Her tongue moved in deeper to overtake mine. Pushing her pubic bone hard into my abdomen, she circled it slowly left, then right, and back again.

We had both gotten to where we were breathing so hard that it made kissing difficult. Moving my mouth to her neck, I nibbled at the skin, tasting the salty sheen of moisture that had collected there. Her actions soon became a little more frenzied. She breathed out a, "Oh my…" and when her tongue found my ear, I too let out a few squeaks of my own. I couldn't help but gasp for air as my hands moved up and down her body.

When I reached the point where I felt I could take no more without exploding, she came to an abrupt halt. It surprised me and I thought something had happened that shouldn't have. But her hands moved to the mattress and she pushed herself up into a sitting position, her flirtatious grin framed by her tangled hair. There was just a hint of perspiration on her upper lip and her eyes flashed. With a degree of poise, she said, "Are you ready for me?"

I only nodded, still trying to catch my breath, my whole body ablaze. Gripping my upper arms, she pushed herself back down my chest, our perspiration allowing a smooth glide to where she cocked her pelvis and forced me inside. Gasping together, our exhalation came slowly, and closing my eyes, we fell into a rhythmic bliss.

***

We made love for an hour, the chime of the grandfather clock punctuating the time spent in ardor. When our climactic spasms waned, she fell forward onto my chest, an exhausted sigh escaping her lips. She lay there with her eyes closed and we panted together. I stroked her hair and caressed her back, sometimes patting her derriere.

"Sterling, that's the best it's ever been for me."

"Well… thanks. Honestly, though, I have to say the same. I want to ask… how you learned all you know? Not that it matters, I'm just amazed and curious. So, just don't…"

"…ever stop?" she said and chuckled.

"Yes, please."

"So, Kinsey."

"What?"

"Reading Kinsey's work made me want to try new things."

"Oh, uh… thank you, Dr. Kinsey, wherever you are!"

"I'm glad you're happy. That was kind of my goal."

"I'd have to be a fool not to be."

She rolled off and lay on her side, facing me. Putting an arm across my chest and a leg over my thighs, she looked over at Sarge who was watching us with great interest.

"What do you suppose dogs think when they see humans having sex?" she said.

"Oh, ummm… nothing. I think they are more interested in the noises we make and what they're supposed to mean. You know… what I mean?"

"Yeah, I suppose. Speaking of noises, sorry, I get kind of loud. Maybe next time you should gag me, that way I don't wake up the entire dorm."

"Well, I should say, I think that was the first time I've ever gotten that loud, myself. But I hope it's not the last."

"Oh, good," she said and giggled, patting my stomach.

"I think we are okay, though. There's a small store room above mine and then the stairwells before the student's rooms start. So, unless someone is in the first commons room listening, like Casper, they are, most likely, asleep."

"Casper?"

"Yeah, the kid in the blue PJ's? He's a first-year undergrad who spends a lot of time in there because his roommate has a girlfriend."

Okay, well, maybe he liked it. Maybe… we'll inspire wet dreams!" she said and laughed.

"Yeah, if I know Casper, that's quite likely."

Claudia rubbed my chest, roughing up the hair, and then after patting it back down, she roughed it up again. We lay quiet for a few minutes, just listening to the noises the building made in the early morning hours. A thought came to me and rubbing the small of her back, I said, "Aren't you afraid you will get pregnant? I mean, maybe we should use a rubber next time?"

"My period is supposed to start tomorrow. I'm not too worried about it this time. It was convenient, that's for sure. I'm usually right on time every month. But I suppose if we were to do it more often, maybe having a rubber on hand would be a good idea. But you know, they are kind of a drag."

"Yeah, but a small price to pay. Especially for what I just experienced." Raising my eyebrows for emphasis, I pushed the hair out of her face.

"You liked it that much, huh?" she said, and grinning, she snuggled closer. About a minute went by and she whispered, "Uh… Sterling? I have to pee."

"Oh, well, I'll have to escort you up to the can and guard the door. Put on the robe and I'll get mine."

"Don't you have something else I could wear, instead? Maybe a long tee shirt or something with tails to cover my butt?"

Oh, sure, there's an extra-large button front in the closet. It's striped, so… I never wear it. It was another gift from my mother—like the robe."

"Sounds peachy, can I get it out?"

"Certainly, you can't miss it."

Claudia stood up and walked off the mattress. I watched her cross the room, noticing that her buttocks didn't bounce, but seemed to only vibrate with each step. I realized she was grinning back over her shoulder at me, and just before opening the closet door, she slapped one of the cheeks and gave me an exaggerated wink.

From behind the open door, I heard, "Oh, I see it, yeah… that's ugly. I mean, no offense to your mom, but what was she thinking?" I heard the rustle of her slipping it on and then she stepped out. It covered her completely, her hands well up in the sleeves. Turning around one time, I saw it hung down just far enough to hide that well-formed bottom.

"Okay? Good, let's get upstairs before I cut loose on your door mat."

"Oh! Don't do that! That's Sarge's territory. Here, let me get my robe."

The shower room and toilets were on the second and third floors in the back corners and just adjacent to the last student room on that level. Casper's room. But it was nearly two in the morning, so I figured we were safe. Walking Claudia up, I checked to make sure the bathroom was free and then sent her inside.

As I stood there waiting, I heard talking from inside Casper's room. The door suddenly burst open and I expected Alex, since Casper was still sacked out on the commons couch. Instead, appearing before me, in all her glory, Sissy stood without a stitch of clothing. She froze, making the 'Oops!' face. Petrified, she didn't attempt to hide her small, perky breasts or the patch of bright blond pubic hair.

"What's going on? I thought you had to pee?" I heard Alex say from within the room. "Hey, say something, Sissy."

His face appeared over her shoulder and seeing me, he said, "Oh…hey Sterling. How's it going?"

"Peachy," I said as the flushing of a toilet was heard. The bathroom door opened behind me and Claudia stepped out. She gave a surprised, "Oh!" before adding, "Hi." I turned to look at her and making eye contact with me, I could see the confusion in her face.

Looking back at the other two, we watched Alex slowly pull Sissy back into the room, saying "Later, gators," as he shut the door.

We stood there a few seconds longer, listening to the whispers filter through the panel.

"Alex, he saw me naked! What am I going to do?"

"Nothing, it's okay. You've got nothing to be ashamed of, Sissy. You've got a great body. I'm sure Sterling isn't going to go around telling people what you look like without your clothes on."

"That's not what I meant, nitwit. I mean, are we going to get in trouble now? Is he going to call my mom?"

"Naw! Think about it goofball, he had a girl up here, too."

"I said, don't call me goofball, goofball!"

With that, we walked away. Sissy wasn't the first. I'd walked into our shower room many times in years past as an undergrad, and later, as a dormitory assistant, to find boys doing communal showers with their girlfriends. As a D.A., I gave them my usual one-minute lecture about the dangers of getting caught by someone who cared. That way, I could say I fulfilled my duties to anyone of authority who might be concerned. Luckily for them, Palance had his own shower room on the floor above.

Claudia and I returned to my room, both of us showing signs of exhaustion. Once inside, she asked, "Can I sleep in this?" I whipped off my robe and fell back onto my bed. Pulling the blanket over me and then holding it open for her to crawl in, I said, "Couldn't think of anything better."

She snuggled in beside me and I realized it was the first time in a long time that I wouldn't have to sleep alone. Sarge came to the bedside and wagging his tail in an almost apologetic manner, rested his muzzle on the blanket, his eyes begging to join us.

"No! No, boy… sorry. Go lay down."

He returned to his bed with Claudia saying, "Awww… so mean. Poor dog."

"You want him up here? Laying on you, farting, panting, and snoring. He also runs in his dreams, so he'd probably have you knocked onto the floor by morning."

"Or, you! He kind of likes me, you know."

"Yeah, sure."

"So, is he actually a guard dog? I mean, if you told him to sic somebody, would he?

"Yes, and yes. But I don't want him to be known as a guard dog. It's better that people just look at him as my pet. He was taught a special word. So, 'sic em' won't do the trick."

"So, what's the word? Can you tell me?"

"Only if you promise never to say it. Well… unless you need too, of course."

"Okay, I promise."

Moving my lips to her ear, I whispered, "Beissen."

She started to say it out loud and I hushed her. "Don't say it! Not even now." Looking back at Sarge, I saw his ears now stood at attention. Claudia slapped a hand over her mouth, and I heard a muffled "Oops!" Then she leaned over and putting her lips to my ear, whispered, "So, like… buffalo? That's so weird."

"No, it's a German word and it means, 'Bite'… like, 'Bite the crap out of them!' But please, keep it to yourself. You will experience a whole different dog if you say it in his presence, and somebody will get hurt. We don't want that kind of trouble."

"Sorry. So, on the subject of trouble."

"Yeah?"

"Are you going to get into trouble, now? For having me in here, I mean?"

"I don't know."

"Those two upstairs obviously saw me."

"Well, they're in the same boat. Oh, speaking of boats, how would you like to go boating?"

"Boating? You mean like with a real boat?"

"Well, yeah. Fake boats aren't that much fun. How about it?"

"Sounds peachy. You've got a boat?"

"Well, it's my fathers. Maybe we could even picnic on the island."

"There's an island?"

"Yeah… and a boat."

"Wow! Neato! But I don't know when I could. Getting kind of busy. Remember, I'm not a grad student."

"Okay, we'll just plan on it—someday."

We lay quiet after that, and soon Claudia's soft, purring snore filled the air, followed by Sarge's from across the room. A certain set of waterpipes rattled. Someone had just flushed the toilet up on second. I drifted off, happy Sissie had finally been able to pee.

XI

Erebus Rages

Sunday mornings were usually quiet mornings. Well, least up until the chapel bell began to peal at nine o'clock. I woke to it, and somebody stumbling down the stairs, followed by the slamming of the front door. Probably Casper, late for mass. I swung my legs out and sat on the edge of my mattress. I had to be sure to get the front door unlocked before ten, that way the returning chapel goers could get back inside. Sarge sat patiently waiting at my door, giving me a look that said, 'Hurry it up, will you!' I felt an unusual stiffness all over my body. Smiling to myself, I looked back at Claudia who rolled over to face the window, mumbling something about Darwin in her sleep. Getting my robe on, I grabbed my keys and went out into the vestibule.

I propped the inside doors open and unlocked the spring-loaded night latch to the outer. Then sitting on the veranda steps, I watched Sarge go about his routine. Other than an old man tottering past the Bell Tower on his way to the service, the campus was empty. The front door over at Loring burst open just as the attendees at the chapel broke into a loud hymn.

Three girls hurried past, one of them being Sissy, who suddenly stopped to stare. Dressed in her best, she looked embarrassed, and I wondered if she was still ruminating about our little episode. I met her pale blue eyes and could see that she was afraid.

"Mister.... ummm... Sterling? Am I okay?"

"Sissy—you look great."

Her expression became irritated and she stuttered out, "I mean about... getting in trouble?"

"That's what I meant."

"Oh...okay, sorry, I thought you..."

166

"Sissy?"

"Yeah?"

"Go to church."

"Oh… okay. Thanks," she said, and giving me a nervous grin, she dashed around the corner of Dyer and disappeared from sight. I heard the door unlatch behind me and looking back, I saw Claudia had it open just a crack.

"Sterling, come in here," she said, scanning the street like she expected Mordechai to appear at any second.

"What? You're dressed, already? Your clothes get dry? I thought we could have some breakfast."

"Sterling, just come."

I did as she asked and opening the door all of the way, the smell of frying bacon wafted out as Sarge ran in, heading for the kitchen. Claudia had pushed herself back into a corner and beckoned me. When I came to her, she reached up and locked her fingers behind my neck, saying, "Pick me up, just like you did last night at Pembrook," then tilting her head to the side, she gave me a shy grin. I put my hands under her derriere and picked her up off the floor. Crossing my arms so she could sit on them, we kissed for a good two minutes before she pulled her face back, saying, "That should last me all day. You can put me down now; I have to go."

"Where? You going back over to Pembrook?"

"Yeah, I need a shower, and I have to study."

"You should stay away one more night. Make Mordechai go into fits about the chance that you might have been kidnapped. Then she'd be expecting a world of hurt for sending you out into the dark and stormy night."

"Naw, I told you, she's just doing her job. She probably won't bug me at all today. Well… except to ask where I'd spent the night. I'll just tell her in the bushes"

"You're too nice, Claudia. You might just be nicer than me."

"I doubt that, but anyway, got to go."

Kissing a fingertip, she touched it to my lips. "See you later, gator," she said and grinned big enough to show that overbite. She then dashed

167

out the door, heading for Pembrook. I watched her go, noticing the carefree manner in which she walked. When she reached the opposite curb of Church Street, she stepped up onto the grass and twirled once, her arms raised above her head. Waving one time, she took off in a trot across the lawn.

Going to my room to feed Sarge, I whistled for him to come. I heard Casper yelp and then, "Hey! Get your nose out of there, you mangy mutt."

He came flying around the corner with a dog's version of a grin on his face. I suspected Casper had gotten his morning goose and could now start his day. I went up and showered while Sarge ate. Meeting a bare assed Alex coming out of the shower room, he held the door for me, smirking.

"Thanks," I said.

"Sterling?"

I turned, leaving the door open about a foot, so I could see him. Not something I really wanted to do, though, as he stood just outside in the hallway, naked, toweling his hair. His pale, skinny body was devoid of fat and I wondered if he ever got any sun.

"What is it, Alex?"

"So… what did you think of my girl?"

"She's a great kid."

"Ummm… that's not what I meant, I…"

"I know what you meant," I said, and scowled.

With that, I shut the door in his face and heard, "Okay, daddy-o."

Time to quit this gig. Just spending the night with Claudia this one time had turned me around. If she and I were going to be together, I needed a place of my own. A place where I could go to the toilet or shower without the company of post-adolescent boys. I could take an apartment over on Saltonstall Street. Daisy Pattingell always had studios available. I had enough saved up from my mother's monthly stipend (which was the money my father had left me) to pay for that. There was certainly enough for a small apartment for more than a year. A wave of sadness washed over me as I comprehended the reality of it. The 'big change' was picking up momentum, and a lot faster than I expected.

Finishing up, I breakfasted downstairs with Bobby Corey, Stan Peters and Lorenzo Rossi. I had to answer what seemed like a million questions, mostly about life as a grad student. Afterwards, I found Sarge passed out on the bed, so I left him to snooze and headed over to the Arkham cop shop. I wasn't sure what they needed me to do in order to charge Lister, but I figured it required a signature. Walking nearly ten blocks to the municipal building, I expected to talk with Jerry who would just be getting off duty.

I met him coming out the front door. His short, reddish-blonde hair showing through the frosted glass caught my eye before he even got the door opened. His haircut was new, a standard side part whereas most cops in the area chose a military style flattop. I wondered if we shared a barber.

"Mr. Sterling Rice, what a pleasure. Had a little action last night, did we?" he said, blocking the entrance to keep me outside.

Glancing back over his shoulder for a brief second, a scowl crossed his face. Pushing out, he forced me down a couple steps so he could close the door. He stopped on the landing, and his face changed from friendly to serious, as he whispered, "Be careful, Sterling, that Lister Whateley is a bad man. As much as that Duncan girl is a problem for us, she couldn't have timed it better for you. I'm a hundred percent sure Whateley would have used that pig sticker if you'd gotten in his way."

The door opened up behind him, and Ralph Hutchins stood there, now out of uniform—a small bruise on his jaw. Chief Solum stood behind him, studying me through Ralph's armpit. Jerry, keeping his face turned to me, rolled his eyes.

"Nice to see you again, Sterling." he said. Then shaking my hand, his eyes locked on mine and seemed to say, "Watch out for this guy." Then he went around me and walked away.

Hutchins followed Jerry down the steps and with a sneer on his lips, he said in a snide manner as he passed, "Morning, Mr. Rice." I watched Jerry pick up his pace like he wanted to put some distance between him and Hutchins. He turned down the alley to where they parked their cars, but Hutchins continued north on foot to the next corner before turning out of sight.

"Sterling, come in my boy, come in," I heard Chief Solum say, and I stepped up as he reached out and guided me in with a free hand. Coming into his office, he shuffled to his chair, his stooped, old body dressed in his church going clothes, an ancient six shooter strapped to his hip in a western style holster. His short grey hair was in disarray and his usual jovial face showed that same look of consternation that my father's had in his portrait at the library.

The Chief smiled at me, his watery grey eyes trying hard to do the same. I stood there in front of him, trying to piece it all together. Something was wrong. His smile seemed more apologetic than the just, 'Happy-to-see-you' kind. Glancing over at the steel bars of the holding cell in the corner, I noticed it devoid of prisoners and the door hung open.

"Sterling... I'm sorry I didn't get that call made this morning. There was no need for you to come down here."

"Why is that, Chief? Where's Lister?"

"Well, don't let this get around, huh? But... Lister kind of got away from Ralph last night. Knocked him for a loop, and well... anyway, Ralph didn't get it as bad as that Duncan girl. Lister damn near killed her. Then the bastard got clean away. I've notified the State boys."

"What happened to the Dun... to Regina?"

"Well, I shouldn't say, at least, not to you. But Lister snuck back to the diner. Must have hid in the alley, waiting for Miss Duncan to take out the trash. He jumped her from the bushes. Cut her up with that damn knife and knocked her around a bit—even broke her leg. Well, I should say... fractured it to the point she couldn't walk on it, anyway."

On the desk before me lay a pearled handled switchblade on a brown paper lunch bag. It was stained red and it looked like blood had run into the initials 'RD', that had been scratched into the nickel-plated end cap. "Whose is this? That doesn't look like the knife Whateley had."

"Oh... that's the girl's. Hutchins said he suspected there was an actual knife fight before Whateley got the upper hand. You know, just like you see in the movies? Hutchins said there was a trail of blood leading away down toward the river. So... we suspect she stuck him at least one time. She can tell you the rest... I think I've said enough. She's over at St. Mary's. You tell em I said you could visit. If they give you any guff, have them call me."

"Okay, Chief, well… if there is any progress, would you or Jerry give me a bell over at the university? Just to help, uh… help us, stay safe."

"Oh, sure thing, Sterling. Yeah, good idea. Watch your back, huh? Hutchins was saying something about a girl you were with? Something about Lister wanting her for something? Even went as far to say you might have provoked Lister into pulling that knife. But… shit, I don't believe that. Lister's just another outlaw from over Dunwich way. You know the troubles we've had from their kind. I suspect Ralph's wife has an influence over him. She's a Whateley, you know? He was still working over in Kingsport in '28 when the Horror came. The only reason he ever came to work for me was because he hooked up with Elvira. Well, anyway… got work to do, young man. Say hello to your mother for me."

That was my cue. Now, I felt compelled to go talk with Regina. She, in all probability, was the reason I was still breathing. Also, I was starting to get a picture of who the good guys were.

"Thanks, Chief. Guess I'll head over to St. Mary's and see how Regina's doing."

"Okay, Sterling. Hey, we might have to talk to that girl. The one you were with… Osborn? Or maybe I'll just let the State boys handle it. I don't know. We'll see."

"Okay Chief, good luck with this."

"Yeah," he said, as his thoughts seem to drift away, his eyes on the switchblade as he scratched his head.

I left the cop shop and walked south on East Street to Pickman which would give me a straight shot west to the hospital. I crossed over to the other side before I got to the corner where the old, dilapidated Witch House stood.

As a kid, I had always kept my distance. It had been abandoned for as far back as I can remember, or—that's what everybody believed, anyway. My mother told me once that it had been slated for demolition the year before I was born. The workmen had found unspeakable things inside, and now, no contractor would go near it. The roof had caved in and the city had gone as far as to erect a high chain link fence around it with signs declaring 'UNSAFE-NO TRESPASSING'

Yeah, unsafe for a lot of reasons other than rotten floor boards and crumbling walls. I just hoped one day it would implode. Then raising a plume of dust into the sky above Arkham, we could all breathe a sigh of relief knowing that the Witch House was no more.

Lyle rented rooms upstairs across the street in an old Queen Anne styled house that dated back to the late 1800's. I wondered if he would be in bed or still up having breakfast. If he saw me pass, I'd give him a wave just to keep him thinking we were still on good terms.

A familiar car sat at the curb across the street in front of the Witch House. I couldn't quite place it. An old, black, nineteen forty Chevy coupe with a cracked back window and a missing hub cap. I pondered it for a minute. The entire curb was free of cars except for that one. Looking up at the curtainless windows in the Queen Anne's turreted tower room, I saw movement inside.

Lyle stepped up to the curved pane of glass at the front, still dressed in his watchman's uniform. I waved and smiled. That's when a second man appeared at the window on his right, and then, I remembered whose car that was—Ralph Hutchins.

Ralph stepped back as if trying to avoid being seen. Lyle did the same without waving. The smile on my face went from being polite to nervous. I put my eyes front and quickened my pace. The hair on my arms stood up and I got that 'being-watched' feeling. Glancing back after passing the house next door, a shot of adrenaline brought the electricity.

Lister Whateley stood watching me from the window on my side of the tower, a bright white bandage wrapping his left hand. I turned away, fighting the urge to make like a striped assed ape and get the hell out of there (something that Silas Martin used to say when I was a kid). I also couldn't keep from looking back a second time, but the windows were clear of watchers.

This situation was getting worse by the minute. How many more bad guys could there be? It was too big for me. I needed to talk with someone—but who? Chief Solum seemed trustworthy, but apathetic. So, that left Jerry.

His expression over at the cop shop told me he didn't trust Hutchins. Jerry was considered to be overzealous, but I wondered if that perspective had been spawned by people that leaned more toward the dishonest. People who were afraid that one day Jerry would catch them in the act. In private moments he had always come off as a regular kind of guy who just wanted to do his job and do it well. He even joked and teased me in a way that wasn't meant to cause any hard feelings. Jerry was a good man with a well cultivated sense of what was right, unlike Hutchins, who was just a bully in uniform. And now, I had seen him standing in Lyle's apartment with the very man who had tried to attack me and Claudia, plus putting Regina in the hospital. So, where was Canaan? I'm sure he was the Shadowman. Perhaps, he was no longer allowed to act alone and had gotten demoted to 'horse holder' so to speak.

Making my way to the hospital, I kept looking back, making sure that the black coupe, or Lister, weren't in pursuit. Reaching St. Mary's with all my parts still intact, I stopped at the top of the steps and scanned the street behind me. My eye caught a red, nineteen fifty MG TC with its top up. It had been parked in a line of cars on the opposite side, about half a block up. It was Jerry's. That was his, 'Gotta impress the chicks' car.

Someone sat inside, holding a newspaper as if reading—more like hiding. I thought to go over there and talk to him. But if he was trying not to draw attention to himself, then I didn't want to mess that up. It seemed ridiculous because no one else in Arkham owned a car like that, but I guess it was a better choice than the squad car. So, walking inside, I went to the nurse's desk. The head nurse asked if I had permission to see Regina and then allowed me upstairs when I suggested she call Chief Solum.

I felt a shock when I saw Regina lying there, her condition much worse than what I imagined. Her leg was cast and hung by its heel in a sling. Her face was covered in bruises and she had a two-inch sutured cut tracing the left side of her jaw. I wondered if her throat had been Lister's target. Her arms showed numerous long cuts that were sutured as well. Both hands were bandaged and splotched with crimson.

173

"Sterling," she rasped out. "Funny you should be here. Come to give me that kiss you never promised?" She tried to laugh, but winced and groaned, her mirth amounting to no more than a rattling whisper.

"Hey Reg… you look like shit."

"Should see the other guy," she said, her voice brittle. "Hey lover boy… how about a little water, huh?"

Finding a half full glass with a bent straw in it, I held it to her mouth and she eagerly sucked at the liquid, her eyes watching my face. Pulling her parched lips from the straw, she said, "Try not to look at me, huh? I'm kind of lacking in the makeup department. Hey… you know that cop friend of yours… Jerry, right? He ain't too bad looking, a real flutter bum, and he was even nice to me. On top of that, he's single. Never thought I'd like a cop. With me like this, I suppose no man's ever going to give me a second look. I'm going to grow to be an old spinster still wearing a pink jacket."

I had quit looking at her liked she asked and focused on putting the water glass back. My eyes didn't stay away for long and I saw she was now staring at the wall across the room. Tears were leaking from the corners of her eyes. Letting out a stuttering sigh, she said, "The bastard cut my face, Sterling… he cut my face!" She started to weep but must have found it too painful. Forcing herself to calm down, the tears still ran in rivulets from her blackened eyes. Looking right at me, she sniffed, and sighed again.

"I'm sorry, Reg, I don't know how to thank you for what you did. It was rather brave, but… we've never had any doubt about you and courage. If there is anything I can do?"

She sniffed some more, and when she found her voice, she croaked, "I suppose a kiss is out of the question?"

Without hesitation, I leaned in and just before I kissed her, I saw hope in her eyes. Our lips met for a moment and pulling away, I wasn't sure what I saw in them afterwards. She seemed to be pondering the effect, and then tossing caution to the wind, she said, "I suppose you and Shirley Temple are on the hook, huh?"

I felt afraid to answer that question because I knew she didn't want the truth. But I gave it to her, anyway.

"Well, I'm not going to lie to you Regina… yes we are."

174

I tried to sound apologetic, but it came out more like a confident declaration. Regina took a deep and painful sounding breath and said, "Sterling…"

"Yes, Reg?"

"Get the fuck out."

"What? But…"

"GO!"

It startled me and as I backed toward the door, the floor nurse appeared, saying, "I'm sorry sir, you should go, Regina needs her rest." Moving out into the corridor, I watched my friend turn her face to the window. There came a loud, unexpected whimper, and as I walked away, I heard the usually unyielding Regina Duncan begin to cry.

XII

Evil Wings In Ether, Beating

I stood on the front steps of the hospital, seething. People passed in and out, but I didn't take much notice. Seeing Regina laying in that bed like that, had triggered something inside me. A dark determination. Something diabolical was unfolding in my world, and sadly, I was inclined to just turn away for selfish reasons. I felt that maybe it was because with Aubrey's abduction, I couldn't do anything but beg for action and hope something would get done. Yet at twenty-four, I didn't have to stand by and just wish. I didn't have to curl up in my bed, bawling my eyes out. I could act. My father had faced something horrible in his life time, putting his very existence on the line to stop a cataclysmic event. He had been gallant. I wasn't sure if this thing happening was of the same magnitude, but because the Whateley's were involved, it could very well be. There was still too much left to be discovered. I didn't think I could do that by myself. I needed information, and more than that—people I could trust.

Jerry's car was still parked where I saw it last. The newspaper would lower once in a while as he turned the pages, giving him an opportunity to look around. I stopped caring that I could screw up his stakeout and walked over.

Moving right up to the window, I stopped and stared down at him. It took a few seconds for him to acknowledge me. Pushing today's copy of the Arkham Advertiser down onto his lap, he tilted his head back over the top of the seat, closed his eyes, and sighed in annoyance.

"Hello, Jerry."

He turned his face to me, glaring through the glass. "Get in, Sterling," he said, and reaching across the small car, he opened the other door. Coming around, I squeezed in and shut it. The day was warming up and

176

I wanted to suggest maybe he open the windows or drop the top. But that would blow his cover. I wouldn't stay long, bodies in small, unvented spaces tended to bring a queasiness.

Jerry wasn't much older than me. Which means, I had to work hard not to be disrespectful of what he represented. He had come from south Boston, a tough, Irish neighborhood. Why he had chosen Arkham, was beyond me, and he wouldn't talk about it. The guy would be a good ally, though, because he had no history with Arkham.

"What do you want, Sterling?"

"Was just up seeing Regina."

"Yeah, I figured that much."

"She's in pretty bad shape."

"I know, I went up there to ask some questions. She told me all she could. You know, Sterling, that girl's got a good side. You know the kind? Tough on the outside, but tender in? She'd be the one to risk climbing the tree just to save a kitten… if you know what I mean?"

"Exactly, I've known that since the day we learned to walk. We grew up together. A tough girl that would stand by you in any fight."

"I didn't think that I would like her, but I was wrong. And to be honest… and don't you say a damn thing to anyone, but… I'd like to take her out sometime, maybe show her that not all cops are buttholes."

"You ought to, Jerry. After she's back on her feet, you should take her on a date. You might be surprised at what you find. Take her out for dinner up in the French Hill district away from her usual hangouts, and maybe, some dancing over at the River's Bend Ballroom. Treat her like she's something other than the trash she probably feels like she is. You never know? Anyway… Jerry, there's another thing I'd like to discuss. Something's going on around here, and I am beginning to think it has something to do with that missing student."

"Elspeth Houghton? Yeah, I've been doing some checking. Seems President Morgan over at M.U. wants to keep that under wraps, though. Not good for university business. He's making it difficult for me… right along with Ralph Hutchins."

"Yeah… Hutchins. Got some news for you about that guy. I got a feeling he's in on whatever's it is."

177

"Careful there... that's a serious accusation."

"What? You don't suspect him?"

"I didn't say that. I'm just saying... You haven't told anyone else, right?"

"That's right."

"Good, then don't. I suspect Chief's okay, but Solum and Hutchins have been together a long time. Ol' Jarvas, might not be making good police chief decisions because of Hutchins' influence."

"What about, Lyle Umberling?"

"What about Lyle Umberling? Okay, so... he's the top suspect on my list. He has too much access to too many things on that campus. And he needs money for booze. So, I figure he'll stoop pretty low for a buck. Then there's the Whateley clan. Dunwich is out of my jurisdiction. Have to rely on the state boys for any crap those degenerates pull outside of Arkham."

"Speaking of state boys, my girlfriend's stepfather used to be one. Anton Kofta?"

"Kofta, you say? And who's your girlfriend?" he asked, taking a pen and note pad from his shirt pocket.

"Claudia Osborn? She was from Dunwich. Moved to Cambridge with her mother when she was five. So, that was about fifteen years ago."

"Yeah, I can do the math. So, she's Elspeth Houghton's roommate, if I remember correctly."

"Yeah, she was with me over at the drive-in when Whateley showed up."

"She's going to have to be careful, Sterling. Keep an eye on her. Whateley wanted her for some reason. Witnesses said Lister mentioned her father, Joseph Osborn? Well, our speculation is that he may have employed Lister to come take her back to Dunwich for a visit."

"That's what I thought at first, but not anymore. So... be honest with me Jerry, how did Lister escape last night?"

"Why do you ask? Don't you think he could have had his way with Hutchins?"

"Well, honestly, no."

"I shouldn't say anything about that. You're not authorized to know. In fact, until you came over to talk to me, you were also a suspect. So, keep in mind, this is pure speculation… but I think Hutchins let him go. Probably had Lister give him a good whack for the sake of appearances. Ralph probably gave him the knife back and the bastard went over and did a number on our Regina. I've been sitting here in my car, waiting for Ralph to make an appearance. If he goes up there to see her, I'm going to be right behind him. I've decided I'm going to get her shipped over to Gloucester. That'll keep her safe until this thing comes to a head."

"Can you do that?"

"Damn tootin', I can do that. Police order. I've got a few friends on the state level... specifically a magistrate whose name you'll never know.

"Peachy! The safer she is, the better. One more thing, Jerry, something I think is going to shake things up. On the way over, I passed Umberling's place. I saw Hutchins through the window with Lyle, and without a doubt… Lister Whateley."

He turned and looked at me, his eyes going to a squint. "You're telling me you seen Whateley at Umberling's? And in the last twenty minutes?"

"Well, more like half an hour."

"Sterling… get out of my car. I've got to go get the Chief and head over there."

He started the motor as I squeezed out of the little door, and before I shut it, he said, "Keep this to yourself, hey? I'm not going to say who told me unless I need to. Be careful, Sterling, especially with that Umberling. If I have to haul his fat ass over to the station for more questioning, I will. Maybe you can keep an eye on him and let me know if he pulls any crap."

"Another thing, just to add a little flavor. I saw Lyle hanging out with the man I think was our peeper. It was a few nights ago. Canaan Whateley? Lister's brother?"

"Why didn't you tell me back then?"

179

"Because, Jerry, I didn't know who I could trust. You... you were still suspect," I said and chuckled.

"Wise ass! Okay, so... makes sense, I guess. Well, seems we've got a lot more to talk about. But right now, I've got to go. The longer I wait, the less chance I have to nab Whateley. Shut the door, huh?"

I did as he asked, and he sped away from the curb, the small tires smoking on the cobblestones. I felt better now, knowing there was someone I could trust on a government level. Someone that seemed dedicated to finding a solution. But I grew nervous thinking about how to handle Lyle. If Jerry arrested him today, then, no problem. If Jerry didn't, then maybe I should call in sick, or even resign from the caretaker's position first thing in the morning. I was fairly safe tonight because I didn't have to work, but I dreaded next week.

I needed to get back to campus and let Sarge out. I wouldn't call the Dean of Students about resigning until after I found out more about what Jerry found over at Lyle's place. Dean Farr had to know, one way or the other, though. First, I wanted Jerry's approval before I told anyone why I was quitting. There was going to be some kind of a domino effect on campus, and I feared I might have to be the one to knock over that first tile.

I walked into my room and Sarge nearly knocked me down to get out the door. I moved with him as he wandered about the green, examining trees and shrubs. I felt anxious. All the anguish I had experienced with Aubrey was twofold now. I needed to calm down, maybe take a nap, or go see Claudia. I was hoping she would be available tonight.

After Sarge's twenty plus squirts and two steaming piles, I went back to work on my dissertation. Skipping lunch, much to Sarge's dismay, I worked until the phone rang. Needing a break, I jumped up and went out to find I was in a race with Casper to answer it. He didn't back off and I had to wrestle the handset from him.

"I got this, Casper."

"Okay, well... I just wanted to help."

"That's just peachy, Casper, but when I'm here, I'll get the phone, capeesh?"

"Yeah, sure... So, some girl called earlier."

180

I could hear a man's voice through the handset, saying, "Hello? Hello?" but before I answered, I glared at Casper and said flatly, "Thanks, Casper." He got the point and walked away, obviously shamed.

"Sorry… Dyer Hall?"

"Sterling? It's Professor Strang, from next door. I'd like to meet with you tomorrow afternoon in my office, let's say… one thirty?"

"That will work, Professor. May I ask what this is about?"

"I'd like to save it for tomorrow, if you can hold out until then?"

"Okay, I'll be there."

"Very well, Sterling. Good day."

My mind was abuzz with questions as I hung up the handset. I wondered if the word had gotten around to all of the important people on campus. Lyle Umberling, was a bad guy. The meeting would offer me the opportunity to announce my resignation.

I remembered what Casper had said about the girl calling and I went into the commons to question him further. He lay stretched out on the sofa, reading as usual.

"Casper, do you ever study?"

He looked up from his book, and a few seconds passed like he had to decide if he was still talking to me, or not, then he said, "Sure, Sterling, yeah, I study. But I'm only going for my BA. I'm a literature major, you know?"

"No, I didn't know."

He finally grinned, "Yeah, daddy-o, I'm…"

"Okay, so what's the message from the girl?"

"Oh, well first, it was for Alex from Sissy, then somebody wanted to talk to Dempsey. Then there were three wrong numbers and finally that girl who wanted to talk to you. So…"

"Enough… so, what did she say?"

"Oh! She was going to call back. I'll just let you get it—like you said."

"Casper, I think M.U. is going to have to hire you as the receptionist for Dyer Hall."

"Really? And pay me money? Wowza!"

"No, not really. Go back to your book."

"Oh… okay," he said, his face full of disappointment.

Returning to my desk, I spent another two hours working from my notes. Then tiring of that, I napped for another hour before the phone woke me. I got there on the third ring. Casper was absent from the sofa and the sound of horseplay echoed from the second floor. Palance hollered down the stairwell from third, "Would you imbeciles cut the noise? I'm trying to study up here. Nothing but halfwits… you're nothing but halfwits!"

The noise came to an abrupt halt. I heard a, "Drop dead, Boris Karloff," and a door slammed shut. Shaking my head, I picked up the handset and said, "Dyer Hall?"

"Sterling?"

"Claudia, hey, what's up?"

"Oh…" she said and giggled. "Just wanted to say, I won't be able to see you tonight. So… how about tomorrow for lunch?"

"Sounds peachy, but I've got a meeting with my advisor. How about after… let's say… two thirty?"

"Okay, I have class from one til then. You might have to wait. Meet me on the steps of the science annex, like last time?"

"Sure thing, see you then?"

"Okay, and Sterling?"

"Yeah?"

"Can't wait!" she yelled into the handset and then made a kissing noise followed by a giggle. There came a click and she was gone. Even though I wouldn't get to see her tonight, my dark mood vanished. Claudia was my ticket out. Her eternal optimism would lift me up. I would feed off of that.

I was falling in love. But that love felt like a balloon tethered to the ground, unable to float free. The string that anchored it was made up of many strands, every one of them an element of discourse that needed to be eliminated.

Returning to my chair, I sat, thinking about a particular idiom. It was that saying about being down so long it looks like up. But you really don't know until you have passed a certain point in any relationship, and one day you look down to see the dark clouds below you and realize that you have risen into the light.

How long have I been lonely and miserable without realizing it?

My mother didn't help matters, and Sandra, neither. It seemed as if they had conspired to take control of my life, utilizing the: 'Tough love' theory of existence. It would be a wonderful thing if my mother could just accept me as I was, and Claudia, as my new love. It would be so easy; but obstinacy reigned.

I would call my mother out and confront her with all the questions I had on my next visit. Maybe even threaten her with no contact if she wouldn't see that things needed to change in a way that both could be happy. We had to get closer or move farther apart. There had to be compromise. We couldn't keep playing by her rules. I wanted to have a reasonable exchange and be allowed to show her the love that I had for her as my mother.

There was still time, she was only fifty-seven. There could be years of happiness before the end. What if I got married and had a child? Would she accept grandchildren? Could she find an inkling of joy from being a grandparent—or would she reject it with the belief that having a grandchild around only made her look old? Did she really want to die alone? The thought made me realize, I had sensed something, but I just might be ignoring it. The way she looked the last time I saw her—frail, pale and shaky.

Getting up I went back to the phone. I hesitated for a few seconds and then dialed the house I had grown up in. Clenching my teeth, I waited. Elsie picked up on the third ring.

"Hello?" she said as if annoyed.

"Mother… mom? It's Sterling…"

"What is it, Sterling? I am in the middle of my singing lesson."

"Just wanted to check on you, ummm… I had a bad dream. I was…"

"I'm still breathing if that's the concern."

"Well… okay."

"Is that all you have? Mr. Levi is waiting."

"Yes…was a little worried is all."

"Goodbye, Sterling. Oh, and Sterling... don't ever address me as mom. What are we, peasants? No. Good day."

As I expected. What was I thinking? I guess I had hope, but I think that was Claudia's influence. I just wanted to grab my mother by the shoulders and shake her. Tuesday would be difficult. But I had almost two whole days to prepare for what I was going to say. If it came down to a screaming match (which was quite possible), so be it.

I fed Sarge early. The undergrads had gathered in the TV room for the Sunday matinée. Giving up on my dissertation for the time being, I joined them, leaving my door open for Sarge to follow if he wished.

Sitting down between Kenny Robinson, who everyone called 'Spanky' and the Drexler twins, I realized too late that they were watching, '*The Son of Ali Baba*', a Tony Curtis movie. So, a running narrative followed soon after I planted my derriere on the sofa. It involved changing the character, Kashma, (played by Curtis) to 'Sterling'.

Kenny was the first narrator to open with, "Princess Azura steps up to Sterling and says, 'Still, you don't trust me, Sterling?' Sterling replies: 'If I have misjudged you Princess, remember only, the slave girl I held in my arms...'" and so on. The rest of them, seeing that I was going to tolerate it, chimed in and the narration went around the room at least twice. Then it stopped being funny, and they gave it up.

Esdra Allen, a fish faced kid from Innsmouth, was in the kitchen boiling up a ton of hotdogs. The counter was stacked with bags of buns, relish, mustard, and ketchup. His father, who happened to be a butcher, had sent them by truck the day before. I, of course, would have thought fish, being Innsmouth was a port and all. But Esdra told me that the people of Innsmouth didn't eat fish. "Help yourselves, fella's, don't want 'em to rot!" he yelled from the kitchen.

I seriously doubted hotdogs would ever remain in Dyer Hall long enough to rot.

All the activity took my mind off my problems. I returned to my dissertation after a couple of hours and ended up falling asleep at my desk. Sarge woke me with a nudge around midnight. Time to pee.

The mist was on the rise as I stood on the veranda watching Sarge's shape move about the college green. Locking the outside doors after, I stopped at the foot of the stairs to listen. Somebody was having a rambling discussion up on second floor about whether Fords were faster than Chevys, and that was backed by the incessant clack of a typewriter rolling down from third. I knew I would miss all this, but life would go on. It would be okay as long as I had someone to share it with. Double locking my door, I lay down on my bed still dressed. Sarge climbed up with me, reminding me that Monday would also be bath day.

***

Coming up out of a deep sleep, I lay on my back, listening. A distant noise, like a bell clambering, lasted maybe all of ten seconds. Not feeling Sarge beside me, I opened my eyes a crack. He sat staring at the door, ears and hackles up. Looking back at me, he wagged his tail and whined. Then returning his gaze to the door, he gave a low woof and growled. I realized that my heart was beating twice its normal rate. It took another two seconds to understand why.

That had been a burglar alarm. The library's burglar alarm. Slipping on my shoes and grabbing my keys, I hurried to the kitchen. The grandfather clock chimed the half hour, and in the dim light of the first commons, I saw it said three thirty-five. I slipped into the kitchen and then took a quick right into the pantry. It had one small window situated at about head height offering an unobstructed view in the direction of the library. The mist had remained thin and I could just make out the bulk of the building in the distance. I rubbed my eyes trying to get them to focus. Yes, the windows in the reference room were ablaze with light. Only Lyle, or the head librarian, could get away with that after hours. A burglar would have known better then turn on any light. Then why the alarm? Either the wiring had shorted or, someone had moved the Necronomicon.

Sarge and I left Dyer Hall by the back door, letting the spring-loaded night latch secure it upon shutting. Walking fast in that direction, I kept my eyes locked on the distant building. I had no idea what I would do when I got there. I hoped that I'd meet Lyle checking the interior and he would say, "Don't worry, Sterling, bumped the case is all. You go on back to bed now. I've got this under control." I was only fooling myself.

185

Sarge ran ahead and I loudly whispered my command to come. He came back and heeled in step with me, an anxious whimper followed by a whine escaping his mouth. In the ground bound cloud, I could just make out his eager eyes as they sought mine.

We stopped at the northeast corner of the building, hoping to utilize the only window on the north side with a view into the reference room. The problem with that, the window now hung open wide enough to allow someone in—or out. Its sill was about a foot higher than my head. So, I thought to stand on the plinth course at the base of the wall to get a look inside. Before I could, voices filled the air and flashlight beams cut through the mist as they moved between the chapel and Dyer Hall, apparently somebody was enroute to the library from Faculty House. I pushed backward into the shrubbery and quieted Sarge.

I recognized the voices of Professor Strang, Alice Payne, and Dr. Corning as they moved past me. Just as they went out of sight around the corner, I heard a car, its engine racing as it sped up West Street from the river. Its headlights played over the wall at the west end of the building, and a red glow raced repeatedly over the same area, telling me that it just might be the Arkham police. Jerry should have been on duty and I itched to meet up with him and share what I knew. The patrol car pulled into sight and screeched to a halt at the curb. The driver quickly set the emergency brake, causing the car to rock. The engine shut down, all lights went out, and the door swung open. I could tell right off by the bulk of the driver, even in the dim light and mist—it wasn't Jerry.

There was the jingle of keys, clanking of handcuffs, and the squeak of leather. I recognized the slap of a holster on a fat thigh—Hutchins. He mumbled as he moved my way, his heavy riding boots pounding on the cobblestones of the walk that led from the street.

"Damn it. Stupid bastard. I told him this wouldn't work. Can't trust a Whateley. I'm always saying… can't trust a Whateley. But, nooo! You think they'd listen. Damn it all to hell."

Where was Jerry? Had something happened to him when he went to nab Lister at Lyle's place? Hutchins' monologue was interrupted by a woman's shriek from the open window. He stopped his blabbering and picked up his pace. I crouched down even more as Sarge let out a low growl. Wrapping my hand around his muzzle, I held it until Hutchins had gone around the corner. I figured it would be safer for me to go inside now with the faculty there. I could tell them I heard the alarm and came running. It was best that I showed up last.

"Oh my god… they took it. They got in and took it. We're in for it now. Who knows what they want it for?"

I recognized Dr. Corning's voice. It was soon followed by Dr. Strang saying, "Officer Hutchins! It's just us, so you can put that gun away. Glad you're here, I think he's dead. That's a lot of blood, and he hasn't moved since we arrived."

Blood? Dead? Worse than I expected. Dashing out of my hiding spot, I ran around to the front of the library and went inside to see them all gathered back in the corner, dressed in assorted pajamas and robes. Hutchins had been standing with his back to me and spun around, his hand going to the butt of his pistol. But seeing it was only me; he turned back.

Alice walked to me and wrapped her arm in mine, saying, "Oh, Sterling, someone took the Necronomicon… and I think they killed poor Mr. Umberling, too. Nineteen twenty-eight, all over again... I tell you… its nineteen twenty-eight, all over again."

I walked her back to the group and stood peering around Hutchins who was gulping air like he was having trouble swallowing a bite of pot roast. "Oh my god… poor man," Alice said as I looked down on Lyle.

He lay on his left side in a pool of blood, his head and shoulders up under the waist high, brass framed case, his right hand clutching his chest where I suspected the wound was. From where I stood, only his right eye was visible, and it was wide open as if in surprise. His hat lay just beyond the top of his head, soaking up his life's blood at the edge of the puddle. The lid of the case remained open, braced on locking supports, the big ring of keys still hanging in the latch. I took another step forward for a better look and Hutchins grabbed my arm, "Hold it there, kid. Watch where you're stepping. Got to get the state boys in here."

Sarge moved up behind the officer and growled. Looking back over his shoulder, Hutchins let out a small gasp and took his hand off me. Alice pulled me toward her and gave the officer a hard look. The others followed suit and Dr. Strang turned his back to Hutchins and whispered something indiscernible in Dr. Corning's ear. I called Sarge to heel as Hutchins focused on removing a notepad from his upper coat pocket. I couldn't help but notice the sweat beading up on his forehead under the bill of his cop hat.

Dr. Strang turned back, and Dr. Corning lamented "I knew we should never have given the watchman a key for that case."

"Oh my god…" Alice said, and releasing my arm, she put both hands to her face. "Oh my god… shouldn't we call an ambulance?"

Hutchins said, "No, he's dead. Crime scene now. I'll be right back."

Walking to Alice's desk in the main entry hall, he picked up the telephone's handset and dialed. A minute passed before I heard, "Sorry to wake you, Chief, got something going on over at M.U. library. Could you come over? Okay, see you soon. Yeah, we are going to need State on this… yeah, I'll call them." Hanging up, I heard him dial another number.

Taking a risk of getting bitched out by Hutchins, I moved to the edge of the blood pool for a closer look. Lyles left arm was under him and part of a brown envelope protruded from beneath his hip. The back flap had been torn opened and from what I could see, it looked like there was a stack of cash inside. The problem was; two, ten-dollar bills floated in Lyle's blood and a third remained sticking half way out of the packet, but bent back over the top to reveal Jefferson Davis glaring at me with an unsmiling face from a fifty-dollar Confederate Grayback, a form of currency used in the south during the civil war. I suspected the stack of bills beneath it were the same. The murderer must have attempted to cheat Lyle and things had gone bad.

Something else caught my eye—a single bloody heel print on the Persian rug style floor runner. It had the same nail pattern as the one I found on the river bank, but not the one from Waldron's Grove. So, the 'he' Hutchins had been referring to, that couldn't be trusted, must have been Lister. I wondered how much of that money laying there, soaking up Lyle's blood, was supposed to go to Hutchins—before the watchman discovered it was grey and not green.

Hutchins reappeared, and seeing I had moved, scrutinized me with a squint. "What are you doing here, anyway, Mr. Rice?"

"It's okay officer," Dr. Strang said. "Sterling's with us."

Alice and Doctor Corning nodded in agreement. Hutchins looked down at Sarge, who eyed him maliciously, his ears back, a pre-snarl curl forming his lips. Changing the subject, Hutchins said, "State police are on the way and so is the Chief. If one of you wants to stay, that's fine. The rest of you can go."

"Very well, officer, I will stay," Dr. Strang said. "Alice, you, Louis and Sterling, should probably return to your beds. Going to be a long day today."

Hutchins replied in a flippant manner, "Yeah, we're probably going to have to close the library for a good part of it to get this cleaned up."

Alice said, "Oh my! That just won't work, officer. The students need to be in here. It's finals. This is so unfortunate. Please understand, this needs to be taken care of as soon as possible. Maybe we could just close the reference room for a little while?"

"Well… we'll let the state boys decide."

"I am going to call the Dean and President Morgan about this. I'm sure they'll have a say in the matter. Alice is right, closing the whole library would propose a serious problem for the university."

Dr. Strang's words were stern. Eyeing Hutchins, he waited for argument. He got none, and Hutchins just went back to writing in his little notebook.

"Okay, I will see the rest of you later? I've some things to discuss with the officer."

We took that as our cue, and I led the way out the front door as Dr. Strang started in with Hutchins, telling him how things needed to be. Going outside, we had just started to turn the corner when Chief Solum's personal car pulled up at the curb. We waved a hello to him as he hobbled to the front steps. He waved back with a, "Hey folks."

I left those two as we passed behind Dyer Hall with 'good nights' all around and just before I closed the backdoor, Alice's forlorn words came floating to me on the early morning air, "It's nineteen twenty-eight all over again, Louis, nineteen twenty-eight… all over again."

XIII

Thus The Living, Lone And Sobbing

I t didn't take long for the campus to come alive with talk. "The watchmen had been killed at the library!" and, "Did you hear that that big, ugly book was stolen?" I couldn't help but overhear from the first commons in Dyer Hall, "Remember that time back when that Whateley guy tried to steal it… what year was that?" and of course, Dempsey, a loudmouthed history student, not knowing I was nearby, shouted from the kitchen, "Yeah, Dr. Armitage will be rolling over in his grave about now, and so will Sterling's dad."

Poking his head out, Dempsey saw me standing there, glaring. With an, "Oops!", he ducked back and a whispered, "Crap." floated out the open door.

Almost immediately there followed a ton of questions. Everywhere I went someone wanted my opinion; I was Dr. Rice's son, after all. Then there were the few who confided in me that they were afraid. "Will there be another horror?"

I went to the library the first chance I got; Sarge hot on my heels. A state police car was pulling away from the curb along with the familiar M.U. meat wagon. Turning north at the corner, they headed back over to the medical school's morgue.

Going inside the library, I saw the heavy doors to the reference room were shut. Something I'd never seen in my lifetime. Two men in dark suits and fedoras, one with a camera, stood just outside, talking with President Morgan and Dean Farr. Alice paced back and forth behind her desk, rubbing her hands. When she saw me, she smiled in a nervous manner and waved me over with an obvious degree of agitation.

"Oh Sterling, the state police are almost done, they've been here most of the night. Cliff, from Lockley Hall, the janitors from the Science

190

Annex and the Liberal Arts building, plus some men from the physical plant, are inside cleaning up right now. I've had so many complaints already from students. Hopefully, it won't be too much longer."

"Hopefully. So, have you heard anything? I mean, about what happened?"

"Well, I overheard a policeman say that Lyle was stabbed to death. Something about a… ummm… pig sticker? The coroner, that man in the dark blue suit, said that it had only been one time, but it had severed Lyle's aorta. Oh Sterling, it's so horrible. Poor man."

"Yeah, um…poor guy. So, you haven't heard anything about the Necronomicon? Who they might suspect?"

"No, nothing like that. They been doing most of their talking inside with the door shut. I only heard what I told you because somebody was walking out and left it open. Whoever wanted that book is certainly up to no good. You know, Sterling, I was about your age when that Wilbur Whateley tried to steal it back in twenty-eight. I was a student of Library Sciences back then. I'm so afraid they are up to the same. We don't have Dr. Armitage around to get us out of it this time, or your father. Dr. Morgan is too old and certainly isn't in his right mind, so he won't be of any help. Don't know what we're going to do… just don't know."

"Don't worry, Alice. If we put our heads together, we can figure something out." I patted her on the shoulder to reassure her. She grabbed my hand and holding it, she said, "I hope you're right, Sterling. I hope you're right. I truly miss Warren."

She had to let go of me because a student walked up to check out some books. "Talk to you later, Alice," I said and walked back outside. Stopping to stand on the steps, I wondered if I should just approach the suits and tell them what I knew. But I wanted to talk to Dr. Strang first, and maybe, Dean Farr. I also wanted to corner Jerry for the latest from his end, but I hadn't seen him since our talk. He told me not to say anything. If I spoke out of turn, I feared repercussions. If he had a plan, I could screw things up. If the state police called me in, though, I would have to spill the beans, whether Jerry liked it or not. I couldn't keep quiet for too long.

Chief Solum, still parked at the curb, climbed out of the passenger side of his car. After tossing a clipboard back inside the old Ford, he made his way toward me across the front lawn as if energized by the whole affair. I wondered if he was happy there was finally some excitement in Arkham.

"Hello, Sterling! Don't worry, we'll get you into the reference room soon enough. I'm sure you've got work to do. I never went to college, but I can just bet it's tough getting one of them Ph.D.'s. Don't worry, son, maybe just half an hour more."

"Thanks, Chief, happy to hear it. Hey, Chief, where's Jerry been? Expected to see him here last night."

"Oh, came to me yesterday morning all hepped up about some discovery he made. Sorry, can't tell you about that, but... he took a few days off and drove down to Springfield. Something about following some leads, or something. He don't get paid for it, though. Can't have my officers out playing detective all the time. I need patrolmen. Hutchins took over his shifts. Now, that Ralph, he's one of them workaholics, you know? He don't think nothing about working twenty-four hours straight. Likes to be in uniform all the time."

I thought, yeah, with a wife like Elvira, I wouldn't want to stay home, either. Chief Solum finished his little spiel with, "I suspect Hutchins will have my job someday. Any-who, Jerry's supposed to be back on shift, tomorrow. You can probably talk to him then. Well... got to get to it. You come back in an hour, we'll have that room open for you and you kids can get back to your studies."

"Thanks, Chief," I said as he patted Sarge's head on his way inside. When I came around the corner of the library to go back to Dyer, I ran into Bobby Corey who had stopped on the walk and was staring down at the well-worn cobble stones.

"Hey, Bobby Corey! What's the tale, nightingale?"

"Look at this Ster, it's the weirdest thing. I can't figure it out. Looks like somebody stenciled that stone in red with some kind of a symbol."

Walking over, I looked down to see what he was talking about. It was another heel print. Same nail pattern I'd seen on the rug. The flat side of the heel faced the green and the Bell Tower, telling me the direction the owner of those boots had been going in.

"What do you suppose that is?" Bobby asked, pointing.

"Uh… no clue, certainly is weird, huh?"

"Yeah, daddy-o! Hey, is the reference room open yet? Heard the watchman got killed in there last night. Got to see that! Somebody said the killer stole that big, ugly book, too! Geez! Finally, some excitement! See you later, alligator!"

I watched him walked away, singing his version of Bill Haley's hit, '*Shake, Rattle, & Roll*', I grinned, shook my head somewhat mystified, and refocused on the heel print. It was right in front of the window, and there were others. They were just harder to see as they faded away toward the opposite edge of the walk, the grouted joints between the stones breaking up their lines.

I would bet you; Lister had come out of that window and made for the river. I suspected the Necronomicon sat on someone's kitchen table over in Dunwich about now. I don't think Lister or Canaan had the ability, nor the schooling, to use the book for what it was intended. The Wizard Whateley that my father spoke of has been long dead—but there were a few others. The theft of the book only confirmed it.

Returning to my room, I tried to work on my dissertation, but couldn't concentrate. The hours dragged and my mind became a whirlwind of thoughts. Jerry wouldn't be back for a day. I may not be able to wait that long. I needed a beer, better yet, a few beers. I also needed to head over and talk with Dr. Strang and then meet up with Claudia. So, no beer, yet. Another agonizing half hour went by before I gave up and headed over to the School of Languages for my meeting.

I heard conversation coming through Dr. Strang's door, and after knocking, he called me in. It surprised me to see Dean Farr and President Morgan, both seated in chairs, everybody smoking, and drinking coffee.

"Sterling," Dr. Strang said as they all set down their cups and stood up as if I were someone of importance. Farr and Morgan shook my hand as Dr. Strang patted Sarge's head and smiled at us from behind his desk.

"Sit there… in that red, leather wingback, right there. Want some coffee or tea? Maybe a cigar?"

"No, thanks, Dr. Strang. So... what is this about?" I asked, my eyes shifting from Strang to Farr and then to the distinguished Morgan, whose dark eyes bored into me intently, hardly blinking.

At fifty something years of age, his dark hair was seriously greyed at the temples. He looked a lot like his much older brother, Francis, one of the three pictured over at the library. He had a close resemblance to Cary Grant. He was tall and walked like a man of importance. His suit was pristine, the red and white striped tie, tacked with the university symbol, was obviously silk. A polite smile braced his lips as he brought his pipe up for a puff.

We didn't have a personal relationship. But we could have, if Francine and I had gotten serious. President Morgan was a no-nonsense kind of guy, and I often wondered what kind of father-in-law he would have made.

"Dr. Strang," Morgan said, "You can do the talking, beings you're Sterling's advisor, and know him best." Taking another puff of his cigar, he blew smoke at the ceiling and looked over at Dean Farr.

"Yes, please do... that's best," Farr said, servilely smiling.

Looking back at Dr. Strang, I watched him lean forward in his chair, the palms of his hand flat on the edge of his desk. They spread out, sliding along the wood and then moved back together. He did this several times before he spoke.

"Sterling... with the death of Lyle Umberling, Dean Farr thought to offer you the watchman's position until we can find a replacement. I begged to differ. President Morgan agreed with me. In fact, we wondered if you'd be willing to give up both positions...caretaking, and Dyer Hall. This would be so you can take up more teaching. Just as you and I had discussed, previously. I personally would like to see you here in the School of Languages building more often. Would you be able to decide at this moment? I'd like to finalize this thing as soon as possible."

I watched him glance quickly at Dean Farr with what appeared to be a look of annoyance. Farr cast his eyes to the floor and sighed.

To take the scrutiny off the Dean, I spoke quickly, "Well, Dr. Strang, I've already given it a lot of thought and... yes, I believe it's time."

"Excellent, young man, excellent!" he said, grinning and nodding at Morgan, whose Meerschaum went to his lips as he nodded back in a

194

respectful manner. A slight smile braced his lips as he released a puff of smoke to the ceiling.

I noticed Dean Farr seemed to be deep in thought and finally his face turned my way and locking eyes with me, he said, "Sterling, even though you are the most experienced of the caretakers, and I thought you could best fill the role of temporary watchman... Dr. Strang and President Morgan have talked some sense into me. I don't wish to lose you, but I understand that you are not here at M.U. to become a slave to menial tasks. Teaching will account for your tuition, so you don't really need to pay a thing to Miskatonic. As you know, we owe a great debt to your father."

"What about housing? Will I have to take an apartment off campus? With no income, how will I pay for that?"

Morgan jumped right in and said, "No, no... we will work hard to find you something within the campus boundaries. There is a room available in Faculty House, and even though having a third-year grad student residing under that roof is somewhat irregular, I don't think we'd have trouble pulling it off."

Dean Farr added, "We need to get Cliff Breckingham to take over for Umberling... with the offer of a pay raise of course, then we can get Austen Ward, your second, to move up into your caretaker spot. Palance Kilham, one of the grad students living over in Dyer Hall, has always shown an interest in your dorm assistant position. He has been your biggest critic over the years, and we suspect he will be eager to push you out. We also feel he may not be the best man for the job, but we have reached a point where we have agreed to give him a trial run. So... Breckingham and Ward will start tonight. Kilham will move downstairs in June, after the summer break starts and take control of Dyer Hall."

"We should have a room ready for you by then," Morgan said as he puffed away on the curved stem of his pipe.

"So... that's that," Strang said. "Now... that's not the only reason I called you here today, Sterling. But the other subject can wait. We can meet again on Wednesday and talk more about your teaching schedule for August."

"Okay, but I'm curious about something."

195

President Morgan stopped puffing and gave me a concerned look. Dean Farr halted the coffee cup en route to his mouth, looking worried like he thought I might throw a monkey wrench into their plans. Dr. Strang sat back in his chair and interlocked his fingers over his chest. The smoke from his cigar, resting in the ashtray, rose in a straight line toward the ceiling. He looked so much like some wise old sage that I had to hold back the grin that so badly wanted to take control of my lips.

"I am a little worried about the theft of the Necronomicon," I said, looking at President Morgan.

He set his pipe on a decorative ashtray standing next to his chair and leaning forward, he brought his palms together and clamped them between his thighs. He projected his face out toward me as if I had his undivided attention and said, "The police are on that, city, county, and state. I know what you're thinking, and yes, I too have a concern about that. Could the thief possibly bring the Horror back? Maybe... haste is of importance here. If I may be completely open with you, Sterling, with the understanding that I trust you as Warren's son—what is said here today—remains here."

"Yes, I can keep my mouth shut."

"Very well, since you've put it that way... We suspect, the missing girl, Elspeth Houghton has something to do with it. I'm sure you know her story, plus everything that your father ever told you. I was around twenty when you were born, I think I was a sophomore at the time. I know all about the Dunwich Horror. My brother is still alive, and even though he is now in Boston and suffering from dementia, I believe if it came down to it, he would be able to help thwart anything that comes our way. I have his journal of copious notes from that time, and I also know your mother... Elsie, has your father's. The ones belonging to Dr. Armitage are tucked away in a safe, which very few people have access to. We are much better prepared than Dr. Armitage was back in nineteen twenty-eight. I suspect the Whateley clan of Dunwich are up to their old tricks again. If they have absconded with the Necronomicon as Wilbur Whateley had attempted to do, back in twenty-eight, we will meet them in unyielding fashion. Sadly, I fear we won't find Miss Houghton alive. I—we—fear she may have been taken for the purpose of sacrifice. Purely speculation, and we are still waiting to hear from the police on the matter. But the theft of that book only serves to bolster our beliefs. We also have a great degree of trepidation that there may be other students abducted in days to come. Dr. Corning has read my brother's and your father's notes and he has reason to believe there will be need for one more, uh… girl, to be sacrificed before they can actually use the Necronomicon for its intended purpose. They will also need a girl to birth the monstrosity. So, we fear two more of our girls may be taken. I have directed the state police to start their search in Dunwich, and deliberately named the Whateley's as the culprits. Miss Mordechai over at Pembrook has been asked to keep a closer eye on her girls. The same for Miss Heinz at Loring. We don't have to worry about the boys. Sterling—we want you to stand with us if need be. Keep an eye out… but it is of the utmost importance that the welfare of the female student body here at Miskatonic be kept in mind. If the word gets out that this university is not safe, well… we could see our lives go down the drain; so to speak. M.U. will fold, and a historical Massachusetts institution will fade away into history. Do you understand what is at stake here, Sterling?"

"Yes, President Morgan, I do."

"Good, okay, Dr. Strang, Dean Farr, I have somewhere to be. Thank you for your time, Sterling, I wish you the best," he said, and got to his feet. We did the same and shook hands all around before he walked out.

Dean Farr didn't release my hand right away, and forcing eye contact, he said, "I will get right to making those arrangements. Sterling, you are free from your caretaker obligation from this point on. We'll talk some more about the dorm assistant's position later. Wish you the best with your teaching." With that said, he patted the back of my hand with his other, released me, and followed President Morgan out the door.

Dr. Strang came around his desk and took my hand. "About what President Morgan said, we can only hope it won't come down to that. But I wholeheartedly believe we have lost Miss Houghton, and seriously fear we may lose more. A university is a prime hunting ground for predators of all sorts," he said, his eyes traveling briefly to the stuffed wolverine, before returning to me. "The carefree attitude of young

197

people as they experience the freedom of their first time away from home, makes them vulnerable. Naiveté prevails, I'm afraid. It's up to the likes of you and me to see that they stay safe. Many of these students come to Miskatonic from other places where what happened back in nineteen twenty-eight is just a myth. But you and I, as well as a few others who have called Arkham home for many years, know better. I know that there are some of the elder Whateley's who can accomplish what that old wizard attempted to do, and Josiah Whateley is one of them. He's the wizard's younger brother and may have been involved with their first attempt. So, what President Morgan said, is absolutely true. They will need one more sacrifice, if, they've used the Houghton girl already, and then someone to give birth. There aren't too many women left in Dunwich that can do that. As you may know, it was Lavinia Whateley, the daughter of the wizard who birthed Wilbur and whatever that thing was that your father helped put down on the top of Sentinel Hill. Elvira Whateley is married to that scoundrel, Ralph Hutchins, who masquerades as a policeman here in Arkham. She got lucky in getting out of Dunwich, unlike her brothers. No woman would ever marry, less cavort, on purpose, with Josiah's two boys."

I stood in awe. My mouth now hung open and I forced it shut. I had a whole new picture of Dr. Strang. Like I said, he had been around a long time, but I had no idea of his level of involvement, or what he knew.

"So, Sterling, we will talk again on Wednesday." Patting my shoulder, he studied my face briefly and then returned to his desk. I felt compelled to tell him all I knew, but Jerry's words kept coming back. I could seek him out at a later time, and then he could pass along to President Morgan, what I was presently keeping secret. I wouldn't be surprised if they already had knowledge of most of it. Thanking Dr. Strang, I turned to leave as Sarge came up from behind the desk and followed me out the door. Moving in a semi trance down the corridor toward the entry hall, I thought of Claudia.

I wouldn't be able to keep my word to President Morgan, I would have to tell her. She could tell me all she knew about the Whateley's and Dunwich. I needed to know why Joe Osborn would send Lister to bring her home, or if that was all a ruse. Now my thoughts rolled like numbered ping pong balls in a bingo cage at full crank. Maybe Claudia had been the intended target at Pembrook instead of Elspeth. If they had sacrificed Elspeth, maybe Claudia was next. The Lister episode at Dean's Drive-In supported that belief. I hurried my pace as the Bell Tower chimed the half hour. The sound of the bells didn't pull my eyes away from the western horizon, where pinkish, mare's tail clouds rose above the trees. That terrible feeling of doom filled me from head to toe. I struggled to push it away in an attempt to put myself in the right frame of mind to meet Claudia.

Dashing around the corner of the annex, I half expected her not to be there. Then I heard, "There you are, hey, kookie! Thought I was going to have to find another boy who looked like a movie star."

Claudia stood at the top of the steps, grinning, hands on hips. I stopped, put on my happy face, and grinned back. It was poodle skirt day, again. This time, light blue with a more detailed poodle. It was a snooty looking dog with its nose up in the air and eyes closed like it was better than all the other poodles. She wore a white, short sleeved blouse (tucked in this time), and her typical bow matched the skirt. Her hair hung in spirals and I wondered if she had made it that way on purpose.

"A new hair-do?"

"Ah… no, just does that after I wash it. Takes a night of sleeping on it and a few brushings to calm it down. Thought I'd make it nice for you."

Walking up the steps I stopped in front of her as a group of students came out the door, one of them, Sissy.

"Oh, hey, Sterling," she said and batted her eyes at me as she passed. Claudia saw it and projecting a mock gasp, pretended to slap me.

"Oh, you're in trouble now, mister."

I looked back to see Sissy and her group had stopped on the walkway, all smiles. Claudia grabbed the front of my shirt and I brought my face back to her to be met by soft lips. I heard Sissy and the others giggle, with one of them saying, "Well, blows my chance, no way I can match that."

Claudia giggled and taking me into a tight embrace, I hugged her as well. It felt so good to hold her, and I experienced a most prodigious sense of contentment. She pulled her face back but didn't let go. Her eyes were lively as she smiled and said, "I have a confession and I think now's the time to tell you. Sterling Rice… I think I'm in love with you." Blushing, she cast her eyes down as several gasps escaped from the mouths of the group still gathered at the bottom of the steps.

"Are you sure about that, Miss Osborn? Because I don't want any messing around."

She released me and bringing her hands to my chest, she rubbed her palms up and down. One hand stopped and played with a button. "Of course, I'm sure, Mr. Rice. Nothing on this earth feels as good as this does."

Looking over my shoulder at the crowd of girls, I said, "You heard that, right?" They all nodded at me and each other, tittering. "Okay, you can all go on now, shows over." They laughed and walked away toward the cafeteria. Heads came together with loud whispering and the occasional glance in our direction.

Looking into Claudia's face, I saw that her eyes had grown moist.

"Okay, Miss Claudia Osborn, I have to be honest with you… I believe I too… have fallen." Giving her a confident smile, she closed her eyes and sighed. When she opened them, I watched a tear slip from the corner of the left one, and she moved to wipe it away.

"No… let me," I said, tenderly blocking her attempt.

I leaned down and kissed the tear where it had stopped on her cheek. I focused on its saltiness and the softness of her skin. Her own lips soon found mine and we held them nearly motionless for several seconds, before I pulled back to ask, "So, why the tears, this time?"

"Just like the last time, silly. Haven't you ever been so happy it made you cry?"

"Well, I suppose… once or twice when I was a kid. This could be one of those moments, it's just… we are not in private right now. I don't cry in public."

"Well, maybe you should, Sterling Rice," she said and bringing the side of her face to my chest, she squeezed and giggled into my arm pit. The door behind her opened and Professor Ellery (the younger) walked out. Looking back, Claudia blushed and stepped back, smoothing the front of her skirt.

"Afternoon, Professor," I said.

"Professor Ellery," Claudia added.

He stopped, and looking at us through thick glasses, gave us a half smile. "Hello Claudia... set for finals? Keep up the good work." He continued down the steps and without looking back, he added, "Good day, Mr. Rice."

I watched him move toward Faculty House and he stopped a second time to look back over his shoulder. "Oh, and maybe find a more appropriate place for your love making?" he said flatly before continuing. Claudia tried not to laugh, but a squeak escaped her tightly clamped lips and I chuckled.

"Love making... he obviously doesn't know anything about true love making... or at least, mine. Maybe he should read Kinsey's book," Claudia said, taking my hand.

"No doubt."

We laughed together and then she spun me around, trying to force me to sit. "Sit down. I want to stay here for a while. The sun's around the corner now, so it won't fry us like a couple of eggs."

"Eggheads is more like it," I said and did as she asked. She sat behind me, one step up. Pulling her skirt over her knees, she had me rest against them as she leaned forward and wrapped her arms around my chest. "You see, Sterling, this way no one can see my thinly veiled private parts. You're shielding them from wandering eyes."

She giggled and added, "I could have worn my petticoat, but I hate those things. I like the freedom of feeling the air moving around my fat butt and..."

"Fat butt? It's anything but... a fat butt."

She laughed at my pun and said, "You think so?"

"Yes, I think so. I suppose I'm one of the few who have seen it and compared to Sally Conklin next door at Loring... you've got the derriere of a mouse—no contest."

"Well, I don't know who that is, but... I'll take your word for it," she said as she massaged my shoulders.

"Claudia?"

"Yes?"

201

"I have something I want to talk to you about. Something serious. I don't want to ruin the mood, but I have to tell you."

"Is it about the dead guy over at the library? Beatrice told me all about it. Said somebody stole that big ugly book. Good riddance, I say. I mean...not about the guy who was killed, but... that book. It gave me the creeps."

"Well, it should. Do you know the history of that book? It has something to do with Dunwich. So... yeah, that's kind of what I wanted to talk about."

"Okay, least I got you talking, and I don't scare that easily. So... let's hear it."

She took out a piece of Dentyne and popped it into her mouth. Then leaning out past my shoulder, she looked into my face and grinned. "Hold tight!" she sang out and spread her knees. I fell back against her and felt the heat.

There came a tell-tale odor that told me she had gotten her period. Wrapping her arms around me again, she put her chin on my shoulder and said, "Okay, spill the beans."

"Okay... so, Saturday night at Dean's, Lister said something about your father being sick. Do you suppose that's true?"

"Honestly, I don't know—but I don't care. There's a real good chance that my father just found out I'm attending M.U. What I don't get, is why he didn't just come here himself, unless he really is sick. But why a Whateley?"

"Maybe a ruse, maybe Lister figured if he could fool you into thinking your father needed to see you because he was sick, you'd go with him without a fight."

"That's the scary part. So, if it wasn't true—what would they want with me?"

I felt a chill as I thought back on what President Morgan had said about Elspeth and human sacrifice.

"That night Mordechai was chasing that peeper about the terrace back of Pembrook, are you sure that wasn't Canaan Whateley?"

"I don't know. It's been years. He wouldn't look the same, right? It was dark, we were on the second floor, and he moved pretty fast."

"I'm for certain it was, and I suspect it was him and Lister who took Elspeth. I have a feeling they thought she was you."

"So... I might be a little responsible for Elspeth being kidnapped?"

"I wouldn't go that far. That's like saying you're ruining the world because you're breathing."

She kissed my ear and squeezed me a little tighter. The warmth of her body took away that chill, coupled with memories of the first time we made love.

"Well, at least we only have to deal with Canaan, now that Lister's in jail."

"That's what I need to tell you, uh... Lister's not in jail. He escaped, or, was let go on purpose. I, and maybe a few others, suspect he's the one who killed Lyle. I think there was some kind of a deal between them. Money changed hands and access was granted to the Necronomicon. Lister's still out there, hiding. I'm afraid it is just a matter of time before he shows up again. Claudia... I feel you're in more danger than you think."

"The police are on it, though, right? I mean, sure, I'll have to be careful. Maybe I shouldn't be out running around after sundown, or going into dark, shadowy places, and stuff like that?"

"What makes me concerned is that he had no qualms about walking right into Dean's front door. Stupid or brave... still dangerous."

I looked at her face out of the corner of my eye. She had fallen into thought. Her eyes were distant. A long sigh escaped her lips, but she remained silent.

"You should call Anton."

"Think so? He'll tell my mom and she'll just worry."

"I'd suggest it. He might have some advice. Maybe he could pull some strings on his end if he had an idea of what's going on over here in Arkham. Maybe get some troopers sent to Dunwich undercover, so to speak; if they aren't there already."

"Like I said before, Sterling, I don't scare that easily. I was hoping for a peaceful life here and I thought that was just what I was getting. Dunwich is like a bad dream that keeps coming back. I could easily just

transfer to another university, someplace too far for this to follow. But…
now there's you."

"So now, I'm the one who will feel responsible if something bad
should happen."

"I'm sorry, but… unless you tell me, right now, to go away… I'm
not going anywhere. I love you, Sterling Rice, and I'm hoping you love
me as much."

I sensed she was waiting for an answer to a question she hadn't really
asked.

"In that case, I will tell you again, I love you, too, Claudia Osborn.
So, I guess… we are staying right here, huh?"

She turned my face to her and kissed me on the lips. Sarge surprised
us by getting up from where he had been laying, and pushing his muzzle
in, started licking our faces. We pulled away, sputtering. Claudia
laughed and clamping the big dog's head in her hands, she pushed her
nose to his.

"Oh, Sarge, I love you too… but don't you get any ideas, mister."

He licked her and scampered away. Stopping on the cobblestone
apron at the bottom of the steps, he did a playful doggie bow. With his
front legs splayed, his rump in the air, and his tail wagging, he woofed
at us. Then charging away, he turned and came back, stopped, and then
repeated it. Running left, then turning right on a dime, he finished by
running in tight circles. Then plopping himself down, he lay on his belly
out in the grass, panting.

Claudia jumped up and I feared she was going to give us her version,
but she grabbed my hand instead. Pulling me to my feet, she took off
running, leaving me no option but to follow. Sarge came to his feet,
barking. People passing, stopped to watch the two fools, and the dog,
make their way to Dyer Hall. Once inside, Claudia kicked off her loafers
and pulled me down so that we lay across the mattress. I kicked off my
shoes, and we remained there looking into each other's eyes. Sarge lost
interest in us and went to his bowl to drink.

"The good news: I got my period. The bad news: no sex until it's
gone. Sorry."

"No, don't be. But just so you know… I don't mind sex with a
period."

"I do," she said matter of factly. "Can't we just lay here, together—quietly?"

"Certainly," was the last thing I remember saying, and Claudia, fighting to keep her eyes open, was the last thing I saw before popping awake much later in total darkness.

The phone out in the entry hall was ringing with what seemed like urgency. My mother's words, 'When the phone rings at three in the morning, someone's dead' rolled through my mind. Grabbing my alarm clock, I held it close to my face and felt a shudder roll up my spine, it was nine minutes after three in the morning.

Jumping to my feet, I hoped to stop the ringing of the phone before it woke the house. Claudia sat up as I turned on my desk lamp. She rubbed at her eyes, blinked and mumbled, "What's the tale… oh, the phone. Geez, must have fallen asleep. What time is it?"

"Ten after three."

"Crap, I suppose I missed Pembrook's curfew, huh? Oh well, going to have to come up with another excuse for the warden."

"I wouldn't worry about that right now; I got a bad feeling that something worse is brewing. Be right back," I said, and going out, I pulled the door shut but didn't let it latch. I found the outer doors to the dormitory secured. So, Cliff was doing his job; much to my relief. Pushing through the inner set, I grabbed up the telephone receiver.

"Hello? Who is it? You know damn well it's three in the morning, right?"

I waited for someone to speak, but there was only a gurgling noise and gasping. I just about hung up thinking it was a practical joke, but then I heard a clock chime the quarter hour. It was my mother's century old Ingram and behind that, the sound of Whip-Poor-Wills. There came a groaning, followed by the sound of someone falling and a handset bouncing off of a wooden floor. The bird's piping picked up its pace. Slamming the receiver down, I dashed back to my room. Claudia was slipping on her shoes when I burst in and she said, "What's going on?"

"Somethings wrong at my mother's, I'm heading over there," I said, grabbing my keys.

"I'm going too, and you can't stop me."

205

She jumped up and Sarge followed. They both ran out of my room and I locked up. Stopping just long enough to make sure the night latch would set when I shut the outer doors, we then flew across the quad.

We were about halfway there before I realized I ran barefoot. By the time we got to the corner of College Street and Crane, we were out of breath and even though wet, my feet had sustained no injury. Passing the cottage next door, we were met by a flock of large birds rocketing away from the area below my mother's window. The flapping whoosh of their wings passed over us as they fluttered away into the sky, their voices silent.

We leapt up the steps two at a time. Only one light lit the front parlor and the door stood wide open. I came inside as Claudia stopped at the threshold; her hands clamped tightly around Sarge's collar. I suspected she was concerned about intruding, not being family, or, having an invitation. But seeing my mother lying there on the floor, I sensed it didn't matter much anymore.

Dressed in her night gown, she lay on her back with one knee up, her head pointing toward us. The parlor rug was bunched up like an accordion as if the heels of her bare feet had ridden over it, again and again. Her right arm lay bent on her chest, the hand forming a claw. Her left had locked onto to the leg of the coffee table, leaving me to believe that she felt if she could keep a grip on something tangible, she wouldn't have to depart this world.

Her eyes were wide open, as was her mouth, but she wasn't seeing anything. In the dim light of the hurricane lamp in the corner, I watched the blueness creeping into her face. Falling to my knees, I pried her hand loose from the table leg, then grabbing her by the shoulders, I pulled her up into a sitting position and shook her.

"Mother! Its Sterling, mother? What's wrong? Tell me what's wrong, so I can help you."

I had never felt such panic in all of my life. Any sense of reasoning left me and moving my mother to my lap, I rocked her as if it would help. I had some sense of Claudia righting the telephone stand and placing the phone back on top. I wanted to lash out and tell her to leave it alone, but a faraway voice in my head said someone should call an ambulance. Then the sound of her dialing, followed by a mature little girl's voice requesting one to come to staff housing at the campus.

Footsteps moved toward the door, and then I was alone. I held Elsie, staring into her face, saying, "Mother? Mother! MOM!" Those words just kept coming out of my mouth and I couldn't stop saying them. Then I felt hands on my shoulders and lips at my ear. I recognized Claudia's voice through her sniffles as she said, "Just lay her down, Sterling. She's gone. We can't help her, now."

"NO!" I said, pulling the body to me. My mother's cheek came against mine and I could feel the deathly coolness of it. I started to weep uncontrollably as the sound of the ambulance filled my ears, granting me reprieve from the sound of my own sobs. Then the attendants were there. A distant voice telling me to let them have her, followed by them peeling my hands loose. Someone tried to lift me under my armpits and pull me to my feet. Getting up, I looked back to find it was Claudia.

Turning away from her, I stood in a daze, watching the attendants through my tears, as they checked my mother's vital signs. The smaller man looked at the other and shook his head. A third came in with a stretcher and then Claudia taking my hand and leading me out onto the porch. We moved to the chairs and she put me into my mother's favorite Adirondack that sat just to the right of the front door. Dr. Goldman appeared on the lawn and ran up the steps.

"Sterling," he said, his stethoscope glinting surrealistically in his hand as he rushed past. Kneeling down beside me, Claudia tried to hug me over the arm of the chair and bringing her lips to my ear, she whispered, "I'm so sorry, Sterling. Sorry that I never got to meet her."

It took me a few minutes to realize her words were subtly telling me that my mother was not coming out of this. I wanted to argue and tell her there was a chance, but the words stuck in my throat. The commotion inside seemed far away. People from the surrounding cottages had gathered on the cobblestone walk, their faces all a blur in the pole lamps illumination, a red light flashing repetitively across them every two seconds. I started to feel an ache in my hands and realized I was gripping the arms of the chair so tight that I might accidently rip them from their anchors.

Then the attendants scuffled passed carrying the stretcher, a sheet draped over my mother's face and body. Gasps rose from the crowd followed by the slamming of the ambulance doors. The red light stopped its incessant revolving and the vehicle pulled away as if they had all the time in the world.

Dr. Goldman was beside me now, his hand on my shoulder. His voice sounded as if he spoke from a drum, "We are taking her over to St. Mary's, Sterling. Can you meet me over there?" I heard Claudia's assuring, "Yes, most certainly."

"Terribly sorry, Sterling," he said and walked away. Bouncing down the steps, he hastened in the direction of the hospital. Claudia stood, and moving to the door, I heard her fiddling with the night latch. I assumed she had set it so we wouldn't be locked out if we returned. Then moving back to me, she peeled my hands loose from the arms of the chair and with a little grunting, actually lifted me out.

"Come with me, Sterling, we need to go over to the hospital."

We walked down the steps as the crowd moved away, boys from Dyer, Sandra Heinz leading a troop of girls from Loring. Along with them, the familiar faces returning to the cottages, Professor Bigley from the School of Medicine with his wife, Peggy, Professor Elery of the School of Science with his wife, Prudence, Dean Farr and Lisa, Cliff Breckingham in a spotless new uniform, Betty, with her skinny as a rail husband, Langston, Myrtle, the head of housekeeping with her new husband, ol' Ross Bailey (a carpenter up from the now non-existent ton of Gowan), Coach Cobb, Dr. Goldman's wife, and ol' Tom Scruggs, the head of the Physical Plant along with his wife, Ethyl, plus Doctor Strang, Alice Payne, Doctor Corning, and young Professor Cecil Ashley from Faculty House.

We moved up the sidewalk along Boundary Street with me in a trance, Claudia's arm around my waist. I vaguely remember Sarge panting behind us as we cut between the Sports Complex and the Gymnasium. It seemed like forever before we walked up the steps of St. Mary's.

Sarge stopped just outside and sat where he could see through the doors. Claudia went to the desk to tell them why we were there. They made us sit in the waiting room, anyway. So, we did that, Claudia rubbing my back, and me feeling glad there was no one else in there besides us.

I remember drinking bitter coffee even though I didn't like the stuff. Some time passed, and then people I knew, but barely acknowledged, came in and then departed. I remember Dean Farr standing before me, speaking briefly with Claudia. I remember a sobbing Sandra who spoke only to me as she passed on her way to the front desk. She became angry, threatening the nurse because she couldn't get the answers she wanted. She stomped out without a word, ignoring Claudia altogether.

Professor Strang soon appeared and patting me on the shoulder, gave me his condolences. He spoke to a nurse, then demanded a doctor, who must have told him what he wanted to know. Putting his hand on my shoulder afterwards, he kissed Claudia on the top of her head and thanked her before going out.

The caffeine helped to bring me out of the shock of the moment. Even though I felt more aware, it still seemed all so surreal. Then we were taken into a consulting room, where Dr. Goldman explained that my mother had suffered a fatal stroke. Nothing could have been done to save her.

I asked why she chose never to tell me; she must have known if she had hypertension. There was a shrug and, "I'm sorry, Sterling." After a minute, I realized there was no way he could have known. He suggested I contact her physician if I had questions, and then suggested we return to the campus.

Sarge had patiently waited outside and hooking up with us as we came out the door, we headed back to Dyer Hall as day dawned in the east. Claudia took my keys and unlocked the outside doors of the dormitory for the day. Once in my room, I sat down on the edge of my bed, feeling exhausted. I watched Claudia walk out and prop the inside doors before disappearing into the entry hall. I heard her dial the phone and a few seconds passed before she said, "Miss Mordechai, Claudia Osborn here." Then she went silent and I figured Mordechai was giving her an earful, but then Claudia continued, "Dean Farr? So, he's been in touch? Okay, okay… then you're aware. Super! Goodbye."

It seemed so odd to hear her conduct serious business in that little girl voice. It made me realize how important her body language and facial expressions were. Over the telephone it would be hard to take her seriously.

She returned and sat down beside me, not saying anything. Then rubbing my back, she looked longingly into my face. I kept my eyes glued to the floor as memories of the early years with my mother, flooded in. That's when I broke down completely.

Claudia wept right along with me. I soon felt an intense anger rise up. Life had deprived me of a chance to reconcile things with my mother. So, I paced and ranted. Claudia just sat on the edge of the bed and listened, eyes wide, occasionally nodding in response to rhetorical questions. Sarge sat in his bed tracking my movements, a look of concern on his face.

It seemed hours went by before I felt cleansed of any guilt or responsibility; real or not. Returning to Claudia, I lay down and cried into my pillow, her hand tenderly caressing my back.

I soon calmed and just lay sniffing. My hand strayed to Claudia's thigh and I patted her. My brain had experienced some kind of subconscious upheaval. I would be okay, though. Nothing much would change as my mother had distanced herself long before this day. I just felt so much like I had been cheated and then sat pondering what clues I may have missed that could have averted this moment. Guilt.

Claudia got up and fed Sarge. Then returning, she held my hand, not saying a word. I felt all cried out by noon and Claudia left me with a promise to return after her afternoon class was over. I remained in my bed, thinking about all that had happened and all that needed to be done.

I knew it would take some time to work through my grief. We had mourned my father for almost a year. I suspected it would be less for Elsie Myra Grangerford-Rice. She had saw to that, and perhaps that had been her plan all along.

Sarge moved up onto the bed, and lying beside me, he licked my face. Then placing his head on my chest, I fell asleep, caressing his thick fur, assuring him with touch and words that, without a doubt, he was the best dog in the world.

XIV

Grave Girdled Ground

I was awakened by the ringing of the phone. The shadows in the room said mid-afternoon. The phone rang a second time, and I wished for Casper to get it, but he would be in class. Rolling out of the jumble of blankets, Sarge met me as I went out, and he moved to sit by the front doors. Picking up the receiver I said in a raspy voice, "Dyer Hall."

"Sterling, Mrs. Samuels here. President Morgan would like to see you in his office. Can you come now?"

"Yes, give me a few minutes."

"Very well, I'll tell him. And Sterling… sorry about your mother."

"Ummm… thank you. Tell President Morgan, I'll be there soon."

There came a click and I stood in a daze, still trying to wake up. I floated in a bubble and nothing seemed real. Yet I told myself it would be alright, everybody would understand. The word would get around fast and just like when my father died, I knew what to expect. Except this time, a kind of loneliness seeped in, making me realize how much I counted on somebody to be there, to be—somewhere. It felt like my mother had been an anchor that I had been tethered to. A regulator that kept me grounded. The tears tried to come again, and I fought them. It dawned on me that I still held the handset. I hung it up and walked out onto the veranda. Sarge pushed the door open with his nose once he heard the knob turn. I could have sworn I heard him sigh as he drained his bladder just outside on the grass. I stood, leaning against a column, watching him, his leg raised high in a kind of balancing act. Instead of running to examine other potential targets, he came right back and sat beside me to stare up into my face, a question in his eyes. He whimpered

211

and put one of his big paws on my leg, kind of like he knew something had changed.

"That's right, boy, things have changed, but don't worry, I'll be alright. It may take a while, but I'll be alright." It was more like I was trying to convince myself than him, figuring if I said it out loud, then it would have to be true. He whined and cocked his head as he studied my face. I patted his paw and he dashed away out onto the lawn. I jumped off the veranda and headed for admin.

"You can go right in, Sterling," Samuels said, when I came through the door. Sarge pushed past and she only gave him a look of disgust before turning back to her paperwork. She would have normally thrown a fit and then demand that I remove him. But today she made an exception. I guess Samuels did have at least one ounce of compassion.

Through his open door, I could see President Morgan on the phone. I slipped inside and he motioned for me to shut the door and have a seat. Rather than take one of the two chairs positioned in front of his desk, I sat at the back of the room where four, large, reddish-brown leather chairs, inundated with brass upholstery tacks, sat in a semi-circle with small, but fashionable tables between them. It's where the 'big-wigs' sat, smoked, and planned. Sitting in front of Morgan's desk was too much like when you got in trouble in school and were sent to the principal.

He said goodbye to whomever he conversed with, thanking them profusely for undertaking some task. His manner led me to believe it had something to do with my mother.

"Sterling! Glad you could come."

Coming around his desk, he walked to me and I got to my feet. Taking my hand with one of his, the other grasped my forearm as he said, "So sorry about Elsie. I made inquiries' as soon as Dr. Strang informed me of your loss. You don't have to worry about a thing... I mean about funeral arrangements or the service. I suspect she anticipated this day as Wilmarth's Funeral Home has informed me everything had been prearranged. That's who I was just speaking with."

"And the cottage? I suspect it will have to be cleaned out?"

"Don't worry about that right now, Sterling. There's no hurry," he said, putting a hand on my shoulder and giving me a look of assurance.

"Elsie's obituary has been taken care of by Mrs. Samuels. The service and funeral will be Wednesday. She, of course, will be interred with your father over in Christ Church Cemetery. Would you like to say a few words that day?"

"Uh… no. Couldn't do that."

"Okay, I understand. Ten o'clock then, on Wednesday. Oh! And Lyle Umberling's won't be until Friday if you wish to know. You worked with him, so I thought maybe you'd like to go up there. Sadly, it will be over in the cemetery on Hangman's Hill. We haven't been able to locate family. The service will be short. The university is covering the costs. The man had worked for us for many years. We are, ummm… going to keep up the impression he wasn't involved in the theft, even though fingers are pointing that way. No sense maligning the dead."

President Morgan still had my hand and squeezing it slightly, he added, "Have to get back to work, Sterling. Thanks for coming over. We'll be in touch on matters of her property and the cottage. Once again, I am terribly sorry. Take time to mourn. I'll see you on Wednesday."

I had nothing to say. Thanking him, I called Sarge and we left. My mother may have been prepared, but I wasn't. I never thought about what I would do when this time came. I could say the hard part had been taken care of; the university was looking out for me. I only had to stand by as a sorrow filled observer. One never knows how they are going to feel. Grief could come as does the mist that rises nightly in Arkham, obscuring one's sight for a short time, or as a tidal wave, dashing you on the rocks. Mine was the latter, and it was unexpected.

I didn't know how to feel about Lyle. I suspected he acted out of desperation. A need for money. He had been duped by the Whateley's and in all probability, through Hutchins. So, I would show up at his interment just to pay my respects, and, with an adequate amount of self-control. Elsie's service was another story altogether. Dread seemed to fill me from head to toe. I would be on display for all to see. So much for my rule about crying in public.

The next few days were a blur. Familiar faces came and went as we progressed through the whole process. The service at the chapel, the burial where I sat with Claudia and Sarge as the M.U. staff and faculty stood behind us. People from my mother's social circles offered condolences but left me at a loss for lack of recognition. Chief Solum, Dean Farr, President Morgan, and Dr. Strang all showed up. Claudia remained with me throughout the whole affair, dressed in a black, short sleeved shirtwaist with pearls around her neck and soft black gloves. Skipping all her classes and breaking many rules, she stayed by my side. Holding my hand, she offered comforting words and hugs during the times I thought I would break. She had even wrapped Sarge's collar in black ribbon and kept him close by on his rarely used leash. He had accepted her, and even though he detested the tether, he followed her commands and managed to behave well enough for the occasion. Nobody questioned Claudia's presence, leaving me to suppose the Q&A would come later.

Mrs. Goldman held a small gathering at their cottage, offering food and drink to the mourners. It became excruciating and I had to flee at the end of the first hour. My post funeral actions seemed based more on keeping face then laying myself bare to the masses. I felt guilty for not showing the people how I really felt. But I put on a good show and excused myself after what I considered to be a reasonable amount of time to stand on the front lawn, deep in thought. Claudia remained inside, I assumed to represent me. Sarge stayed with her, not fighting the lead still attached to his collar. There was a trust now and I was glad for it. I needed to be alone.

Going to my mother's cottage, I sat in her chair on the porch and wept with my face in my hands. Eventually Claudia showed, released Sarge from the leash and came to stand behind me, rubbing my shoulders and not saying a word. Sarge lay at my feet, his muzzle on his big paws, one eye on me. Soon the people began to leave the Goldman's cottage. When the last of them departed and their hosts came out to stand on the porch, Claudia, I, and Sarge, left my mother's cottage and headed for the dorm, thanking the Goldman's as we passed.

"If you need us, call us, Sterling," Mrs. Goldman said, wiping her eyes. "Yes, do so," the doctor added solemnly, raising a hand in goodbye. Claudia left me on the Dyer Hall veranda with a hug, a kiss, and a promise to reappear later to check on me. I watched her go and

Sarge started to follow, until he realized that I wasn't. Returning to sit beside me, whimpers and whines filled the air until I took him inside.

The dorm was as quiet as the catacombs that ran beneath it, and going into my room, I shut the door, pulled the shades and undressed in the dim light. Lying in my bed, with Sarge's head on my chest, I ruminated. Occasionally his eyes would travel to my face and a slight whimper would escape his lips as he tried to understand what was going on. It would be a long night.

***

Friday came and leaving Sarge in my room, I made for Hangman's Hill. Claudia had a class she couldn't skip. So, she promised to meet me later. Passing my mother's cottage, I noticed someone had shut all the curtains. I felt hollow inside as I studied the place, knowing that Elsie no longer moved within. There would be no more Moonlight Sonatas floating out on the evening air. Just a silent cottage that I had once called home.

I hadn't received any word yet as to whether I could expect help in cleaning out her belongings and was at a loss as to what I would do with them once I did. Too much work. Pushing it out of my head, I turned the corner and walked up Boundary Street to the hill.

Moving through the woods, I came down the other side and passing through the rusty, wrought iron gate, I saw the pine casket sitting next to a mound of earth. The pastor from West Church stood talking with Dean Farr. Looking east down the slope, I could just make out the Arkham police car through the lichen covered trunks of the ancient oaks. It had been parked along Boundary Street and I saw Chief Solum with Jerry making their way up through the trees, talking, and gesturing with their hands.

Once they arrived, we all said our hellos. The pastor started in with a short eulogy, read a few words from his bible, and that tied it up. The gravediggers struggled to lower the box into the hole with ropes. So, Jerry, and I, lent them a hand.

Dean Farr moved down the hill, talking with the pastor, Chief Solum stumbling along behind. Once Jerry and I finished, we moved to follow the others, the cemetery men muttering thank you's at us as they began to shovel in the dirt.

"Sorry to hear about your mom, Sterling. Two funerals in one week. Must be tough. Sorry I couldn't make it to your mother's."

"That's okay, I figured you were busy."

He stopped walking about halfway down the slope and grabbing my arm, I slid to a halt in the leaves and turned to face him. "Yeah, I was kind of busy. I also wanted to say…" and lowering his voice, he continued with, "I worked it so I could get Regina moved down to Gloucester. Made up a story to tell the Chief and had to finagle a way to haul her. The state police are aware and provided me with a car. Solum and Hutchins only know she left St. Mary's, but they're thinking Springfield. If the Chief finds out about me falsifying my report and lying, I'm in for a bit of trouble. So, keep your mouth shut, will you?"

"Certainly, it's not like I don't need a friend right now—an ally—so to speak? You're definitely him. So, can I ask… what about Lyle's murder? That's what it is, right?"

"That's Hutchins' baby. He snapped it right up. Probably so he can control the outcome. I'm doing my own unofficial investigation. What do you know about it? Heard you showed up at the crime scene."

"Matter of fact, I did. I overheard Hutchins saying, 'I knew this wouldn't work' and mentioned Lister Whateley."

"Oh boy! That's it, right there. Where were you when you heard that?"

"Just outside the library window, hidden by the fog. He passed me, making tracks for the library's front door. I was maybe, oh… ten feet away?"

"You might have to testify, Sterling. That little bit of information is enough to hang Lister and put Hutchins in the hoosegow. I'm going to call the state boys again today. Stay safe, Sterling." Without another word, Jerry moved away to join Chief Solum in the car.

I could see the pastor had left Dean Farr standing in the road and was now passing through the gate at the church's meditation garden. I joined the Dean in a walk back to the campus.

"Well, that's two in one week, Sterling. Hope we don't see any more for a while."

"Yeah, that's about all I can take."

"How are you feeling? Pretty bad, I imagine. I remember when my mother died."

I didn't say anything. My good memories were few. The heavy feeling in my gut would be there for some time as I adjusted to the change. My only regret was that our relationship hadn't been better, or maybe, that I hadn't tried harder to make it that way.

"I'm glad you came up here. It'll save you a trip to my office," he said without looking at me. With all that had happened, his statement left me to wonder what else might be coming.

"I wanted to tell you that Palance Kilham is ready to take your D.A. job right as we speak. There's been some discussion, and the powers that be, would like for you to take your mother's cottage. President Morgan wanted me to pass that along. Does that suit you?"

"You mean... to live in?"

"Yes, of course. That way we won't have to clean it out and if you're going to be teaching more this August, it certainly solves your housing problem. As long as you feel you can live there... lots of memories, I imagine. It is your boyhood home, is it not?"

"Well... yeah."

"So, will you take it?"

I didn't answer right away. Images came rushing in like a mob of people all trying to get through a door at the same time. I knew the answer would be yes, but there seemed to be a need to evaluate the situation.

"Sterling? Do you need more time to think about it? President Morgan and Dr. Strang would like to move on this by Friday of next week. So..."

"Yes, I agree. I mean... I will. I did grow up there. It is my home, too. It's just... I never thought I would ever be the master of the house, so to speak."

"Good, good. I'll inform President Morgan and he can deal with the board... not that they matter much in this kind of a situation. Not like it's going to cost M.U. any money."

Reaching into his pocket, he produced two keys on a small ring. One had a small piece of white tape on it, and in my mother's handwriting I saw, 'FRONT DOOR'. That would be the duplicate. The other was older and tarnished—my father's. Handing them to me, he said, "Hand off your Dyer Hall keys to Palance when the time comes, will you?"

"Certainly," I said, and the conversation turned to other things, mainly his planned fishing trip coming up in June. We separated at the Bell Tower and I returned to my room. I could move out anytime, I just had to let Palance know. He would take over and move his meager amount of property down the stairs. I felt bad for the boys. I wasn't sure if I should gather them all together for a prep talk or just let it sneak up on them. It fell into the category of: 'Thing's You Don't Like, But Will Be Good For You' That is, for them, not me. I expected a rebellion.

Casper must have picked up the mail. A pile of letters, mostly sympathy cards, lay piled on the floor just inside the door to my room where he had shoved them through the crack at the bottom. Sarge jumped off the bed, where he had been shredding one of the envelopes. Inside I found what was left of a condolence card from cousins over in Aylesbury. It smelled slightly of bacon fat.

Stacking the envelopes on my desk, I saw one of them came from the Independent Bank of Arkham, a manila envelope that hadn't been posted. I supposed it must have come by courier. Taking it with me, I went out and sat on the steps as Sarge did his thing. The formal letter within stated that my 'Trust' had become solely my own. I would have to go over and sign some papers. My father's money would become mine, my mother no longer the middleman. I didn't care. Other than food and clothes, it could just stay in the bank until it fell to dust. Maybe I could buy Claudia a gift, or Sarge, a new collar. Otherwise, it wouldn't hurt for it to just sit.

At the bottom of the letter, it informed me I would also have to make an appointment and go to the office of P. H. Geares, LLC, up in the French Hill district. There would be more papers to sign in order to take possession of the estate. The mantel clock, by which my mother regulated her life, and my father's boat, were two of those things. More property to be responsible for. Time for a yard sale. Send it all away. I didn't care. Well… maybe not the boat.

Stuffing the letter back into the envelope, I heard Sarge let go with that familiar woof and dash off toward the science hall. Claudia had just cleared the buildings steps and plodded my way, smiling as if she had a secret. Sarge danced around her, looking for the moment he could goose her. She still hadn't reconciled with her petticoat and the blue/brown pleated skirt blew in the breeze. There was a long sleeved, white angora sweater of the 'Fluffy' variety that emphasized her chest, and a light blue cardigan that she wore like a cape.

The raw ache in my gut was replaced with relief. I couldn't have been happier to see her. I remained seated as she walked up. Without a word, she tilted my face up with a finger under my chin and kissed me.

"How are you feeling? Any better?"

"Yeah... now that you're here."

She smiled big in an embarrassed sort of way, and batting her eyes, she leaned in and kissed me a second time.

"Well, I'm glad to see you, too," she said. "Had this horrendous test... so glad that's over. The pressure is off now. How was that guy's funeral?"

"Okay, if you want to call it that. Lasted all of ten minutes."

"Poor, old guy. What a life. Oh well, let's go inside, I have something I want to show you."

Once in my room, she laid her book on my desk. I kicked off my loafers and sat on the edge of my mattress, wondering what she had to show me. Sarge moved to his bed and started licking his balls, bringing a giggle from Claudia.

"Do you ever wish you could do that?"

"What? Lick Sarge's balls? No way!"

"No! I mean lick your own, silly."

She got to laughing and reached the point where she had to sit in a chair at the desk to keep from falling over. I too laughed so hard that I cried, not so sure it was because of the humor. Claudia noticed. To redirect her attention, I said, "But you know... he seems to like the taste. I don't think I'd want that. I mean, just the thought of my... ummm... in my own mouth. Well, you get my drift, right?"

Claudia stopped laughing and just sat grinning at me. She had baited me into this, possibly to cheer me up. Moving over to stand in front of me, she cupped my cheek and stared longingly into my eyes. I placed a hand on hers and said, "Hey, maybe we can just forget about who can lick their private parts, okay? What did you want to show me?"

"Oh, I'm not going to forget about it, but... what do you think of this?"

Letting the Cardigan fall to the floor, she pulled the angora sweater off over her head. She sported a rather risqué black bra that looked too small for her. "I stole this from Elspeth's dresser drawer. It's one of those Beau Bras by Lovable. I'm a thief now—all for you. What do you think? Like it?"

"Like to see it off of you."

"First, tell me you like it."

"Oh... I love it. Kind of small for you, though, isn't it?"

"It does hurt a little."

"Yeah, thought so."

She laughed, and with eyes twinkling, she undid its hooks and flung the brassiere. It draped over the back of my chair and then slithered off to fall behind. Before I could comment about how grateful I was that she had become an underwear thief for me, she was straddling my thighs, her eyes locked on mine. With her knees on the mattress, she rose up and pushed her breasts into my face. Throwing her arms over my shoulders, she demanded that I kiss them. I certainly was not going to deny her that, and my lips and teeth explored every inch. Tilting her face upward, her moans crescendoed to the ceiling.

When it seemed Claudia had all she could bear, she settled back into her initial position and went to opening my shirt. "I still have my period, so... still no sex, but! There are other things..." Winking, she grinned and peeled the shirt from my body. Then sliding backwards off my legs, she kneeled on the floor to unbutton my fly, the grating noise of my zipper loud in the room.

For a brief second, her eyes found mine and a mischievous grin formed her lips. Then taking a firm grip on the cuff of my slacks, Claudia whipped them off, taking my underwear with them as if she was pulling a table cloth out from under a full setting of dishes. My erection burst into view and stood at attention. Claudia's eyes changed from seductive to delighted as her eyebrows rose and her mouth formed a perfect 'O'.

Pushing in between my knees, her lips came up to find mine and we kissed passionately as she massaged my chest. She then surprised me by brusquely pushing me down onto my back so she could lie on top of me, tonguing my ear and gnawing at my neck.

I hadn't put my hands on her since she opened my shirt, but I felt that's how she wanted it. Claudia wanted to make it my day. Anything I tried to do for her would only disrupt her plans. Once again, she was going to have her way.

Her lips soon made their way down to my chest and stomach, where she stopped to run the tip of her tongue slowly around my belly button. I felt at any moment that the fire of lust would consume me and there would be nothing left but a pile of smoldering ash. My whole body spasmed and she stopped to study my face with sleepy eyes, saying in a matter-of-fact fashion, "Like I said—I'm not going to forget about it." Returning her lips to my quivering abdomen, she worked her way down.

XV

Dimly Rushing, Blindly Going...

We lay on our backs on the sheet, me without a stitch of clothing, and Claudia, still naked from the waist up. "How are you feeling?" she asked, "Better, I hope. I was kind of working toward pushing those blues away—least for a little while."

"Yeah, I know you came here to work your magic, but honestly, sex or not, I'm just really glad you showed up." I pushed the hair out of her eyes and saw the gratitude there. The clock told me we had been at it for almost an hour, or should I say—she had. I still felt spent, but in a satisfying sort of way. Something I had never experienced before Claudia. I wondered if I should also be grateful to Dr. Kinsey.

Sarge, still in his bed, stopped nudging something around on the floor with his nose and looked over at us, his tongue lolling. After licking his lips, he began to pant.

"What do you suppose he's thinking right now?" Claudia asked.

"Perhaps, we are a couple of idiots because we don't do it quite like he would?"

"You mean, doggie style? I wouldn't mind doggie style. Well... after my period, anyway."

"So, maybe next time, huh?"

"Okay, next time. Gives me so much to look forward to," she said and giggled. Then tweaking the end of my nose, she rolled onto her side, to face me.

"Well, it's a good thing dogs can't speak English. I'd be afraid Sarge would go around telling everybody what I look like without my shirt on."

"He might just tell somebody that your boobs are real, and that there isn't one single falsie in your purse."

"But I don't carry a purse?"

"Well… there you go."

She laughed and pinched my thigh. Then throwing her arm over my chest, she kissed my cheek. "Sterling, I love you."

I looked into the black pools of her pupils; the dim light having brought them to full dilation. They were searching mine as she waited for a confirming response.

"I love you, too, more than anyone... ever."

"I'm truly happy to hear that. I remember when I first saw you, I thought to myself, 'I wonder if that boy would like me.' I asked other people about you, but I guess I didn't ask the right ones. No one seemed to know—or care. Some said you were stuck up. I just really hoped if I talked to you that you wouldn't be mean. Then that day outside the library, you were. I thought maybe I should give up on that dream. But then you looked at me in a way that told me that I might be reading you wrong. Now, here I am. This is the second time we have been together without our clothes on, and you just told me that you loved me. It's kind of… well… a lot more than I hoped for."

Her hair had fallen to cover one eye, so, I rolled onto my side to face her and blew it back. She blinked and allowed it to return. "You know, I have some Dentyne in my skirt pocket?" she said and then gave me a quick kiss with a look that said she hoped I caught the humor. I grinned to let her know I had, but had to add, "Yeah, speaking of breath, maybe you should get yourself a piece, while you're at it." Claudia mocked a pout and poked me between the eyes with a fingertip.

I said, "You know… I think I'm the lucky one here," and moving my finger to her right breast, I ran it over the silky soft skin. She trembled slightly and her eyes closed for a second before she murmured, "That tickles."

I moved the finger up to her arm and rested my hand there. "Yep, there is no doubt… I'm the fortunate one in this relationship."

She started to say something, then thought better of it. Rolling over onto her back again, her hand found mine. We lay in silence, staring at the ceiling, our hands clasped and resting on the inside of her hip. I could feel her pulse through the rough wool of her skirt, and it told me her heart was doing double time.

I thought about the past few days, and how next week, about this time, I'd be back in my childhood home. I would miss Dyer Hall and suspected the residents would miss me. Palance wasn't such a bad guy, but he wasn't Sterling Rice. I hoped maybe some of the boys would stop over for a visit. The thought of taking possession of the cottage brought yet another thought, I was also the proud owner of the boat I had coveted since childhood.

"Claudia?"

"Yeah?"

"Remember I asked you about going boating?"

"Uh-huh?"

"How about... we go soon?"

"So, you have a boat and you want to take me boating? Sounds peachy. Can we have a picnic, too?"

"Sure, why not. I can get food from Betty over at the cafeteria. In fact, I'm sure she'd pack the lunch in a real basket if I asked."

"What is she, like... your mom? Oh... sorry," she said, and closing her eyes in dismay, she sighed heavily.

"No, it's okay. Yeah, kind of like my second mother, anyway."

"Sounds cool. So, when? Saturday? Can we go Saturday? I need a break before next month's finals roll around. Not that I'm worried, it's just, it's always such a hassle."

"I get it. I was there, once."

"I suppose I'd better get dressed and get back over to Pembrook. I do have some studying to do and I need to call home. It's been a while. Anyway, where's Elspeth's bra?"

We both looked around the room and she startled me by shouting, "Sarge! You naughty dog!" and then she giggled. He lay in his bed, the bra between his paws, his tongue working over the inside of a cup. When Claudia had vocalized her dismay, he looked our way briefly, gave us what could only be described as the perfect canine smirk and then returned to his treat.

***

Friday soon rolled around, and I left campus to take care of my business at the bank. Sarge went along to keep me company. The amount of money that my father had accumulated over his life, plus the insurance policy, amounted to a great deal. More than I anticipated. Elsie had barely made a dent in it. I knew she didn't care about the money any more than I. Her life had been all about my father—and status.

After the bank, I walked up to the French Hill District to see P.H. Geares. I hadn't made an appointment, but I figured if they wouldn't let me in to see him, I could simply make arrangements to come back later. I got in right away, and no one said a word about Sarge.

Geares was a tall, thin man with ashen features and no sense of humor. More like an undertaker than an attorney. He led me and Sarge into his office and sitting down in his chair, he opened a file folder that lay centered on his desk. It held no more than five sheets of paper. I took one of two leather chairs that faced the desk, and Sarge stretched out behind me on a fancy Persian rug. He groaned once as if in anticipation of the boredom to come and lay with his muzzle between his front legs.

Mr. Geares cleared his throat and began to read. He informed me that both my parents had left me all of their property along with a couple of E bonds, and much to my surprise, my father's blue, 1944 Oldsmobile. He told me that my mother had it stored away in McCabe's barn at his farm just outside of Arkham. She and my father had never driven it much. I figured there wasn't a kid in Arkham that wouldn't love to have it, but I wasn't one of them. I could care less. I planned to sell it. Maybe McCabe would take it in trade for a few more years of boat storage.

The Peterborough Speedster was the one thing I vowed to keep; it came with memories. The Oldsmobile—not so. When Geares finished, he gave me a big brown envelope which contained copies of those five sheets of paper as well as boat and car keys. Then bidding me good day, he showed me out, saying, "If you ever need a good civil lawyer, look me up." I walked out hoping I never would.

Strolling back through Arkham, I was in the best mood I had been in since my mother died. I felt all cried out, but that hollow, 'unfinished business' feeling hung in there. I expected there would be bad days to come where there would be more tears, especially when I went over to the cottage to check things out. That would have to wait until Sunday.

Claudia and I were going boating tomorrow and I planned on asking her to help me clean up the place. I feared the memories that may come when I boxed up my mother's more personal items. So, I wanted Claudia with me when that happened. But then I thought it odd because, before this year, I never wanted anyone to be around during those moments.

Two blocks from Dean's Corner Drive-In, Jerry passed me in his MG, going up the hill. The car skidded to a halt on the cobblestones and then reversed. He whipped it backwards into a narrow alleyway, pushing through the shrubbery that clogged its opening. He shut off the engine and the air grew quiet as I stared confused at the still waving bushes. The MG had disappeared completely; Jerry was the master of concealment. About ten seconds passed before, "Sterling, get your ass in here," emanated from within the green.

Pushing through the neglected privet and spirea shrubs, I did as he told me. It was a good thing he had the top up or he'd be cleaning twigs and branches out of that car for months.

"Get in, and leave that damn mutt outside."

I did as he asked, detecting urgency in his voice. Sarge got the hint and lay down under some ragged looking hydrangea on the passenger side where he attended to his grooming.

I squeezed into the MG and Jerry said, "How are you feeling? Boy, I remember when my mother died. Hard thing to take. The ol' man's still alive, though. Sometimes wish it were him and not her. Going to have to head back to Southie someday and see the old lush. Anyway, I wanted to tell you to be careful. The Whateley's have been seen around, and Hutchins has been acting weird. The state boys have an investigation going and that includes him. I think he feels them closing in. He won't even talk to me now, and the chief can't seem to get a word out of him. Just a matter of days, my friend, just a matter of days. Hey! You wouldn't be interested in a job, would you?"

"Nope, got other plans. Not that you cops are a bad bunch of guys. It's just… I'm built more for academia."

"Well, I need to say that there's no doubt in my mind that Hutchins is going away, probably that new prison up in Cedar Junction. I suspect he hasn't a clue that we're on to him. The Chief is going to have to fill in, and it looks like a lot of overtime is coming my way. Damn! This department is just too short handed for the size of Arkham."

Sarge jumped up to look in the window, his paws on the door.

"Would you get that fucking dog off my car? That mutt's scratching my paint!" I wanted to remark that if he was so concerned about that, maybe he should reconsider not driving through bushes. Better not, though. Bad time to lose an ally. Rolling down the window, I said, "No, boy," and pushed him away. He returned to his bush but kept his eyes on me.

Jerry had his eyes on me too, glaring. Then shaking his head as if in disbelief, he continued, "So… figure on a deposition very soon, and then a trial by jury. With your testimony, we are guaranteed a guilty verdict. You'll get a notice in the mail, or I'll just hand deliver it. Okay, well… that's it. Watch your back for Hutchins, and keep an eye peeled for those Whateley's. Give me a call if you see or hear anything worth my time, okay?"

"Sure thing, Jerry. Whatever you say. You suppose Hutchins might actually come after me?"

"Wouldn't put it past him. He'll try to catch you breaking the law or trump up a charge. If he ends up in the hoosegow, you're going to have to watch out for that wife of his too. She's kind of weirdsville—if you know what I mean. So… okay, I'll be in touch."

I didn't say anything, and he reached across and opened my door, sending me the message to get out. I did, and as I shut the door I started to say, "See you later," but he interrupted with, "Oh, and Sterling, stay close to that little girlfriend of yours. You do understand that she's not safe? Any one of those hooligans might try to use her against you. Now, Hutchins is kind of a candy ass, but he can make trouble by keeping the Whateley clan informed through Elvira. Edna Belsh over at the telephone office told me that there have been more than the usual number of calls coming out of Dunwich to Hutchins' place. A few of them from Osborn's mercantile. Your girl's an Osborn, if I remember correctly? Oh, and don't say anything about ol' lady Belsh, huh? She's scared to death as it is. Can't tell you what she's been hearing over that telephone line, but take my word for it—it's no good. Least we know where that Necro… Necromom… Where that damn book is! Okay, said too much already. See you later."

I had been standing there, my mouth hanging open. Along with that hollow feeling, there came an increased fear for Claudia. I think mostly because Jerry's word was official. I felt the anger rising up and imagined myself, tommy gun in hand, taking out the entire Whateley clan as they stood unsuspecting on the porch of Osborn's store. I honestly didn't know if Osborn's had a porch—but I didn't care.

Jerry started the car and shoved it into gear. I stepped back into the bushes, pushing my dog along with me as the red MG rolled away through the branches and leaves. Then calling Sarge to follow, I broke through the green into the street and headed for the cafeteria to see Betty.

She wasn't in her office, but since the door stood open, I used her phone to call McCabe. Surprisingly enough, he answered. I asked him to prep the boat for tomorrow and he assured me it would be ready by nine sharp. The slur in his voice left me doubtful. Whiskey made people forget things, making me think maybe I could use some of that about now.

Moving back through the kitchen, I found Betty doing her favorite thing—preparing dessert. Cutting cake slices, she carefully placed them on little plates. I snuck up behind her and said, "Boo!" but she hardly reacted.

"Sterling, my dear!" she said, and putting down her knife, she gave me a hug. "So sorry to hear about Elsie. It was so very… unexpected, huh?"

"Yeah, the saddest part was I didn't get to say goodbye. The last time I saw her, we had a big fight."

"Oh, my goodness, unfinished business. Never good… never any good. So, are you here for supper? You can eat at the faculty table, you know?"

"No. I mean… not here to eat. Got to get back to the dorm, getting behind on my work. But I do have a favor to ask."

"Oh, anything, Sterling. You must feel so lonely now. Sandra's in here a lot. But… oh, wait! Rumor has it, you've got a new girl?"

Betty gave me her, 'You naughty boy!' look and chuckled in a husky manner. "So, some Shirley Temple look-alike, I hear? I keep an eye open for her to come in, but I guess, she don't. Must be a Pembrookian's, huh? They have their own kitchen over there. A bunch of stuck-ups if you ask me. So, what's the favor? Ask, and you shall receive."

"Claudia and I have a date tomorrow. We want to picnic."

"Is that her name? Claudia? What a lovely name. Anyway…yes, I can make you up a nice basket, got a couple of the old ones back in storage for faculty outings. The wives like them. You are certainly entitled to one."

"Thanks, Betty. Can I pick it up about nine thirty in the morning?"

"You bet, kiddo. Oh my! This will be fun. I'm going to surprise you, okay?" she said, grinning and clapping her hands.

"Okay, I'm going now. See you tomorrow. Right after breakfast?"

"Yep," she said and reached out to wrap her beefy arms around me kissing me on my cheek. I pecked her back and gave her a quick squeeze. Stepping back, she took my hand, saying, "You've always been like a son to me, Sterling. Your father was always so kind to me, and I know Elsie tried and even though I don't care for those stuck up… well, if you ever need anything, you let me know, okay?"

I noticed her hazel eyes had grown moist and I felt the need to flee before mine did too. "Thanks again, Betty. I am always grateful that you came to work at Miskatonic. See you later…"

"Alligator!" she said, finishing it. Laughing, she slapped at her thigh and turning back to her desserts, she pushed loose strands of gray hair back inside her hairnet, wiped her eyes, chuckled, and said to herself, "Alligator—that's so funny."

I realized the room had gone quiet. Betty noticed the quiet too, and spinning around, she pointed her cake knife at the gawking workers and yelled, "Get back to work! This ain't no sideshow. The students will be here in fifteen minutes. We got some goulash to get done, and Benny Mitchell, you get that damn stogie out of your mouth, this instant!"

229

XVI

Daemons, Out Of Green Waters, Rise

The grandfather clock chimed ten and leaving my desk, I moved into the TV room. Friday nights were quiet until curfew because everyone was out on the town. Casper took advantage of Alex being away and stayed up in his room. I watched the weather to be sure we wouldn't get rained on tomorrow. The weatherman said, partly cloudy, but no rain. I called Pembrook and got Beatrice.

"Who? Claudia? She's in the shower. Is this the Tony Curtis guy?"

"Sterling."

"Sterling? What kind of a name is that? Are you, sterling? Like— shiny? Like—a knight in shiny armor? Oh, daddy-o, Claudia sure thinks so."

"Beatrice, could you please have Claudia give me a bell over at Dyer?"

"Certainly, big daddy. You know that you're four years older than she is, right?"

"Yes, I know."

"I'd like to date a grad student. Anyone over there you can recommend? Haven't dated in a decade. Dated in a decade… ha! That's funny, don't you think?"

"Beatrice… just tell her I called."

"You can talk to me, you know? Claudia won't mind. I'm kind of cute too, and…"

"Thanks, Beatrice," I said, and hung up.

I whistled Sarge out of the room and went out on the veranda. Sitting on the steps, I waited. The ground mist floated just above the grass. Another foggy night here in Arkham. All the lamps had been lit, so it

230

appeared Austen Ward had taken his task to heart. I felt a slight tug in my chest. I was already missing my job.

Cliff Breckingham, looking sharp in his brand-new watchman's frock, came into sight around the School of Science, a large, silver flashlight in his hand. I wondered if anyone told him what was going on. The Whateley's would probably leave him alone since they got what they wanted. Lyle's murder made me realize how dangerous the wielding of those keys could be. I trusted Cliff could handle it.

He must have saw me backlit by the porch light, so he waved. I waved back. He was full time now, and by a stroke of luck, his oldest son had landed the custodial job over at Lockley Hall. Good luck to the both of them.

Sarge came back up and whined after licking my face. I found it odd, but I figured he, like me, was missing Claudia. Going back inside, I returned to my work, waiting for her to call. Half an hour passed and still nothing. Going to the phone, I just stood there, staring at it. Even though our plans were certain, I felt I needed to hear her voice one more time before the day was over. I had to know she was okay. If she didn't call soon, I was going over there; Mordechai or no Mordechai.

Esdra came in and giving him a two second glance, I said nothing and turned my gaze back to the phone. Moving up the stairs, he stopped and leaned over the railing. Looking up, I found his fish-like face and googly eyes, unnerving. I wondered why anyone from Innsmouth would send their kids to university. It was a rather courageous step on his part. Esdra got a lot of crap for his looks, but he gave it right back.

"What's the tale, nightingale? Not going to ring just because you're staring at it."

"Oh, thanks for that, Esdra."

"You're welcome, Sterling. Good luck. Oh! Sorry to hear about your mom." He gave me a patronizing grin and showing his sharp, little fish teeth, he ran up the rest of the stairs to the second floor.

Tired of waiting, I gave in and dialed the dorm. "Pembrook! Home of the most beautiful girls in Massachusetts. Beatrice, here. How may I direct your call?"

"Beatrice… what? Are you sitting on that phone?"

"Oh, Tony, you do love me after all."

"Beatrice, get Claudia."

I heard Claudia ask, "Who is it, Triss? Did you say, Tony? Triss, is that Sterling? Triss, give me that phone."

I heard them tussling and Beatrice say, "No! It's Tony Curtis, and it's for me."

"You girls quit that, and hang up that phone or use it properly," Mordechai's voice cackled from the background.

"Yes, Miss Mordechai," the two girls said in patronizing unison, with Beatrice finalizing the event by saying, "Miss Mordechai, I have a question…" her voice fading away.

"Sterling, what's up? Everything okay?" Claudia asked.

"Uh, yeah, just wanted to hear your voice one more time before I hit the sack."

"Oh, you're so sweet. So, are we set for tomorrow?"

"Yeah, maybe about ten?"

"Sounds peachy. Can I meet you on the green in front of Pembrook?"

"Sure, Betty's making us a picnic lunch, complete with basket. I'll pick it up after breakfast."

"Cool! Can't wait. Okay, got to go, the Warden's giving me the eye. Probably because I'm standing here in just a towel and talking to a boy at the same time. Do you get the picture?"

"Uh, yeah."

"So, are you getting excited, now?"

"Claudia?"

"Yeah?"

"I also wanted to be sure, about… well, I had a talk with one of the Arkham cops. The Whateley's have been seen around. So, be careful, huh? Lock your dorm room tonight—and the windows."

"Don't worry, my dear, Captain Mordechai is on top of it. All hatches have been battened down. We're safe here at Pembrook with our appointed watchdog. She reminds me of one of those… what are they called? Oh yeah! Dobermans! That's it!"

"Okay… I'll see you tomorrow?"

"Yeah… and Sterling?"

"Yes, Claudia?"

"Love you."

I heard tittering, like a crowd of girls were standing behind her. After looking around and up the stairs, I said, "I love you too... more than words can say."

"Bye-bye," she said softly, and before hanging up, I heard her say to the others, "What? You're just jealous!" Then with a click, she was gone.

I heard Esdra's low chuckle come from the second floor and a door slammed. Palance's deep voice rolled down from third, yelling, "Quit slamming those damn doors or you're going to regret it! Got me?"

One more reason to have a place of my own. Least my telephone calls would be more private. Returning to my room, I went back to work with the occasional intruding thought as to how I might prank Esdra for eavesdropping.

Locking the doors at midnight, I figured the amount of noise taking place in the TV room, and up on the second floor, indicated the majority of the residents had returned. I kept hearing Palance's deep voice addressing one thing or another, telling me he was already taking control of the chaos that was Dyer Hall. I went to bed and fell right to sleep, only to be startled awake with a nightmare. Lister Whateley had been standing at the foot of my bed, a hunting knife the size of a small sword raised above his head.

Taking my alarm clock in hand, I held it close to my face and saw it was only three minutes after ten. Sarge lay on his back in his bed, his feet in the air, snoring like crazy. Rolling off the mattress, I went to a campus side window and pulled back the shade. Nothing but fog with scattered spots of light behind it. I got a terrible sensation that evil was lurking out there and wished I could see as far as Pembrook to know if a certain room light was still ablaze. Wiping the post dream sweat from my upper lip, I crawled back into my bed and comforted myself with memories of Claudia as I drifted off.

I woke up to the sound of somebody stomping down the stairs, yelling, "Got to go. I don't want to miss the bus," followed by the slamming of the doors. Sunlight snuck in past the shades and Sarge paced the floor between the bed and the door. Sliding off the mattress, I pulled on my robe and took him out, unlocking locks in the process. Traces of fog lingered, but the sky showed clearer than I expected. A good start to the day. The excitement I felt almost overrode that foreboding, and I stood there trying to will what remained of that dismal sensation away.

Back inside, I grabbed my bag of toiletries and went up to shower. Sarge followed instead of waiting by the closet door that kept him from his bag of food. I climbed into the shower and surprisingly, he followed me in. I wasn't sure if human shampoo was good for dogs, but I took advantage of the situation and gave him a good scrubbing.

Afterwards, I toweled myself and him dry. Doing a quick shave, I took almost half an hour to manage my hair, adding a little extra pomade in anticipation of boat driven winds. Back in the room, I fed Sarge, dressed in dungarees, my olive-colored work shirt, heavy socks, and old loafers. Then moving into the kitchen, I had a quick bowl of somebody else's cereal and milk. Making a quick stop back in my room, I grabbed my brown leather bomber's jacket. Figuring I might need my wristwatch, I found it buried beneath an assortment of things in my desk drawer. Slapping it on, I wound it up and set it to the grandfather clock in the entry hall. It was nine-forty. I had twenty minutes to go get the picnic basket and then—Claudia.

Grabbing my keys, I called Sarge so we could head over to the cafeteria. Betty met me just inside the back door of the kitchen, basket in hand. "Saw you walk past the windows. Have fun, hey kiddo?" she said, and winking, she turned back to the kitchen turmoil issuing orders to anyone she thought might be slacking off.

Sarge and I jogged toward Pembrook and crossing Church Street I saw Claudia sitting by herself almost in the center of the big dorm's lawn. It reminded me of that painting, 'Christina's World', perhaps because it showed a girl alone in a huge space. I had to push out of my mind, though, that the real Christina had a degenerative muscle disorder and had actually been dragging herself back to her farmhouse across the field. The complete opposite of Claudia.

Sarge ran up and started licking her face and then danced around her. Stopping, he gave me a look like he thought he should be rewarded for his discovery.

234

Claudia grinned and got to her feet as I walked over. Her pedal pushers were denim, and she wore the same light, tan jacket over a red and crème colored plaid shirt, a red bow to match. She had chosen bobby socks and sneakers for the day. A wise choice since we'd be off the beaten path; so to speak. For the first time since I met her, she wore earrings. A tiny blue gem punctuated each earlobe. I assumed it was a birthstone.

She closed the small paperback that she had been reading, leaving me to believe she may have been there awhile. Catching a glimpse of the title before she shoved it in her back pocket, I saw it was, '*Star Man's Son 2250 AD*', a story I knew and liked by Andre Norton.

"Good book?"

"Yeah, kind of scary though. I mean, Hiroshima wasn't too long ago. But it's just science fiction. Hey, you know us biology students, can't get enough of science, even the fictional kind. So… good morning, Sterling."

She tilted her head back for a kiss and bending down, I gave her one. Then dropping the basket, I picked her up. After putting her arms around my neck, she wrapped her legs around me and I squeezed her tight. She squealed happily and squeezed me back with what I considered to be an extraordinary amount of strength. Pulling her face back from my shoulder, she stared into my eyes for a few seconds before giving me a quick kiss on the end of my nose.

She dropped her legs down, as a clue to let her go, and moving to the basket she said, "Let's see what we have here. Some sandwiches… oh! BLT's, yum! Apples, oranges, a thermos of… let me see…" Twisting off the top, she nearly shouted, "Lemonade!" And then added, "Oh, and there's chocolate cake! Even a table cloth and napkins. Your other mom thinks of everything." Pushing Sarge's nose out of the way, she closed the lid.

"Yeah, Betty's been feeding me for years. She knows what I like."

"So… shall we?" she said, putting the two handles together and picking up the basket before taking my hand.

"Can't hardly wait for my boat ride."

"Well, don't expect too much. It's been a while. My father would never let me drive it... uh, pilot it. So, when I got mad at him, I'd sneak down and take it out. I suspect he knew, but never said a word."

"That's funny. He probably didn't want your mom to know. So, anyway, we can start out slow, and maybe, by the end of the day, do a fast run up the river just for the fun of it"

"I don't know about that. There's a lot of snags in this part of the Miskatonic. The little freight haulers have a tough time getting through without damage. Don't want to rip the bottom out. It's only been mine for a day."

"Oh, so it's yours now? Peachy!"

"Yeah, they read my mother's will yesterday. I got everything, of course. Boat, furniture, beds, rugs, the ancient mantle clock from the last century—and a car."

"A car? Wow! So, yeah, maybe we should take it easy with the boat then. Especially if we want to go for future trips with—our children."

Her statement came as a confession. Claudia was in this relationship for the long haul. I felt something I hadn't felt for a while. Joy. It mounted and rode my angst like a cowboy breaking a bronco. I found myself grinning and she noticed. "What are you grinning about? Do you have a secret? Tell me."

"Oh, it's nothing. Nice day, huh? Perfect for a picnic," I said, trying to change the subject. "We should go out to the island. There are some good places to picnic out there. One is a nice little glade right in the center. We could spread out the table cloth and eat, and then maybe..."

"Make out?" she said, grinning and raising her eyebrows several times.

"Yeah, that too."

My spirits soared as we strolled, her hand holding mine as they swung forward and back like a pendulum. We had to go around and walk outside the wrought iron fence that ran along West Street. Then we cut back east on Main, to go down the path I had taken the other day. As we stood waiting for traffic to pass, the Arkham squad car rolled by. Thinking it might be the Chief, I waved. But Hutchins sat behind the wheel and raised a hesitant hand in response. He slowed as he turned north to cross the Garrison Street Bridge. He must have been out for the

Chief on business. Probably trying to present an image that he still sought Elspeth's kidnappers. His presence quashed my stratosphere bound mood, but I didn't tell Claudia.

We were soon through the warehouses and on the river bank. Stopping just outside the east end of McCabe's boathouse, we studied the river.

"So, that's the island over there, huh?" she said, pointing.

"Yeah, that's it. Devils Altar Island they used to call it. But I haven't heard that for years. Kind of scary, huh?"

"Kind of exciting; don't you mean?"

"Okay, I'll go with that. There's a massive flat stone sitting on two smaller ones, outside the glade, on the downriver end. They say Indians used it for rituals. The, um… Pocumtucks tribe… or something like that."

"Well, we should go look at it while we're there, don't you think? Wish I'd brought a camera. We could take pictures of each other standing on it, or something. Beatrice has a Rolleicord I could have borrowed. Don't know how to work it though. But I'm pretty smart. I suppose I could have figured it out."

"That's okay, maybe another time."

"She'd probably want to know where I was going if I'd asked. Beatrice is not one you want knowing your business."

"Yeah, so do you want to wait here, and I'll bring the boat around to you?"

"Sure, Sarge will stay with me."

Setting the basket down, she fell cross-legged onto her derriere in the grass. Then calling Sarge over, she had him sit next to her so she could give him a good petting. Before I walked away, she leaned over and whispered in his ear as her eyes came back to mine. "Get moving!" she said, "We're going to tell each other secrets while you're gone."

I thought he would follow when I walked away, but he just sat there, taking in all the attention. I felt a pang of jealousy. Sarge and I had been together so long, our bond was unbreakable. But he had taken to Claudia without a second thought. Something I would have to get used to. It seemed silly that I felt envy toward Claudia—all because my dog loved her too.

"Be right back," I said.

I noticed more heel prints and boat keel marks in the sand where I had seen them before. There were so many, it had become one big quagmire of markings. I wondered if maybe we should forget about going out to the island. I didn't want to disappoint Claudia, who would probably want to continue anyway, even if I told her of the danger.

Going into the boathouse, I went to the end stall. As requested, the boat now sat in the water, tied at the bow. I had to assume McCabe had charged the battery. Looking things over, I saw he had placed two life jackets, a can of fuel, and a paddle inside the Speedster just in case the motor quit. Sitting on the bench seat behind the wheel, memories flooded in. My father's face, my mother with her hat, and the river glimmering in the sun.

"Sterling, be careful!" rang in my head, and I actually looked back, fully expecting to see my mother seated behind me. But there were only the swallows fliting in and out along with the pigeons cooing in the rafters.

Taking the key Geares had given me, I stuck it in and turned. The motor sputtered, caught, and quit. A second time brought better results, and with light blue smoke rising, the old Johnson purred at an idle.

Getting out, I untied it from the mooring post, and pushing it away, I jumped back in. When I cleared the sides of the stall, I turned it out into the river, briefly giving it the gas so I could idle down river toward Claudia. Rising to her feet, she brushed herself off, and picking up the basket, she walked to the shore. Sarge moved ahead of her, walking out into the water.

"Wow! Neat boat—old boat."

"Still a good boat," I said, as I helped her in. Sarge hesitated, splashing back and forth, and then with a few false starts, he leapt in. Shaking water on everything, Claudia shirked back, squealing her dismay as he moved up to sit behind the windscreen.

"Which way?" I asked, "Up—or down toward the ocean?"

"The ocean. Let's see how close we can get."

"Well, we can go clear to Kingsport, but that might take a while."

"To the ocean!" she shouted and laughed. Shielding her eyes from the sun, she pointed in the direction she wanted me to go.

"Okay, there are life jackets if you want them."

"Lifejackets? Geez, Sterling, I'm a swimmer! Lifejacket, my butt," she said, and moved aft to sit with her back against the transom. I put the picnic basket amidships and returning to the pilot's seat, I pulled slowly away, heading down river. We soon passed under the Garrison and Peabody Street Bridges and passing the small beach outside the French Hill District we saw a group of young people had gathered there. They shouted, waved, and then mooned us. Claudia laughed at the line of untanned bottoms and said, "Shall I moon them back?"

"Nah, save it."

"But I can show them a moon not so pale?"

"I knew it! You do tan on the roof at Pembrook."

"Yeah, but don't let it get around, huh? So, shall I?"

"Don't want you falling out. That would kind of ruin the day."

"Party pooper," she said, and pretended to pout.

After a while, the ocean came into view with its mammoth freighters going in and out of the port. I could see a small freighter, the familiar, 'SNAG RUNNER' being loaded for its late evening run to Aylesbury and some small towns in southern New Hampshire. Turning mid-stream, I headed back.

Sarge's paws were braced against the top of the windscreen as he sought the airstream. It blew his ears around and pushed his lips into a grin. Glancing aft, I saw Claudia sitting placidly, her face tilted to the sun, eyes closed.

Turning my attention back to the river, I noticed the east end of the island was quite overgrown with trees, shrubs, and thickets. They hung out over the water and I saw where a small boat could probably slip in underneath them and not be seen. I thought to pull in and dock to keep my boat out of sight, but Claudia said, "Don't stop, not yet, keep going… go up by Dun…Aylesbury. Yeah, Aylesbury, and then come back. I should be hungry by then."

"Aye, aye, Captain."

Picking up speed, I moved away, keeping an eye open for snags and sand bars. Looking toward the boathouse, I saw McCabe's old pickup parked outside, and McCabe himself standing, studying the west wall of the building. With a can of paint hanging from one hand, and a brush in the other, he looked our way. I waved and he did the same with the paint brush. Something else caught his attention, and setting the can of paint on the ground, he moved to the river bank to stare up toward the island.

Looking over my shoulder, I caught a fleeting glimpse of the Arkham patrol car parked on a rise in the road on the other side of the railroad tracks.

Hutchins was out of the car, walking down the access road to the boat dock on that side. The city had their flat bottom police boat moored at the ramp. Sometimes the Arkham cops would patrol the river within the city limits. I figured with Hutchins, it was more like an opportunity to catch, and harass, skinny-dippers.

I thought to turn the Speedster around and go back to see what he might be up to, but that would have been too obvious. My boat finally cleared all obstacles and I accelerated up the middle toward the bend in the river.

"Whoopee! Go Sterling, go!" Moving to the front, Claudia stood with Sarge, gazing over the windscreen, hair and ears wild in the breeze.

In no time, we were three fourths of the way to Aylesbury. The countryside changed quite a bit; becoming wilder, the river widening out. At one point, for a short minute, the shiny dome of what I knew to be Sentinel Hill came into view, its standing stones obvious even at that distance. Whateley country. Time to turn back.

"Turning around! So, hold on."

"Yeah, good idea, starting to get the heebie-jeebies, or... maybe I'm just hungry."

Changing places with Sarge, she slid over and threw her arm around my shoulders. Taking my eyes off the river for a second, I watched her face as she took in the scenery. She caught me looking and smiled. Putting a cheek against my upper arm, she placed her other hand on my leg, and I felt her release a sigh.

"This is so cool, Sterling. I have never been on a boat before. I feel so... free."

"I know what you mean. It's been a long time for me, but I still remember the days my folks and I spent boating on this river."

"I can only imagine. When I went home to Cambridge for the summer, last year, I spent most of the time shopping with my mother or hanging out in the house with her and Anton. No boating. No amusement parks. No, nothing. That was okay, I guess. They were always laughing and joking. We never got tired of each other. It made me happy, but even a few outings would have been nice. What about your folks? Or should I be talking about this? I mean, with your mom, and all."

"No, I mean... yes! It's okay. I never felt that close to either of them, even though I wanted too. If I have regrets, it's more because I never got to have what you have. I always hoped, somehow, my mother and I would have at least a few happy moments before she died. I actually feel a tiny bit envious of you."

Pushing the throttle lever forward, I slowed our speed as we approached the island.

"Oh, don't be jealous. We had our moments, too. Arguments, disagreements, and there were times when we didn't talk for hours. But it never ended without remorse and apology. Anton was always the one to be the voice of reason. I will be forever thankful for having left Dunwich and my real dad behind. It was the best choice my mom ever made. Marrying Anton was her second. You and I should be together as much as possible, Sterling. Because... well... maybe I'll rub off on you."

She laughed and her smile was infectious. We grinned together and then she tousled my hair. "Yuk," she said, and laughing, she wiped her now greasy hand on her pedal pushers. I wanted to take her in my arms right then, but with one hand on the wheel and the other on the throttle, I didn't dare.

"I think you've already rubbed off on me," I said.

"What? I didn't hear you."

"I said, you already have rubbed off on me. I think we got a good start. I feel... rather hopeful."

"Yeah, you rubbed off on me too," she said, wiping her hand on her pants again as if she couldn't quite free it of the pomade. She then lightly punched my shoulder to let me know she was teasing and said, "Don't get me wrong though, hair oil or not, I'm happy too." Kissing the index finger of her other hand, she pressed it against my cheek. "Why don't we go to the island now? It will be better for talking, and I'm kind of hungry. I was so excited this morning that I spent too much time getting ready and missed breakfast."

"Well, heading there now, hold on. I'm going to pull up onto that little stretch of sand."

Trees hung out over the water and before they blocked my view, I noticed the patrol car hadn't moved, and the police skiff was no longer at its mooring. I presumed Hutchins had gone up river to harass the mooners.

Sarge now lay in the middle of the boat on the floor. As soon as the keel scraped bottom, he leapt over the side and splashed around in the shallow water. Having had enough of that, he ran up on shore and squirted a couple of saplings. I got out and pulling the boat onto dry land with Claudia still inside, I tied the anchor to the mooring rope and dropped it behind a fallen log. She grabbed the basket and in clumsy fashion, made her way over the windscreen and out across the prow. Jumping off onto the sand, she fell to her knees, nearly crushing the basket.

I went to help her up, but she said, "I'm okay. Kind of a klutz if you haven't noticed already. Something you're going to have to get used to if you're going to be hanging around with me."

"I can do that... get used to it, I mean." Throwing an arm around her waist, I supported her as we moved up the slope to the path.

"This looks so cool. I want to see that altar stone. I've seen the one up on Sentinel Hill. It' so weird. I was with Bridget Bishop. We were only five at the time. She laid down on it and I got such a bad feeling. I remember thinking that any minute, wicked people were going to pop out of the woods and stab her through the heart."

"Yeah, well... let's go to the glade and get set up, then we'll go and see this one."

"Sounds peachy," she said, as Sarge reappeared running down the path toward us. Seeing that we were coming, after all, he did an about-face and ran back.

We went up a small incline as the path snaked through the undergrowth and trunks of ancient trees. Circling to the right, it straightened out and sloping down, opened into that small glade I was telling Claudia about.

The sun hit the open space just perfectly. Birdsong filled our ears, and squirrels scrambled, jumping from oak tree to oak tree, trying to put some distance between us and them. Sarge, taking his attention from the chipmunks scurrying through the undergrowth, put it on the airborne creatures flinging themselves through the branches overhead. Prancing back and forth, with tongue lolling and eyes focused upward, he disappeared down a path on the opposite side of the clearing.

Claudia skipped to the very center, and stopping, looked back over her shoulder at me and said, "Will this do?"

"That's fine, you couldn't have done a better job in finding exact center."

"Yeah, well… all us biologists know how to do that. You're lucky for having found me."

For more reasons than I could say.

Walking over, I helped her spread the cloth. She sat down, crossed her legs, and started pulling items from the basket, arranging them in an orderly fashion in front of her.

"I thought you wanted to go look at that altar?"

She grinned with embarrassment and looking up, said, "Yeah, I did, but I've changed my mind. I just realized how famished I am, and when I saw these BLT's, it set my mouth to watering. Is that okay? People can change their minds, right?"

"Hey, you got no argument from me—calm down. I'm not going to fight over food."

"Good, let's eat."

Throwing her head back, she closed her eyes and laughed. "I'm so used to Pembrook rules. Get in quick, grab your food, or go hungry. Always show up on time for meals, or… expect to eat at the cafeteria."

243

"Well, these sandwiches are going to be here until you or I eat them. So, you don't have to worry. Well, I guess... Sarge could be a problem."

"Yeah, I suppose the only time I have to be careful outside of Pembrook is when I'm around your dog with food, right?"

"Good thing he has manners, or should I say, obedience training."

"Peachy!" she said, and pulling the paperback from her pocket, she let it fall. Then dropping down onto her side and resting on an elbow, she unwrapped a sandwich with her free hand. After looking it over for a brief second, she sank her teeth into the stark, white bread. The BLT began to disappear rapidly. Sitting down across from her, I took one from her orderly arrangement and did the same. With her sandwich nearly gone, she swallowed a bite and belched. Her eyes grew big and she tried to cover her mouth.

"Sorry, it's so good."

Claudia blushed as a shorter version of the first burp escaped her lips. We had spent time together naked and here she was, still shy about belching. To make her feel better about it, I cut loose with one that echoed through the trees, and then cocking an eye, I said, "There, now we're even."

She laughed, belched a third time, and went back to eating. Wiping mayonnaise from my chin, I turned my attention to the landscape and other things. There was evidence other people had been there. A burnt patch showed someone had lit a bonfire, maybe last year. Beer cans and other assorted pieces of partially burnt trash lay at the center. A piece of newsprint hung in the brambles at the edge of the clearing, and a candy bar wrapper whirled on the breeze. If Claudia wanted to make love here today, I feared we might suffer an intrusion.

Several minutes passed without words. I watched Claudia start in on her second sandwich with the occasional shy grin coming my way. The newsprint rattled through the underbrush, catching my attention a second time. The breeze gusted and the newsprint floated to us along with some other trash. Rolling and spinning across the ground, it rose skyward and reaching up, I snatched it out of the air with my free hand.

"Good catch," Claudia said, her words sputtering through a mouth full of sandwich. Taking the last bite of mine, I spread the paper flat out on the tablecloth. It was a single piece of print which made up four pages after being folded in two. Turning it to the front page, I got a shock. '*The Dunwich Flyer*' it read across the top. My eyes rose to meet Claudia's.

"What? What is it? Show me," she said.

Rotating it around, her eyes got big. "Geez, how'd that get here?"

"Don't know, but... I'd like too."

Turning it back so I could read it, I saw the date, 'April 14th, 1944' and then the headline: 'FAVERSHAM GIRL MISSING, FEARED TAKEN' I physically shuddered and Claudia scowled.

Faversham was a small town just south and east of Dunwich. The article told of a fourteen-year-old Gertrude Dent who had gone off looking for a lost lamb. She never came home. Her bonnet had been found in the woods, along with her makeshift shepherd's hook. The ground was torn up like there had been a struggle, and spots of blood had been found. It also recounted a girl missing from Aylesbury the year before, and five months after that, a second teenaged girl who had been home alone in an isolated farm house north of the Aylesbury Pike.

Claudia had been watching me intently and when our eyes met, I said, "I didn't know Dunwich had a newspaper?"

"Yeah, if you want to call it that. Four whole pages printed in a shack. Some guy called Earl Hoadley had founded it. Didn't last long, maybe ten years. I was long gone and living in Cambridge when Anton came home one night and told my mother that he had gotten some news about Dunwich. Hoadley had disappeared. Somebody had seen him out walking the road to town, but I guess he never showed up. He'd made a lot of enemies. But people of Dunwich don't want anybody outside of there to know their business. That guy was doing just that. He was telling the world, or at least, Worcester County."

"So, he just dropped out of sight?"

"Something like that. Anton was still with the state police at the time. But the war just got over and that's all anyone cared about. My mother used to tell a story that her great grandmother had told her, something about a preacher man by the same last name. He had disappeared from there too. But that was way back in the seventeen hundreds. My grandmother, before she died, used to joke about how Earl Hoadley had come to seek revenge on the citizens of Dunwich for doing away with his relative. But I don't know if that's true or not. My grandmother really liked telling whoppers."

"Well, this edition is almost eleven years old."

"So, published the year before he dropped out of sight."

"Yeah, he wrote about missing girls and that included Aubrey even though he didn't say her name. Seems like a lot of people went missing from over that way."

Our conversation was cut short by a single bark from the downriver end of the island. It was not a, 'Hey, Sterling, I'm having a great time chasing squirrels,' bark—more like one of surprise or fear. Then came a steady stream of barking that was cut short with a yelp.

"Sarge is in trouble," I said, and dropping the newspaper, I got to my feet.

"What is it? Do you suppose he fell in a hole? Or… are there bigger animals here?"

"I don't know, but I'm going to find out."

She stood to follow me, and I said, "Maybe, you should stay here."

"Why? What if something happens? I mean, like if you wouldn't be able to drive the boat. I can't drive a boat." I could hear the worry creeping into her voice.

"Well, let's not get ahead of ourselves. But you saw how I did it, right? And if something does happen, McCabe is right over there painting the boathouse."

"I don't want to leave without you."

"I get that, but it should be fine. Just stay here. If something happens, run down to the shore and yell like crazy. McCabe could bring his own boat over to help you."

"Okay, but I'm kind of nervous about this. I really do want to go with you."

"Just give me a sec', huh, Claudia? I'll be right back."

I walked away before she could say any more. My concern for Sarge was overwhelming my ability to reason, but I didn't care. I needed to go and help my dog. Moving to where the path started, I stopped and peered into the trees. The smell of an outside privy assaulted my nose.

Something caught my eye just off the side of the trail. Stepping through the underbrush toward it, I came into a tiny opening to see many issues of the *Dunwich Flyer* stacked next to an old log. Someone had placed a fist sized stone on top to keep them from blowing away. There were burnt matchsticks, gum wrappers, and the butts of homemade cigarettes littering the ground under my feet. Wondering about the stench, I peeked over the top of the fallen log to see, as expected, I had stumbled onto someone's makeshift toilet.

I got the feeling that someone was watching me other than Claudia. Turning around, I forced myself to act as if indifferent to their presence. Moving back to the path, I stopped at the edge of the glade to see Claudia standing with hands on hips.

"Well, see anything?"

I started to speak, but a breeze came up and that candy bar wrapper floated by me only to stick in a patch of weeds. I saw, 'Big Time' in large white letters on a purple background.

"What's wrong, Sterling?" Claudia said with some urgency.

I decided not to answer, fearful she would hear the panic in my voice. We needed to get off that island. The birds that had been singing up a storm suddenly went quiet. Claudia's face dissolved into horror and her hand came up to point in my direction.

The sound of boots running on packed earth came from behind me. Everything seemed to slow down as I started to turn. The odor of tobacco, perspiration, and dirty laundry joined the outhouse smell. Out of the corner of my left eye, the end of a heavy stick swung into view. They missed my head but hit my shoulder at the base of my neck instead. Fireworks filled my vision and I felt myself going down with the odd thought, 'At least they missed my noggin!'

They had hit me hard enough to push me toward unconsciousness. I dropped to my knees and then tilted right on my way to the grass. I caught a glimpse of a dark figure coming up behind Claudia. Through my haze, I watched as an arm came around her chest to pin her to them. In their other hand, a dirty white rag that was pressed to her mouth. I tried to speak, but all that came out was a strangled "Hey…" before I fell away into darkness.

XVII

Ghoul Guarded Gateways

A sharp blow to my right hip brought me out of a chaotic dream. Opening my eyes, I recognized the floor of my boat and its cherry wood, varnished middle bench, at my feet. Somebody had just dumped me inside, my wrists and ankles tied. I lay in a semi fetal position, my shoulders toward the front.

I remained still as someone moved about the Speedster, cursing under their breath. There came a familiar creak as they climbed into the pilot's seat and tilting my head back as far as it would go, I could see it was Canaan Whateley.

Because he had his back to me, I figured it was safe to rise up enough to scan the area. We were drifting just a short way out from the point of the island, the force of the river's current pushing us back toward that patch of sand. I heard another motor whining and watched the police skiff move perpendicular from the island toward the boat ramp on the other side of the river. Hutchins.

A shout ripped the air and looking toward shore, I saw McCabe jumping up and down, waving his arms, like he was trying to get the officer's attention. Canaan muttered, "Ah shut your mouth, you old drunk. That fat pig ain't going to help you."

A single loud bark then floated to me above the sound of the Speedster's idling motor. Without giving any thought to Canaan, I lifted my head a bit further to see Sarge burst from a thicket. He was dragging a piece of broken branch tied with a short rope that was looped around his neck. I suspected they had snared him to keep him out of the way. Seeing me, he began barking. There came an, "Oh, shit," followed by, "What... oh, no you don't."

248

Canaan grabbed a fistful of my hair. I could smell chloroform as he tried to shove a dirty white rag against my mouth and nose. I pulled loose and got to my knees to face him. It was awkward and I struggled to keep upright. He was facing me back over the bench top, still trying to grab my hair. The pomade was making it difficult. The boat rocked, and I fought to remain vertical as my hair slipped through his grip each time. I could hear Sarge splashing his way to the boat, and Canaan's face told me my dog was getting close.

"Damn it all to hell! Damn dog," Canaan said, and whipping around he hit the throttle. The front of the boat rose as it moved away from Sarge. I fell back, twisting and squirming, trying to get back on my knees. I thought to push myself overboard in order to escape, but the way my hands and feet were tied, I would surely drown.

I finally got my derriere up on the middle seat and before Canaan could turn and renew his attack, I saw through the windscreen an old skiff moving just ahead of us. Lister sat at the back, his hand on the control arm of the outboard. The psycho was looking our way and laughing. At the front of his boat, I could just make out Claudia laying on the bottom with her head resting on the foredeck. She was obviously unconscious

Canaan changed his tactic of trying to seize my hair to grabbing the back of my neck. Jerking me forward, he shoved that rag against my face. I tried to avoid it by turning my head from side to side, but he stayed with me. I felt myself going under for the second time as Canaan latched onto the front of my jacket and pulled. I fell forward into my original spot. The last thing I remember was the motor drowning out Sarge's frantic barking as we moved west toward Dunwich.

***

A sharp rattling purr filled my ears and my head vibrated, leaving me to feel like it was going to explode. I couldn't straighten out my legs and coming out of my fog, I realized a new piece of rope had been added. It ran from my wrists, down between my knees to my ankles. Any hope I'd had about slipping my bonds was quashed. I would remain as I was until they cut me lose—or killed me

I could feel the waves slapping against the hull, and the smell of hot oil told me that Canaan was pushing the old outboard to its limits. Raising my head, I recognized the river bank from our earlier run to Aylesbury. I felt addled, and not wishing for another dose of chloroform, I dropped back and lay still. They wouldn't have brought us here if they meant to kill us. Or at least—me. If I was to be dead, they would have done the job back at the island and just taken Claudia. So, I may be there to serve some purpose. The thought renewed my hope for escape, and I felt my anger welling up. That was good. It would help carry me through.

The sound of the Speedster's motor soon slowed. I heard the skiff's outboard still whining at full throttle, but it was now behind us. Seconds later, it too cut back to an idle. I felt the Speedster turn toward the south bank and we floated into an alcove under some overhanging trees. The engine quit and the boat jerked to a halt as it ran aground. It began to rock back and forth and then came the sound of heavy boots hitting mud followed by the sucking squish as they moved away.

"Pull him out of there, Canaan, and drag his ass up to the wagon."

"Well, he's kinda heavy, Lister, and my shoulder still hurts from where that old cow of a house ma wacked me with that poker over there at the school. You're going to have to help me. I'll be damned if I'm going to do it by myself. Had a tough time getting him in that damn boat as it is. So... let's get that girl in the buckboard, then the two of us can haul his heavy ass up there, together. Hear me, big brother?"

"You always were a pest, Canaan. If I didn't need your help right now, I'd beat you raw. I'll let it go because you got that Houghton girl all by yourself, even though she weren't this Osborn girl—like you were supposed to get."

"Well, how's I to know? They looked damn near twins."

"Yeah, so you screwed the pooch on that one."

"Well, you screwed up the deal by getting a tray bent over your head. You know... that Houghton girl could be my wife 'bout now. Ain't fair you got your wife way back when you was a young 'un. I don't see why I couldn't have the Houghton girl for mine."

"Ah come on, little brother. First of all, you ain't got no money. I gave Pa a hundred dollars for mine way back when. Cousin Alijah gave him nearly three hundred dollars for that Houghton girl. So, you ain't getting shit until you can pay like we did."

"Well, I suspect Alijah's happy now—even though I ain't."

"Yeah, but the old man ain't either. He ain't got no one for the sacrifice, you idiot. You were supposed to get this Osborn girl and bring her back for her pa. It were ol' Joe that paid us to grab her and bring her home to Dunwich because he's gone sick. He knew, damn well, she wouldn't come on her own. Then, you show up with Doc Houghton's niece."

"Well... we got the right one now. Pa's going to pay us good money for these two as soon as Ol' Joe pays him. Pa's got to buy more cattle with Alijah's money, as you know. So, we need two more girls and maybe... we can snatch a third. Then I can finally buy me a wife. I seen a sweet little thing up there at that school, that..."

"Canaan, how you yak on! Why don't you shut up? Those state cops are still poking around. It's only going to get harder to grab more girls, and all because of you."

"Well, Lister, I..."

"Shut it and go drag that son of a bitch least part way out that boat while I haul that girl's fat little ass up top."

The discussion ended and I heard Canaan making his way back to the Speedster, mumbling threats against his brother. Fear had put a knot in my stomach, but my anger kept it in check. I feared for Claudia more than myself. I hoped they would put us in the same wagon, least that way I would know that she still had breath in her body.

Canaan came up to the boat and stood quiet for a moment. I suspected he might be trying to figure out how to get me over the side. I kept my eyes shut so he'd think I was still unconscious. He pulled on the rope that ran between my wrists and feet. Opening my eyes a crack, I saw he had it with both hands, his feet braced against the hull. I started to move his way, but it hurt like hell. When he got me to the gunwale, he tried to lift me out. I tried to play dead as much as possible. After banging my head against the gunwale once and dropping me several times, he stopped to take a breather.

251

"Damn you, Lister Whateley," he mumbled. "You and your money-makin' schemes. Just once I'd like to beat your ass. Then we'd see who's the better man." The boat rocked hard on the portside and I heard a sulfur tipped match being struck against the gunwale cap. The smell of tobacco smoke followed, and I figured Canaan had decided to take a cigarette break and had planted his derriere on the side of the boat to wait for Lister.

My mind raced for ways to get us out of this situation. If the state police were still poking around, like Lister said, I wondered if we might be lucky enough to be discovered. These Whateley's were inept and seemingly accident prone. I found myself hoping it would be by Canaan's error that we might escape.

"What you doing, Canaan? Why ain't you got that fella out of that boat yet?" I closed my eyes again and tried to quiet my breathing.

"Waiting on you, big brother. I tried but... no go. You get that girl in the buckboard?"

"Yeah, I did, you worthless piece of shit. Going to have to do this all by myself, I'm guessing. Come on, let's get him out before that girl wakes up."

"Why don't you see if you can get him all by yourself.... let's see how you do,"

I heard the sound of a slap. The boat rocked back again as Canaan slid off the gunwale. Opening one eye a crack, I saw them facing off. I wondered if they would fight and maybe kill each other, or at the least, disable one another. Problem is, I'd still be tied up.

"You want to dance, little brother? Go on, give me your best shot. You'll get the same as you got last time."

"Someday, Lister, someday..."

"Ah shut it, you been saying that all your life. I'm still here and still kicking your scrawny ass. Now grab this son of a bitch and let's get him up to the wagon."

One took my feet and the other grabbed me under my arms and they lifted me out. Then I was being carried, the sucking of their boots in the mud soon changing to clonking on hardpack.

Canaan said, "This one ought to be coming around soon, don't you think?"

252

"Yep, I 'spect he's there already. Keep him tied. Maybe just cut that rope 'tween his feet and hands. That a way, we can stretch him out in the wagon."

"Sure smells pretty for a man. Maybe I ought to get me some of that sweet-smelling water."

"Won't do you no good, you'd still smell like a pig sty on a hot summer day."

"Ah, up your ass, Lister. You don't smell no better."

I felt the sun on me now as they lay me in the ruts of the road on some kind of a tarp. The tension of the rope between my hands and feet gave way as they cut it. My legs straightened out and I desperately fought the urge to scream as cramps assaulted my calves. The canvas rattled and cracked as they rolled me up inside. Grabbing me, they swung me upwards. I felt the side wall of the buckboard on my back as I was rolled inside. My motion was stopped by something that felt soft, like a bag of feed—or a body. Claudia.

The smell of urine and the sound of breathing came to me through the heavy fabric. That brought me some relief. If old man Whateley needed to sacrifice her, it would be best for these two to show up with her alive.

They rolled me so I faced away from her and then their voices faded. There came the sound of horse's tack and Lister's voice a short distance off, "Go right on ahead, you old nag, step on my foot. I ain't beyond knocking you down, you know."

They were dealing with the two horses at the front, getting them ready for the haul. That's when I heard Claudia whisper, "Sterling?"

"Yeah, Claudia, it's me."

"Oh, I'm so glad. I thought they killed you. I'm so afraid, Sterling. I peed my pants... how embarrassing. We got to get away."

"They got me tied, I can't do anything."

"I got loose... I can slip my hands out, now. They got me wrapped in a tarp. Maybe I can get you lose."

"Don't try anything, yet."

"When?"

"Quiet, they're coming back."

Their boots clonked and scuffed on the road as they moved toward the wagon. I felt the buckboard lean left and then the springs of the seat at the front squeaked as someone climbed aboard.

"Want I check them again, Lister?"

"Yeah, good idea. Maybe give them the rag one more time."

I heard Claudia's tarp rattle as it was pulled aside. "She's still out Lister, maybe she's dead?"

"Better not be dead!"

"No, wait... I see her tits rising, so she's still breathing."

"Don't you worry about her tits... check the other one."

I listened to him walk around the back of the wagon and prepared for whatever he might do. Pulling the canvas aside, he snapped my ear lobe and I tried hard not to gasp.

"Okay, just flicked his ear and he didn't move none. Still breathing."

"Good, now get on up in here, so we can get going. Got damn near two miles to go to get home."

"Should have taken the good road," Canaan said with a cynical tone.

"You stupid son of a bitch, Canaan... and what? Be seen by half of Dunwich. Or maybe that policeman that's still sneaking around? Saw him just yesterday, walking down the road, plain as day. He was over by the Frye's old place, just strolling at his leisure. You'd think he belonged here. And you see that hog leg he's been carrying? Got to be a forty-four at least. Blow a hole in you big enough to push a melon through. We got to take this here backroad for a reason. So, shut your hole, and get on up here."

He did as Lister told him, and the buckboard jerked forward, the wheels squeaking on poorly greased races. I would be surprised if we got even a mile on such a poorly maintained wagon. It bucked and tilted left then right as the wheels fell into ruts. Lister swore constantly, and Canaan just laughed at his brother's grumbling, stoking the fire of discontent.

At one point the buckboard listed so hard to the right that I was forced onto my back, the canvas flipping open. Cracking an eye, I could make out the brims of their hats and then Canaan surprised me by whipping his face around.

254

I didn't move a muscle, hoping he couldn't see the glint of my eye. The dome of Sentinel Hill rose up behind him and then the sun disappeared as we moved into a forested area. A strange odor that had been just barely noticeable before, now filled my nostrils as if its source were the soil itself. A dead animal, rotten eggs, and vomit, kind of smell. I thought about my father's stories and his mention of that very thing around the hills of Dunwich. I never gave it too much attention at the time, but now, I would never forget it.

There came the frequent call of a Whip-Poor-Will, the constant croaking of frogs and the cackling call of owls in the gloom; all of that backed by the sounds of the buckboard. Eventually there came other odd noises. Rumblings resonated from the mountain side coupled with an occasional odd crackling noise that echoed through the trees around us. I could have sworn it was lightning, had it not sounded like it was coming from the ground below us. Listening hard to try to decide what could have caused such an odd clamber, I heard a dog barking.

Even though it was faraway, the late afternoon breeze had carried it to my ears. It only sounded for maybe half a minute, but it rang familiar.

"Tarps open, Lister, and that feller's over on his back now."

"Yeah, that last rut probably gave him a toss."

"You want I should put him out again? I can reach him real easy like."

The next thing I knew, the rag was hard against my face, and I swirled away into blackness for the third time. I rose and fell in and out of consciousness. It became a kind of dream-like state with me finding myself in familiar places. One time in Dyer Hall, one time in my mother's cottage, and then with Claudia on the green. That was followed by dark shadowy figures looming up and me getting pushed into the river. I felt like I was drowning and struggled to take a breath every time I surfaced. Then a terrific jolt, and I rose up into consciousness. The wagon had stopped, and now there were coonhounds bawling a short distance away backed by the whisper of the breeze through the pines.

People were talking. My eyes popped open and I peeked out past the edge of the canvas, through a crack at the bottom of the wagon's side wall. I recognized the grimy dungarees of the Whateley brothers standing with somebody in a yellow dress covered in tiny blue flowers.

There was a woman. Her voice was soothing and oddly familiar. I felt myself drifting away again just as the plank of the side wall was lifted from its cleats and dropped to the dirt. One of them rolled the edge of the tarp back to expose me to the light. Seconds passed, and then the woman gasped and said, "Oh, my! Lister, why him?"

She got no answer to her question, instead Lister said, "Just shut it, woman, or I'm going to smack you so hard you'd be feeling it for a week. Canaan, you take that other side off, and then you come back over here and help me get this bastard down into the cellar. And no bitching, hear me? Then you can come back up and get that girl. She don't weigh nothing. I'm sure you can handle that, right?"

I heard and felt the board on the other side being removed and dropped on the ground. Then they pulled me out of the wagon and carried me inside. I was overwhelmed with food and spicey smells, but mostly that of bacon. All of that was backed by the stench of decay as if the house were rotting away. I opened my eyes a little and caught sight of crème colored wall paper and ramshackle shades pulled part way down over open windows. Then it grew dark again as boot heels thunked heavily on open wooden stairs.

"Light a lantern, Canaan." Lister said, and then came the shock of being dropped on the floor. I couldn't help but groan and Canaan snickered. There came the sound of a lantern chimney being raised and the hiss of a match sparking to life. A dim glow filled the room as an old railroad lantern now swung in someone's hand. They leaned me back against a cupboard and Lister's mean, yellowish eyes gleamed in the light as he crouched close and cut the rope that bound my wrists.

I gasped from the pain as my arms fell to my sides. Taking my right hand, Lister lashed my wrist with a rope that had been threaded through an eye bolt in the ceiling over my head. He then hauled me up about a quarter of an inch off the floor as Canaan tied the other end to a second eyebolt that stuck out of a ceiling joist across the room. With my derriere just barely off the floor and my right arm stretched to the ceiling, I couldn't do much but swing and groan. Canaan reached out and cut the rope that bound my ankles with that bone handled Barlow knife and the blood flowed into my feet, adding more pain to what I was already dealing with. That's when I noticed the filthy bandage that wrapped Lister's right hand and the large rusty spot at its center. Regina's handy work, no doubt. I hoped for gangrene.

I squirmed, trying to find the most comfortable position. Almost fully awake now, I realized I sat in a small cellar. I could see directly up the stairs and that woman now stood at the top, in shadow, huffing and whimpering. Her dress was ankle length and looked like something the pioneers might have worn. She never looked directly at me and acted like she could expect a good slapping if she did.

"Suppose that'll hold him, Lister?" Canaan asked.

"Don't you worry about it none. He ain't going nowhere, and even if he could get up, he can't reach the knot. We'll just keep that cellar door locked when we are not down here. I 'spect he won't be with us long, anyways. Pa will tell us what to do after he gets a look-see. Maybe we can have a little fun with him later."

He poked me in the chest with a gnarly finger and said, "What do you say there, boy? Waking up, are you? Don't you try to get away, now. I'll do to you what I did to your friend back in Arkham. Funny how she thought that little knife would help her. Shoulda stuck it up her fat ass." He cackled a laugh and I thought how I could have easily kicked him in the balls. As bad as I wanted to, I knew it would be a mistake. The last thing I needed was for them to start beating me. If they left me alone, I figured I could just get to my feet and there would be the possibility of loosening the knot at my wrist or getting to the other end where it was tied to that eyebolt.

"Take his shoes Canaan… and his stockings, too. Then get some of that bacon grease upstairs and pour it on the floor all around him so he can't get no grip. Maybe the rats will come and he can have a good ol' time trying to keep them from chewing off his toes."

So much for my plan.

Canaan yanked my shoes and socks off and threw them in a corner by the stairs. The woman now stood two steps down from the top, her hands rubbing at each other. "Lister," she said, "Got something I need to tell you. It's important… from your Pa."

"Aw shit, what now, woman?"

He took the stairs two at a time, and she backed up out of sight as he came. I heard her whisper, "Lister, your Pa stopped by after you took off this morning. He tol' me, he found Ol' Joe dead from his sickness. So, there won't be no more money coming from him, unless your pa can find where he's stashed it. Lister, Josiah's figuring it must be somewhere in the store."

"Aw hell, what we supposed to do about that girl? He better find that money or we grabbed that little hussy for no reason."

"He said he'll be coming around this evening for supper. He'll tell you of his plans for her, when he does."

"Well, goody, goody," Lister said with sarcasm. "Canaan, git your butt up here and get that grease."

Canaan set down the lantern and after turning up the flame, he went up into the kitchen. He was soon back with a small tin bucket full of hot bacon grease. "Pull your knees up there, boy, if you don't want this on your feet." He dumped it on the floor all around me and I felt the heat of it.

"There, try to stand up now. Go on, do it. This ought to be funny."

"Naw, you just stay put, or I'm going to have to stick you," Lister said coming down the stairs. "That's enough, little brother. Got to get that girl inside and up the stairs to Elvira's old bedroom. Go on now, go get her."

"Okay, but if I can't lift her, you are going to have to come and help."

"Aw shit, Canaan, you're such a damn weakling. Go get her! She don't weigh nothing. Have my woman help you, she ain't doing nothing right now but fretting."

Canaan stomped away up to the kitchen. I heard the bucket hit the floor, followed by some muttering and then discussion between him and the woman.

Lister said to me, "Now, you just stay put. Don't try to get away. This will all be over for you, soon enough."

I decided to speak, keeping in mind that I shouldn't piss him off or it would be over for me sooner than that. "So, Lister, what's your plan for me and Claudia?"

Lister lowered himself down onto a dubious looking kitchen chair along the wall and said, "Oh, don't you worry about her, we'll think of something. As for you, well… my pa wants to come around and see what your daddy spawned. You know they ruined his brother's plans way back 'fore you were born, and then they had to go and kill my cousin Wilbur, on top of that. Now my pa's going to finish it. He knows as much as the ol' Wizard did. Maybe he can use you for something. You ain't going to get out of this alive though, that much I can tell you."

He showed a wicked grin in the light of the lantern, his snake like eyes going wide. But his glee didn't last long as there came a pounding of feet and Canaan shouting, "Lister! Lister!" and stopping in the doorway to gaze down at us, he took a deep breath before declaring, "The girls gone, Lister! She damn flew the coop. I can't find her anywhere!"

XVIII

In The Night Wind, Madly Flying

A wave of relief washed over me. If Claudia could find someone to help us, we might get out of this thing yet. Lister jumped to his feet, knocking over the chair. He held his knife like he might just use it on Canaan.

"You stupid son of a bitch, Canaan, you let her get away. Didn't you check her ropes?"

"Yeah, I checked them."

Lister seemed to fly up those stairs and using his free hand, he grabbed his brother's shirt at the chest, pushing him backwards, saying in a slow, deliberate manner, "When you looked at her last—did you check those damn ropes?"

"Well, she was…"

Lister pushed him to the left and there came a slap, followed by an "Oomph!" The familiar sound of someone getting punched in the stomach. This was followed by a crash and a body hitting the floor. The woman came from the right, passing the open door, her arms out like she wanted to help Canaan. Then another slap and she gave a loud, painfilled yelp that was followed by a whimper.

"There you go, woman, you can have one too, for just being here."

She began to cry and dashed past the door going the other direction. A door slammed and small feet pounded up wooden stairs. Things went quiet for a minute with only the sound of Canaan trying to catch his breath. "Come on stupid, get to your feet. We're going to have to go and try to find her. Got to get her back before Pa shows for supper. If she ain't here at this house, all hells going to break loose. You better hope he don't bring his gun cause he just might shoot your toes off for good measure."

260

Canaan groaned and with a voice much different from before, said, "We can find her. She don't know these hills like we do."

"Hell she don't, you idiot! She was born here. If I remember correctly, she did a damn good job of keeping up with us when we were kids. I got a feeling we ain't going to find her, or at least, before Pa gets here."

"We got the dogs, Lister. We got the dogs. We can turn them loose and they can hunt her down."

"What the hell you saying? Those hounds are good for nothing. Maybe hunt down an ol' raccoon or take up space under the porch. The dogs, hell, might as well sacrifice them, instead."

Lister walked to the cellar door and looked down at me. "Stay put there, shit-heel. We'll be back for you later." With that, he slammed the door and I heard him throw the heavy bolt.

Their footfalls moved away and then I could see their legs outside a small window set at ground level on the west side of the cellar. The dirty glass let in a small amount of light to shine on racks of jars full of fruits and vegetables. It flickered as the two brothers moved back and forth, then their voices melted away and it grew quiet.

I tried to get to my feet, but like they planned, I couldn't get a grip on the floor. I tried to use my free hand to pull me up on the cupboard, but I slipped, and it went palm down in the pooling grease, splattering me and the cupboard. Pretty soon bacon fat covered just about everything.

Clever idea to use the grease. I just hoped those rats wouldn't make a showing. I suspected if they did, it would be about sundown. But I had a bad feeling I may not last that long. My right arm started to numb up, and I could only find relief if I sat still.

I hoped even more that Claudia could find someone to help. I suspected she had a good distance to go before finding another house, and it was questionable whether whoever lived there would stand with us against the Whateley's.

I heard the creak of the second-floor stairs. A door opened and closed, and I watched a shadow move across the strip of light that showed at the bottom of the cellar door. It came back and stopped just outside like someone was listening.

After what seemed like an eternity, I heard the bolt slide and the light flooded in. By the time my eyes adjusted, the woman was half way down the stairs. She stopped briefly at the bottom and even though her face was still in shadow, I knew she was staring. My nose filled with the scent of lavender and my ears, the snotty sound of her breathing.

"Who are you? What do you want? If Lister catches you down here, he's just going to beat you some more."

She didn't answer as she shuffled to me, stopping just short of the ring of bacon grease. The lantern light flickered over the little blue flowers on the calico dress and her hands played with a silver necklace; its blue stone gleaming. It looked familiar, but I figured there were a lot of those around, the cost of a buck at any drugstore. A child's necklace.

She lowered herself down onto her knees, her round face coming into the light of the lantern. Her hair shone light brown and had been done up in the style of a milkmaid with braids pulled to the back of her head to form a bun of intricate weave. I stared at her face, trying to piece it all together. The nose, the lips, the milky skin, and the freckles. Her blue eyes stared as if she had a secret. Then a slight, sad smile broke her lips and it all flooded in—Aubrey.

"Aubrey? AUBREY! Is that you?"

"Yes, my dear Sterling, it's me."

Confusion hit me like a freight train. I didn't know how to react. I felt like I may pass out again as I watched a tear roll down her cheek. My own welled up and I fought to hold them back as my bottom lip started to quiver. Now would be the worst time to go soft. But every emotion possible filled my head to bursting. The grown-up version of that little girl spinning on my lawn so many years ago, now, kneeled before me.

Throwing all caution to the wind, she flung herself forward to wrap her arms around me. I grabbed her with my free arm and squeezed as she sobbed into my shoulder. My own tears soon overflowed down my cheeks to soak her hair and dress.

"Aubrey... I can't believe it's you. I thought I'd never see you again."

"Oh, Sterling," was all she sniffled out.

She must have realized her weight would be hard on my arm. So, pulling back, she moved to her original place, her dress now covered with bacon grease. She wiped the tears from her face and chuckled in a nervous manner. Reaching out she touched my cheek and said, "Sterling, my dear Sterling. You've finally come."

"Aubrey, why are you in this place? How did you get here?"

"I'm Lister's, now. Have been for a long time. Ever since they came for me that night back when I was a little girl."

"You're Lister's? But you were kidnapped?"

"That was a long time ago, Sterling, and now... I live here. At first, I believed you would come and rescue me. When you didn't, I gave up trying to come back to you. I miss my mom, Sterling. But I 'spect she's dead now. Probably from missing me too much. They say a broken heart can kill you. You've heard that, right?"

I didn't want to tell her how true that was. My aunt committed suicide my sophomore year at M.U. My uncle, Theodore Rice tried to drink himself to death and succeeded in getting run over by a freight train. I watched Aubrey's lips move and heard her words, but there seemed something odd about her. She seemed far away and detached, like she lived in a dream. I imagined that eleven years of life with Lister Whateley had pushed Aubrey over the edge. In order to numb the pain, she had retreated inside herself.

"Aubrey, why didn't you try to get away?"

"Lister wouldn't let me. I tried to go when I got tired of playing his wife. But he wouldn't have it. He told me he loved me so much that if I left him, I would die, and then he would too because he couldn't live without me. I didn't want anyone to die, Sterling. Now they are going to kill you, and I only just found you again. You know, I'm not really his wife. That's just what they say. That's what Josiah says, and don't nobody go against Josiah. There weren't no proper wedding."

The tears returned and she covered her face with both hands. I reached out and touched her arm. "Aubrey, can you untie me? I need to get out of here before they come back."

"They will just catch you, and then they'll kill you right away. They're going to catch that girl, you know? You just need to believe me on that, Sterling."

"No. I'm not going to believe that. There's still a chance. Claudia knows this country. They will never find her before the police get here. And they are coming, I'm sure of it."

"Nobody's coming. Nobody came for me, and nobody's coming for you. It's all lost, Sterling. They're... they're just too powerful. Our time is over. But Lister says after they sacrifice some girls, Josiah is going to make it so I have some babies. I want babies, Sterling. It has been so long since they promised me."

"Just untie me, Aubrey, and then you can come back with me to Arkham."

"No, Sterling, it's no use. Just remember, though, I love you. If the world were a different place, I'm sure we could have been happy, but...."

She didn't finish, and kissing a finger, she pushed it against my cheek. Then getting to her feet, she dashed back up the stairs and shut the door, bolting it like before. I heard her return to the second floor and the house grew quiet again.

Sitting in the dim light of the lantern, I listened. Sunlight soon angled in the window, telling me late afternoon had come. I could hear the birds and the occasional bawl of a hound. Floor boards creaked upstairs, and it sounded like mice scurried around behind the boxes piled in the corner.

I tried untying the knot, but it had been tripled. Wiping some of the grease on my wrist, I tried to pull my hand through the loop, but Lister had been smart to tie it tight. I went back to trying to stand, realizing after a while, even if I did, I still couldn't reach the other end of the rope. Growing tired of trying, I sat still, thinking of Claudia. Had the end really come? My time with Claudia had been so short. I wasn't going to accept that, not while I still had a single breath left in my body. I would have to trust Claudia. There was a real good chance she could outwit these people.

The sun soon left the window and the room darkened. There came a rustling noise and a loud squeak from somewhere to my left. The rats had come. Searching inside the cupboard with my free hand, I found an old wooden spoon and prepared to defend myself. As I waited for the first to appear, there came a loud knocking at the front door.

Aubrey came down from the upper floor and moved across the kitchen. I heard her pull the latch and the door squeaked open.

"Where's Lister?"

It was an older man's voice, gruff and deep. Heavy boots creaked the floor boards of the kitchen, followed by what sounded like something heavy being dropped on the table. Something like a stack of newspapers or—a book. A large book like, the Necronomicon.

"He ain't here, Josiah, he went to… to get that girl."

"What the hell's all over your dress, woman?"

"Oh, spilled a little bacon grease on me at breakfast."

"A little, hell! Woman that looks like… Oh, forget it. Get me some coffee."

I heard her move away and a chair being pulled out. "Where'd Lister go to get her? Australia? He should've had her here by now."

"I don't know, Josiah. He brought that fella and told me he was going out to get that girl."

"That boy here now? Where is he?"

"Lister's got him down in the cellar."

"I want to get a look at him."

The chair slid again, and the cellar door opened. A tall man stood at the top. Air rushed down the stairs and brought his stink with it. Stomping down, he stopped in front of me. Then picking up the lantern, he held it close. He had Lister's face, except old and wrinkled. His beard was white with age and three times as long as his boy's. His black eyes in the lantern's light, barely showed any of the white. I felt that I sat in the presence of evil, and I wondered if he had the looks of his brother— ol' Wizard Whateley.

"Well, looky here. You be that Rice feller's son, hey? I met your daddy way back when the Wizard tried to help the Old One's break through. They stopped them though, sure enough. But they's coming back, and now I'm going to be the one to help shepherd them through. There's no one to stop them now. That little girl that my boy's grabbed.

That Osborn girl? She be your girly now, if I reckon correctly. She's going to help me do it. Her pa paid good money for us to nab her and bring her home. Shame he had to go and pass on before we got the right one, thanks to that no account, Canaan. But no never mind. I'm figuring I can just use her for the first sacrifice up on the hill. Be real nice if she were a virgin, but I 'spect, she's not. She'll work out just fine. It's the blood that matters. You looking like you want to say something to me, boy?"

"What can I say?"

"Well, whatever you want, I'm supposing. Famous last words and all?"

"Okay, what are you going to do with me?"

"Well, I had no idea whether you'd be coming to our little gathering or not. I figured I could just kill you if you did, kind of revenge for poor little Wilbur. Oh, I guess he wasn't that little, huh? But now I'm thinking you might be worth something. Maybe a ransom or… who knows? But there's always money to be made. It's taken me damn near ten years to get enough of it to buy all the cattle and the property that I be needing to make a home for what Lister's woman is going to bring into our world. They'll be special ones, mark my word."

"Well… I'm going to rain on your parade. That little Osborn girl, she bested your boys, and the reason she's not here is—because she got away."

"What? You lie. No one bests Lister, he's a clever one, he is."

"I couldn't have heard better news that moment Canaan ran in to tell us… now let's see, how did he put it? Oh yeah, 'She's flew the coop'. I think those were the exact words he used."

I tried to sound confident, but I came off more like a little kid confessing something to an angry father. The old man crouched down and back handed me. It wasn't one of those light ones either. It rattled me. The pain in my jaw took a while to go away and I had trouble seeing straight.

"Well, boy, if what you're telling me is true, it don't matter. We'll get her back."

He was seething, I could tell, and a split second of worry flashed across his brow. Standing, he turned and stomped up the stairs.

Aubrey had been lighting lanterns, and after placing one on the counter next to the dry sink, she moved out of sight to the right. When Josiah reached the top he said, "Woman, is that true? That girl run off?"

He walked in the direction she had gone and then I heard a slap. Aubrey gasped and whimpered.

"Go on, tell me. Don't be holding back now."

They soon appeared just outside the open cellar door, Josiah was holding her by her upper arms, his face in hers. She pulled lose and backed up a step, rubbing her cheek. Josiah followed and grabbed her in a bear hug, his large hands going to her derriere.

"No Josiah, don't do this. I'm Lister's woman. You know that. I'm Lister's," she said as his hands manipulated her through the dress.

"Don't tell me what to do. Lister's property is my property. Been a long time since I had a woman and you're just the sweetest thing. Maybe I should take a little taste before the boy's get back with my prize. Then maybe I'll sample her too before I bloody up that stone with her innards. Too bad we got to keep you pure. Got to have us a virgin, you know? For the birth? So, you're going to get your young-uns very soon."

A surge of anger rose up in me and I blurted, "Let her go, you bastard."

"Awww, shut your hole, short timer," he hollered back, and reaching out, he slammed the door. It didn't latch and slowly swung back open. I saw he still had Aubrey in a tight embrace, his face tilted down into hers. She turned, looked at me and then closed her eyes. Josiah brought a hand up to fondle her breasts and a sob broke from her lips.

"I been yearning to see them little titties of yours, but I'm guessing Lister be back soon and there ain't no time for a girly show." With that, he shoved her, and she sat down hard on the floor.

He turned to the table and picked up what he had dropped there earlier. For a brief moment I saw it was what I had assumed it to be. He walked toward the outside door, saying, "I'm going home to get my gun. That girl better be here when I get back this evening, because if I have to go out there and find her myself, there's going to be hell to pay."

Then he was gone. Aubrey got up off the floor and finding a chair, she sat down where I could see her. With her face in her hands, she wept.

How she could have put up with this day in and day out for eleven years was beyond me.

"Aubrey, come down here and untie me. You can do it. You could get a knife and cut the rope. We can head down to the river and take a boat back to Arkham."

"No use, Sterling," she said through her tears. "Even if we get away, it won't matter, not if they bring in those Old One's they's always going on about. They's going to wipe the face of the earth clean of good folk. We are all going to die. Don't you get it, Sterling?"

"That won't work if they don't have a sacrifice, or someone to birth some little monster."

"They'll catch that girl… that Claudia. Even if they don't, they'll just get someone else. They were going to use me, you know? Way back when."

Her face came out of her hands and she looked at me. Even at that distance I could see the intense anguish and fear, her light skin now mottled red, her mouth, a sad scowl. My heart ached for her.

"Lister paid his Pa to keep me as his wife. I 'spect Josiah just wasn't ready. So, he let Lister have me for the time being, but now that he has the big book… I reckon the time has come."

"Well, he won't be able to use it if he's in jail, or better yet, dead."

She stood up and came to the door, her face back in shadow. "I thought about that, Sterling. I wanted to kill Lister a hundred times over. He tried to rape me on my thirteenth birthday, but Josiah put a stop to that. They had a terrible fight, and Josiah put Lister on the floor with a butcher knife to his throat. I talked Josiah out of killing him. I should have let him do it, cut his throat, I mean. There'd be no one to do the dirty work if he did. So, Lister did everything he could to me, well… short of poking me natural-like. You know? Where a man pokes a woman when they want to have a young-un? Then, he let Canaan have me once to do the same. That only made things worse between them. Now Canaan wants his own woman. But he's got no money to pay Josiah for her. That brother ain't good at nothing. He's always messing things up. I want to kill them all, but… I'm not a killer. Like I said, I don't want no one to die."

"There may not be any other way, Aubrey."

"I think I would have to have a real good reason to kill somebody. I'm not sure right this minute what that would be."

"Aubrey, think about it. If it's the end of the world, cutting me lose isn't going to change anything. You said if you did, he would kill us both. Well, if those Old One's are coming to wipe us out, we are going to die soon anyway. Least we'd have a little time together. It won't take anything to get a knife and cut this rope. Then we can go. Least that way, we can say we tried."

"You've got a girl, now, Sterling. Am I going to matter that much to you? I mean if we do get away?"

"Aubrey, let me say this, I love you. You have been in my thoughts every day for eleven years. But I love you like a sister. A very dear sister. My relationship with Claudia is different. You'd like her, Aubrey, she's a great girl. But just so you know, nothing will ever change how I feel about you. Claudia may be my wife someday, but you will always be my Aubrey."

She walked down a few steps, stopping short of the glow cast by the lantern. Now, almost indiscernible on the stairs, she spoke, a disembodied voice in the dark, "Sterling, I've been waiting so long to hear you say those words. I knew even back when we were kids, I could never marry you. But being with you was enough. And now that you said those words, I have to say, I love you too. It's important to me that you know that."

She grew quiet for a few seconds, but the silence didn't last. Soon a low keening escalated into a kind of a growling groan that soon faded. Aubrey sniffed several times and sounded as if she might start crying again. But it all came to an abrupt halt, as if she had suddenly gotten a grip on herself. I found her eyes in the dark, their wetness reflecting the dancing flame of the lantern.

"Aubrey? Are you alright? Aubrey…"

"Shush, Sterling!" she said, and moving into the lanterns glow, she stepped to the eyebolt in the joist just above her head. She reached a hand toward it but stopped short. Her fingers just fluttered there as if the rope that bound me were a viper waiting to strike. Jerking her hand back,

269

she turned and dashed up the stairs with a growling, "Oooh!" I just sighed and shook my head.

She returned to the second floor and I had no idea what she might be doing up there. Time seemed to drag. I felt we were fast running out of it, though, and my thoughts were marked by a Whip-Poor-Will as it started to pipe just outside. A second bird joined in and then a third. By the time Aubrey reappeared in the kitchen, a whole flock had gathered, and a raucous chorus ensued.

Aubrey had changed into a blue calico dress with a floral print and white trim. She carried a dirty white flour sack, partially full of something I assumed to be clothing. Setting it on the table, she moved to the counter. A drawer came open and I heard the clink of metal against metal. She reappeared before me with a paring knife in hand and avoiding the pool of bacon fat, she cut the rope at the halfway point. Then helping me to my feet, I skated in the grease until she was able to pull me free of it.

"I daren't cut that rope at your wrist, least not down here in the dark, anyways."

"Let me have that knife for a second." She handed it to me, and I cut off the rope, throwing it and the knife across the cellar.

"Grab my shoes, I'll meet you upstairs."

I made my way up, trying not to slip and fall. Grabbing a stained dishtowel, I sat down in a chair and wiped my feet free of the bacon fat. Aubrey came up with my loafers and socks. Dropping them on the floor, she said, "I packed a few things in this here bag, can't carry too much. But I took my favorites. Gosh, Sterling, do you hear them birds? Something bad is going to happen. Something real bad, I'm sure of it."

I stood up and she threw herself into my arms. I embraced her and she whispered, "I didn't think I'd ever be holding you again. I just wished I wasn't so afraid."

"Don't think for one minute it's any different for me. But we got to go. It will be dark soon and if they find us gone, the first place they'll look is at the boats. I've got to get help for Claudia."

Through the open window came the sound of someone running. Aubrey pulled back and a, "Oh shit," slipped from my lips as Aubrey's eyes grew wide with fear.

"Oooh, I knew this wouldn't work," she said.

Tossing her bag out of sight under the table, she went to stand in the doorway to the front sitting room, all the while muttering to herself, "Don't be afraid… don't be afraid." Soon her hands were at her cheeks and she started to weep. Turning her head from side to side, she expressed a mournful "No… no… no…" over and over again.

I slammed the basement door shut and locked it. If they thought I was still down there, I could hide and maybe jump who ever came in. Grabbing a ceramic rolling pin off the counter, I went to stand where I would be on the backside of the door when it opened. I could get in at least one good lick before all hell broke loose. If it were Lister coming back, I'd have to hit him hard enough to put him down, and then I would have to tie him up. I might have better luck if it were Canaan. I figured he would cry uncle a lot sooner than Lister. I just might have to use my four years of boxing experience from Wentworth. I had laid out many a fellow classmate, and I hoped I still had the knack.

As I stood waiting, listening to Aubrey agonize over the situation, I noticed the stamp on the rolling pin read, 'Compliments of Osborn's General Store'. Well, maybe Claudia's father might be useful to us after all.

The door whipped open, blocking my view of Aubrey. Lister ran in alone, panting heavily. The stink of his perspiration rolled to my nose, mixed with what smelled like he might have crapped his pants. He left the door open, allowing me to remain hidden.

"Aubrey! Damn it! Canaan's dead. Shit! Canaan's dead!"

Peeking around the door so I could calculate the distance, I saw he had moved to lean on the table with both hands, gulping for air, his back to me.

"We almost had that girl up by the glen, but she had that damn dog with her… that Rice kid's dog. It killed him, Aubrey. I seen all the blood. I swear it tore out his throat like it was nothing. That girl just stood there, hollering at me that I was next. Then she sicced that damn mutt on me. On me! Damn it all! I had to run all the way here with that critter on my trail. Think I shit my pants. Lost my knife somewheres, too, or I would have cut that mutt, but good. Go get me my gun out of that parlor closet. The ten-gauge double gun, you know the one. It's loaded, so don't worry none about grabbing no shells. Just bring the gun. I'm going downstairs to get that kid. Damn... you hear them birds out there? That's the loudest they ever been. I 'spect they're waiting on that Rice kid to die, and I'm going to be the one to see to it. Go on now, get that gun, damn you!"

Aubrey stood frozen in place, her hands still at her face, her eyes as wide as they could get. I feared she might glance at me and give my position away. But her eyes remained locked on Lister, staring as if she had lost her comprehension of the English language.

"Too it, woman!" Lister said, and picking up a salt shaker, he flung it at her. She ducked, but it had missed her completely, shattering on the wall alongside the doorway. She snapped out of her fear induced stupor and scrambled out of sight into the parlor.

If she actually handed that gun off to Lister, there would be no getting away. I knew a ten gauge was the mother of all shotguns. It could literally blow a man in half. But it was no good at a distance. That would be the only thing that could save the day; putting a few hundred yards between Lister and us, or better yet, not letting him get his hands on it in the first place.

I literally vibrated with nervous excitement. I heard Aubrey struggling with the doorknob in the other room. Between the rattling and the Whip-Poor-Wills, I calculated I should be able to get over to Lister without being heard. Coming out from behind the door, I took aim and swung as hard as I could.

"Hey! How come that boy's shoes..."

I'd forgotten my loafers. They still sat on the floor next to a chair. Lister took a step toward them, and the rolling pin missed his head to bounce off his left shoulder. I heard a distinct *snap!* Osborn's complimentary rolling pin, flew from my hand and walked right across the table top, flipping end over end to embed itself in the plaster of the wall. I had hit him so hard that I had lost my grip and now stood weaponless.

Lister screamed like I had never heard a man scream before. I had broken something, but that didn't stop him. He turned and pushing the palm of his right hand against my chest, he straight armed me back to the wall between the windows. Without even thinking about it, I threw a right cross and then a left, both times connecting with his jaw. He got a look of surprise on his face and wobbled a little, but that was all. He shook it off and came right back. I glared into his snake like eyes, wondering if he was even human, and for a mere second, I thought of the Wilbur monster.

Lister's palm slid up my chest and his fingers tightened around my throat. Banging my head one time against the plaster, he then tried to choke me out. The blow merely dazed me because of all the adrenalin coursing through my veins. It was the lack of air that was going to do me in. I tried to peel his hand from my throat, but he held firm.

His left arm dangled at his side, totally useless. So, I punched him where the rolling pin had made contact. That broke his grip and he screamed even louder than the first time, spraying me and the plaster with spittle. Letting go of my throat, he turned and staggered across the room as I slid down the wall, gasping for air.

At first, I thought he might have been heading to get that shotgun, but he stopped at a sideboard just outside the parlor door. Pulling open a drawer, he let it fall to the rough wood of the floor with a bang. The contents spilled out and reaching into the pile, he brought out a sheath with another large hunting knife stuck in it. Because he couldn't use his left arm, he put the leather scabbard in his teeth and glaring at me, he bit down and pulled out the knife.

I was wrong—it wasn't a hunting knife—it was a fighting knife, the Bowie type. An Arkansas Toothpick as my mother had called it. One thing she had been fond of doing, much to my dismay, was reading me tales of the old south. I remember one of them had been about the James Bowie/Norris Wright feud. She had described that weapon to a T.

Spitting the leather scabbard out onto the table top, Lister said, "I'm going to gut you like a pig." Then he held the gleaming blade up in front of his face for effect, his eyes crazy with hate.

I lurched to my feet and looked for something to fight back with, or at least, something to help hold him at bay. He came slowly around the table, gripping the knife in a way that convinced me he knew how to use it. I grabbed a broom from the corner and held it so I might push the knife away when he came at me. Standing with my back to the open front door, I thought to dash outside. That's when Aubrey showed up, her blue eyes frantic with fear. At her hip, she held the short, massive double barrel, its muzzle pointed toward Lister's back.

"Stop it, Lister—stop it now," she said.

"You shut your hole, woman."

"Lister, I want to say something to you and you gotta let me."

"Fuck off, I told you! Can't you see I'm busy butchering your boyfriend?"

"He ain't my boyfriend, Lister, he's my cousin, and I love him." Looking directly at me, her demeanor changed and the fear seemed to melt away. Her eyes turned to slits as she cocked the hammers on the shotgun, then adding in a cold, flat voice, "My one good reason."

I felt the concussive wave of the explosion as the cannon belched fire from both barrels. Smoke rolled into the room and time stood still. Aubrey went airborne as she flew backward into the parlor from the recoil, the gun clattering to the floor. At the same time, Lister's midsection disintegrated in a cloud of red mist and bits of flesh. Pea sized lead pellets peppered the wall and broke glass as they rocketed through the window. I felt the spray of his life's blood on me as my derriere hit the floor, my ears ringing like the four-alarm bell at the Arkham firehouse.

I just sat in shock, staring at Lister who now lay on the floor across the room, his body spasming. His face still had that look of surprise. The din of the birds, outside, had risen to a fevered pitch. His eyes locked on mine and then they seemed to glaze over as his features relaxed. Blood poured from his mouth and nose, propelled by whatever air was left in his lungs. It was the proverbial death rattle; a rather wet one.

The noise of the Whip-Poor-Will's changed abruptly from frenzied piping to what sounded like a sea of screeching laughter. I watched through the door as they rose up in one massive, pulsating cloud of feathers and rocketed into the dusky sky, that demonic cackling laughter loud enough to overpower the ringing in my ears.

A chill rode up my spine as the screeching din dissolved away into the distance above the tree tops. I thought of a conversation I'd had once with Doctor Strang about the myth of the 'Psychopomp'. Those fleeing birds now had me convinced that it wasn't a myth at all.

Fearful for Aubrey, I scrambled to my feet and went into the parlor. She sat cross legged, head in hands, sobbing. "Aubrey, are you hurt?" Looking up, she pointed to her ears and shook her head to signal her deafness. I nodded in return and kneeled beside her, putting a hand on her back. Comforting her with words would have been the right thing to do, but my brain had gone on hold from the shock, and besides, she wouldn't be able to hear them anyway. So, I just rubbed her back, the both of us gazing into the kitchen through the settling smoke. We stayed like that for a long time.

Aubrey finally got on her knees, and turning to me, she threw her arms around my neck. With her lips to my ear, she said, "Is he dead? He's dead now, right? I killed him, and he ain't coming back."

"Yes, he's gone now." There came a few seconds of silence before I pulled back and said, "You did the right thing, Aubrey, don't worry— you did the right thing."

She gave me a weak smile with a slight shrug. "Like I said, Sterling, I would need a real good reason to kill somebody, and well… he sure gave me one. I couldn't let him hurt you."

The smile fled her face and she cast her eyes down. I watched her lower lip quiver, but before she could fall back into sobbing, I helped her up and walked her out past Lister who now lay in a large pool of blood. Sitting her on an old chair outside the door, I went back in. Taking the cloth off the table, I threw it over the body.

Having spent many an hour, hanging out over at the School of Medicine's morgue, dead bodies didn't bother me all that much. I had, out of curiosity, snuck in many times to observe the medical students work with cadavers. That was Palance Kilham's thing. It had been more the shock of seeing someone nearly blown in half that unsettled me. A person going from being very much alive to—very much dead.

Lyle Umberling's murder trial had now gotten a whole lot more complicated. I wondered if Aubrey might be convicted of a crime for having killed Lister. I had my doubts, but you never know about the courts. I would do everything I could to be sure she wouldn't see the inside of a jail cell. It had been self-defense, plain and simple. Besides, Aubrey still remained a victim of an abduction, so who in their right mind would convict her? I came and leaned in the doorway to gaze down on her. I saw the girl with who I used to play. Still a little girl in a grown woman's body. I knew in my heart that she would have to be looked after.

We needed to find a phone and call somebody. I worried about Claudia having to be out in the dark but felt the comfort of knowing she had Sarge with her. Grabbing the lantern off the counter, I moved out to stand in front of Aubrey. She sat calmly, her hands in her lap as she stared off into the woods. The scene left me to wonder if that had been the reason for the chair. How many nights had she sat out there in the dark doing that very same thing, listening to the hill sounds, the Whip-Poor-Wills, and smelling the sulfurous stench of the Dunwich landscape?

"We've got to go, Aubrey. Josiah might be coming back with that gun anytime now."

She looked up, but it seemed she didn't see me. She smiled, but more at the familiar sound of my voice than me. Returning her eyes to the woods, she said, "They got him, Sterling. They took him straight to where he belongs."

"Who's that Aubrey? Who got him?"

"Those terrible birds, they came to catch his soul, and they got it. So…I'm free now, aren't I? I'm finally free. I'm just afraid it might be too late."

She looked up at me again and the smile returned. In the light of the lantern, I saw a glimmer of recognition in her eyes. "Do you remember that time when you and me were out catching those little butterflies? Those yellow and white ones that were always flying around your mama's flowers? You wanted to take the lid off the jar and let them go so they wouldn't die. We always had so much fun, didn't we? You and me… Sterling and Aubrey."

Her face dropped, the smile slipped away, and a single tear rolled down her cheek. Afraid to face such profound grief head-on, I turned away to look down the dark lane, blinking back my own tears. I watched as two tiny pinpoints of light came over the hill and moved toward the house. My hearing was almost back to normal, and I picked up the definite sound of an approaching automobile. Did Josiah own a car?

"Aubrey, we've got to go, someone's coming."

She didn't answer me and remained where she sat. I grabbed her arm to tug her to her feet, but she pulled away. "Don't, Sterling. Don't you see? I'm free now. Nothing can touch me. I can just sit here in my chair and not worry about who might be coming."

The skewed logic of her statement troubled me, but my concern would have to wait until later. We needed to get out of sight. I blew out the lantern, and set it on the steps, then grabbing Aubrey under her arms in a kind of embrace, I brought her to her feet. She didn't fight me this time, instead she wrapped her arms around my torso, and smiled into my face. It was like she thought I wanted a hug. Picking her up, I carried her out of sight around the corner, her feet dangling.

Standing her up against the wall, I peeled her hands loose, and snuck back to peek around the corner. The car was moving slowly and just before stopping in the yard, the headlights switched to bright, to shine in the open front door. There seemed to be something official about that black, nineteen fifty-four Ford. It was the same kind of an automobile the state police used. The driver sat alone up front, but I noticed movement in the back. That's when the driver got out to stand behind the open door. Looking toward the house, he waved a large silver flashlight around, shining it on different things. He dressed like the Whateley's, but he lacked the beard.

Walking forward, he made sure to stand just back of the headlights. Pushing his hip length jacket aside, he hooked a thumb in his belt as light glinted off metal. The badge pinned to his shirt, gleamed, and so did the large revolver, holstered at his right hip.

"Stay here, Aubrey, don't come out until I tell you."

"Who is it, Sterling? Do we have guests? I'm not ready for guests. The house is such a mess."

"Just stay put," I said as the plain-clothed cop called out, "Massachusetts State police, you in the house, come on out." His right hand stayed close to the gun, making me afraid he might shoot me by accident. So, I yelled out, "Don't shoot, I'm coming around the corner. Please, don't shoot me."

"Come out then, but keep your hands where I can see them."

I stepped into view with my arms straight up, trying not to move too fast. I watched him unsnap the holster, but the gun remained inside.

"Who are you?"

"Sterling... Sterling Rice."

He followed me with the flashlight beam as I moved out into the yard. "Sterling Rice—from the university over in Arkham?"

"Yeah, that's me."

A recognizable bark sounded from the back seat and a car door swung open. Sarge jumped out to race across the dirt yard. Claudia crawled out behind him and shouted, "Sterling! Oh my! You're still alive. Oh, geez! I think I'm going to pee my pants again."

Sarge hit me running and almost knocked me down. With his paws on my chest, he licked my face. I noticed the dried blood coating his muzzle and the fur on his chest. I tried to get a hold on his collar to look him over, but he broke loose and danced around me, barking excitedly. He must have caught sight of Aubrey standing back in the shadow and he stopped. A chest deep growl rolled out and I said, "No boy! Sit!" He did as told, but kept his eyes on her, his ears at full attention.

Nobody else seemed to notice his reaction as Claudia shouted, "Oh, Sterling, I'm so glad you're okay." She ran to me, flinging herself into my arms. Picking her up, she wrapped her legs around my waist and kissed me hard. She stank of pond water, the woods, and the putrid odor of Dunwich soil. There was also the tell-tale smell of urine. Her face was streaked with mud and her hair was filled with twigs and leaves. Pushing her chin to my shoulder, the tears came, and she wept.

I watched the policeman put his hand on the grip of his revolver and moving up to stand just outside the door, he shined his light inside. After a few minutes, he turned and started toward us. I set Claudia down and we met him halfway. She wiped her eyes with her left hand and keeping a tight hold on me with her right, she said, "Sterling, this is Officer Colbert. Ummm... Sean. He's a friend of Anton's. He saved my life."

"Well, I don't know about that," he said "It was more like that dog of yours. Anybody else here besides you, Mr. Rice? You see that Lister Whateley anywhere about?"

"He's not going to give you any trouble."

"How's that?"

"Well, he's kind of… dead."

"Oh? How'd that come about? You kill him?"

"No, his wife shot him, but she was defending me. He's in the kitchen, covered up with a table cloth."

"Who's that back there," Claudia asked, pointing toward the corner of the house.

Officer Colbert's hand returned to his holster, his flashlight coming up to illuminate Aubrey who had stepped into view. Sarge came to his feet and walked over to her, stiff legged, ears back, his tail flagging danger.

"That's Lister's wife. It's okay, she's not dangerous. You remember I told you about Aubrey Rice, my cousin?"

"Aubrey? I thought she was… oh, forget it."

"Sarge, down boy," I commanded as he followed her across the yard, sniffing at the hem of her dress. Officer Colbert eyed her as she came, and said, "So, you're Aubrey? Aren't you that girl that went missing, years back? Twelve, if I'm not mistaken. Well, I don't know what's going on here, but we'll get to the bottom of it. I'm going to step inside while you have your little reunion. You said Lister's dead, right? And there isn't anyone else in there?"

"Yeah, well, unless his father shows up. Josiah Whateley was here some time ago and said he would be back—with his gun."

"Oh, don't worry about him. We grabbed him earlier, carrying a big ol' book that was stolen from the university library over in Arkham. I think he's going to jail for a while. The charges just seem to be piling up."

I couldn't keep from grinning; the relief was so overwhelming. Officer Colbert disappeared into the house and I turned back to find Claudia and Aubrey in tight embrace, something I suspected was initiated by Claudia. Reaching out, I rubbed both their backs at the same time, and then wrapped my arms around them.

After a moment, we separated and stood looking at each other in silence. Aubrey had said nothing the whole time, and now, she just smiled, looking back and forth between Claudia and I. Colbert soon came out carrying the shotgun and said, "Well, he's dead, alright. These ten-gauge doubles really do make a mess. I got to get some of the other fella's up here. I can't leave until they show. One of the boys will take you back to Arkham. Miss Osborn, you should go to the hospital and get checked out. The same for you Mrs. Whateley, you might…"

"Rice," she said, sounding aggravated. "Miss Aubrey C. Rice. I ain't never been no Whateley."

XIX

Things I care Not To Gaze Upon Again

We sat in Claudia's examination room at St. Mary's. The big hand on the wall clock was just one click away from five in the morning. It had been well after midnight before one of the troopers finally got around to driving us back to Arkham. The trip itself was close to an hour. Aubrey had been taken to another room, and I imagined she was being subjected to not only a physical examination, but a psychological one as well.

Claudia had called Pembrook to explain to Mordechai what had happened. The warden sent Beatrice with clean clothes and later had to be ejected by hospital staff for being too loud. We suspected she must have gone back and told the whole university about our ordeal. Students started showing up in droves, all risking a curfew violation just to see how we were. Eventually the head nurse had to station a large, mean looking orderly in the entry hall to keep things under control.

Not knowing who else to call, I woke up Dr. Strang who had come right over after calling Dean Farr. We had a brief discussion and I gave him my keys so he could take Sarge back to my room. Chief Solum had shown up for his two cents worth and told me that McCabe had called in what he had seen, and also that Hutchins had dropped out of sight. The patrol car had been found abandon next to a telephone booth two blocks up from the cop shop.

I had been treated for rope burns at my wrists and ankles. They couldn't do anything about the massive, purple mark that saddled my left shoulder or the finger shaped bruises where Lister had clutched my throat. Luckily for me, nothing was broken.

It was Claudia who had suffered the worst. She had a stitch in her earlobe (where her earring had been torn out), and a brace on one finger for a dislocation. There was a tiny bandage on her left cheek, and some gauze pads taped to her knees, elbows, and her right calf where she had a small gouge from climbing a rock. Her hands were scratched and cut, and she was positive there must be a ton of bruises all over her derriere.

We sat joking about different things, with me sitting on a chair and her on the edge of the examination table. She wore a child's striped hospital gown which she had trouble keeping closed at the back. We decided to wait there as long as we could in order to hear what the doctor had to say about Aubrey. That gave Claudia time to tell me about her ordeal after escaping the wagon.

"So, anyway, Canaan didn't tie me very tight and I got out of the ropes he had used on my wrists, and when they were messing with you at the boats, I untied my ankles. They had me wrapped in that stiff, old canvas tarp, making it hard for them to see what I was doing. Canaan didn't bother to check my ropes that last time because he got so distracted by my boobs. Geez! Never thought they'd save my life, well... unless I fell on my face. You know how clumsy I am, right? Anyway, when I was sure they were all inside, I just tumbled out of that tarp and off the wagon. It wasn't easy at first because my eyes needed to adjust to the light, and then there was that stuff that was on that rag. I think... chloroform?"

"That's what it was, alright. I'd know that smell anywhere."

"Yeah, it's made from seaweed and... well, it made me kind of sick and dizzy. How about you? I know they used it on you at least once because you were there... and then you were gone when I whispered at you.

"Twice actually, and..."

"Anyway," she said, giving me the big-eyed look that told me to shut up and let her finish.

"I got across the road into a big field of long grass, and finally into the woods. I headed toward the Corey's place, but soon Lister and Canaan were close by, running up and down the road. So, I doubled back and headed toward where the Bishop's house used to be before the Horror smashed it. I was thinking maybe I'd hide in our old tree house, but they saw me cross the road about half a mile up. So, I ran down

282

toward the Devils Hop Yard. I snuck past them by crawling through the bushes and ended up where the stream runs into Cold Springs Glen."

"So, what about Sarge? Where'd you meet him? They must have snared him or something back at the island. I suspect he broke free and followed us upriver."

"Uh-huh, that's the really weird part. He came running down the stream bank when I popped out of a thicket at the north end of the Glen. He stopped like he didn't recognize me at first. But then he must have caught a whiff of me because he ran over and started jumping all over me. He knocked me down once because he's so big. I got a hold of that piece of cord they used to snare him and untied it from the broken branch. Then I used it like a leash and we ran back into the Glen. But that's when Canaan showed up. He must have come down from the road through Frye's old farm to head me off. I didn't know what to do because I'm too small to fight. So, I said the magic word and let go of the leash. It's like you said, Sterling, Sarge just went crazy. I mean, I never saw a dog get like that before. First, he grabbed Canaan's arm, but when Canaan grabbed him back, Sarge went right for his throat.

He got Canaan down on the ground and just started jerking him through the grass as he walked backwards. Canaan was kind of gurgling and trying to fight him off. I've never heard flesh rip before and then… all that blood. I screamed a little and thought I was going to puke. That's an awful sound, you know?"

To comfort her, I reached over and rubbed her thigh below the hem of her gown; the part that was free from bruises. "So, when did Lister come in?"

"He must have been trying to sneak around behind me. When I finally talked Sarge into letting go of Canaan, I realized Lister was standing on the edge of the clearing and must have been a witness to Sarge's killing of his brother. We just stood there staring at each other, kind of like back when we were kids. I said, 'Beissen!' and Sarge knew just what to do and chased Lister down along the stream bank and back up into the woods. I didn't want to stand around looking at Canaan lying there all bloody and gross with his eyes open. So, I ran down to the road that comes into Dunwich from the south. By the time I got to it, Sarge was back. There was no fresh blood and I didn't hear any screaming. So, I figured Lister must have gotten away by climbing a tree or something. Sarge and I ran up the road toward the Corey's place. I figured I could use the phone and call somebody, but that's when I saw Officer Colbert's car coming. He was turning east toward Sentinel Hill at the T intersection. So, I waved him down and when he saw the shape I was in and all the blood on Sarge's fur, he didn't waste no time calling someone on his radio. I told him what had happened, but I guess the police chief over in Arkham had gotten that call from McCabe. The chief must have called the state, who sent out, ummm... what is it? Oh! An all-points bulletin. So, Officer Colbert was already looking for us. The rest—you already know."

Claudia stopped talking and sat gazing at the wall, her eyes glazing over. Then she shuddered. After that, she slid off the table and came to me. Sitting sideways on my lap, she threw her arms around my neck, trying her best to avoid my bruises. Then laying the side of her face against my good shoulder, I heard her whimper and sniff. Turning my face to hers, she gave me a look of embarrassment as the tears rolled down her cheeks.

"Its emotion, I'll be okay in a second," she said apologetically.

She had been upbeat during her story telling, but I had started to wonder at what point she might break. I also knew my turn was coming, I just needed privacy. After a minute's worth of weeping, she wiped the tears away with a heavy sigh. "Sorry, I just needed to do that. I guess I'm trying to be too strong, but it might be better if I let it all out. I imagine watching Lister get shot might have been a little disturbing for you, huh?"

"Yeah, it's not a common thing at M.U. You think about all those movies where people are getting shot. They just fall down, no blood, no guts, no nothing. Well... in real life, it's a whole lot messier. Aubrey shot him with his own gun, and a big one at that. You saw that cannon when Colbert brought it out. My ears are still ringing. I don't think that particular memory is going away for a while."

"So... it was Aubrey who shot him, huh?"

"It's so ironic that he told her to go get the gun. I guess he didn't think that she might use it on him. She told me earlier that she would

284

need a real good reason to kill somebody. After Aubrey laid him out, she let me know that, I was that good reason."

That's when I choked. The tears welled up and my bottom lip quivered. Taking a minute to compose myself, I watched Claudia from the corner of my eye. She seemed poised, waiting for me to fall apart. But I pulled myself together and gave her my best smile. She kissed my cheek, her eyes showed sincere, and she said, "It's okay, Sterling, it's just us in here."

"Yeah, well, don't worry. The time will come."

"Okay," she said, and lightly kissed my lips. "So, changing the subject, how did Aubrey end up there—at Lister's? I mean, were Lister and her really married?"

"No. From the way I understand it, the Whateley's were in the kidnapping business. I suspect since pickings were slim there in Dunwich, they were grabbing women from all over—or should I say, girls. Josiah snatched Aubrey first. Lister had to pay a hundred dollars for her. Then Josiah changed his mind and decided to use her to birth the monstrosity he wanted to bring into the world. So, Lister could use her however he wanted, he just had to keep her a virgin. Then the others followed. Josiah was putting together a bank roll so he could buy cattle and get a house and farm big enough for them to use after Aubrey gave birth to the new Wilbur, and whatever came with him. As for Elspeth… well, your father, ummm… Joe, getting wind of what the Whateley's were up to, paid Josiah to have you kidnapped and brought to Dunwich. Canaan just grabbed the wrong girl, is all. So, Lister's cousin, Alijah Whateley, offered Josiah three hundred dollars for Elspeth. The mean old bastard wasn't going to pass that up. Joe threatened to turn Josiah in to the law if he didn't get Lister to bring you, or his money, back. But about an hour after Canaan and Lister went off to grab you… and me, Joe died from whatever had made him sick. We just made their job easier when we showed up at the island. They were already setting things up, waiting for dark so they could snatch you. I guess Josiah decided long before they got back that he was going to use you for their first sacrifice."

"Geez, just the thought of that is so gruesome. I could be dead right now!"

"Yeah, that makes two of us."

She repositioned herself and straddled my legs, facing me. Throwing her one arm over my unbruised shoulder and slipping her other behind my back, we just held each other in silence. There came a knock and because Claudia's derrière was hanging out, she jumped off and stood facing the door, her back to the table.

"Come in," she said, giving me her, 'What, now?' look.

The doctor walked in and closed the door. An old, gray-haired man in his late fifties, he projected an air of professionalism. Producing a clipboard, he gave us his practiced smile.

"Sterling, how are you feeling?"

"Okay, still a little shook up, I guess."

"If you start having trouble with what you witnessed, I mean with the shooting, we can help. We have new people on staff now that can deal with that type of thing. Claudia, same for you. How are you feeling?"

"Just peachy, Doc. I think I'll be okay."

"Very well. Now, for Aubrey. Sterling, I'm afraid we are going to have to commit her to the asylum."

"The asylum? Isn't that for criminals?"

"Oh, don't worry. Aubrey won't be with the criminals. She did commit a crime, but we've determined she's not in her right mind. She'll get treatment there. It's not the asylum of the old days if that's what you're thinking. If she improves, she can leave there and live the rest of her life outside of a hospital. I've got a feeling you'll be keeping tabs on her, right? She told us you were very close as children. Is that true?"

"Yes, we are very close. So, can't she be released into my care, or something like that?"

"Do you think that would be a good idea, right now, with your schooling still in progress? Give it some time, Sterling. Let's see how it goes, okay?"

"Okay, but like you said, I'll be keeping up with how she's doing. The sooner we can get her out of there, the better, right?"

"Most certainly. Claudia, you, and Sterling are free to leave. I believe we've done all we can for you. Check back in a week or so, let me know how you're doing—or you can go see Dr. Goldman. Your choice. Okay, good morning to you both."

He gave us that smile again and exited the door, leaving it open for a few seconds while he spoke with someone in the hall. Claudia had already turned to the table to gather her clothes when he poked his head back in. Spinning around, she pushed the gown closed at the back, giggling. I stood up automatically to block any view from the outside and saw Jerry standing out there, looking over the doctor's shoulder.

"Sterling, an officer wishes to speak to you? May he come in?"

I threw a wave at Jerry and said, "Can it wait for a minute? Claudia wants to get dressed. Hey Jerry, how about we meet you out front?"

"Officer?" the doctor said turning to look at the uncomfortable Jerry.

"Sure thing, meet you out front."

The doctor let a slight smirk push past his stoic lips before pulling the door shut. So much for professionalism.

"Do you suppose that cop saw me?" Claudia said.

"Probably not."

"Okay, but I'm just going to pretend that what you're telling me is true, and that he's not thinking about my fat, little, bruise covered butt right now."

"Just get dressed, will you? I really want to get out of here, and now, I'm expecting the third degree from Jerry. Plus, I too, am thinking about your derriere."

"So, now I'm going to have to stand there while you talk to him, knowing he just might have seen it."

"Claudia, please!"

She giggled and started dressing, putting on a little show for me as she did. That included singing a made-up song to the tune of 'The Good Ship, Lollipop' with sexual references. It made me feel better, and not so much because it was highly seductive, but because it was actually very funny.

When we got out to the waiting room, we found Jerry reading an early edition of the Arkham Advertiser and drinking coffee from a paper cup. He got up and shook my hand, and then hesitated before shaking Claudia's. She grinned and looked away, embarrassed.

287

"Why are you blushing, young lady?"

"Oh, nothing. Just had a thought... anyway, what's the tale, nightingale?"

"Yeah, Jerry, what's cooking? You look like you have something important to tell us. Not bad news, I hope?"

"Well, you made the paper," he said and showed us the headline with a picture of Josiah Whateley being led up the steps of the Worcester County jail by Trooper Colbert and another officer. The photo appeared to have been taken just before sunrise, the flashbulbs of early-bird photojournalists, giving Josiah Whateley's face a devilish look.

"So, everything is good, actually. Josiah Whateley confessed to everything. Even going as far as to brag about how they kidnapped your cousin and the other girls over the years. Seems he was supplying most of Dunwich with reluctant brides. Sadly, there's evidence that some of the girl's families might have actually sold them to the Whateley's. If there's any bad news, it's that he's sworn to kill you and Aubrey if he ever gets a chance. Said it right in front of his lawyer and a room full of policemen. But I suspect he won't live to see parole. Old men usually don't. Judge Crawford called before I left the station and said there won't be a jury hearing on this. Chief Solum sent me over right away to let you know. With Lister and Canaan dead, and Josiah already in the pokey, we only have to grab Hutchins. He and Elvira have disappeared. At first, we thought, dead. But the Whateley's wouldn't harm their own kin, so... probably not Ralph either. The state has put out an all points on them both. I have a feeling I know where they are, but I'm not saying right now. Oh! And we also found Elspeth Houghton. Kind of worse for wear, so we sent her to Boston General. Alijah Whateley tried to make a run for it. The state boys caught him down there in Holden where that tornado touched down back in '53. He stole a car, but he couldn't drive worth a shit... easy catch. He's stuck in Worcester County jail with Josiah. That big, ol' book got sent back to the library, so President Morgan was really happy about that. Said it's worth thousands of dollars. Ol' Josiah was ranting on about finishing his brother's work, something about ol' Wizard Whateley and that time back in nineteen twenty-eight. Said they were going to sacrifice Miss Osborn up on Sentinel Hill. Also said that would be the first step in bringing The Old

Ones back... whoever the hell that is. He was still ranting when I left. Can you believe that shit? He hates you, Sterling. I mean, he really hates you. The old fart was rambling on about how a dog killed his nephew right here in Arkham, some guy called Wilbur. Supposedly in the same spot where ol' Lyle Umberling was murdered. And now, your dog killed his son, Canaan. Is all that true, Sterling? If so… that's some crazy shit."

"Yeah, it's true. Every bit of it. I'll have to tell you all about it someday. Maybe over a beer at the Clubhouse."

"Okay, got to go, need to get some sleep. I'll keep that beer in mind. Later, gator."

He walked away after tossing the newspaper on a chair. Then stopping at the door, he turned and said, "Oh, by the way, Regina's back. Think I'll stop over there and see how she's doing before I go home. Anyway, thought you might want to know."

We followed him out, making haste in case the receptionist tried to corner us about the bill. We went directly to my room. Sarge expressed his glee in seeing us. He wanted out to pee, but he still had Canaan's blood all over him. Using the water from his dish, Claudia held him while I wiped away most of it with a wet towel. After getting him presentable, I sent him out. He came back in a matter of minutes like he had been away from us for too long.

The three of us then fell asleep together on my bed. Claudia and I were exhausted. Sarge just seemed grateful for an opportunity to lay with—or—on, somebody. We awoke to a pounding on the door. I jumped up as Sarge started barking his head off. The clock said three forty in the afternoon. The pounding didn't stop, and remembering I was now safe and back in my own room, I yelled, "Who is it?" I imagined Hutchins standing just outside, his revolver leveled at the door.

"Who is it, Sterling?" Claudia asked, rubbing her eyes and yawning.
"Don't know. Afraid to look."
"Oh, just do it. Who do think it is? Lister, back from the dead?"

The pounding got louder, and I got angry. Sarge must have sensed my state of mind and started clawing furiously at the bottom of the door. I still had dorm responsibilities and shouldn't go off half-cocked on anyone. Whipping it open, I faced the unexpected.

Epochs Uncounted

Palance Kilham looked down at me with a face only a mother could love. His deep set, dark eyes, under bushy eyebrows searched mine. His high forehead showed pale in the light from the overhead. Sarge growled, sniffed at his leg, and then returned to Claudia. I just grinned, glad my dog had decided not to raise a leg to Palance's.

"Hello, Palance, what's the tale, nightingale?"

Palance always spoke in a slow, but intelligent manner unless he was yelling at the undergrads. I think he actually liked doing that kind of thing and might even look forward to the moment the boys misbehaved. He topped out at six foot-five and dressed like somebody's butler.

"Hello Sterling," he said, his voice low and resounding. "Hope I'm not intruding."

Claudia moved up beside me, wrapping my arm in hers as she smiled up at Palance.

"Oh, I see that I am. I'll keep it short—even though girls aren't allowed in Dyer Hall. Anyway, Dean Farr told me to work it out with you. How soon will you be vacating your room?"

"Well, you may have heard, Palance, a friend of mine was assaulted at the local diner and nearly died. My mother passed away. My work partner was murdered. Claudia and I were abducted, and other assorted things. Even Sarge suffered at the hands of some pretty bad guys. So, you know… there just hasn't been time to figure that one out."

He just stood looking down at me, his eyes moving back and forth between Claudia and I. It was the first time I ever saw his mouth just hanging open, a look of amazement on his face. Then I saw the red creep up the pale skin of his long neck.

"Well, you just let me know, Sterling," he said, as he turned to the stairs.

"Wednesday, Palance, Wednesday."

"Very well, I won't trouble you. Sounds like you have more serious things to deal with."

I shut the door and headed back to bed. Claudia had a different idea and stopped me by sandwiching my waist in her hands. Looking up into my face, she said, "That was weird, huh?"

"Yeah, that's Palance. Gets along well with dead bodies."

"What? Are you kidding me?"

"No, he's a Med student. Works over at the morgue."

"Well, anyway... Sterling, I think I'm going to head for Pembrook. I need a hot shower. On top of that, I have a paper to complete for tomorrow. I'm afraid I may not get anything done because of the much-anticipated attention from my fellow inmates, I mean... dorm mates. So... unless you want me to stay?"

"Well, silly, of course I want you to stay. But I also understand school just didn't stop because real life intervened. When will I see you again?"

"Tomorrow, of course."

She then jumped up into my arms and wrapping her legs around my hips, she kissed me like she did the very first time. Then finding my eyes, she cocked her head to the side and said, "Love you."

"And I, you, or do I need to say it?"

"I need for you to say it, please?"

"I love you, Claudia Osborn—with all of my heart."

"Thank you."

I set her down, and in the process of trying to find my hand, she grabbed my wrist instead. I yelped, trying not to swear. "Oops! Sorry," she said and grabbing my fingers, she squeezed them, smiling up into my face apologetically. Then out the door she went. I followed, stopping at the veranda steps as she skipped toward the street. Sarge came to sit beside me, watching and whining. She stumbled over something unseen and looking back at us, she laughed. Then doing a single twirl at the curb, she threw us a kiss and dashed off. I watched until she bounced up the steps at Pembrook.

When I got back inside, I grabbed my shower kit and calling Sarge to follow, we went upstairs for our much-needed shower. After making sure we didn't leave a trace of Canaan's blood in the basin of the shower stall, we returned to my room so I could dress. Since it was Sunday, I decided to head over to the diner. Grabbing a jacket because the evening had cooled quite a bit, I strolled my usual route. My mind still buzzed with all that had happened and every time that picture of Lister's guts being blown out, popped into my head, I forced it away by thinking of something sweet, nice, or innocent. I looked over my shoulder every hundred feet or so, just to be sure Hutchins wasn't creeping up on me. I had to trust Sarge to alert me to any foes. I figured it might take a while before I got comfortable again.

Dean's Corner Drive-In was busy as usual on the outside, but nearly empty on the inside. Three car hops worked frantically to keep up, with Becky in the lead. They buzzed in and out of the door as I walked up, tending to the many family cars filling the lot. They had no time to chat with the drivers of the few hotrods lined up along the north edge. But all the James Dean wannabes were getting a different kind of attention in the form of dirty looks. Mothers and fathers scowled and grimaced in their direction, unaware that their children threw secreted glances of admiration from backseats.

Sarge flopped down in his usual place; much to the dismay of the carhops. I walked inside and utensils clanked down as applause rose from the grill. Dean and his two cooks were letting me know they had seen the newspaper, and my question about where Regina might be, dissolved away as I was met by her grin from across the room.

Regina sat sideways in my favorite booth, her casted leg sticking out and resting on a chair. In front of her, sat a pile of paper napkins next to a basket of cheap metal service. She had been busy rolling napkins around spoons, knives and forks, and there was quite a hefty stack starting to overflow the table. Just beyond them, catchup, mustard, and relish bottles, in chrome wire carriers, waited to be filled. A pair of crutches lay in the seat on the other side, their rubber tipped ends poking into view.

"Everything's on the house today, Sterling," Dean shouted as I walked past.

"Sure thing, Dean, but you're going to have to come up with something more original than that from now on." He gave me his usual salute and grinned, showing his dentures. Juan and Miguel smiled shyly and gave me a short wave.

"Well, look who's here," Regina said, and reaching under the table, she pulled the crutches off the other seat and sent them clattering to the floor. "Don't know who's those belong to, someone must have left them behind. So, have a seat, Pete. It's your spot anyway. So…like wow, Sterling, you came to see me. Treated you pretty badly at the hospital last time, I know, but don't worry, you still get me cranked, daddy-o, don't you know? So, what's buzzin', cuzzin'?"

"Heard you were back in town, Reg."

"Yeah, Gloucester is a drag. Oh! You knew I was there, right? Well, nice hospital, anyway. A whole lot bigger than ours."

"Yeah, I know about it and how you were secretly transferred. Wasn't so sure I'd find you here at Dean's."

"Yeah, you know me. Better here than home. Still live with my mom, you know."

"Now that's one thing I didn't know."

"Yeah, she's kind of sick right now. Don't really want to be there, but I do feel bad for her."

Regina seemed a little more subdued than usual. The stitches on her jaw couldn't be hidden. The area under her eyes still showed a brownish-green from the bruising. She tried to hide it with makeup, but there was no hiding what Lister had done to her. I could see the cuts on her hands had healed, but a white gauze bandage still wrapped her bicep, a couple of sutures visible. She would tough it out, that was Regina's style.

"So, you're getting better? All of your battle wounds are healing?"

"Yeah, but it makes me low," she said, fingering the bandage. "I see you have a few of your own?"

"Yeah, rope burns. You heard Claudia and I were taken, right? Kidnapped over to Dunwich by Lister. Claudia suffered a little more than I, mostly after her escape. But she's a tough one, too."

"Well, a girl's got to be tough if she's going to make it in this world. You know, I stuck that son of a bitch good! Right through the hand. But he just kept coming. If I ever see him again, he'd better run the other way."

"Oh, you're not ever going to see him again. He's six feet under. I watched my cousin Aubrey blow him nearly in half with his own gun."

"You're shitting me? You saw it?

"Well, yeah."

"Killed by a woman with his own gun?"

Regina perked right up at that and then gave me a sly smirk. "I guess I can stop watching my back so much now, huh?"

She looked relieved. I decided not to say anything about Hutchins. I had to be sure to tell her later, though. I just didn't want to ruin the moment. I had a feeling that my fear might be more paranoia than anything, and perhaps Hutchins didn't really present that big of a threat. He'd be too busy hiding.

"So, you going to eat? I can get up and serve you. You want a burger with some fries?"

"Well, Reg, I had considered it, but..."

"Hey, old man, give Sterling a burger with some fries on the side... and a milkshake! A chocolate one! Oh, and cook one up for Sarge, will you? It's on me."

"Sure thing," Dean said, "How about you, Reg? Want something?"

"Naw, you know I hate your cooking, you old geezer," she said and sneered before throwing Dean a wink.

Dean flashed a grin at us and chuckled before he returned to the grill. Then talking in hushed tones to Juan and Miguel, they all took turns looking back at us, grinning as if they had some secret.

"So, you must still be with Shirley Temple, huh? Got kidnapped together and everything."

"Yeah, I think it's long term. If you know what I mean."

She got quiet as she fiddled with a spoon, her eyes on the table top. I expected some kind of cynical remark, but looking back at me, she said, "Well, I'm happy for you, Sterling. Not easy finding someone who gives two shits about you. I mean, not you in particular, but..."

"I got it, Reg."

She didn't say anymore, and a few minutes passed in awkward silence as I watched her play with that spoon. I wanted to say something clever or helpful. What came to mind could be easily misunderstood, but I thought, ah, what the hell.

"Reg, I want you to know, I give two shits. Maybe not the way you want me to, but I do. I'm grateful that you defended us by bending that tray over Lister's head, and I'm sorry for what happened to you. That kiss I gave you at the hospital was sincere and deserving. Maybe not for what you want from me, but deserving, none the less. If there is anything I can ever do for you, well, besides you-know-what, let me know, huh?"

"Yeah, I know."

"Burgers up, Reg! Want me to bring em?"

"Naw! I'll grab em Dean. I still work here, you know."

I jumped up, hoping to help, as she struggled to get out of the booth, her poodle skirt hiking up to reveal black, lace trimmed panties, but I saw she could care less. She lost her grip on the booth and started to tumble backwards, but I caught her.

She laughed and said, "Such a he-man! Probably should fall down more often when your around."

Once on her feet, she did a quick walk to the counter, throwing her casted leg out in front for momentum. She struggled with the tray and fearing she may not make it back to the table, I met her halfway.

"Here, let me help you with that," I said, but she stopped and gave me a look of defiance. She needed to prove that she could still do it. I started to turn away, but she said, "Sterling," and setting the tray on the table next to us, she threw her arms around me and held me in a way that told me it wasn't for sexual gratification. Simply a need for human contact.

I looked over at Dean, who saluted me with his spatula and winked. An older couple, sitting over in the other corner, had their eyes on us, and I heard the woman say, "Oh, Elmer, look, isn't that sweet." I heard Elmer grumble something as Regina pulled away. Grabbing Sarge's burger from the tray, she unwrapped it and tossed it out the door. He had been on his feet watching us, trying to determine if Regina's hold on me was civil, or not. He caught the burger and one half of the bun, the other half sailing by. The old woman applauded in her glee and nudged the old man who grumbled some more.

Regina picked up our tray and hobbled back to the table. Sarge made short work of the other half of the bun and sat waiting to see if there might be more coming his way. I followed Regina back to our seats and the old woman said, "This is the most entertainment we've ever had here, huh, Elmer? We should come more often." The old man just grunted and took a bite of his hamburger.

Sitting down, Regina pushed everything already on the table over to the wall to make room for my food. I offered her the milkshake and she accepted without argument. What she had said about giving 'two-shits' kept coming back. I wanted to say more about that, maybe even list those people who did. Then, what Jerry had said over at St. Mary's came to mind.

"So, my friend, Jerry, the cop, tells me he saw too it personally that you got transferred to Gloucester."

"Oh, yeah. Wasn't supposed to talk about that with anyone."

"I know you don't like cops, but I think that guy has a thing for you."

She looked down at the table as if searching for something that wasn't there. A slight smirk broke her lips as if she reflected on a pleasant memory, and then looking up, she said, "Another thing that I'm not supposed to talk about. But that guy's a big tickle and a real flutter bum. So... you don't need to tell me. He kept hanging out in my room down there in Gloucester and would bring me anything that I wanted. I really put him to the test. And honestly... and don't you say anything to anyone, Sterling, but I missed him when he left. Weird, huh?"

"Well, I know it's not so great for your reputation, but things can change."

"Yeah—just like this subject! So, some fish faced kid was in here earlier going-on about you, said you quit your dorm job. Is that true? Next thing you know, you'll be quitting your lamplighter job, too."

We talked for the longest time. Conversing about life in Arkham, reminiscing about when we were kids, and laughing about some of the stupid things we did. She didn't hit on me once. We were just two friends, hanging out together. I would never look at Regina Duncan the same way ever again.

By eleven that night, she'd finished her assigned tasks. Picking up a jacket from the seat, I noticed it wasn't the pink 'Arkham Harlots' jacket, but rather, a man's red and black plaid, bomber. I had seen it somewhere before, just not sure where. Pulling it on, she hobbled out on her crutches, looking a little embarrassed because of it. I walked with her across the lot, noticing the sneers on the carhops faces as we passed.

"So, you're leaving work early, that's not like you," I said as we approached Garrison.

"Well, Sterling, life isn't all about work, you know?"

I realized she was going in the wrong direction to be heading home. I started to say something as we rounded the corner and then I saw Jerry's MG parked at the curb with the top down. He sat behind the wheel in civilian clothes. He started to get out, but then froze when he saw me. Regina grinned. Tossing her crutches in the space behind the front seat, she said, "Well, if it isn't my knight in shining armor." Jerry just grinned and looking at me, said, "And… if it isn't, Sterling Rice." I suddenly remembered who the jacket belonged to.

He reached over and opened the other door for Regina. She turned and threw her arms around me, "I'm so glad you're safe," She said, pecked my cheek, and then fell backward onto the seat, nearly landing on Jerry. Pulling her good leg in, she whipped her casted one up to rest on top of the door before closing it. More black lace. She raised her eyebrows at me several times, grinned, and then leaning back, she kissed Jerry. Righting herself, he shoved the shifter into gear. Together they grinned and said, "Later, gator!" as the MG shot away toward the Miskatonic.

I ended up running back to the dorm with Sarge in the lead and me thinking how problems can turn into benefits. Chief Solum passed me in the patrol car, wearing a uniform, something I had never seen before. He smiled and waved before heading up into the French Hill District. The Chief must have given Jerry the night off. I couldn't stop grinning and mounting the veranda at Dyer Hall, I reminded myself that I was supposed to be afraid about being out after dark.

XXI

A Dark Universe Yawning

Monday morning found me and Sarge in Dr. Strang's office. He and I discussed the kidnappings, the Necronomicon, my teaching schedule for the fall, and finally, my dissertation, but only after his curious examination of my bandages. Two hours later, I sat in President Morgan's office with him and Dean Farr, drinking coffee and receiving apology after apology. They expressed hopes that I would remain and teach at M.U. regardless of the trouble. After yet another careful examination of my bandages, which of course, brought more expressions of remorse, they sent me on my way with best wishes. Grateful to get away, I went to sit on the green in the sun and mull over all that had been said.

I spent part of my afternoon sitting on the lawn of the quad playing ball with Sarge and cloud watching. Sarge soon got tired of the ball and coming to me, rolled over onto his back for a good scratching. I worked my way through his thick fur with the occasional glance toward the entrance of the Science Hall. I had Claudia on my mind, and then, just like that, she appeared. Coming around the large brick building, she walked between an older man and woman.

Neither of Claudia's companions were much taller than her. The man wore a beige trench coat with a grey Homberg perched on his head. The woman had a flowered scarf tied over her well coiffured hair. Her knee length jade colored coat contrasted her white gloves as well as the black purse hanging from her arm.

They walked straight to me and Claudia said, "Thought that was you! Of course, who else has a giant dog at M.U.! Sterling, this is my mom, Moriah Kofta, and my dad, Anton; of course."

I got to my feet with as much couth as I could muster. Sarge rolled onto his paws and cozied right up to Claudia. Anton reached out his large hand to me and said, "Happy to meet you, Sterling."

Taking it, I met his eyes and said, "Same here, sir." Trying to be proper, I reached out to Claudia's mother. "Happy to meet you, Mrs. Kofta." She hesitated, but then took my fingers for a light shake before pulling back.

"You can call me Moriah," the woman said.

"You can also call the wind, Moriah," Claudia added and giggled.

"Hush! You…" Moriah said and gave Claudia a playful shove, the red running up her neck in a flush. Anton chuckled and threw Claudia a look that indicated her little joke might have something to do with his influence.

Moriah composed herself and said, "Claudia has told us so much about you. We actually could hardly wait to make your acquaintance. We know a little about your father, Warren. He was a good man. So sorry to hear about your mother."

"Thank you," I said, starting to feel a little awkward about being the center of attention.

Claudia came to me and we embraced, holding off on the kiss. She felt really good in my arms. So, I just held her. When it started to go on a little too long, she tilted her head back, winked, and returned to the spot between her parents. I marveled over the change in her appearance. It was the first time I'd seen her in a long-sleeved shirtwaist style dress. It was sky blue in color and sported a lighter blue trim. Her headwear was of the same color, something my mother had referred to as a cloche hat, a style straight out of the twenties. Her purse matched her mothers and she too wore white gloves that stretched to her elbows. The scratch on her left cheek was healing well, and I doubted it would leave a scar.

"So, Sterling… hell of an ordeal, huh? Those Whateley boys—one bad bunch," Anton said. He smiled to show me teeth that had seen better days. Even though short in stature, he had a bulldog quality to him, and I wondered if he was just as tenacious. There was a jovial glint to his eyes, and he was quick to smile.

"Yes, damn glad we got through that," I said, realizing I had just used profanity in front of Claudia's parents. I was thinking poor excuse for an English major, but they both chuckled.

"Yes, and a big thanks to Sarge. Claudia's quite fond of him."

"Yes, quite fond," her mother said. "We are so grateful for the both of you."

They smiled at each other and then at Claudia who patted Sarge's head and scratched under his chin. That got his rear foot to thumping and Moriah to laughing. The noise she made was high pitched and seemed exaggerated. Claudia looked up at me, rolled her eyes, and changing her demeanor, said, "Just so you know, Anton had a lot to do with getting us out of that mess over in Dunwich. He and Officer Colbert were pretty tight when Anton was a trooper."

Claudia threw an arm around her stepfather's waist and gave him a good squeeze. A boyish look crossed his face and he blushed. He kissed her hat and lay his cheek on the top of her head for a second. Claudia turned and gave Moriah a grin before stepping over beside me. Taking my hand, she seemed to be facing off with her mother in mock defiance. Moriah gave her, what I assumed to be a, 'Yeah, so what?' look and stepping over to Anton, she took his beefy hand in hers.

It was Anton's turn to roll his eyes. He blurted out, "Yeah, Claudia was keeping me informed. Right after that Houghton girl got kidnapped, I put a bug in ol' Sean's ear and he took it upon himself to be in close proximity to Dunwich. He was always anxious for a good collar. He'll probably get Captain for this. You know, back in forty-two..."

"Anton, you promised, no shop talk. It makes me so nervous and I just want to bring Claudia back to Cambridge where she'll be safe."

I felt Claudia squeeze my hand. Out of the corner of my eye, I saw her look hard at her mother, before saying, "I'm okay here. Those people are in jail... or dead. Besides, I'm not sure I'd go back, even if you tried to make me."

I looked directly at her now as she smiled at her mother, a smile that didn't reach her eyes. Solid defiance this time. Her mother gave her a stern look, but it softened quickly. "Oh, Claudia. Sometimes you're just like your father. Joseph was like that, you know?" Moriah gave me an unwavering look after her statement and I just smiled and shrugged.

"He's dead now, lung cancer they say. Isn't that right, Anton? Smoked like a fiend. Oh, how I hated that. Now, I suppose I'll get possession of that store. It used to be an old church, you know? I remember when the steeple collapsed in a thunderstorm. Thought I'd die from fright. Not a safe place to raise a girl child, I'll tell you that much. Of course, now I'm wondering if Miskatonic University is…"

Anton blurted, "So, Claudia, we're going to get out of your hair now. Call us sometime, huh? Let us know how you're injuries are healing."

"I'm okay, really I am."

"Maybe you and Sterling can come home for a few weeks this summer. How about it, Sterling?"

"Sure thing, Anton, love to."

"Okay, back on the road."

Claudia let go of my hand and hugged them both in turn, getting a kiss on each cheek. "Okay, so long for now," he said. I saw Moriah's eyes well up with tears before he turned her around and ushered her back toward Church Street where I assumed their car was parked. Then I heard Moriah say just loud enough for me to hear, "We're not in her hair… are we, Anton? We're not in her hair."

I saw him pat her on the back and whisper in her ear. They turned and waved again before picking up their pace. Sarge sat in front of us, watching them go, then staring over his shoulder at us, he looked like he felt cheated because his new friends were leaving.

"You know, Sterling, I love my parents, but I'm so glad they are heading back to Cambridge, now."

"Well, you stood up to her. So, that was a good thing. But are you really like your father?"

"Maybe, I don't remember. But I am twenty years old, so not a child anymore. But I suppose if you really think about it, I'll always be her child—no matter how old I am." Whipping off the hat, she shook out her hair.

"I suppose that's true. Just remember, though, and I can say this now that your parents are gone, don't put too much distance between you and them."

"You don't need to tell me, Sterling Rice."

"Yeah, I know, but I wanted to," I said, and gave her the same look she gave her parents when she first took my hand and crossing my eyes, I stuck out my tongue.

She slapped me with her hat, and then tried to jump into my arms. But the long dress kept her from getting her legs around me, and they dangled as we kissed.

When we finished, I lowered her feet back to the ground and she said, "Been waiting all day for that."

"Same here, and I want some more."

"I want more than just that... and I want to get out of this ridiculous dress." Pulling off her gloves, she stuffed them and the hat into the purse. I cringed at the sight of her hands and said, "Geez, those still look bad. Are you sure you want those gloves off?"

"Hey, there's no blood, and I took some aspirin, so... I'm peachy."

She wrapped her arm in mine and we walked toward Dyer Hall. I watched her parents in the distance as they climbed into a blue Ford parked on the street in front of Waldron's Grove. They soon pulled away, Anton's hand coming out of the window in a wave. Raising mine in return, I wondered if they had seen us kissing.

XXII

Skies Once Dark, Are Now Beaming

By late morning on Tuesday, I had completely packed up my room. Claudia and Esdra (of all people) helped me carry boxes to the cottage and we stacked them on the porch. Returning to Dyer Hall, afterwards, Claudia and I sat to rest on the front steps. Esdra left us to go inside, and Claudia glanced back as if making sure he was out of sight before she stretched her body out along a step and put her head in my lap. She grinned up at me like she had a secret, and then she stole a kiss, before saying, "Weird kid, huh? I mean... nice kid, just weird looking."

"Yeah, he's from Innsmouth. I saw a family portrait in his room. There's quite a resemblance among his siblings. Big family too, must be fifteen brothers and sisters."

"No! You're kidding me, right?"

"Nope, big families are pretty common over in Innsmouth. My father had known some student who spent some time there back in nineteen twenty-seven. As the story goes, this guy started some kind of an investigation into some weird crap that was going on. Then, he just disappeared. That's all I know. But like you said, nice enough kid, just kind of a fream."

"Speaking of family... Sterling, I'm exhausted and I stink now after carrying all those boxes. I think I'm going to head over to Pembrook for a shower."

"So, no tour of my mother's house, or... bed?"

"I'd just fall asleep before we even got started."

She snatched another kiss and getting up, patted Sarge, saying, I'll give you a bell. How about that?"

303

"Fine, leave me to my own devices."

"Poor boy," she said, and patted me like she would my dog before trotting away with a giggle. Looking back over her shoulder, she added "Later, gator," and promptly tripped over her own feet. Catching herself before she fell, she threw her hands up in disgust, turned her face to the sky and shouted, "Why me?" before breaking into a laugh.

After cautiously crossing the street, she took to skipping as she moved over the grass of Pembrook's lawn. I watched her grow smaller as she got closer to her destination, her ungainliness, my only concern on this bright, sunny day. Waldron's Grove had been taken back by the amorous and as far as I knew, it no longer harbored any threat.

I still had the evening hours to fill before bed and I could either go to the cottage and unpack, work on my dissertation, or go visit Aubrey at the asylum. They had built a new wing, years back, for less dangerous inmates, and had changed the name, removing the '...For The Criminally Insane' from the sign. I felt reluctant to go up there, but I wanted to see my cousin. It still felt odd that she was back from the dead and that I could be with her just about any time I wished. It was hard for me to fathom that she had been held captive so close to home all these years, but hadn't tried harder to escape. It made me realize there was a whole lot I didn't know about being somebody's prisoner. I supposed that at the tender age of twelve, she knew compliance hurt a lot less than resistance. Evil men had stolen her childhood. I felt the anger welling and wished for Josiah Whateley to suffer.

I decided to go to the asylum, but debated whether I should take Sarge or not. The intruding thought that I would have to walk back in the dark put that to rest. I hoped to be able to leave him at the door before I went inside. Then maybe Aubrey and I could stroll the grounds with him in tow.

It took me a good fifteen minutes to get there. Then we spent another ten minutes just looking at the place from the street. Getting up the nerve to walk up to the guard shack, I found the guard to be quite an affable fellow who became even more so when he discovered we were there to see someone who actually had visiting privileges.

He petted Sarge for a minute, telling me what a great dog he must be before directing us up the long curving walk to the main entrance. We strolled to where the pathway forked, and then took the newer section to the front door of the W. Peaslee Psychiatric Hospital wing.

Another guard sat on a chair at a small table just under the roof of a vast portico atop a massive set of limestone steps complete with an Italian style balustrade. He smoked and read the same copy of the Arkham Advertiser that had Aubrey's story in it. He was a nice enough guy and couldn't have been happier to take charge of my dog while I went inside, telling me he had one of his own. I gave the command for Sarge to stay and he lay down next to the man's chair, sighing out his discontent at having to be left with a stranger.

I stepped into a well-furnished sitting area full of burgundy sofas, love seats and cushiony armchairs. Coffee tables with magazines and end tables with shaded lamps completed the space. The receptionist was an elderly woman with large glasses. Her hair was pulled so tight behind her head in a bun, that it seemed to be trying to pull her eyes shut. She sat to my left behind a large desk that was more like a lectern placed atop a short platform. The top was so high, I could have rested my chin on it.

Looking up at her, I smiled, and she said in a pleasant voice, "Can I help you?" I felt the relief of knowing it was probably not the angry sounding woman I had spoken with on the phone.

"Hi! Uh… yeah, I'm here to see Aubrey Rice?"

She looked at her list and then giving me a genuine smile, she pointed to a door behind her, to the left. "Right through there," she said, and then dialing the phone, I heard, "Send Aubrey Rice down to the visitors lounge, please." Her face went blank for a moment and then she asked, "I'm sorry sir, and you are?"

"Sterling Rice."

"Thank you," she said and repeated it into the phone. After hanging up the handset, she leaned forward, looked down at me, smiled, and said, "I hear from the ladies that you're all she talks about. Lovely woman, our Aubrey. Don't expect she'll be here long. Please sign the book just inside before the orderly lets you through. There's a garden outside the door at the far end of the hall, so you may walk there, if you wish. It's a lot more private than the visitor's lounge. Aubrey… such a sweet girl, so sad what she's gone through."

I smiled and nodded before going inside and put extra effort into shutting the door as quietly as possible. A large man in a white uniform stood behind a wall of bars. He didn't smile. His large blubbery lips didn't seem to move when he growled out, "Sign the book." Glancing right, I saw it lay open on a podium. It asked for a name and address. I wrote 'S. Rice' and 'Miskatonic University' with an indiscernible cursive. Turning back to the man, he narrowed his dark, close-set eyes as he opened the heavy gate. I hurried through and he slammed it, grinning when he saw the noise startled me. "In there," he said and pointed to a door leading into a large, high-ceilinged room, "And no monkey business, or I'll walk your butt right out of here—personally."

I forced a submissive kind of smile and kept my smart-ass remark to myself. He controlled this space, and arguing, or giving my opinion, wouldn't help anything. Going into the basketball court sized room, I sat at one of ten long tables. The walls had been painted white and the tall windows were curtainless. There was a one-way viewing window on each end of the front wall, up under the ceiling, and I wondered who might be watching.

In the far back corner, an older couple occupied an entire table. A woman sat facing a disheveled man dressed in a crème-colored gown. They both studied me for a minute and then returned to their conversation.

The large black clock on the wall, protected by a metal cage, told me that twelve minutes had passed before I heard a commotion in the hallway, coupled with conversation. Aubrey soon appeared at the open door with a large woman sporting a lab coat, name tag, and clipboard. I presumed she was a doctor. They had been holding hands. Their talk stopped when Aubrey saw me. The doctor released my cousin's hand, patted her on the back, and said, "Let Charlie know when you're ready to go back up, okay, dearie?"

Aubrey's eyes were glued to me and she only nodded in response as she rushed my way. I stood up and prepared to catch her. She did slow her forward motion a little before reaching me, and throwing herself into my arms, she began to cry. The woman, still standing in the doorway, smiled, nodded with satisfaction, and walked out. The other people were looking at us as if annoyed, and then turning their attention back to each other, they brought their faces closer together over the table top.

I thought Aubrey would never stop shedding tears and I fought back a few of my own, with only one or two squeezing by. "Let's sit down, huh, Aubrey?" I said, but she didn't answer and squeezed me tighter. So, I just stood there, holding her, feeling the coarseness of her cream-colored frock where it lay at her slender waist. I realized that it felt weird to hug her now that she sported a womanlier shape, compared to how I remembered her at twelve years of age. Something, I guess, I would just have to get used to. Her hair hung free, smelling of baby shampoo. Her body spasmed for a few seconds and then it all stopped, just like she had turned off a water faucet. I felt relieved. She let go of me, backed up, and rubbed at her eyes. Then shrugging, she said, "Sorry… I… I don't know what got into me."

"It's okay, I understand," I said, before taking a step toward my seat. She grabbed my arm and whined, "Let's go out to the garden, I want to walk." Her eyes strayed to the older couple, than back to me.

"Okay, show me the way."

She grinned, jumped in place, and clapped her hands lightly several times before wrapping her arm in mine. Hurrying me to the door and out into the corridor, she acted just like she did back in nineteen forty-two. Taking my hand when we were half way to the garden door, she almost skipped as she moved, looking back at me with a little girl grin on her face; an expression implying that they have a secret—even if they don't.

"Bring her back to this room, when you're done, hey fella?"

"I can bring myself back, Charlie. Don't get pushy. This is my cousin—you know!"

I heard a muttered, "Yes, mam," and looking over my shoulder at the big man, I watched him back up to the wall, come to attention like a sentry, and cross his arms at his chest, his eyes seemingly focused on the wall across the corridor. He didn't seem to want to argue with Aubrey, and it made me wonder if it might be policy, or perhaps, she had faced off with him earlier. Maybe he knew she had shotgunned a man to death, and he feared he may be next. She seemed to have the upper hand, and I felt glad for it.

"That Charlie, he's really a big pushover," she said. "Don't let him scare you."

She grinned at me and her eyes seemed to sparkle. The way she spoke made me think that she just might be alright, after all. I suspected there would be an official diagnosis, it's just—I figured I wouldn't be the one to get it.

Opening the outside door, she towed me down the steps into a flower garden filled with walking paths, benches, and little wooden bridges over narrow, bubbling streams full of large goldfish. The daffodils and tulips were already showing their colors. A tall chain link fence enclosed the area with a tall arborvitae hedge surrounding it on the outside. A small section at the front was left open so the patients could sit on benches and look out over the vast front lawn stretching out toward Arkham.

We walked toward the west side of the enclosure, holding hands, and making small talk. When we finally got around to the front side, we stood looking down on French Hill. In the distance, I could just make out the roof of the Bell Tower back at M.U. I turned to speak, but Aubrey had drifted away; and I don't mean in the physical sense. Her eyes were open, but unblinking, and her lips had gone slack. Her grip on my hand remained solid though. There was no way I could break away without peeling her fingers loose.

Looking at her made me think of a hand written letter I had received from a friend at the beginning of my second year as an undergrad. There had only been one correspondence, and understandably so. He had been a roommate who had quit school to go off and become a soldier. Benjamin Reed had been killed in the battle of Pyongyang in Korea shortly after I received it. He had mentioned the 'Two-thousand-yard stare' that many of his fellow combatants had exhibited after a fight. 'Shell shock' was the word my father had used.

There came a bark and I looked to see Sarge with his front paws on the railing of the portico above us, his tail wagging like crazy. I figured he must have heard us talking and coming to investigate, saw us at the fence. He ran down the steps and came around on the outside walkway to where we stood.

It brought Aubrey out of her trance and she said, "Oh! Look Sterling, a doggie! Hello, doggie. Oh, you're such a big doggie."

Sarge clawed at the chain link, danced back and forth, and then started digging to get under. "Sarge, sit," I said sternly. He did as commanded, his ears erect, a warbling whine rising up from his throat. Aubrey knelt down and reaching her small hand through the fence, she petted him and rubbed his ears. He licked her hand and she giggled. "Do you know this doggie, Sterling?"

"Yes, don't you remember? This is my dog, Sarge. He came with me today. He was with us that night at Lister's."

I realized too late that it might have been a mistake to bring that up. She confirmed it by pulling her hand back, standing up, and wrapping her arms around my waist from the side. Laying her head against my upper arm, she began to weep.

Not knowing what to do, I patted her arm with my free hand, mentally chastising myself for not thinking first. I figured it might be best if I let her be the one to bring up the past from now on. That way, she could be selective about what memories were brought into conversation.

After a few minutes, she stopped and grew quiet. The guard on the veranda now stood at the balustrade, watching. Movement at a second story window showed the doctor observing through the glass. Sarge had calmed down and sat watching us through the wire, his tongue hanging out and dripping. His keen eyes watched my every move. I grew self-conscious and started to feel it might be time to go. I could always come back on another day, hoping that Aubrey might be better by then.

I ushered her away from the fence and she took my hand, Sarge whining through the wire. We walked to the middle of the garden where the flowers bloomed. Sparrows hopped about on the stepping stones, and a robin hunted the grass for early evening worms.

"Sterling, do you remember those baby birds we found up in the woods on Hangman's Hill? Those little sparrows? They were so small and helpless. You were afraid to hold them because they were so fragile.

I remember you told me I should be the one to hold them because you were too rough."

Aubrey stepped to face me and taking my other hand, she cocked her head and smiled kindly, adding, "Sterling, you've never been too rough." Then she threw her arms around me for the third time and hugged me tight. Feelings boiled up inside me and I lost control. A single sob broke from my lips and I pressed them into her hair to try to block any more that might try to escape. My quiet tears spilled out onto the top of her head and she must have felt them soaking her scalp. Leaning her head back, she studied me before saying, "Oh Sterling, you're crying. Don't cry, Sterling. Everything is going to be okay. I'm here now. Aubrey is home."

She wiped away the wetness from my cheeks with her fingers. I stepped back and pulled a handkerchief from my pocket and held it against my nose. I felt embarrassed and was glad the other strollers were a good distance away. Aubrey grew tired of waiting for me to wipe my eyes and taking the hanky from my hand, she did it for me. Tenderly dabbing at my cheeks, she smiled up into my face. After completing her task, she handed it back and then stood on her toes, kissing me on my forehead. I stood there, feeling sheepish, and probably looking it too. I had broken my rule and cried in public. All because of Aubrey. I decided it wasn't such a bad thing after all, and maybe it was a rule that I could do without.

The sun had dropped below the horizon and somebody turned on the pole lights set at each corner of the garden. A Tiger Swallowtail seeking a roost for the night, fluttered by. Aubrey's eyes locked on it and she gave chase. It rose a safe distance above her head, but she still followed, laughing, and jumping, as she clapped her hands up toward it. Then running back to me like a child, she jumped several times in place, her hands steepled at her chin. Her eyes were wild with excitement, and she said, "A Tiger Swallowtail! It was a Tiger Swallowtail! They're so pretty! So... big!" Grabbing my right hand with her left, she hurried forward and when the length of our arms played out, she stopped, standing sideways to me. When her eyes found mine, she spun herself back in a familiar dance move, wrapping herself inside my arm before spinning back out to her original position.

"Do you remember learning to dance? Aunt Elsie taught us, remember? She thought we were pretty bad. I didn't care, it was so much fun."

"Yes, I remember."

"You didn't like it. But you did it anyway. You did it for me. I will always love you for that."

She let go of my hand and twirled just like Claudia did, except Aubrey kept spinning until she nearly fell over with dizziness.

"Aubrey, time to come in," someone called.

I turned to the steps and saw the doctor standing just outside the door. She waved and Aubrey stopped and looked at the woman as if confused.

"Time to go home, Sterling. My ma's calling me in for the night."

Taking my hand, she tugged me to the building. "I can play tomorrow. Can you come back?"

"I don't know yet. My mom may not let me." I said, fishing for a certain response.

"Well, okay, but you tell Aunt Elsie... it's okay. I can be out til dark. If she says no, then maybe the next day, okay?"

"Okay," I said.

We arrived at the bottom of the steps and she squared off to face me from about a foot away. Grabbing my upper arms, she leaned in and pecked me on the lips. "Okay, my sweet cousin, got to go in now. See you soon, and... don't forget about me, huh?" and then whispering, "I know she's not really my ma, but I think she likes it that I make like she is." Aubrey winked and then turned away.

I just smiled and watched her jump up the steps one at a time, her feet tight together as if in a game. Then disappearing through the open door, the woman stepped in behind her and pulled it closed.

Standing there alone, I wondered what to do next. Deciding I had better leave the same way I had come in, I walked up to the landing, only to be met by the doctor coming back out.

"Sterling, right?"

"Yes, that's right."

"I'm Alma Peaslee. I'm looking out for Aubrey while she's here."

Alma stuck her hand out, and I shook it. Then we had to move aside to allow others to come in from the garden. Standing at the railing together, we waited for the steps to clear of eager ears before speaking again. When we were finally alone, she said, "Sterling, because you are family, I wanted to talk to you about Aubrey. She isn't going to be with us too long here at the hospital. Maybe a week... two at the most. We need to meet state requirements. She's not a danger to herself or anyone else. Her cousins, on her mother's side, over in Aylesbury, have agreed to become her guardians. Do you know them?"

"Uh... not very well. I mean, they've been friendly toward me and my parents. Like, when we used to meet at gatherings and things like that. But I don't know them all that well."

"Okay, I suggest that maybe you try to open up lines of communication with them. Maybe send a letter or give them a call. Reintroduce yourself; so to speak. I'd like, if you can, to have as much contact with Aubrey as possible. I know you're a grad student over at M.U. So, you're very busy. Do you suppose you can make time for Aubrey?"

"Yes, certainly. I have my own place now. Aubrey knows of it. She spent time there back before she was kidnapped. It's my folk's place. So, she should be comfortable there if she were to come over for a visit."

"Good. Anybody else live there, or...?"

"Just me and my dog. I have a girlfriend, Claudia, she will be there quite often, I imagine. But they know each other now. Claudia is smart, kind, and understanding, so it shouldn't be a problem."

"So... she would be good company for Aubrey. Okay, I'm going to give you a telephone number."

Writing it out on the bottom of a sheet of paper on her clipboard, she ripped it off and handed it to me. "I've got to get upstairs, so I'll let you out the side gate where your dog is. That way you can avoid the walk around—and Charlie."

Chuckling, she ushered me down the steps and to the gate. Unlocking the large padlock that secured it, she ushered me through and relocked it. Then smiling through the chain link, she said, "Keep in touch, Sterling."

"I will, you can count on it."

I tried to catch her eye to bolster my sincerity, but she had turned away, her attention back on the clipboard. Sarge danced around me as we made our way down through the old trees scattered around the immense lawn. He nosed at my pocket as we moved through the dusk, checking to see if I had brought his ball.

My mind was other places though, processing all I had just heard and experienced. Whip-poor-wills called to each other across the park-like space, bringing unpleasant memories and adding to my apprehension. The guard waved and smiled as I passed his shack, a bare bulb hanging above his head, illuminating yet another copy of the Arkham Advertiser.

Walking down the lane that threaded its way through the three acres of lawn that bordered the public street, I glanced back. I thought how the place had changed over the years. Someone had made an effort to bring it into the twentieth century. It was not the old, scary building, towering above Arkham like it used to be.

Walking down the middle of the dark streets in the French Hill district, I kept Sarge close. I'm sure he didn't know what the fuss was all about, but every single man standing alone under a streetlamp, or suddenly emerging from a car, heightened my unease. Checking each time for any resemblance to Hutchins, I hurried past.

A block from the Baptist church on Powder Mill Street, headlights lit me up from behind. A car had come around the corner and moved toward me at an idle. I didn't look back. The hair on my neck stood up and I made for the curb to my left. The vehicle pulled up next to me and I actually expected the sound of gunshots as I spun to face it.

I felt the tension run out of me as I glared into the face of Jerry McClean. He grinned at me through the open window above the Arkham Police logo. An unfamiliar man in uniform looked past him from the passenger seat.

"Sterling! How's it going? Walking alone at night, I see. Not a good thing in this, uh, how do they put it? Oh yeah—dark town." He laughed and added, "Heading for the dorm? Jump in, I'll give you a lift."

"Jerry! Boy, am I glad to see it's you."

"Why? Afraid of something like… maybe an ex-cop on the run?"

313

He laughed again, the light from the dash board showing me the wink I might have otherwise missed. "I got Sarge with me... sure you want him in the car?"

"Ah hell, Sterling, it's not my MG. If he pees on the seat, Arkham will foot the cleaning bill. Besides, he wouldn't be the first."

Opening the door, I let Sarge jump inside and then climbed in after him, taking a whiff and finding Jerry hadn't been kidding. Probably drunks who couldn't hold their bladders.

The other officer turned and studied me over the top of the front seat. Jerry said, "Sterling, this is Dan O'Meany. A friend of mine from over in Boston. He's our new officer on board."

Looking at him in that new uniform and cap, I could see he may have been just a little younger than Jerry's twenty-six years.

"So, Hutchins replacement?" I said as I shook Dan's hand.

"Hell no... mine! The news is—Chief Solum is going to retire at the end of May—guess who's going to be the new police chief of Arkham? Yours truly!"

"Well, congratulations. Couldn't be happier for you—and Arkham, for that matter."

"Going to need a new hat if your head gets any bigger," Dan said, with just a touch of Boston Irish.

"That's enough out of you, rookie. Hell, I won't be wearing a hat anymore, anyway, not if I'm chief. Chiefs don't have to wear hats, and if you're not careful, I may have all the patrolman wearing berets. Just like those Beatniks. How'd you like that?"

"Fat chance, boyo," Dan said, and sneered.

"So, yeah, Sterling, I plan on hiring some more troops—if you're interested? Sheriff department's handling a lot of our calls right now, but I'm hoping to change that."

Why was everybody always trying to get me into a uniform?

"No thanks, Jerry, didn't get an education just to waste it. I'm not a street warrior like you."

"Jerry McClean, street warrior," Dan laughed out. "Just like The Batman in those Detective Comics."

"Boy, I'll be glad when I get you trained and I can be away from you... boyo! So, Sterling, some news for you," Jerry said, pulling up in front of Dyer Hall. "It's been reported that Hutchins and his wife have been seen over around Kingsport. So, we're not out of the woods yet, my friend. But tomorrows a whole new day. Well, for you anyway. For my buddy, O'Meany, here… it's another day in hell."

Jerry laughed and reaching across, tapped Dan's cap on the bill, knocking it down over his eyes. Dan slapped his hand away and reset his cap. Then looking at me, he said, "Nice meeting you, Sterling."

"Good luck with your training, Dan."

"Known this guy too long…" Dan said, and flicking Jerry's earlobe, he finished with, "…to ever be concerned."

"Thanks for the ride, Jerry, and again, congrats on the new position."

"See you later, gator."

Turning back to his trainee, I heard, "So… Officer O'Meany, let's go see if I can get you killed before your shift ends."

"Fat chance," I heard Dan say as Jerry hit the gas and sped away up Church Street.

Strolling over to the dorm, Sarge and I bounded up the steps two at a time. From the corner of my eye, I caught the smolder of a cigarette over at the Loring Hall veranda. Sarge gave a low woof and whoever it was, took a deep drag and the glow lit up their face.

Sandra.

With the porch light off, she sat straddling the railing like one would a horse. She was dressed in her light blue house coat and fuzzy slippers. I could see her legs were bare and I thought it odd that she would be without her usual pajama ensemble.

"Hanging out with cops a lot these days, huh, Sterling? Heard about what happened. I, uh… wanted to say, I'm sorry. But you are safe now, so…"

"Yeah, Claudia and I—and Sarge—are safe."

"That's what I meant. Still spending time with that imbecilic undergrad, are you?"

"Yeah, we are, uh… how do they put it, oh yeah—in love."

"You never were with me. I guess, you just like them younger."

"Claudia's twenty, and if you can remember your arithmetic, that's only a four-year difference. Oh yeah, and it's a very mature twenty."

"Do you think you could have ever loved me, Sterling?"

"No, Sandra. You made it too hard. But I wouldn't worry about it if I were you. There's got to be some condescending, goddess worshiping nitwit, out there, somewhere."

"Sterling, could we just not go to that place, tonight?"

"Certainly, as long as you can stop bashing Claudia."

Taking the last drag of her cigarette, she flicked it away to glow in the mist free grass, a thin wisp of smoke spiraling to the sky. Sliding off the railing, she walked over to Dyer and moving to the end of the top step, she sat down. Leaning back against the newel post, she didn't bother to close her robe that was now gaping at the front, showing more skin than usual.

I could tell she wanted to talk. So, I surrendered, and sat at the opposite end, keeping a safe distance between us. Seeing me planting my derriere on the porch, Sarge dashed off to check his favorite spots, ignoring Sandra altogether.

The porch light glistened off her cheeks and I could tell she had been crying. I fought the urge to comfort her. She had never shed tears, even once, while we were together. But neither had I. It took some time spent with Claudia to make me start feeling human again. I wondered if I had shown that frailty with Sandra, would it have made a difference in our relationship? I doubted it.

"So, since when do you smoke?"

"Since I left you. It hasn't been easy and…"

"I left you—remember?"

"Okay, true, but well… there's just been this terrible feeling. I think it might be loneliness."

"I'm sorry. But I think, maybe… I'll just say it, Sandra—you frighten people."

"What do you mean? I thought we weren't going to go there?"

"I'm not. But if you want the truth, there it is. I'm not perfect, but that's part of the problem. No one is, Sandra. If people are always feeling like they don't measure up, well, what can you expect? When I realized I was working my derriere off to be the perfect boyfriend, I threw in the towel. So, that's where we are now."

"Do you... do you think if I treated people better... I mean, I guess I had no idea I wasn't. But anyway, do you think you and I could ever get back together?"

"No. It's too late for us. I met Claudia and I can assure you, if we ever break up, it would be her, leaving me. I am twenty-four now, Sandra. That's almost a quarter of a century worth of life, and I am more than willing to spend the rest of it with her."

She wiped at her cheeks and I caught a glimpse of her desperation. I felt pity, but I needed to stand strong. Sandra would endure and adapt in order to get what she wanted. I really didn't need to worry about her. However, what Betty had called my nurturing side, wanted to reach out. I suspected that's just what Sandra was working toward. That was her ploy. But I wasn't going to budge an inch, not for something that had been merely a moon cast shadow to what I had now.

Sandra flipped her shoulder length blond hair and then dropping her chin, it fell back to frame her face. She looked at me out of the tops of her eyes with an all too familiar expression that said, 'I'm yours, if you want me', and rotating on her derrière, she pointed her knees in my direction and the gap between them widened enough to show she wore nothing underneath.

She raised her chin, and then her eyebrows, cocking her head, she awaited my response. My anger boiled over, and my eyes locked on hers. I stood up, and whistling Sarge to me, I said, "Cheap move, Sandra. Because you're so willing to stoop that low, I'm willing to say, I've had what you got, and... I don't want any more."

Sandra pulled her robe closed, and with a look of disappointment, she rose and stepped down to the walk. With the look of someone who had just lost a game, she said, "Well, Sterling, it was worth a shot. I figured it may not work, but... I had to try."

Walking away toward Loring, she looked back over her shoulder and said, "I'm going to say this much, Sterling Rice... that quality you have to resist the greatest temptations, must be a gift from your mother. If you didn't get anything else, least you got that."

I didn't know what to say. I resolved to let her have that one. I still had to decide if it contained even the tiniest grain of truth. The odds seemed to be in her favor.

"I am sure you will be happy with Claudia."

"Well, I'm sure when you see us together around the campus, you'll know for yourself."

"Sterling, this conversation served its purpose. I won't be around to see that. I'm leaving M.U. Transferring over to Brown. You helped me make that decision tonight. I need to start a new life. One where people don't know me. If I change, like you suggested… that just might give me the edge I need to get what I want."

She stepped up to the front door at Loring and stopped to stand in the shadow. I knew she was taking that long last look. Then, she was gone, and I heard her throw the bolt. Sarge had moved up beside me and sat gazing in that direction. Then bringing his eyes up to mine, he made a kind of throaty whine, and put a paw on my leg. I believed it to be his way of telling me I had done the right thing, and could I please have my supper, now?

It turned into another typical night, but it felt strange knowing it would be the last one in my room at Dyer Hall. I fell asleep fully clothed, on a bare mattress, in an empty room. The only thing to carry away in the morning: a half-finished bag of dog food, two dog bowls, and my shower kit. I would bequeath all my food, remaining in the kitchen, to the boys.

I awoke at three in the morning from a nightmare. Aubrey had handed off that shotgun to Lister as he had asked, and it was the blast from both barrels that woke me in a heavy sweat. I sat up shouting, "Wait!" and looking around my room, I felt the relief of knowing it had been a dream.

I looked at Sarge who lay on the bed next to me. With his ears at full attention, he sniffed as if he could smell my fear. I dropped back down to my pillow and he put his head on my chest, still watching me out of the corner of his eye. I ran my fingers through his fur and rubbed his ears, but I wished for Claudia. I wanted to hear her coo to me in that sweet voice of hers and tell me how everything was going to be alright.

In the morning, Palance met me at my open door and handing off the keys to him, he walked inside, a small box under one arm, a typewriter under the other. Stopping to look around, he said in his deep voice, "Could use some paint." Looking back at me standing in the doorway, he added, "Thanks, Sterling." Giving him that index finger salute, I gathered up my few things and walked out.

Claudia had a class at ten and then would be free all afternoon. She said she would meet me at the cottage. Setting the dog food and other stuff just inside the vestibule of Dyer, I made a quick trip over to Gott's and picked up a six pack of Meister Brau beer. Then on second thought, I grabbed some sandwich makings and a quart of Butter Brickle ice cream. I stopped back and grabbing the other stuff, I labored my way over to the cottage. Arriving at nine on the dot, I struggled to find the key and then unlocked the front door.

Stepping in, I expected the clock to chime the hour and looking that direction I saw the hands had stopped at one minute after three. I found it odd because that had been the time of my mother's death. Looking at that spot on the floor, the memory of my arms around her frail back came into my head and circled like a vulture. I shooed it away and moved the coffee table back to its original spot and straightened the rug. I could tell already that it was going to be a long day.

The place had taken on a musty smell. My mother never liked open windows, even on the days where it sweltered. She would just sit in front of a fan, assuring me that the heat in the southern states was worse. But I had a say now, and I proceeded to open every single window in the place.

Not having been up on the second floor in over seven years, I creaked up the stairs to look around. There were three rooms up there, but only mine was furnished. Peeking inside, I saw it hadn't been touched since I moved out. Stacking a bunch of old seventy-eights on the rotund spindle of my phonograph, I turned it up loud to push away the quiet. Returning to the first floor, I started cleaning. I had worked my way into the kitchen by the time Claudia rang the doorbell. Time for a break.

"Welcome to my humble home—now," I said as she stood in the doorway looking around. Instead of tight denim pedal pushers, she wore cuffed dungarees and a well-worn, blue work shirt, untucked, with sleeves rolled up. She was ready for work. Fashion a bandanna over her head and she was, Rosy the Riveter. Kicking off her loafers, she padded across the floor in stocking feet.

Putting down my rag and the cleaning solution, I gestured as if I was offering the house to her and said, "So what do you think of my palace?"

"I can hardly believe you have your own house. Privacy at last. I see you're cleaning? Going to have to get good at that, you know. Not just one room anymore, and no housekeepers."

"Oh, I could have a housekeeper, I just have to ask."

Claudia chuckled, came to me, and fell into my arms. We kissed and then she tilted her head back and I just stared into her face. She gazed back, and then gave me a shy look like being adored just might require some getting used to.

"So... how can I help?"

"I was hoping you could go upstairs and dust everything, and maybe—mop the floors?"

"Sounds like a drag, but I can do that. Well, least we'll get to see who's the better cleaner."

"Is that necessary?"

"Just for fun, Sterling... just for fun. Don't be a poop."

With that, she grabbed a rag, a half bottle of furniture wax, and a feather duster before dashing up the steps. I went outside to start on windows. Mrs. Goldman, dressed for socializing, hollered out to me as she crossed Crane Street, moving toward the sports complex.

"Sterling! Finally moving in, hey? Stop by sometime and have some wine with Dr. Goldman and I. We'd like to hear about your ordeal. You're the talk of the campus." That was followed by a barely audible, "Just like your father." She picked up her pace, and smiling back over her shoulder, she finished with, "Okay, I'm off for a Bridge date, we are sure going to miss Elsie and her violin. Good day, Sterling."

"Thank you," I yelled.

Talk of the campus? Just like my father? Not really what I wanted, but it couldn't be helped.

Bringing my attention back to my task, I swung the skirting panel up at the side of the porch, the hinges squeaking from disuse. I hooked it in place to keep it from crashing down on my head and pulled the old ladder from the space underneath. Putting it against the side of the cottage, I went to cleaning every piece of glass in that wall. Music rolled out of my bedroom window just above my head. Frank Sinatra sang, *Begin The Beguine*, one of my favorites. Claudia sang along and I imagined her dusting away as she did, maybe throwing in a dance move, or twirling. Without a doubt, I knew she wouldn't be able to make a living as a singer, but at least she sounded happy doing it.

Finishing with the east wall, I went inside and after a quick drink of water, I went up to see her. Topping the narrow stairs, I heard Judy Garland start to warble out, *Over The Rainbow* followed by the squeaking of bed springs. Coming in, Claudia grinned at me from the blanket covered mattress, her hands pillowing her head. The quilt now lay crumpled on the floor, and I figured, she, like me, felt it needed a good washing.

"Hope you don't mind, I needed to rest. The quilt was musty, so I pushed it off."

I noticed her pink anklets had her name embroidered on them. I pointed and said, "Your mothers handy work?"

"Yeah… she loves me. Just a little overprotective is all. It's just like I'm one of the rich girls over at Pembrook. It's all cool. Hey, lay down with me, will you?"

"Certainly."

She slid to the edge and I stretched out beside her. The single bed, being too narrow, forced us to lay with an arm hanging off the side. She hummed to the song, her right hand holding my left. I stared around the room at all the things I had abandon. The baseball bat propped up in the corner, the worn and rusty Radio Flyer against the far wall, and the framed pictures showing pastoral scenes that my mother had hung around the room. They contrasted the wallpaper and I remembered when my mother had taken a day to paper the space set aside for me. I wasn't allowed to pick the color or the design. She had chosen cartoon kids in leather helmets piloting colorful biplanes on a cream-colored background. I felt a sudden need to leave.

"I want to make love to you, Sterling, right here—right now," Claudia said, rubbing my chest and grinning.

"No. I mean, I do, but... not in here." Getting up, I walked to the door.

"Where are you going?"

"Downstairs for a beer and maybe a sandwich."

"Sounds peachy, got one for me?" she said, and getting up, she followed me out.

"Of course, I've kind of stopped thinking in terms of just me."

"So, now you're thinking in terms of us? Oh... and Sarge?"

"Well, Sarge has always been me."

She caught up with me at the landing and said, "Hmmm, I think I get it. That whole abstract thing that poets are always going on about."

"Yeah, kind of."

"Thank you, Mr. Kerouac."

I sneered back over my shoulder and she giggled. On the way into the front parlor, Claudia stopped to look into my parent's bedroom.

"This is where your folk slept, huh? Fancy-schmancy. Nice linen, smells like my perfume."

"Yeah, you and my mother had that in common."

"Too bad I never got to meet her."

"Yeah, too bad," I said, wondering if Claudia could have melted the ice woman that had been Elsie Grangerford-Rice.

Wondering about Sarge, we found him snoring away on the sofa, something I thought I'd never see. "Made himself right to home, huh?" Claudia said.

"Yeah, he was deprived for years. He used to live here; you know? My mother probably tortured him after my father died. This is his revenge, I'm sure."

Moving back to the kitchen, I began making the sandwiches. Claudia playfully pushed me aside and took over.

"I can do this."

"Maybe so, but I want to do it for you," I said. "I mean, you practically cleaned the whole upstairs."

"Let me do this for you—please?"

"Okay, but..."

"But nothing, grab some beers and I'll meet you on the porch," she said, grinning big enough to show her coveted overbite.

Leaving her to it, I grabbed a couple cans of cold beer and an opener. Moving out to the front porch, I said a hello to Austen Ward who was turning on the pole lamp in front of my cottage. He grinned, said hello back, and then moved out of sight to do the others. I slid my mother's Adirondack chairs across the boards of the floor to the west end in order to face the setting sun. Planting my derriere in one of them, I swung my feet up onto the short wall that served as a railing and opened the beers.

Claudia soon arrived with a plate full of sandwiches and Sarge close behind. Handing me the plate, she sat down to discover her legs were not long enough to put her feet on top. Sighing in mock despair, she turned her chair toward me and put her feet on the arm of mine.

"Pew! You mean I'm going to have to eat my sandwich and smell your feet at the same time?"

"Ah come on, they're not that bad." I just grinned and handed her a beer and the sandwich plate.

"Not much of a beer drinker, actually. Not much of a drinker, at all. But this is kind of a special moment, don't you think?"

"Exactly, so, drink up," I said as she doled out sandwiches.

"Yes, your highness," she said and laughing, she tore off a piece of crust and tossed it to Sarge. He missed it and had to pick it up off the floor, but then sat close enough so we could just hand him his share.

We watched the sunset as we ate. Pinkish mare's tail clouds rose up in the afterglow. Déjà vu slithered in like a secretive little snake to wrap itself around my brain, but slipped away before I could capture it. Despite the picturesque scene, a foreboding washed over me, and I wondered what might be coming next. I shuddered and Claudia noticed.

"Hey, I saw that. You okay?"

"Yeah, happens sometimes. You might just have to get used to it."

"What's that supposed to mean?"

"I'll tell you later."

"Okay, don't forget, or I'm going to bug you til you do."

Sipping my beer, I watched the horizon fade to dark blue. I so wanted to enjoy the moment and not worry about the bad stuff. Pushing it out of my head, I smiled over at Claudia and her mayonnaise mustache. She swallowed the bite she had just taken and licked her lips. Then giving me a shy smile, she turned her attention back to her half-finished sandwich.

Students passed in groups and in couples with the occasional, forlorn looking, lonely heart deep in thought as they strolled by. Some I knew, some I didn't. Those that knew me, waved, and commented on my new abode, which really wasn't that new at all. Most didn't know that I had grown up in this house.

Alex and Sissy came walking up Boundary Street from the direction of Hangman's Hill. They were holding hands and having the usual disagreement. Stopping on the walk adjacent to where we sat on the unlit porch, Alex took Sissy in his arms and they kissed in an overly passionate manner. His hands strayed downward and pulling up her poodle skirt from behind, he massaged her derrière through white cotton panties. I couldn't help myself and shouted, "Alex Ryan, you unhand that woman's derriere, this instant!"

Sissy shrieked, pulled away and glared in our direction. Alex shoved his hands deep into his pockets, tilted his head to one side and threw us a grin. Claudia broke into a fit of laughter, and I stood up to make sure they saw who it was.

Alex sang out, "Who is that? Is that you, Sterling?"

"Yeah, caught you, didn't I. You can't escape the watchful eye of Sterling Rice, you rogue."

"Is that the Tony Curtis Guy? Alex is that…"

"Yes, didn't I just say it was? Gosh, Sissy, you…"

"Don't say it, Alex, or you will be walking home alone. Hey, Ton... uh… Sterling. What are you doing over there?"

"This is where I live now."

"Oh," she said and whispered something to Alex, who looked at her, then back to me, saying, "Okay, we got to go, I just saw Palance go into the School of Medicine. We've got maybe an hour, at least, before he heads back to Dyer."

Taking Sissy's hand, they took off at a run for the dormitory. I turned and watched them go, feeling kind of sad.

"Wasn't that sweet? I'll just bet you those two will be married within a month of their graduation. How much you want to bet?" Claudia said.

"No bets, not a gambling man." Sitting back down, I took a drink of my beer and just grinned at her.

"Ah, come on, just for fun, Sterling, don't be a poop."

"Okay, five Washingtons says no, and they break up senior year."

"Peachy! Okay, agreed. Five buck says they get married just out of college and get divorced by their second year."

"That sounds kind of pessimistic, coming from you."

"Oh, come on, I can't be positive one hundred percent of the time, that's just ridiculous."

"Very true… oh sage of the Miskatonic."

"Oh, give it a break," she said and chugged the last of her Meister Brau before adding, "Those two just gave me an idea. I'm going inside."

"But…"

"Just give me a minute, huh?"

She got up, skipped across the porch, and I heard the screen door slam. I watched Sarge get up to follow, and stopping, he stared through the mesh. A lamp came on in the dining room, silhouetting Claudia as she moved toward the kitchen. Sarge lay back down to watch the campus. I finished my beer and shouted, "Claudia, could you bring me another brew?" No answer. Another minute passed and all remained quiet in the cottage. That foreboding feeling came back and I walked over to gaze through the screen door. Sarge's head came around and his tail thumped slowly on the boards, his large brown eyes watching me.

I stepped into the parlor and called, "Claudia?" No answer. "Claudia!" I called again. Sarge now stood just outside, whimpering his concern. Fearing the worst, I hurried into the dining room only to skid to a halt from what I saw on the heavily waxed boards of the floor.

A trail of clothing led to my parent's room. Claudia's dungarees, followed by her blouse, her bra, and finally—her flowered panties. No socks, but that made sense, she would never give up her socks.

A light breeze stirred the curtains, Nat King Cole crooned *Unforgettable* from the second floor, and floating out through the bedroom door came a seductive, "Marco?"

Acknowledgments

I would like to take a moment to acknowledge H. P. Lovecraft whose stories I have spent a lifetime reading, most likely, curled up in a chair in the corner of my room with just enough light to read by, but not so much to disrupt the mood. My mother would sometimes question my mental state, often asking, "How can you read that stuff?" and then shuddering, walk away. I would have been hard pressed to explain that I didn't fear the dark as she, and so many others, did. That it would take more than the twilight upon the land to send me fleeing indoors, always keeping to myself that I just had to go out there and see what made that scary noise. I craved the thrill of it and was willing to take the risk to get it. I desired to shudder. I desired for my hair to stand on end. Life would have been just too boring otherwise. Books of dark fiction could do that, and the list of authors capable of suspending my disbelief is long and distinguished. But this is Lovecraft's moment, and this novel is my tribute to the renderings of a man who I felt was (and still is) one of the best.

327

R.C. Davis is a novelist and poet who came to the Midwest of the USA with his family in his childhood years. While he grew up in a small town within the rolling hills that form the western banks of the Mississippi River, his interests in people, places, and genres are very cosmopolitan in scope. R.C.'s love for writing and telling stories comes second only to family, music, his dogs, and nature.